NIGHT GODDESS

T STEDMAN

ACKNOWLEDGMENTS

Thank you to Diane Burke and Imogen Hayes and to all the readers that have been with me right from the beginning. Before I wrote a single word, I had a whole series in my head. This was the book I wrote first as it was freshest in my mind. I wrote the central plot and then shelved it. I was glad, as I'd come such a long way with my writing. I'd be lying if I didn't say it's been emotional.

<u>*The Royal Families*</u>
<u>*Of Atlantis*</u>

Dubonnetti
Bonaci
Santalini
Florianna

<u>*Of Murrtaine*</u>
Borge

'Born of Chaos, Nyx is the goddess of the night. A shadowy figure stood at the birth of creation. Moving the entire universe in her joyful dance, drunk on honey and dreams.' *(Taken from the ancient tome of* The Arawans. *Carried from Atlantis)*

PROLOGUE

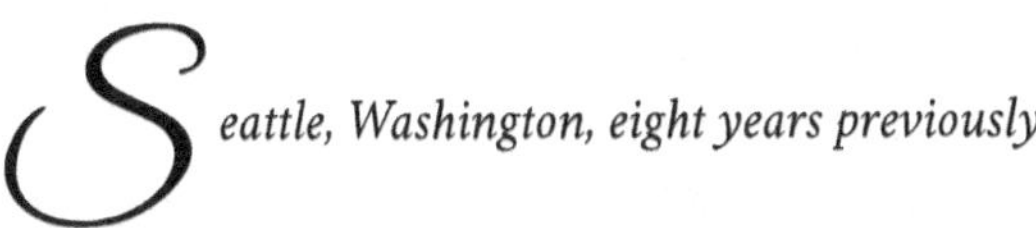

eattle, Washington, eight years previously

"ARE you absolutely sure the boys are ready, Seville? So much is at stake. A wrong move and the chance will be gone for eternity." Lord Croll shook his head and looked out of the anteroom window. The very boys he referred to were playing a rough game of football in the bitter cold with nothing but thin vests to protect them.

A harsh life but emotional attachments were still some-times formed. He recognized the boy Seville favoured playing on with a limp from a nasty gash in his thigh. He was taller and so much more serious than the others, as if he were on a mission already. "What of your star pupil? You've invested so much and would part with him so young?"

Seville paused and frowned slightly. Then continued as if the comment had never been made, "Now is the perfect time, sire. They are entering puberty. It is time to assimilate them into society."

Croll studied him for a long moment. Then, satisfied that his judgment was not clouded, continued to pace, mulling over his words. His robes skimmed the floor as he went, revealing a Roman sandal strapped up a muscled, heavily tattooed leg. "Would it not be expedient to wait until they were strong, grown, sexually active men, able to protect themselves to obtain such a powerful prize? There will be many adversaries, Seville."

Seville inclined his head. "That is indeed true, sire, but younger minds are so much easier to erase. They are older than their years and their training complete. We will be able to place them where they can grow, unaware of their former lives, and in doing so they will be far more effective agents. Their cover will be so effective that they even believe it themselves. And with one hundred percent human blood, they will remain under the radar of Atlantean scouts also scouring the area. They are hidden, lethal and their will is mine."

Croll let out a sigh and smiled ruefully. "You have great faith, Seville." He couldn't argue with the logic, but he was still uneasy. Seville set too much store in not just one small platoon of boys, but one boy in particular. He hoped he could live up to it. Their sect had almost died out over the last century. Everything had been invested in this last intake of boys. There were no second chances. He narrowed his eyes. "How do you propose to keep in contact with them?"

"I won't need to. In recent years we have taken advantage of twenty-first-century technology. We will be able to track their whereabouts and call them in if necessary. I am also confident in a new contact who will aid us in securing the sacred blood, then all we need to do is wait and let the Siren's nature do the rest.

To the casual observer, our boys will have ordinary lives. They will go to school, enter colleges, get jobs, become slackers – all the usual things boys of their age do. Except their true nature will sleep. The academy here will be like a distant memory. Nothing more than a shaky start in life, like a children's home or orphanage."

Croll was impressed. It was a good plan. "And if a boy should find one?"

Seville bobbed his head. "When," he corrected. "The closer the boy gets to the center of Atlantean power, the more effective he will be."

Croll smiled. He was of course referring to the Orb, the ancient source of Atlantean wealth. His great god of fire was indeed with him. The Scythians had waited patiently for centuries for this chance. "It is time to exorcise the parasite demons cast down from the heavens," he said placing a hand on Seville's shoulder. Fanaticism shone from Seville's eyes. No Scythian lord ever had a more faithful servant. "You will receive your reward in the beyond."

"It is time to scourge the earth of all that doesn't belong here, along with their hybrid offspring. We will cast them out like the demons they are. We will take their hidden power source and offer it to the Almighty Ares as the spoils of war." His face hardened. "Just a simple meeting of a boy and a girl and the world will be ours again."

SEVILLE INSISTED on attending the boy's mind-wipe personally. He was the last to attend the infirmary to complete the process. A short procedure that would induce sleep, then when he awoke he would be in his new life with only hazy memories and dreams of what came before.

The tall boy entered, bowed and sat in the dentist-like chair when indicated to sit. It hissed backwards and clamps immediately restrained his head, ankles and wrists.

He was already impressive. Not just in stature for a boy of

his age but in his strength of will. Seville had singled him out from the beginning and treated him the harshest of all in an already grueling program. He'd been deprived of food, sleep and pushed to the point of exhaustion, and still he didn't crack. He was handsome and softly spoken. He could sing and play several instruments all to give him more opportunity to cross paths with a Siren, rumored to gravitate to such things. He was a protégé any master would be proud of.

His clear blue eyes stared ahead of him waiting for what was to come as if he'd waited for it his whole life.

The medic approached with the syringe containing a drug to aid the process that would erase his memory. For a moment Seville thought sadly that he would not remember him after this day, although he didn't reveal such a weakness. Instead, he said, "Are you afraid?"

The boy's eyes went straight to his and held a steely determination. "No." Just a one-syllable answer and nothing more.

Seville's heart swelled with pride. He nodded once to the medic and the shot was given in the top of the boy's arm.

Seville watched in gruesome fascination as the machine buzzed and the boy's eyes slowly closed. He vowed at that moment that this one would receive the upmost care and receive the sacred blood before all others.

 *resent day*

LANDING WOULD BE in twenty minutes. Phoebe was forced to come out of her nostalgic daydream to use the loo quickly before the 'fasten seatbelt' sign came on.

After washing her hands, she checked her reflection for any changes brought on by the water. A girl couldn't be too careful. With nothing to see, she ran her hand through her mass of red curls to tidy them back into place and pulled a face at how freckly and pale she looked. Then she went back to her seat. The clouds of the western seaboard were already billowing around the wing so she clicked her seatbelt, figuring it wouldn't be long now.

Excitement tickled her stomach as she looked for the first sign of land out of the window. Or maybe it was a little bit of fear. This was her first real time away from her family – more importantly, the first time since she was a little girl that she'd ever been apart from Connor, the young Irishman, employed by her parents to look after the horses. She'd spent every available moment with him since she was a child. He knew all her grisly secrets, every one and never judged her.

Once, when he was just a teenager, he'd whispered he was really there to watch over her. It was the perfect thing to say at a time when she needed it. Things didn't come easy to a troubled girl who felt a freak. In a stiff, well-to-do family who took very little notice of her, Connor made her feel somehow special, and she loved him for that. That made him forever her rock.

It was strange, she hadn't thought of that day for a very long time. It was the same day she'd seen the *brown man*. The one who'd appeared in the grounds of her house while she'd been riding her pony. It was the day of her sister's birthday party. Afterwards she'd fantasized he was an Arabian prince come to ask her father for her hand in marriage. He'd known who she was and introduced himself as, *Ghazi Sistani.* She'd said the words a thousand times, but she'd never seen him again. It had been an uneventful meeting that she'd probably built far too much in her mind, but it had always stayed with her. Perhaps because he said he hoped to meet her again one day.

She shook her head not sure why she was getting so introspective. This was a trip of a lifetime and she should live for the moment and not in the past. Connor was just a phone call away and promised to be on the first flight out to Seattle should she need him. It was her gap year. Something every girl should experience before she tied herself down with a job or university. If she liked it, there was always a possibility she could go to university in Washington. She planned on checking it out while she was there.

However, if she was really honest, something about the place just called to her. As a visual artist, there was something about the dark, rainy far corner of the US that she couldn't shake off. Sometimes she thought it was because of its music history, and that definitely was a plus, but there was something more, something she just couldn't put her finger on.

A rough bump dragged her back to her surroundings and she realized the plane had landed. Her hands gripped the seat arms as a wave of nerves engulfed her. *Here goes. This is it.* Somehow, instinctively, she knew her life would start here.

Baggage Reclaim and Customs were negotiated fairly quickly, and she walked through into the airport to see her old school friend, Maggie, jumping about and waving her arms with her cardboard sign saying, "Phoebe Ray".

Phoebe grinned and pulled her suitcase over to her friend who flung her arms around her jumping up and down, squealing. She was exactly the same as she remembered her. Deep auburn hair bounced in large curls that needed a good brush and kind brown eyes alive and creased with laughter. It was impossible not to get caught up in her enthusiasm and she jumped up and down with her.

"Come on, Phibs. It's going to be so great. I can't wait to show you round and introduce you to everyone."

Phoebe smiled indulgently at the use of her old nickname, given to her at school for the tall stories she told. She didn't mind it. She was just excited to be there.

THE APARTMENT where she was to stay was bought by Maggie's English parents and rented out as an investment, but Phoebe suspected it was to keep an eye on their wayward daughter, ensuring she had a safe place to stay. Either way, it was a wonderful chance for her to have a base while she explored and used the opportunity to sketch and photograph the area. A fine drizzle had now set in, giving the late afternoon light a blue, melancholic hue, and she longed to get out with her camera. "Can we go for a walk?" she said, still staring out the window.

Maggie grinned. "Still the same old Phibs. Guess you should stay up as late as you can before you crash."

Phoebe didn't even unpack any of her things. She just tossed her bag on the bed of the room Maggie pointed to and quickly fished out her camera. "Right, ready."

The apartment was in First Hill. Once a place for the wealthy, it was now an arty, happening neighborhood, with green open spaces and close enough to downtown.

The girls walked slowly arm in arm while Phoebe took in all the new sights and smells. It was exhilarating and she just knew she would love the place already.

"How's the gorgeous Connor?" Maggie said, waggling her eyebrows suggestively.

Phoebe nudged her playfully. "Hey, it's not like that." It was true; there had never been anything between them (Not that she hadn't tried). She'd badgered him unmercifully when she was younger. The boy just had a resolve of steel and eventually she'd given up and they'd settled into a close friendship that more resembled brother and sister. He was now in his twenties, she was nineteen and he was her best friend in the world. Didn't mean she wanted anyone else to have him though. She scowled playfully at Maggie who threw her head back and laughed, understanding immediately. "Fair game, Phibs," she teased.

Phoebe pretended to have the hump, but the girls at school had often teased her about the 'gorgeous peasant' whose eyes never left her whenever they went home.

Something caught her eye. She paused, put her camera to her eye and clicked. A cool beanie-headed busker strummed a ballad on his guitar.

"So what's the plan?" Maggie said, and nodded her head towards the busker. "Are you here for the music?"

Phoebe laughed. She was incorrigible. "Nooo!"

They continued to amble along. "I'm not sure really. I want to take some photos, see the sights. I might take a look at the university."

"Ooooh, so you might be staying a while?"

Phoebe studied her friend. She had that calculating look which meant she was hatching something. "What?"

Maggie shook her thoughts away and speeded up their pace. "Come on."

A yellow bus with a blue roof was just easing into the curb. Maggie pulled her along and they both jumped on.

They plonked into their seats and a wave of fatigue washed over her. She guessed the jet lag was beginning to catch her up. "Is everything okay? Where are we going?"

"It's all good. We've just got to hurry, that's all. If you're staying you'll want a job, right?"

Phoebe bobbed her head. She had some savings and planned on seeing how it went but, thinking about it, she supposed a job would be a great idea to make her money last. Then she narrowed her eyes at her friend. "What job?"

Maggie grinned, grabbed her hands and bounced in her seat. "It's going to be great, Phibs. We can work together. I've got a job in a bar downtown, and there's a girl leaving this Friday." She sat back in her seat, anxiously in thought. "I just hope it hasn't been given to anyone else yet."

Everything was going so fast, and Phoebe's head was certainly not firing on all cylinders. She eased back into her chair and decided to just go along with it; frankly, she was too tired to argue with Maggie when she was on a mission.

THE BAR WAS IN A BASEMENT, quite dark, with low ceilings. Nothing fancy, just beer, music and sticky carpets underfoot. It was already fairly busy. Phoebe guessed it was probably later than she thought. It was twilight so evening was creeping on.

Maggie said hello to various long-haired hippy-looking blokes and several girls she guessed already worked there. "Where's Bob?" Maggie stopped to ask.

The blond, heavily charcoal-eyed girl nodded towards the bar. Phoebe followed her line of vision and saw a youngish man with a till receipt in his mouth while he appeared to be doing something with the till.

"Come on," Maggie said, holding her hand and pulling her through the crowd until they stopped at the bar in front of him.

The man's eyes flicked to hers then looked at Maggie. He frowned and took the paper out of his mouth. "It's not your shift tonight."

"No, I know. I wanted you to meet someone." She yanked Phoebe so she literally bumped into her. "This is my friend, Phoebe. She's from England and she's staying a while. Did you give someone Kim's job yet?"

His eyes did a visual sweep of her that made her feel uncomfortable. "I'm trying out someone tonight." He scanned the room just as there was a load clang and a crash – the contents of a tray hitting the floor on the other side of the bar. Then he looked at her deadpan, as if he was gathering patience. "Come Friday. Don't be late. We'll be busy."

Phoebe felt bewildered. *Did she just get a job?* "What time?" she stuttered.

"Just come with Maggie," he said, bobbing his head in her direction. Then he walked off quickly, leaving her dazed.

CHAPTER 2

The bar was a live music venue called The Reptile and the coolest place ever. Phoebe started on the Friday and worked the hardest she'd ever worked. It was the busiest night of the week. Thursday to Sunday had a different band every night. The rest of the week it was an ordinary bar. Phoebe thought it the most exciting place in the world and longed to snap the scene and its patrons with her camera.

At last Phoebe could take a minute's break with Maggie at the edge of the room. "Who are they?" she said, nodding her head towards the band performing on the low stage.

Maggie nodded appreciatively. "I thought you'd like them, they're Blunderbuss. I know them."

Phoebe opened her eyes wide in surprise. "Seriously? They are so good." They really were a great little alternative rock band. They were not bad-looking either, dressed in jeans, baggy t-shirts with the obligatory long hair. However there was one of them that stood out. The lead singer was the tallest, had the bluest eyes, with dark curly hair almost to his waist. Everything about him seemed to ooze sex appeal. A perfect face, a lean body and a great rock voice. "Who's he?" she said, almost to herself.

Maggie giggled. "Careful, Phibs. That's Drew Stone. Everyone loves him."

She wasn't surprised. The guy was obviously a star and could probably get any girl. She put her drink down on the bar as their break was over. "A girl can dream, can't she?"

Maggie laughed and shook her head as if she didn't believe her for a minute. "Come on, if you want to continue to ogle lover boy we'd better not get the sack."

The days passed pleasantly after that and Phoebe quickly settled in. Lots of bands played The Reptile and a lot of them were pretty cute. Some were more punky and others more like a throwback from the seventies. She was known as Lady Ice, the English girl, and hit on regularly. She kind of liked that they thought her posh, even if she felt far from it.

It was a great job because it gave her the opportunity to get out with her camera during the day. The weather, normally drizzly and grey, gave the perfect light for the melancholy black and white style so typically her.

There was only one problem with her new life. Most of the time she felt like she was being followed. She dismissed it as silly at first, but no matter where she went, she always saw the same car – well the same three cars to be exact. It was probably from a lifetime of avoiding her parents, but she noticed a lot of things other people didn't.

Today would have been no different had the car not stopped and an older gentleman got out. Two burly men in suits got out of the front and the three began to walk in her direction. For a moment her heart thumped, then she wasted no more time and broke into a run.

Her feet pelted the wet pavement, and she cut through alleyway after alleyway. Finally she took a peek over her shoulder and began to slow down. Her breath was hacking through her lungs and her throat was sore.

Dropping down to a walk, she put her hand to her thumping chest in relief and was able to catch her breath. They hadn't followed. However, looking around her, she had no idea where she'd ended up. Tall, grey warehouses were either side. Somewhere in her mad scramble to escape she'd managed to find her way into an industrial district.

There was nothing to worry about, she told herself. All she needed to do was go back the way she came until she recognized somewhere or saw a cab. She wiped the sweat from her brow with the back of her hand and began walking. Now she had time to think it felt kind of silly. The men could have simply been going towards a shop or a bar. *Why on earth did she take off like that?* Her flight reflex had kicked in before she had time to think.

Now she'd calmed down, she took in her surroundings. This place was kind of cool. A creak came from some corrugated iron peeled back at the boarded-up entrance to a warehouse. Taking the lens cap off her camera, she went in for a closer look. First she listened for any signs of life. Water dripped inside and the wind rattled up in the mettle rafters. She checked left and right. There didn't appear to be a soul around. What was just a light breeze outside whistled up under the eaves like a gale. The few broken windows high up reminded her of ghoulish eyes, made worse by the teeth-like metal and boards trying to bar her way in. The place literally screamed horror film; don't go in, but photo opportunities didn't come much better than this. After thinking for precisely one second, taking another look around, she peered in.

It was a cavernous space with debris and abandoned rusting machinery scattered all over. Steps went up on the far side to a glass galleried area missing several panes.

The approach of a car made her slip inside and look through a hole to make sure the men hadn't found her.

It wasn't the same one and the breath she hadn't realized she was holding came out in a blast. Her nerves felt shot to pieces today.

Now inside, the place was amazing. Putting her Nikon D810 to her eye, she began clicking. Her feet crunched over broken glass and the whole building sounded like it was moaning at the invasion. It seemed to go perfectly with the feel of the shots and she tried to capture its essence. Titles for the pieces were already appearing in her head: "Long gone", "Seattle seen".

When she took the camera away from her eye she found she was at the bottom of the metal staircase to the gallery. She tested the state of them with a stamp of her foot. They seemed sturdy enough. With a clang on each step she began a slow climb – snapping with her camera as she went.

The room at the top had been an office that looked down on the floor below. An old metal sign propped against the wall said, "Danger: Moving Machinery". It must have been some kind of factory before.

Her foot kicked against something and she glanced down. An old shoebox with 'Grants Loggers' written on the stained cardboard and an old tatty boot gave away what it made. She took a few more shots.

Then, after a few small steps, she froze.

Rain began pelting the roof and the small hairs stood up on her neck when a voice said; "Can I help you, iimr'atan shaba?"

CHAPTER 3

*P*hoebe jumped and turned to face the voice. Her eyes were wide with fright, but the Middle Eastern man was smiling. He put up both his hands as if she was pointing a gun at him. Then she realized she was still holding her camera out in front of her and lowered it slowly. "I'm s...sorry," she stuttered. "Someone was chasing me. I was hiding." Despite being caught trespassing, she couldn't help feeling there was something familiar about him.

It was more than his black wavy hair with hints of grey and beautiful coffee skin. The expensive black clothes and leather jacket that showed he was no factory worker. It was more his poise and the way he carried himself that warned she shouldn't be all the way out here alone with him. *The brown man.*

The man tilted his head slightly but his eyes went to her camera as if he didn't believe she was running for a second.

"Oh yeah... I'm a photographer," she explained. "I know you, don't I?"

He was looking at her intently, as if gauging her for any lies.

"I'm sorry, are you the owner?" He was no vagrant, that was for sure. "This may sound silly, but did you come to my house in Surrey once to meet with my father? Bently-Ray is the name."

"This place belongs to my brother." Then he smiled a little. "Ah, little Phoebe Ray on the little horse. You've grown up."

Phoebe half smiled, half frowned. "Yeah, what are the chances?" Even as she said the words it occurred to her that the odds of her bumping into the same guy in a warehouse on the other side of the world were slim to none. Her mind began to race with any logical explanation for the coincidence and she kept coming up with nada. Even if she supposed he was in one of the cars that had been following her, it didn't explain how she managed to run to a place owned by one of his family, unless he was lying. Either way, she was acutely aware that he was blocking the only stairs to the way out.

He seemed to guess what she was thinking and gestured the stairs with his arm. "May I offer you a lift somewhere?"

"No!" she snapped a little more loudly than she would have liked. He was being polite and charming but her alarm wire had been tripped and she had a bad feeling about the whole thing.

He bowed his head again. "Apologies, as you said you'd been running, I thought you may be lost."

"It's okay, I'll find my way," she said, pointing awkwardly at her camera again. "Better get on. My friends will miss me," she said, side-stepping slowly in a wide arc around him.

His hand disappeared into an inside pocket of his jacket and he pulled out a small card.

"Take this. It is a rough area and a little remote," he said, offering her his card. "If ever I can be of service ..."

Weirdly, it did nothing to reassure her. The encounter

had unsettled her as a kid, finding him alone in the grounds of her house. He'd known exactly who she was and seemed so exotic and strange. She'd never forgot him. Now he was doing it again for a different reason. She snatched the card, rushed down the stairs and across the factory floor.

Now the once-interesting, rusty machines seemed to grab at her clothes as she ran and old sacks and flattened boxes caught at her ankles. She stumbled and tripped several times in her haste to get out.

As soon as she clambered out of the boarded-up door, she breathed with a sense of relief. The heavy shower had passed and the world had brightened. She took a moment, although her heart still thumped and sweat trickled down the side of her face. The crumpled card dug into the palm of her hand and she glanced down. It said simply *Ashur Elazar* and a mobile phone number. That wasn't the same name he'd said on their first meeting. That was Ghazi Sistani. The name was printed in her memory banks. She flipped it over and it was blank. Something about him wasn't right.

Suddenly it felt really important to get out of there and she began to run again. She ran and ran until her steps took her back to busy shops and she got her bearings.

Phoebe fell back into a walk and tried to act normally again. Just when she relaxed enough to think she must be losing her mind, a cream sedan glided slowly past her. Another car she was sure she saw on a regular basis. "For fuck's sake," she whispered, and took off again. Hopping on a bus, she didn't stop till she reached the safety of her apartment. The whole day unsettled her after that and she couldn't get the brown man out of her head.

NOTHING out of the ordinary happened for a while. Her life settled down with work taking up most of her time. Drew

Stone's band appeared a couple more times, and her heart skipped when she realized he often came in as a customer too. Her skin prickled whenever he passed by. It was the weirdest sensation, but he never looked at her. It was frustrating.

Phoebe knew she wasn't conventionally beautiful but she'd never been ignored before. It kind of hurt and knocked her confidence a little.

It made her think of Connor, her go-to person for reassurance and straight-talking; her personal safe zone. It was still quiet in the bar so she tapped his number on her phone.

"Whatsup?" came immediately.

She let out a breath of relief at the sound of his deep voice. "Nothing, just homesick."

"Is everything okay?"

She felt foolish to tell him she felt like she was being followed, a weird guy had given her his card when she'd been trespassing, and the only guy to catch her eye in weeks didn't look in her direction. It all seemed a bit petty now. "No seriously, I'm fine."

"I think I'll come and visit," he said after a pause.

Her manager caught her eye and raised his brows as if she was slacking.

"Okay … gotta go," she said quickly.

THE NIGHT PASSED SLOWLY. The band was good, but her mind was a million miles away.

"Phibs! Maggie said, snapping her fingers to get her attention. "We're all going to Sasha's after work. Wanna come?"

Phoebe's eyes tracked to the blond punk-looking guy next to her with one side of his head shaved and the other left long. He was dressed in what could only be described as a pair of striped pyjamas. She instantly recognized him as the bass guitarist from Blunderbuss and stiffened.

He smiled. "Loosen up, Lady Ice." His look was playful.

She found herself grinning despite herself. "I'm a bit tired and I won't know anyone."

Maggie rolled her eyes.

The guy bowed theatrically. "I'm Glen of the band Blunderbuss."

She giggled. "I know who you are."

"Well then, you will know someone." Then he straightened up as he was being called. "Seriously, we'll all be there; it will be a blast. Gotta go." He nodded at both girls and disappeared into the crowd.

Phoebe continued to watch the space he'd occupied before the crowed swallowed him up. If he was there, the chances were that Drew Stone would be too. Her heart thumped; if ever there was a chance to speak to him, tonight would be it.

Maggie bumped her shoulder playfully with hers. "I know what you're thinking," she sang. Then she must have read her scowl because she laughed.

"I was just thinking that Glen seemed like a nice guy."

Maggie smiled knowingly. "He is." But the look she gave her meant she saw straight through her.

IT WAS late by the time they got there. Between twenty and thirty people were sprawled out in the living room with beer cans strewn everywhere. Led Zeppelin's "I'm gonna leave you", was being strummed on an acoustic guitar. Scanning the smoky room she could see it was full of mainly stoned musicians and a few girls – some she recognized from The Reptile.

The atmosphere was thick with smoke that lay in lines on

the air. People were engaged in long, deep conversations conducive to musicians winding down. Usually about chord changes, the meaning of life, the universe, crap like that. It seemed to go with the territory. She could tell most of them would probably be crashing out where they were.

Maggie had disappeared off somewhere as soon as they got in the door and there was no sign of Glen. Her heart sank. She should have gone home. Exhaustion rolled over her and she looked for a place to sit. The apartment wasn't that big so, in the end, she wadded up her jacket for a pillow and lay down next to the wall in the living room.

It was kind of relaxing to be there but not take part; watching the easy way they conversed and their hands gestured lazily. Most were getting really comfortable and a few were nodding off already.

She made up her mind to stay the obligatory hour and then slip out and walk home. Her eyes felt heavy and she allowed them to close.

"No, Steve, I'm beat. We'll go later."

Phoebe immediately became alert, and peeked through her eyelashes. It took her a moment to get her bearings. She must have slept and turned as she was now facing the wall. Her hackles rose sharply as she became hyper aware of the presence nearby.

It was him. Drew Stone, and he was very close. *Oh my god.* He was lying right behind her. Surely he must see that she was hyperventilating and her heart hammering through her chest. *Shit, what should she do?*

Holding her breath, she remained stiff as board in the hope that her heartbeat would follow suit and he would think she was asleep.

"Lift up!"

Her eyes went wide and she remained frozen. Surely he

was talking to someone else. She was too scared to move just in case.

She felt a gentle nudge to her shoulder. "Lift up!"

Now unable to pretend otherwise, "What?" she said, leaning up on her elbow and turning blearily to look at him.

"Here …" He offered her a small cushion for her head.

For a moment she stared into his blue-grey eyes. It was the first time she'd seen them properly. In fact, it was the first chance she'd had to look at him square in the face. He was everything she expected: beautiful cream skin, too perfect for a boy, surrounded by an enviable abundance of thick hair hanging in loose curls. Then, realizing she was coming over weird, she took the cushion, saying, "Thank you," and returned to the same position, facing the wall far from asleep.

He shuffled closer.

Her eyes flashed open. Drew Stone was literally spooning his body with hers. A guy she had never really met and barely spoken to. Her body just lit up. He was almost touching her but not quite, but she was agonizingly aware he was there. In fact every hair stood up to meet him.

His hand appeared in front of her face. He'd stretched out his arm under his head and rested it across her pillow.

Phoebe knew what it was. It was an invitation.

She swallowed hard, now aware of every inch of him. His warm breaths moved her hair gently and tickled her neck. His chest expanded and touched her back in gentle rhythm. Then there were the bolts of electricity that shot down her thighs to her toes, and places she was desperately trying not to think about.

Not sure what she was doing exactly, she lifted her head. Then his free arm came across her waist and his other went under the pillow and rested at the crook of her neck. When he tugged her into his lap it felt like he completely encased her. Everything that had tingled with electricity now pooled with warmth, luxuriating with satisfaction at being touched and wanting more.

Her heart rate tripled and all she could think was *oh my god, oh my god* ... over and over.

He was there, Drew Stone, a living, breathing, hot guy she'd been crushing on for ages, without so much as a single conversation, touching her, affecting her, everywhere.

CHAPTER 4

Somewhere in the deepest, darkest recesses of Phoebe's mind she knew she shouldn't allow this. The sensible part of her didn't want to come across as easy. The good girl should have got up and walked away, but she didn't. Instead she lay there and enjoyed this closeness for the first time. The fact that he was a gorgeous rock musician every girl in Seattle would kill for the chance with was only a part of it. The longer she lay in his arms the more relaxed she felt and the more he pulled her into him. With micro movements of her own she moved in closer to him until time literally had no meaning. God only knew how long they laid there bathing in the body contact.

Then, before she knew what happened, she felt him move to get up.

"Come on. Let me find you somewhere more comfortable to sleep."

With the beautiful warmth behind her now gone, without thinking she rolled onto her back and looked up into his ice-blue eyes looking down at her. "Come with me," he said quietly. His hand reached down for hers and she paused while she looked at it in a state of shock. Then, in a sudden impulse, she took it and he pulled her up to her feet.

Keeping her hand in his, he led the way. Stepping through the sleeping bodies, cans and bottles. They went down a short hallway with three closed doors leading off of it and came to a stop at the furthest one. He turned a key in the lock, switched on the light and she followed him in.

Inside was a messy bedroom that looked like it belonged to a student. Big flyers and posters covered the walls; vinyl record sleeves were all over the floor and a guitar leant against one wall next to a pair of bongos.

She still hadn't said much at all. Maybe she was at home in bed in England. She frowned, not knowing if she preferred that or not.

Her eyes tracked to the narrow bed where Drew waited for her to look at him from the other side. "It's small but it's clean."

The reality of the situation was now hitting her and she looked at the door. She was alone in an apartment, in a strange city with a sexy man who was looking at her quizzically – as if he wasn't sure what she'd do either.

He quirked an eyebrow. "Do you wanna get in?" He pulled back the quilt a little in invitation.

She stood immobile and looked at the grey light out of the window. It would be morning soon.

Drew seemed to read her mind. "You can just crash for a couple of hours then I'll take you home."

A smile played on his lips as she studied him. Then she looked at the bed and back at him.

He laughed on an exhale, turned and sat on the bed and began to untie his boots. Then he pulled his shirt over his head. The curls of his dark hair almost reached down to his waist and fell forward into his face as he removed socks. A spectacular tattoo of an angel with vast open wings covered his back with indiscernible writing across his surprisingly muscled shoulder blades. In fact he was in really good shape. It was hard to tell under all the baggy clothes he wore.

Phoebe became aware when he was running out of clothes to remove, so she edged towards the bed.

"Turn off the light."

Stopping dead and still unsure, she watched him slip under the covers completely naked.

Oh dear! Her mind raced.

He smiled seductively with his eyes low. "Light!" he reminded her.

Before she knew what she was doing she flipped the light and pigeon-stepped towards the bed until her eyes became accustomed to the light. When her leg bumped its sides she perched and removed her own boots and jeans. Then, leaving her t-shirt and panties on, she slid between the sheets and faced away from him. Her blood pumped so hard it was throbbing in her ears as she pretended to try to sleep.

Laughter bubbled from his chest as he pulled her back into him as he'd done before. Except this time the warmth came from his smooth skin and his long, hard, aroused *OMG!*

"That's better," he said lazily into her hair.

It struck her then that while her heart was beating a military tattoo and threatened to burst out of her chest, this was probably a nightly occurrence to him. And with someone different every time. It was a sobering thought.

However, he snuggled in closer, with his head on the same pillow and his warm, sensuous mouth merely millimeters from her neck. She briefly wondered if he was aware of the effect he was having – or whether or not he cared.

The only person she'd ever fallen asleep with was Connor, and he'd always been a gentleman and fully clothed. This guy was anything but.

The truth was that she had always been wary of the opposite sex. *Was she pretty enough? Would they like her? Were they only after one thing?* In her case, when she came near a man she liked, she felt certain changes. In fact, things started to shift with any extreme emotion.

As a child she'd referred to it as her evil inside. Connor had seen it a few times and tactfully shielded her until it passed and never referred to it. The only time she'd tried to broach the subject he dismissed it with a wave of a hand saying, "Ah, Ireland is full of young Fae. I seen it all the time growing up." However, as sweet as that explanation was and while she could ignore it as a child, it was getting increasingly harder the older she got. It seemed a given that the minute they saw her transformation they'd run a mile. She was like a gremlin that you could absolutely, on no account, get wet. Her eyes changed, her teeth grew and she had no idea what lurked in her chest.

And so she'd kind of put up a wall of indifference around herself. Hence the apt nickname, Lady Ice.

Somehow, this guy – Drew Stone – who she'd been happy to ogle from afar, had ridden rough shod over her wall. And here she was with him in bed almost naked, breathing invitingly on her neck, obviously waiting for her move.

Drew groaned and snuggled even closer – his mouth now next to her skin behind her ear.

Bloody hell! Terror began to rise with the familiar weight and shift in the evil in her chest. Her gums ached as her teeth began their slow descent. *Oh no!* But heat rushed to the pit of her stomach and crept between her legs making them scissor.

She writhed and turned in his arms. Her mouth was no more than an inch from his. The dawn light spilling into the room was now tinged orange as her transformed vertically slit eyes homed in on his mouth.

The weight rested on the walls of her chest and she looked at the door. If she didn't run now it would be too late. This was the strongest it had ever felt and she was losing control. Phoebe looked back at Drew, whose eyes were closed.

Heat stung her cheeks and her breathing was becoming deeper as the weight in her chest grew.

Drew's arms came up into her hair and he brushed her mouth with his. The lower half of her body pushed into his involuntarily and her teeth strained and extended to their full length. "I should go," she said sounding unlike herself, but unable to move. Her body simply wouldn't obey.

Instead he nipped her lips with his. Copper hit her tongue as her teeth bit into her own mouth. The small kisses were asking permission for something more and it was terrifying. A fear like being at the edge of a huge precipice—one that once you stepped over there was no going back and no knowing what would happen.

Although, as she nipped his lips in response, the feeling of him taking advantage of the poor little rich girl far from home began to disappear. When the transformation hit she was far from weak. In fact she felt very much in control. It made her feel powerful. Maybe it was him who should be wary.

That was when his tongue entered her mouth and tasted her blood.

It was obvious when he stopped kissing her and licked his lips slowly. Then, as if he was testing something, he put his mouth to hers again.

Memories from her childhood flashed in her head. Times when she'd freaked out other children by changing at will to scare them.

His tongue ran across her lips to bring her mind back to him. There was no freaking out today. Instead, he pushed into her mouth more forcefully and she ceased to care. Accepting him finally, she kissed him hard and wet. Sensuous and exploring initially, it built to become something demanding and fierce. Heat seared through her whole body and the weight in her chest became unbearable.

Drew groaned as she pushed him over onto his back unable to help herself. Her desperate hands ran all over his chest. He found the hem of her t-shirt and began to pull it up until she had to wriggle out of it. Then his well-practised hands went straight behind her back and adeptly unclipped her bra. It fell loose immediately in front of her and he helped pull down the straps until he could throw it away.

His thumbs rubbed over the peaks of her breasts while he rolled her over onto her back. She gasped as his hands began to move down her body and he began to kiss and nip down the side of her neck to her breasts.

Phoebe clutched at his shoulders, pulling him and positioning him roughly. Then, before she knew what was happening, her tiny panties were ripped from her. He was there at her core and pushed inside her without hesitation.

They both gasped. Then he began to move, slowly at first, until something appeared to possess him and he worked himself to a merciless rhythm.

Her mouth found the soft part of his shoulder to muffle her moans. It struck her again that she hadn't even strung more than two words together with this man, but he was beautiful, and at that moment she didn't care how many women he'd had. He sure as hell wouldn't have had anyone like her. The idea of it just ramped her higher.

Her face was aflame and she moved her grip with her teeth higher to the soft part of his neck.

The weight surged in her chest.

Drew seemed to recognize it in her and pulled her leg across his hip and pushed into her even faster.

She answered by threading her fingers into his hair and pulling him to her more tightly. Then she pushed down her heel into the bed for extra leverage and began to move her pelvis up to meet him.

He groaned his approval – his mouth next to her temple. "I knew you were hot," he whispered, and his hand cupped her butt cheek helping to grind her to him. Her lower legs now had him clamped behind the knees.

He seemed to revel in being trapped and held her tightly by the small of her back and her hip.

Her gums ached and the evil bubbled, determined to come out.

His strokes were now hard, pounding her into the bed that was creaking and hitting the wall.

Something was unfurling in her stomach and her resolve to control whatever it was, was dissolving fast.

Surrender seemed inevitable and she felt herself begin to float.

"That's it," he said, with his mouth provocatively next to hers.

Then something snapped and instinct took over. "I'm sorry," were her last sane words. A hot mist left her and surrounded them. What ever it was came from the depths of her and was as hot as hell.

Everything that followed seemed to be disjointed and in slow motion. The next minute she was staring down at him on his back while she straddled him. He uttered the word, "Fuck!" Then all she saw was blood.

A thousand thoughts came in a split second.

For a moment she wasn't sure whether she'd killed him. Then he groaned. Relief came with the waves of ecstasy that seemed to leave her and wash over him. In her blindness it seemed like they were one person.

An oily warmth came over her tongue and down her

throat and she realized her teeth were now clamped to his neck.

Fear stabbed through her, but the instant she attempted to fight it he clutched her to him more tightly.

Clearly, he was enjoying whatever it was they were doing. She wanted to quantify exactly what it was but she couldn't. All she knew was it was what she wanted, and evidently what he wanted too. It was ownership and giving of self, all rolled into one, and she soared.

Her orgasm unfurled and shot through her, systematically covering every inch of her. As if his blood was charging every cell in her body one by one in a torrent.

With surprising strength, he seemed to lift her and put her over onto her back where he engulfed her and pushed into her in slow, measured strokes. A gasp at her ear told her he was there and he tightened inside her, all around her and shuddered.

Her nails scraped down his back and he threw his head back and let out a long sigh of, "Phoebe!" and collapsed on top of her.

They both lay breathing hard while their heart rates returned to normal. The sex had been mind-blowing, but instead of concentrating on what she undoubtedly should – like what he was going to say about her doing her "Daughter of Dracula" act, all that she could think of was that in the height of pleasure, he'd said her name. They'd never been introduced and, up until then, she'd had no clue that she'd even been on his radar. Despite knowing she should be pleased or the very least flattered, all she felt was unease.

A last shudder pulsed through him. He didn't let go of her or spring off to go straight to the bathroom, which she noted.

After a few more minutes her ordinary vision returned and her teeth receded back into her gums, until all that was left were two sharp points level with the rest of her teeth. "Are you okay?" she said cautiously. "Did I kill you?"

Drew leant up on his elbows with great effort. Miraculously, there wasn't too much damage to his neck, just two perfectly circular holes. His eyelids were low and he had a smear of blood across his mouth and cheek, but he was smiling. He nodded slowly, his eyes tracking from hers to her mouth which when she licked her lips, she was sure were as bloody as his.

A flicker of concern crossed his face and, for a moment, she thought he was going to reject her. It was weird to think otherwise – after all, she'd proved she was a freak and he didn't exactly know her. However, she couldn't help thinking that she had some sort of claim over him now. There was something about this whole situation that made her feel like he was hers.

"You're wild," he whispered, his eyes still straying to her mouth.

"I know."

It seemed to satisfy him and he attempted to sit up but didn't quite make it and flopped down next to her with an, "oomph!" as the air left him.

Now lying side by side, she asked again if he was okay. She despised coming across as paranoid instead of vixen but she couldn't help herself.

Drew attempted to sit up but flopped back down again and laughed. "Wow, it just keeps on giving."

It helped soothe her fears a little. Although it occurred to her that he was light-headed because of blood loss. Without looking at him, she slipped out of bed and went towards the adjoining room she guessed was a bathroom. The small space contained just a small shower, basin and sink, and gave her a moment to gather her thoughts. *He hadn't run away screaming yet.* She reached into the cubicle and turned the shower to cool – her preferred temperature. With a ragged breath she walked back into the room.

At first sight of him propped up on pillows, she was shocked. Strangely it wasn't all the spatters of blood. It was how flushed he looked. She hadn't had that much experience of this kind of thing but even she knew this wasn't usual.

He laughed lazily. "I'm burning up. What did you do to me?"

Phoebe approached the bed quickly. "Let me help you into the shower."

With her arm through his, she managed to get him to his feet. He swayed a little and leant on her. "Whoa!" he said, bringing his hand up to his forehead.

"Let me help you."

He didn't argue, and allowed her to lead him slowly to the bathroom and into the shower. "It's cold," he said, putting his hand in the spray to test it before he got in.

"You need it like this," she said, nudging him gently.

With a small shrug like he wasn't convinced, he stepped in with a sharp intake of breath at the shock to his system.

She joined him and turned the dial up a little to make him relax.

The cubicle was small and not really meant for two. However, Drew was still wobbly and leant against the wall. His eyes were closed and his chest rose and fell with deep, uneven breaths.

It gave her another chance to check his wound and it was healing fast. Still, she watched him closely. In all honesty she had no clue what was happening to him, or whether what she was doing was enough. It wasn't the kind of thing you could rock up to the emergency room and say, "My boyfriend feels faint because I think I drank all his blood."

Boyfriend! That was hardly true. They'd barely spoken.

As if he knew what she was thinking, he half opened his

eyes lazily. "I'm Andrew by the way. Everyone calls me Drew."

The air left her on a single blast of laughter. The tension between them eased a little. "I know who you are," she said, rolling her eyes. *Who wouldn't?* The guy was a local celebrity. "I'm Phoebe." Then she frowned when she remembered he'd used her name.

"Pleased to meet you, Phoebe." He was smirking as he pulled her between his legs and rested his arms on her shoulders. He put his head on an angle and searched her face. "Don't worry, I'll be alright soon. I'm already feeling better. I had no idea you were such a wild cat." Then he rested his forehead against hers as another wave of something hit him.

They remained silent for a few moments, but Phoebe was anything but relaxed. The tingle she felt under her skin was the signal that her black tiger-like markings were beginning to emerge on her skin.

Her eyes flashed to his but they were closed. Momentarily relieved, she did what she'd practiced since she was a small girl.

She concentrated just as Connor had taught her.

Looking down at her feet, she worked her way up, one limb at her time. When at last she reached her face, she let out a slow breath and opened her eyes. Now completely recovered, his eyes were wide open.

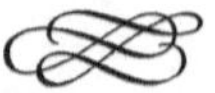

CHAPTER 5

*P*hoebe froze.

Drew didn't say a word for what felt like ages, but he was clearly thinking. His mind whirred in front of her.

She braced herself for the inevitable humiliation and rejection. Instead, her jaw dropped open.

"Does this mean you're my girl now?" He shifted uncomfortably. "Coz, I gotta say, I don't like the idea of you doing that with anyone else."

After a moment of absolute stunned silence she stammered; "I won't … I mean I don't … It's easy to kill someone," she ended with a frown. *Is it possible that he hadn't seen any of her transformation?* Her past attempts at sex had been fumbling failures, usually ending with the guy literally running out of the room. And that's without the full dental impact.

Drew threw his head back and laughed loudly. "Yeah, I get you." His face became serious again. "Lets get dressed and I'll take you home."

She went to protest. "It's okay, it's light now. I'll be fine."

Quite honestly, she needed to process this.

He held her chin. "Hey, are you brushing me off?" His eyes narrowed but he was playful.

Hers went wide. "Oh no, I didn't ..."

He grinned, "Come on, the fresh air will do me good." He took her by the hand and led her from the shower.

They both went into the other room and got dressed – him a little more slowly and shakily than her. He was forced to sit on the bed a couple of times, as he started to sway. When it passed, he continued to pull on his jeans and boots.

After a last check round, she left the room with him. Although she thought his cheeks still looked a little flushed.

Everyone else in the flat appeared to be sleeping. They'd almost reached the hallway to the front door when a few began to stir. A clatter of cups came from the small kitchen and someone wolf whistled.

Busted.

"Yeah, yeah, we'll see you guys later," Drew said, but he was smiling.

Phoebe was sure being seen creeping out with a girl wasn't news and kept her head down.

When they got outside into the cool air, he put his arm around her shoulder. "You cause quite a stir, you know that?" he said, with a smile next to her ear.

They began to walk, but she was puzzled. *No she didn't know that.* She wanted to question him further. "Aren't they used to seeing you with girls?"

He shrugged. "Yeah," he conceded. "But not Lady Ice," he finished, bumping into her playfully.

It felt weird being seen as some sort of ice queen. Nothing seemed further from the truth. It proved no one really knew her here. It was a timely reminder that, despite spending a couple of hours together, she didn't know him either.

Drew walked her up to her building's door. They stopped and faced each other. "Here we are," he said.

Not knowing what else to say, being in unchartered territory, she found herself saying, "Do you want to come up?"

He looked around, bent down and kissed her gently and unhurried. His hand cupped her face and his thumb rubbed along her cheekbone. "Get some sleep. I'll see you later."

It was kind of a relief. Rolling around in the sheets was one thing, but taking a boy where you live and actually having a conversation was a whole other thing entirely. She smiled. "Okay."

He nodded once and jogged down the few steps back onto the pavement. "Later, Wild Cat!" he called, grinning at her as he walked away.

She couldn't help laughing.

Pretty soon his attention was taken up by his phone, which he put to his ear. A last wave of his hand and he disappeared around the corner.

Phoebe must have stood on the steps of her building for quite some time. The whole last twelve hours had been unreal. Excitement and absolute terror churned around in her stomach when she admitted to herself that she had a boyfriend and he was gorgeous. *Was he her boyfriend? He'd said he wanted her to be his girl, hadn't he?* She shook her doubts away. Nothing was allowed to ruin the best night of her life – one she'd remember for ever.

A sleek black car went past slowly. The kind of speed you did when you were looking for a house number. It sobered her instantly and she turned and went inside.

Making sure the door clicked behind her, she spun around and slammed straight into an enormous chest and looked up into a familiar brown face. "Good morning, iimr'atan shaba!"

CHAPTER 6

*E*xactly one month later

PHOEBE STILL FELT like she was being followed. The morning Drew walked her home had been no different. They hadn't hurried, even in the dreary grey morning light. People had their own lives, started up cars or clattered rubbish bins as they began their day.

Instead of feeling tired, she felt exhilarated and hopeful as she bounded up the four flights of stairs, fumbled with her keys and opened the apartment door. "Maggie," she called. "You home?" It was early but she just couldn't wait to tell her about her wonderful night.

The door to Maggie's bedroom opened and she stood bleary-eyed in the doorway, blinking and trying to wake herself up. "Phoebe … Is that you?"

Phoebe frowned. Something about her was off.

Before she could ask her more, Maggie flew at her and crushed her in a hug. "Thank god, where have you been?"

Phoebe was becoming more and more irritated at the mom act. "At the party, remember? I should be asking what happened to you – leaving me there with a bunch of people I didn't know."

Maggie broke away from her slightly to look into her face. It was all getting weirder by the minute because her expression was so odd. She was frowning at her as if she'd lost her mind. "Connor!" she shouted over her shoulder.

Phoebe wasn't sure what troubled her more – the grilling she was getting, or that Connor walked out from Maggie's room in his boxer shorts. Then, instead of the pair of them explaining, Connor cleared his groggy head and said, "Where the fuck have you been? We've hunted high and low for you!"

Irritation was now giving way to anger. "You can pack it in with your sick jokes. Instead of poking your noses into my personal life, how about you two explain how long this has been going on for?" she finished, glaring at them.

"A month!" the pair said simultaneously.

Phoebe tried to process what they were saying, but nothing seemed to compute.

"Where have you been all this time, Phoebe?" Maggie said more gently.

The look of concern on Maggie's face took the wind right out of her sails and she allowed her to lead her into the living room where she sat down with her on the leather sofa.

"Can you make us all a cuppa tea, please, Connor?"

He nodded, still looking pissed off, which fired up Phoebe's anger all over again. "I don't get it. You and Connor?" She wasn't sure if she was angrier with him for being with her closest friend or that they'd kept it a secret from her.

"How about you go first, then I'll tell you all about it?"

Phoebe stared at her in confusion. She was talking to her

as if she was a kid who'd had a bad fright. Nothing was making sense anymore.

Connor came back with the tea and put a mug in each of their hands, then sat in the armchair opposite.

Phoebe searched his face for a full minute. He was drinking his tea but his eyes never left hers and he looked really angry. The last time she'd seen him like this was when she'd run away as a kid after an argument with her parents. He'd found her after a long cold night in the barn, but instead of hugging her and being pleased to see her, he'd scolded her and told her what a selfish little madam she was, and if it had been up to him he'd have smacked her arse.

She sagged and sighed deeply. "Look, I'm sorry okay." She turned to face Maggie again. You disappeared as soon as we got there. I was tired; I lay down for a bit. Then I was with Drew ..."

"Drew Stone!" Maggie cut in. "You've been with Drew Stone all this time."

Phoebe frowned at the pair of them in exasperation. "Yes, okay. So I should have texted or something." Then she threw a sharp look to Connor. "I had no idea you were here."

Then she faced Maggie and said more kindly, "I just waited till it was light and he walked me home."

"That's it? That's all you've got to say?"

All Phoebe could do was try to open and close her mouth in confusion. "I don't get it. You stay out all the time," she said eventually.

Connor came over, knelt by her feet and took her hand. "So you went to the party, spent the night with Drew. Then what happened?" He was speaking softly and directly with the same expression Maggie had.

"I told you, as soon as it was light Drew walked me home."

Both he and Maggie looked at each other, then when she went to say something he shook his head.

"What! What is it?" she said.

"We spoke to Drew, Phoebe. We've hunted everywhere. He was the last person to see you … a month ago."

There was stunned silence after that. Phoebe ran through what he'd said over and over. She looked at his face to judge if he was going say "gotcha" any moment, but he was deadly serious and so was Maggie. "But I don't get it?" she said.

"What happened, Phoebe, don't you remember anything?"

She just sat and shook her head slowly, thinking maybe this was a dream – one of those anxious ones where the answer is right there but you just can't reach it. "I don't understand. Drew bought me to the door downstairs just now."

"No, Phoebes," Maggie said, holding her hands too. "That was a month ago. No one's seen you for a whole month."

Connor went to stand up but Phoebe held on. "Where are you going?"

"I need to call someone, Phoebes. A doctor, your parents." Then he flashed a look she didn't understand at Maggie. "There's some other stuff you need to know."

She was tired and wrung out. The night without sleep was now catching up with her fast. She just couldn't process it all. "Like what?" she said, wearily.

"Let's put you to bed first," Maggie said, pulling her up and leading her to her bedroom as if she had trouble walking.

Phoebe looked over her shoulder at Connor. He gave her a weak smile but looked worried sick.

"Connor will just make a few calls while you sleep. Then you'll wake up and everything will be better."

She nodded and allowed Maggie to lead her away to her room. Everything looked exactly as she left it. Her make-up was scattered over her dressing-table. The hairdryer was on her bed. Even the towel she'd last used to dry her hair was in a heap on the floor. She turned to face Maggie, utterly bewildered.

Maggie pulled back the quilt for her and she slipped out of her boots and jeans and meekly got in. Then she drew the blinds and bent down to stroke her head. "Sleep!" Then, without another word, she left and closed the door behind her.

IT WAS three hours later when she woke. For a full minute she basked in the memory of the amazing but strange night she'd spent with Drew. Then the events that followed when she got home came crashing in. There was always the hope it was a silly dream where she hadn't slept and become over-wrought. Somehow, she didn't think so.

With a brick in the pit of her stomach, she dragged herself out of bed and padded to her small bathroom. The mirror revealed nothing except dark circles and stale makeup. She looked like shit. A shower didn't make her feel much better either. Even though she felt like crawling back into bed, she pulled on some slouchy jogging bottoms and a t-shirt, took a deep breath and ventured out of her room.

Hushed tones were coming from the living room.

Connor was the first one to see her. "Hey! Feeling better?"

Phoebe nodded. Then her eyes swept the room and stopped dead at Drew. He looked beautiful, rested, his hair washed, his faced shaved. He certainly didn't look like a man who'd been up all night. He gave her a small smile and put up a hand in greeting. "Hey."

She stopped herself from turning and running back to her room. He was the absolute last person she wanted to see her in this state.

Maggie appeared and put a cup of something hot in her hands, but she put it straight down on the coffee table. "What's going on? What's he doing here?"

"He's been worried about you, Phoebe. He's been looking for you as much as we have."

Phoebe put her head in her hands. "Stop it. Just stop it. I don't know why you're all doing this, but it's not funny, okay."

Connor marched over and held out his phone to her. "The date of the party was third of September, right?"

Phoebe shrugged.

"Ring anyone, Google anywhere and look at the date."

Looking up at him wearily and sighing loudly, she did as he asked and tapped the phone for the *Daily Mail*, the *Telegraph*, then she just plain Googled: 'what day is it?' They all said the same thing: Sunday fourth of October. "But I don't understand?"

Everyone was looking at her with concern. There was no making fun of her today. All she could do was put her face in her hands and burst into tears.

THE NEXT COUPLE of days were a blur. There was no work because she hadn't showed up for a month and they'd replaced her. Connor insisted on staying, and she wasn't allowed anywhere on her own. They were calling it her blackout, and they were all concerned that it would happen again.

The fun seemed to have gone out of her life overnight. All she wanted to do was sleep; it just wasn't like her. Connor seemed to be on the phone all the time, and Maggie kept giving her these long sympathetic looks, which were starting to drive her mad. The only good thing about that whole time was that Drew seemed to still be on the scene. It was really surprising given who he was. He must have girls queuing around the block to spend some time with him, and yet he phoned or texted pretty much every day and took his turn with everyone else to accompany her anywhere.

It started to occur to her that maybe Drew was babysitting her like everyone else and didn't feel for her in the way she wanted him to. Since their unexpected night of passion he'd given her nothing more than a chaste peck on the cheek to say goodbye.

This particular day she woke up and lay in her bed feeling low and numb like she did pretty much every morning. Rain was already spattering on the window and the day was dark and grey to match her mood.

Glancing at the clock, it was still early. Maybe by the time she'd showered and dressed it would stop. The need to escape the apartment was overwhelming.

After showering, she dressed in plain blue jeans and a navy blue sweatshirt, tied back her hair in a ponytail and didn't bother with any makeup.

Phoebe closed the door to her room and crept to the door before anyone noticed her. Maggie was clattering in the kitchen and she could see Connor on the phone – slipping into his Irish lilt as he often did when he phoned home. Briefly she wondered what the crisis was that seemed to be taking a lot of his time these days – although she wouldn't wait to find out today. This was the best opportunity to get out alone. Her camera was still on the table next to the door so she grabbed it and slipped out.

The freedom was exhilarating. She skipped down the last of the steps and was almost at the street door when it opened and Drew walked in. A smile immediately lit up his face. "Hey! I was just coming to see you. Where are you going? Want some company?"

Actually, she didn't, and for a moment she didn't know

what to say to him. The whole idea was to get out alone so she could breathe. But a small smile played on his lips that totally said he didn't expect a "no" in a million years. Nobody had probably ever said no. Instead, she had to laugh. "Just out to take some pictures. Has it stopped raining?"

Drew turned to walk back with her towards the door. "Yeah, wanna see the sights?"

Phoebe smiled at him and opened the door. The smell of having just rained hit her nostrils and she breathed it in. "Yes, but not the kind of sights you're thinking."

They skipped down the few steps to the street. "Hey, wait up!" Drew said, limping slightly. "Old war wound."

It was something she didn't know about him and guessed there was a lot. He was smiling so she slowed down so he could catch up. "Come on, old-timer."

He laughed and they started to walk casually along the sidewalk in no particular direction towards the busier part of town. "You sure you can handle it?" she said, looking at him sideways.

He narrowed his eyes at her. "You? ... Definitely."

The simple worlds made her swallow hard. Whatever had hurt his leg was soon forgotten while she processed his sexy banter. Not knowing how to reply, she faced forward and they headed just where the fancy took her. They settled into an easy pace. It was the most relaxed she'd felt since she'd been back – that is, until his phone rang.

He put his phone to his ear and looked away as he spoke. "It's okay, she's with me."

Phoebe's heart sank. This whole thing wasn't funny anymore, and she took off at a run. She ran full sprint and had no idea where she was going. Block after block she went until the buildings seemed greyer, seedier and kind of familiar.

She slowed down to a walk. It was the place where the

warehouses were, where she'd met the strange Middle Eastern-looking man again.

After a moment of gathering her thoughts, footsteps came up behind her and she swung around. *Drew.*

"What the hell are you doing taking off like that?" He was limping again and breathing heavily, in obvious pain, which pricked her conscience a bit.

Guilt just added to her frustration. "I needed some space, Drew. You're all smothering me."

He softened and bobbed his head, pulling her into a hug. "Look, I get it, I do, but you have to give it some time so we can figure this thing out."

Phoebe pushed out of his grip, exasperated. He was acting like they'd been together ages when, in reality, it had been one night. Everything was so confusing. She didn't know if she could trust anything anymore – and that included her own judgment. Although she had to remember none of it was his fault. "I'm sorry, Drew. Nothing is making a lot of sense at the moment."

He nodded and exhaled loudly. Putting his arm around her shoulder they began to walk again. "What is this place – why here?"

Phoebe nodded. "I know. Bleak, isn't it." She frowned up at the building she went in the last time. "I came here before … to take pictures. There was a man – a foreigner." Then she sighed and continued walking.

Drew pulled her back by the arm. "You met someone?"

"Yes." She nodded in the direction of the warehouse. "I went in. He was a relative of the owner. No big deal." She shrugged out of his grip. Glancing up at his face, he didn't seem convinced.

They continued to walk and she took out her camera and took some external shots of the buildings. Then, when she had taken enough, they started back to civilization.

After walking in silence for quite some time, Phoebe just had to ask. "Sorry, Drew, it's really nice you're spending all this time with me, but we spent one night together. And you're … you know … you?"

By then they'd reached the shops again, but Drew didn't seem to care and pulled her into his body and circled his arms around her. He laughed, burying his nose into her hair. Then pulled away so he could look into her face. "You have quite an effect on a guy, you know?" He waggled her chin playfully and kissed her on the mouth.

Phoebe accepted the sweet closed mouth kiss and her eyes fluttered shut. Her temperature rose sharply and she couldn't help but be reminded of the night of the party.

That's what he appeared to be telling her – that the one night they spent together was enough to keep him hanging on. While it was flattering, she wasn't sure if she believed him.

As they walked on she noticed he was limping again. "Your leg – are you OK?" She immediately felt guilty having made him run.

Drew gave her a squeeze. "Ah, it's just an old stage injury. I'll get the doc to fix it up. It'll be fine."

"Too much stage diving, eh?" She giggled.

He looked at her curiously with head at an angle, but he was smiling. "Something like that."

They turned the next corner and she was surprised to find they were back where she lived. The brownstone apartment block was set back on the pavement with steps leading up to the green double doors. The other side of the road was a construction site hidden by huge grey hoardings. Before she could protest that she wasn't ready to go back yet, a large sleek black car slowed down next to the curb. Instead, she quickened her pace and gripped Drew's hand trying to drag him with her.

"What is it?" Drew said, his limp making him too slow.

"That car! Don't look!"

But it was too late. It pulled up and the huge driver got out and went to open the back door.

"Come on!" Phoebe shouted.

But Drew was watching the tall, distinguished-looking man get out of the back seat.

Everything appeared to slow down.

The gentleman had long wavy grey hair to his shoulders. He wore an open long black coat over a sharp grey suit that was beautifully tailored. Everything about him shouted "very important person".

Despite his smart appearance, something inside her was urging her to get away from him. It occurred to her that he could be the mafia or something, and she broke away from Drew. He didn't seem to want to move, and she ran to the top of the steps alone.

"Phoebe Ray?" the man said, in slightly accented English.

CHAPTER 7

*D*rew finally found his legs and moved between the two of them to protect her halfway up the steps. "Who wants to know?"

Phoebe felt terrified. With the confusion of the last month, and knowing she'd been followed the whole time she'd been in America, the guy could be anyone. Logic wasn't her primary function right then and she was ready to run.

The man held up a hand to steady her as if he knew. "Please don't be alarmed. I am your uncle … Your Protector, Connor, called me. Can we go inside and talk?"

Drew looked at her as if the decision rested with her. "Connor will be inside with Maggie," he reminded her softly.

Why was he looking at her like that – like it was her who'd lost her mind? She looked nervously at the driver who was easily six and a half feet tall and obviously acted more as a bodyguard.

"Reeve can stay here," the man said, as if he'd read her mind.

Drew finished climbing the last of the steps with his bad leg and picked up her hand hanging loosely at her side.

"Okay," she said eventually.

The man smiled and inclined his head. Then he spoke quickly to the driver in a language she didn't understand and began to climb the steps to join her.

There was no lift in the building and they were on the top floor. As they climbed the eighth flight to reach the fourth floor, Phoebe felt bad for Drew, but was glad that the older stranger would be too knackered to pull any stunts.

When at last they came to her door, it opened before she could reach for her keys. Connor gestured her in and shook the guy's hand as if they knew each other. The whole thing was more bizarre by the minute.

They filed into the small living room. Maggie looked unusually nervous and offered them all a drink. The man declined but thanked her and appeared to be taking in the furnishings of the small room. Connor pointed to the armchair for him to sit, and he and Maggie remained standing.

Phoebe sat on the sofa with Drew and watched the man closely. He seemed particularly interested in some of the black and white shots she had printed on the wall. They were just random people and some unusual buildings she'd discovered locally. "These are yours?" he said.

Phoebe nodded.

"They are interesting." He continued to study them through narrowed eyes.

It was disconcerting, as if he were scrutinizing her. "What do you want?" she blurted.

He returned his eyes to hers and smiled kindly. "Forgive me, my name is Alfonzo Bonaci – your uncle," he said, inclining his head in way of a greeting.

Phoebe wasn't sure how she should reply. "My uncle," she said flatly. Then she looked at Connor, a little exasperated. He wasn't looking fazed or surprised at this man's visit at all.

In fact, he seemed much more concerned at her reaction at that moment. "You know him?"

He nodded. "Kind of."

Her head hurt and she rubbed her forehead. Everything felt jumbled up. She knew she'd been adopted but, as far as she'd been made aware, she was alone in the world. "I don't believe you."

The man remained completely unrattled. "You are Parthenope Riadne Teles Bonaci."

She was already shaking her head. "No. You're wrong. I'm Phoebe Ray. I have no living blood relatives … They told me." Tears were pricking the back of her eyes. She didn't want to hear any of this, and she certainly didn't want Drew to think of her as some kind of weak, damaged, charity case.

"Your host family was instructed to keep your cover. The reality is, you have a very large family. You have four full-blooded sisters and two half brothers."

Phoebe held up a shaky hand. She wasn't sure whether it shook from fear or anger. "Why haven't you contacted me before?"

Alfonzo inclined his head again. "I do not blame you for being cautious. It is a good survival skill. We only become involved when your safety is compromised, or when you're past eighteen and suitors begin to appear." He gestured his hand towards Drew.

She looked angrily at Connor, who looked a little uncomfortable at her accusatory glare.

"Until such a time it is safer to leave you hidden where you are."

"But I'm fine!" A lump was coming up in her throat and she wasn't sure why. Okay, she'd lost a month somewhere, but she didn't know this guy professing to be her uncle at all. Connor was her best friend in the world. If he knew all this, then he'd been keeping something monumental from her. The look in his eyes, not wavering for a second, proved she'd guessed correctly.

A lone tear tracked down her cheek, which she wiped instantly away with the tips of her fingers.

"Who have you been with for the last month, Phoebe?" Alfonzo said.

With a slow blink, she focused her attention back on the stranger. "You don't think if I knew I would have said?"

The man studied her for a moment, then he addressed Connor. "I think she should come home with me to her family in Ireland."

"What? … I'm not going—"

"Phoebe!" Connor snapped. It brought her up sharp. He rarely raised his voice to her. "Hear him out. It's important."

She glared at Connor but all she wanted to do was cry, and that made her even angrier.

"With your family you can be properly protected," Alfonzo continued. "Given recent events, I think it is the best option."

"I don't understand?" Her head was in such a jumble that she didn't even know what to ask first.

"Let me put your mind at rest and answer a few rudimentary questions. When you get to Ireland, everything will be made clear."

Phoebe watched him closely. "I doubt that."

Drew gripped her hand and she looked up into his face. It was the first time she'd remembered he was there. He smiled kindly. "You got nothin' to lose, babe."

She smiled weakly, unconvinced. However, it did make her realize that they may have only really spent one night together, but he'd stuck around through everything with her. That kind of made him special.

She nodded to Alfonzo. "Go on."

He sat back in his chair to get more comfortable. "You come from a very ancient royal family, Phoebe. The Bonacis have been around on earth since before the city of Atlantis was destroyed."

Phoebe frowned. She wasn't exactly a brainbox, but she sure has hell knew that Atlantis was a story that no one really believed. *And royal?* She almost laughed.

"You have physical differences compared to your human family growing up," Alfonzo said.

"Human?" She flashed her eyes at Connor, who was looking at her steadily. Then she returned her gaze to Alfonzo. This was all getting too weird.

"You belong to a hybrid race whose descendants colonized this planet ten thousand years ago. They came from a water world, which is why your body goes through certain changes."

Phoebe shifted uncomfortably remembering the dark bands that came out all over her skin when she got wet. It was true that she'd always felt different, *but an alien?*

"You have to understand that now you are an adult you are in constant danger. There are many who seek you. Some are your own people, but a greater danger exists from the governments and organizations who seek to control you for your power."

The lost month did spring to mind, but even if someone did kidnap her, it was very difficult to believe she had anything someone would want. She wasn't even in charge of her own life these days.

"And you have no memory at all." Alfonzo nodded as if he knew exactly what she was thinking.

"Do you know what happened to me?" Everyone else had skirted around the issue since she'd been back, putting it down to a blackout or something, but that still didn't explain where she'd been.

He paused as if thinking something through. "Something similar did happen to one of your sisters. Except it was a whole year. And the person believed to have taken her implanted false memories and wiped her mind prior to that completely."

The thought filled her with horror. *A whole year just gone.* "Why would somebody do something like that?"

Alfonzo sighed deeply and shook his head. "Power." Alfonzo leant closer to her in his chair. "There are five sisters, of which you are one, and there are five royal families. Each of you fulfils an ancient prophecy to marry into each of those families. The first of your sisters was claimed by the royal family of Dubonnetti and because he was first he was made king, but in order to hold the crown securely he needs all of the sisters. The other families would like the crown for themselves or at the very least to diminish the king's power by taking a sister for themselves. You see, they each vie for supremacy. The humans can't make up their mind whether they want to use you for power to bargain with or simply destroy you, which would end our civilization as we know it. You are the last of the sisters, Phoebe. Everyone is looking for you. In a sense, everything rests with you and whom you choose to give your allegiance. No one can force you. You alone must choose. It is the code we live by and has been the way with us for ten thousand years."

Phoebe was struck dumb with information overload. What could she say to all that? She wanted to laugh but the seriousness of the faces around her sobered her. "Choose?" she said warily, looking at Drew beside her. It felt strange to think of him when in reality she'd known him for five minutes.

He hadn't said a word but regarded her closely.

"Can't they go ahead and do it without me? They've done without me all this time."

"Our enemies are closing in. We need to investigate who took you and why they didn't keep you. There must have been a reason. And who's to say they won't return?"

Phoebe's eyes darted to Alfonzo. She hadn't thought of that. In fact she'd done her damnedest to not think of it at all.

"Everyone you love will be in danger as well," Alfonzo said, his eyes straying to Drew.

"We hardly know each other really," Drew said, then he grinned at Phoebe.

She couldn't help grinning back and blushing. It was the first time he'd hinted at the hot night they'd spent together.

"I'll take it that you have not taken the Siren's breath as you are still alive," Alfonzo said. "That is unless you too are Atlantean." He tilted his head slightly as if assessing Drew physically. "You are tall," he said, with a bob of his head.

Drew laughed in his infectious way. "I'm a hundred percent homo sapiens, man."

Phoebe giggled. It all sounded so bizarre. Then again the sex they'd shared wasn't exactly conventional. It immediately sobered her.

"Do you have a piece of unusual jewelry?" Alfonzo said directly to Drew.

For a moment, Drew looked taken aback. As if the last thing he expected was questions to be directed at him. Then he shook his head. "No, I don't think so."

"Anyone?" Alfonzo said, over his shoulder at Maggie and Connor.

Connor pulled out the blue necklace Phoebe knew well.

"Anything like this stone?" Alfonzo said, pointing.

Drew shook his head. "No … Like I said, a hundred percent human."

Phoebe looked at each of them, but mostly Drew. It all seemed odd – the subject, his choice of words, everything.

Alfonzo narrowed his eyes. "For now, you can assume the role of Protector – along with Connor, it should be fine." Then he spoke directly to her again. "You must understand, that although you appear to have taken a lover, a mate exists for you in the world – one you are destined to marry."

Everything was now getting way out of control. Alien races, new families and most of all at that point, the assumption that she and Drew were an item. The guy needed to shut the hell up before Drew was completely put off her. "I'm not responsible for any of this," she found herself explaining to him fast.

Then as if all her fears had come true, he cupped the side of her face with his hand. "Look, you got a lot to think about. I'm gonna go and give you some space."

All she could do was swallow and nod when what she really wanted was to grab onto his hand and scream, "don't leave me". Right then he was the only sane person in the room.

As he went to stand, Alfonzo added. "Now you have come into her life, whether you are with her or not, you will be in danger. As her Protector you should accompany her to Ireland – at least until her husband is found."

Drew's eyes widened as if things had gotten way out of his league.

Alfonzo stood as well, signaling the party was over. It was a relief. Phoebe needed to process all this. Not just what she'd been told about herself – the jury was still out on that one – but what had really happened between her and Drew, and what he'd come to mean to her. It was the first time she'd really thought about it. To her it was only yesterday. To everyone else it was old news. That still hadn't sunk in. Someone knew what happened to her during that month.

Maybe these new people – her supposed family – knew the answers.

Alfonzo paused at the door. "A car will be here to collect you tonight at nine." Then he glanced at Drew. "With the amount of Atlanteans in this city, news travels fast. I don't rate your chances if you choose not to come."

CHAPTER 8

*P*hoebe probably should have questioned Connor further but he'd disappeared to make arrangements. It was just as well. Her head was a mess and she wasn't sure if she could handle any more surprises. So when Drew left to go and get his leg checked out, Phoebe escaped to her room. She was pleasantly surprised when he returned; she'd expected him to run for the hills. Instead, they spent a restless day together as if both of them needed to process what they'd learned. There was no meaningless chatter, nor any chatter, come to that. In the end they just tried to sleep, but it evaded them both.

Thoughts whirred around her head of a family she never knew. That she was royalty, and that Drew was still there despite sex only ever having happened the once. It hadn't been exactly conventional – which brought her right back to her physical weirdness. *Argh!* She was going crazy.

The revelations were probably blowing Drew's mind too. Even though he must surely think her uncle was mad, he had seen her transformed and it must be making a weird kind of sense to him.

Then there was the warning Alfonzo had issued that affected them both. She was sure Drew hadn't bargained for that when they'd got together that night. He hadn't seen beyond a bit of fun. He was a "nothing heavy" kind of guy. Now the decision of whether they'd go was killing them both.

Drew sat on the edge of the bed and finally broke the troubled silence. "Look, I'm going to the club. I need to speak to a couple of people. I'll meet you at the airport." He pulled on his boots and walked towards the bedroom door.

Phoebe watched him sadly. "I understand." She'd been surprised he'd stayed this long.

He paused but didn't turn. Then, when the door clicked shut behind him, Phoebe turned her face into her pillow and sobbed. It still hurt.

THE CAR ARRIVED, as promised, at 9 o'clock sharp. Phoebe had nothing to lose. Her bag was packed and by the door. From the window she could see it waiting and wondered where it would take her. Somehow she knew that once she got into it, life would never be the same again.

"It's time," Connor said, softly, from behind her.

Phoebe turned and looked up into his earnest face. He'd known it all along. Even though there was a part of her that wanted to be angry with him she found that she couldn't. She was worn out with it. Connor was the one constant in her life – the one that always got her through the hurt and the disappointments. He'd been the buffer between her and the siblings she never got along with and the peacekeeper with the parents who never understood. She'd always been the black sheep and he'd taken the role of the strong, brotherly, defender. But, as it turns out, it was all a lie. She felt numb, partly due to shock and a whole lot to do with a sense of loss. The evidence of her being a freak had mounted up until Drew couldn't take it anymore. The last image of him brought a lump to her throat. "Guess we should go."

Connor nodded.

Maggie appeared next to them and pulled her into a tight hug. "Love you, Phoebes. I'll see you as soon as I can."

It was the first time Phoebe had given her full attention to her old friend all day and realized that she'd been present for all the bizarre revelations too. She was mortified and nodded, unable to talk. She wanted to crawl under a rock and die.

Maggie held the tops of her shoulders and gave them a squeeze. "It's okay, Phoebes, when you were away Connor explained a lot of things, so when the guy came today I kind of knew anyway."

Phoebe wasn't sure if that made her feel better or not. She opted for not. It seemed the whole world knew before she did.

Connor hurried things along and guided her with an arm around her shoulder. "I'll keep in touch," he said to Maggie, giving her a meaningful kiss on the lips.

The door closed behind them and they descended the stairs quickly.

The same driver from earlier was already standing next to the car. He opened the door and they slid into the soft leather seats. The car came to life with a gentle purr and they glided into the evening traffic in the direction of the airport.

The muted town lights and people going about their blissfully ignorant lives went quickly past. It was raining again; the outlook poignantly bleak to match how she felt.

Her breath caught in her chest for a moment in fear.

She really was venturing into the unknown.

Out there was a new family, possibly just like her. She ran her tongue absently along her upper teeth, over a pointed canine. It was now level and hardly distinguishable from the others. It seemed symbolic of her whole life.

Phoebe turned in her seat to face Connor – equally lost in thought. This would probably be her last chance to speak to him properly. "You knew all this and you never said a word?" She couldn't keep the hurt from her voice. "How long have you kept this from me?"

With a slow blink and a sigh he looked at her but didn't seem angry, only resigned. As if this day was always going to come. "I've known from the day I met you."

Her eyes widened and her face contorted in horror. "You're not serious. You were fifteen years old … ten years, and you never thought to give me a clue?"

He continued to look at her steadily, unblinking and firm.

Phoebe knew she was probably being unfair to him, but she felt so betrayed by the one person she thought she could trust implicitly.

"I'm a Protector, Phoebe. I was born one. It's what I was always meant to be."

Phoebe didn't bother to reply. He may as well be telling her he was a secret agent – no, scratch that, she would have found that easier to swallow.

Connor seemed to read her mind. "There are lots of people in our world, Phoebe. Many have a particular destiny to fulfill. You have yours – to be a Soul Breather – one of five powerful beings crucial to the kingdom and I have mine. The difference with you is that you are the last."

All she could do was shrug. He'd lost her at Soul Breather.

"Because of your importance they put me with you from a very young age to watch over you … until it got too dangerous to hide you any longer."

With every word he only disappointed her further. "So

none of it was real. You were just paid to spend time with me," she said flatly, desperately trying to hide the wobble in her voice at the end.

Connor turned his whole body to face her and picked up her hand. "Please. No. Don't ever think that. I loved spending time with you. You were a breath of fresh air compared to the life I could have had."

Phoebe snatched her hand from his and faced out the window again. Connor didn't say anything else and she felt him relax back into his seat. All she wanted to do was cry. Nothing in her life had been what it seemed. No wonder her parents gave her no real love and her siblings resented her. Her thoughts always came back to Connor. The strong, fearless, serious boy she'd adored ever since she could remember. A tear rolled down her cheek and she looked blindly out of the window so no one saw it. She sniffed and wiped it angrily away.

It was a relief when a plane rumbled overhead and she realized they were at the airport.

They didn't stop and were waved straight out onto the large parking area with small jets all in a row. It made her wonder for the umpteenth time, how powerful these people were.

They came up to a small private jet with a coat of arms on the tail and the words Dubonnetti Industries across the fuselage.

"Miss?" the driver said as he opened her door.

She got out slowly, determined not to look at Connor, to the loud engines piercing her ears and the aviation fuel hitting her nose.

The driver already had her bag and held out a hand for her to climb the steps to the plane. A beautiful Barbie-like stewardess greeted her with a beaming smile at the top. "Welcome to the Royal Dubonnetti," she said, holding out a hand indicating for her to enter the plane.

"Phoebe, wait!"

She turned sharply to the clatter of footsteps on metal behind her.

Drew.

He slipped past Connor coming up the steps behind and came up sharp in front of her. *Thank god!* Before he could open his mouth she threw her arms around his neck and clung to him, breathing in his heavenly smell.

His heavy bag clunked to the floor and his arms squeezed the life out of her.

Briefly her eyes held Connor's over his shoulder, but his expression remained blank and unreadable when he squeezed past and entered the plane.

Phoebe just closed her eyes and pulled Drew to her tightly. "Are you mad?" she whispered against his chest.

"About as mad as you," he said, looking into her face grinning. Then he wiped her tears away with the pad of his thumb and fingertips. They were tears of relief that he'd actually come. Despite knowing all the weirdness surrounding her he'd actually turned up, just like he said he would. It helped soothe the deep hurt and betrayal she felt about Connor. It was just what she needed.

Everything got pushed to the back of her mind when they entered the plane. With Drew's arm still around her shoulders, Phoebe relaxed a little and took it all in with wonder.

"Sweet ride," Drew said in her ear.

She looked up at him as stunned at all the leather and chrome as he was.

The stewardess indicated two cream leather seats next to each other. "Fasten your seatbelts. Can I get you a glass of champagne?"

They glanced wide-eyed at each other. "Yes please!" they said simultaneously. Then they took their seats.

"How's your leg?" Phoebe said, suddenly remembering.

Drew hit his thigh with a closed fist. "Good as new. Doc fixed it up."

The plane began to taxi along the runway and Phoebe gripped Drew's hand, more grateful than he'd ever know.

CHAPTER 9

After twelve hours, the plane touched down in Galway Ireland to similar cloud and drizzle to what they'd left in Seattle. It was now around 5 p.m. Phoebe stood in a tired daze with Drew at the top of the steps in the shrill hiss of engine noise. However, cutting through the smell of fuel was a fresh breeze that smelled earthy and clean.

Another car waited for them below. The driver held the back door open and, after checking each other was ready, they descended the steps and got in. Connor sat in the front with the driver, which was partitioned off by smoked glass.

The airport was considerably smaller than Seattle and they were soon whisked away in the blacked-out car with a minimum of red tape. Neither of them had been to Ireland before and so they sat quietly absorbing the rolling green countryside and narrow winding lines. They travelled north for about an hour, spotting the ocean a few times until a large, imposing, grey stone mansion came into view.

"Is that it?" Drew said.

Phoebe leaned across him to see more clearly. "Oh my god, it's a castle."

The car took them up the long shingle drive bringing them closer. The nearer they got, the older and more bleak the building looked. A feeling of dread was fast overruling the butterflies in her stomach.

Alfonzo had told them they were some kind of royalty. She guessed this was the family pile.

The car came to a standstill right outside the huge double oak doors, which opened immediately. Several young men and women, all dressed in white shirts and black trousers, swarmed around the car and took out the bags.

The driver opened the door and they both slid out the same side and stood looking up at the gothic, moss-tinged stone. Every corner was dotted with the scary faces of winged gargoyles that reminded her of old horror films.

A more senior-looking man, dressed in a black tailcoat, bowed in front of Phoebe. "Good evening, Your Highness … Sirs," he said, with a nod to Drew and then Connor.

The butler turned with a "follow me" and the three of them traipsed up the few stone steps and in through the oak doors after him.

The hallway was lit for nighttime but it was so dark with wood walls and furniture, it was probably lit in the daytime too. The butler continued on, past a grandfather clock, endless dusty taxidermy on shelves, to a wall that moved at the press of a button. Steel doors opened to reveal a lift.

Drew and Phoebe widened their eyes at each other. Connor looked unfazed, proving he'd been there before. It made her blood boil all over again.

"Welcome to Ballygowan Castle," the butler said, pushing the button.

The lift doors closed and, after a jolt, Phoebe grasped Drew's hand when her stomach turned and she felt them go downward instead of up.

It took less than five minutes for the lift to settle and the doors to open. Standing in front of them was a tall, greying man; strikingly similar to the one she'd met in Seattle. They took a step out and the doors closed behind them. The man came forward and immediately grasped Phoebe's hand and kissed it. "Daughter," he said.

Her heart stopped and she looked up to Drew who smiled sympathetically.

"Forgive me," the man said, shaking his head as if to clear emotion riding him.

When the smile returned to his face, she extricated her hand and smiled weakly back.

"I am Sebastian, your father." Then he turned to Connor and shook his hand warmly. "Nice to see you again, Connor. It seems such a short time since you stood here as a young boy," he said in an accented voice.

Connor inclined his head. "It's nice to see you again too, Your Highness."

"Thank you for delivering my daughter to me safely. If you follow my man here, he will show you to your quarters."

As he walked past to go with the butler, Connor's eyes held hers. They held no apology for obviously being there before. Phoebe's eyes stayed glued to his, accusingly, until Sebastian brought her attention back to him.

"And who do we have here?" he said, addressing Drew.

"My name is Drew, sir. Er, Your Highness," Drew stammered, making her smile.

"Ah," Sebastian said, with a slow nod of understanding she wasn't sure was accurate. It wasn't even clear to her yet what exactly her status was with Drew.

"Follow me."

They looked at each other and walked towards the top of the marble steps. "I expect you think the house is strange being upside down. You see, we don't live in the upper part, we live down here."

It was the exact moment when they reached the top of the steps and Sebastian held out his arm as if he was presenting what was in front of them.

The two of them stood speechless.

There in front of them was the largest, most unusual cavernous room they'd ever seen. In fact it looked like a huge black rugged cave carved out of the mountain. A million small white lights twinkled like stars over the ceiling and walls. Huge black chandeliers hung all over. "The size of that TV," she whispered to herself.

"It's an aquarium, I think," Drew said next to her, as amazed as she was.

Then it hit her. "Oh my god, Drew. It's the sea!" She was pointing and looking like a complete idiot.

Sebastian chuckled. "Yes, it's the sea. You are now below sea level. Down here, we no longer have to pretend what we are," he continued softly, giving her the time to take in the whole room. All the tables and soft, plush-looking sofas were arranged like a huge lounge around the most beautifully ornate black fountain. Unlike the human world, water was obviously central to their lives and welcomed into the room instead of shut outside.

They gradually descended the sweeping black and grey marble steps. Tucked away to the right of it was what could only be described as a bar.

"Used for grand gatherings and celebrations," Sebastian offered in way of explanation.

Directly opposite was an arch in the rock, which appeared to go off into a tunnel.

Phoebe was just wondering where it led to, when a man came out of it in strong, graceful strides. In fact, he was the most striking man she'd ever seen. He was tall with black, wavy hair to his shoulders. His beautifully pale pink shirt fit his lean frame perfectly, tucked into the tailored black trousers covering his perfectly proportioned legs.

All she managed to do was stare as Sebastian introduced them to Dante, the king of the Alantean nation, and he drew her close to kiss her cheek. A waft of some beautiful cologne mixed with something potently male surrounded her and he pulled away again.

"Good evening, Phoebe Ray," he said, smiling, eyes twinkling with mischief, in the most gorgeous Irish accent she wasn't expecting.

Suddenly it registered what Sebastian actually said. This guy was an actual king, and she didn't know whether she should bow, curtsy or what. In the end she did some kind of cross-legged awkward squat.

The king laughed and held her arm as she wobbled. "Honestly, no need, Phoebe. But I do appreciate the gesture," he finished laughing, making her blast red.

Drew held out his hand and introduced himself.

Dante took his hand and shook it warmly. "I've heard good things about you."

Then Dante turned his attention back to her. "We've waited a very long time to see you, Phoebe. I'm so glad you decided to make the trip," he said, inclining his head.

He seemed so serious all of a sudden that she felt she had to fill up the space. "I wanted to check everything out – you know, what the other guy said. It's kind of something every adopted kid wonders about, don't they? Where they're from?" she was gabbling on and she knew it. She looked up at Drew for a little reassurance and he smiled back at her kindly.

The king was watching her curiously. "I'm glad. I'm afraid it's a little more involved than that, Phoebe." Then his face lit up again. "I expect you'd like to meet your sisters."

Phoebe gripped Drew's hand and swallowed. This was all too much.

"Come on, they're dying to meet you."

Dante started to walk to the opposite side of the large lounge. There, a large group of people were gathering and sitting down in the chairs. Her heart pumped. Everything was going way to fast, it was overwhelming.

As they neared, a woman stood and Sebastian met her and guided her towards them with his arm around her shoulders.

Phoebe's jaw dropped. She couldn't decide if she was beautiful or not, but one thing she was sure of was that she definitely wasn't human. She was human-like, with long blonde hair to past her waist, but her cheek bones were a little more pronounced and her brown eyes larger than was normal with almost no whites. Her limbs were very long and willowy, and she moved gracefully – almost like she was floating.

"May I present Naomi, your mother," Dante said, gesturing with his hand.

The woman bowed her head slowly and smiled in a strange way that didn't move the rest of her face, but Phoebe felt a warmth emanating from her. Then the woman exchanged a look with her father that lasted too long. It seemed just like they were talking, but nothing came out of their mouths.

Sebastian finished with a slow blink then faced Phoebe again. "Your mother would like me to apologize for her and explain that she cannot talk. But if you are willing, she would like to talk to you straight to your mind?"

Phoebe remained blank, not sure how to respond. All that came out was a nervous laugh and a glance at Drew like she'd entered a mad house.

He answered with a squeeze of her hand

Sebastian and Naomi waited expectantly.

She shrugged, not sure how much weirder it could get. "Sure!"

Suddenly her mother seemed very close. *Welcome, my daughter. I didn't want to startle you by addressing you like this straight away.*

Phoebe's hands flew to her temples.

Naomi smiled and nodded. *Please don't be afraid, it's the way of our people. The voice doesn't travel well through water and so we have no need for vocal cords.*

All Phoebe could do was blink in utter shock. Briefly, she wondered if that meant she could do it.

With practice, yes. Naomi answered, causing her to recoil in horror.

"You read my mind?"

Only your surface thoughts, but it is possible for me to enter for deeper understanding.

Phoebe shook her head manically. "No, you're alright."

Dante stepped forward and she was glad of the distraction, but again the look to Naomi said he was having one of those creepy unspoken discussions. "Come," he said, guiding her with his hand at the small of her back. "It's a lot to take in on your first day. Come and meet your sisters and their partners."

The disturbing meeting with her mother was soon relegated to a dull ache at the back of her mind as Dante gently steered her towards the rest of the family. The thought of genuine sisters excited her and terrified her at the same time – *Would she like them? Would they like her?*

"Sadly, your sister, my wife, the queen, is not here to meet you. She is in Murrtaine."

Things were beginning to slot into place. So this man had married her sister. The name of the place was not familiar, but there was no mistaking the look of love that crossed the king's face.

Squeals, and two children pushed between them. "Whoops! Sorry, Daddy." One was clearly chasing the other. "Ow!" followed, then, "Give it back!"

"Hey! Come on yer rascals. Come and meet your aunty."

The two children stopped what they were doing immediately and walked over, clearly interested in the newcomer.

They were beautiful children, she guessed around seven or eight years old. They had hair similar to Dante's, black, curly and shiny, and the most unusually stunning green eyes and olive skin any girl would die for.

"Xavier and Alexia," he said with a hand on each head. "Say hello to Aunty Phoebe."

"Hello, Aunty Phoebe," they said like they were at school repeating a teacher.

Phoebe grinned. "Pleased to meet you," she said, shaking both their little hands. She couldn't help but be charmed by them. Suddenly, she envied the sister she'd never met. It seemed like she had it all – a handsome husband, beautiful kids and living as a queen in a castle.

"My sister is very lucky," she said, trying to keep the bitterness from her voice. "Two beautiful children."

"Three," Dante said, with a small bob of the head. "You'll meet little JJ in time. He's with his dad."

Phoebe's eyes widened, but she didn't say anymore. *So the relationship wasn't all a bed of roses.*

Dante searched her face as if he knew what she was thinking. Then she suddenly remembered her mother had read her mind and hitched a breath in shock. "Sorry," she blurted.

To her relief, he laughed easily. "Come, you have others to meet."

The next to stand and greet her was a small woman of a

similar height and build to her. But where her own hair was wavy and fiery red, this girl's was dark brown, and she had similar green eyes to the children's.

Before she said hello, her eyes tracked upward to the huge man standing next to her. Not only was he the size of a house, but every part of him was toned like he was an athlete or a soldier. Although his hair was a little unruly in black waves to his collar, possibly ruling that out. His duck-egg blue eyes were smiling with his grin that showed two perfectly pointy canines.

Her hand went to her mouth.

"Sorry, I didn't mean to scare you," he said. "I'm Keenan Santalini. I'm afraid we're all this big."

Phoebe regained some of her composure. He didn't seem to make the connection to his teeth so she didn't say anything. "No, I'm sorry. You didn't scare me, honest."

He grinned again, showing her another flash of teeth that looked far larger and sharper than hers. "This is Lacy, your sister and my mate."

She looked at him curiously again, at the use of the word mate instead of wife, but eventually rested her eyes on the beautiful-looking girl in front of her who was putting out her hand.

Phoebe shook it, but all she could do was stare. The beautiful well proportioned face, the hair, eyes and petite frame. She was so like her when she got up close. Apart from the different hair colour, there was no doubt they were sisters. "Pleased … pleased to meet you," she stammered.

The girl laughed, a beautiful musical laugh that matched her completely, and pulled her into a hug. "I know it's all strange, but we were all the same at the beginning," she said next to her ear.

They pulled apart and Phoebe decided she liked her immediately. There were a thousand things she wanted to ask her about what she meant, but there simply wasn't any time. A line had formed and Dante wanted to move her along.

They smiled regretfully, and Phoebe took a step to the next person.

A stunning blond with eyes that were so pale blue they were more like clear water. She was beautiful but she remained expressionless. It hit her that she was very similar to her mother, in that the muscles weren't moving in her face. Then, no sooner had she had the thought, her face transformed into the most beautiful smile. She looked just like an ice princess from a fairy tale. "I'm Isla," she said, and pulled her into a tight hug. "I'm so pleased to meet you. You have no idea."

"Thank you ..." she said, trailing off when she realized that the man next to her had been siting down and was now standing up. Every inch of him appeared to be unfolding into the tallest man she'd ever seen – even bigger than the last one.

"I want you to meet my husband, Phoebe. Prince Darres Borge."

Despite his size, he wasn't as muscled as Keenan. He was lean though. Phoebe had to snap herself out of silence but he bowled her over. From his poker-straight black hair that reached his waist, to the faint stripes still clearly visible licking up his neck and circling his forearms.

Phoebe was speechless. His overall appearance was like some huge, war-paint-covered, Native American. She wasn't afraid of him. Even though he clearly wasn't human, some-thing in his coal-black eyes put her at rest.

The strange smile proved he knew exactly how she was feeling. *Welcome, Phoebe. Be at ease. I myself know how strange it can feel coming here for the first time.*

His beautifully accented voice drifted through her mind

like a light breeze. It made her feel better instantly, and she longed to ask how someone like him was once a stranger here. It also occurred to her that even amongst all the strangeness, he still managed to stand out.

I am a pure blooded Murr. He pulled Isla to him and she looked up adoringly with her hand flat against his chest. *We live together in my birth place of Murrtaine with our two boys. Keefa! Dannon!* he called, but his lips never moved.

Phoebe followed his line of vision to two more boys, slightly larger than Dante's children. They stopped what they were doing immediately and looked at their father. The whole thing was amazing considering no other person in the room heard it.

The boys jogged over.

Greet your Aunty Phoebe as a prince should, Darres said. It was stern but said with obvious love.

Yes, Papa, the little psychic voices replied. Then the two of them bowed low from the waist. *It is an honor to meet our mother's sister,* they both said.

Phoebe looked at Darres, amazed and delighted. She hadn't come into contact with many younger children growing up, and the ones she'd met here were adorable.

She felt a squeeze to her arm and gasped, "Where are my manners. This is my, …" she wasn't sure exactly what to call him and just went for his name, "Drew."

Drew leant forward and shook Darres's hand. "Drew Stone, sir."

Drew wasn't short at six three but Darres still towered at least another head above him.

Darres was looking at him strangely. Phoebe guessed it was one of those weird internal conversations. However, just as her eyes began to track to the next person in the lineup, Drew appeared to crumple and grab his head. "Drew! she shouted, and tried to catch him before he hit the ground.

Before she knew it, Keenan and Dante had her side, and a stranger helped with the other.

Drew appeared to be coming out of it and began to stand a little dizzily at first. Then he shook his head. "Sorry, I don't know what happened." Dante passed him a handkerchief and he dabbed a small rivulet of blood running from his nose.

As he spoke, Phoebe was watching him closely. All the while he hadn't looked away from Darres, whose eyes narrowed. Then he tracked them to her. *Sometimes the experience of psychic speech is too much for humans.* However, his attention then went to Dante.

Phoebe watched him a long moment after he stopped talking to her, wondering why she got the impression he wasn't telling her everything.

All such thoughts were pushed out of her mind when Drew noticed and hugged the next man in the line-up, smacking his back loudly. "I can't believe it … you … here," he said, holding him at arms length and then pulling him into his body again.

Relieved the drama had passed, Phoebe couldn't help smiling. The two men had obviously met before and were clearly thrilled to see each other. She wasn't sure where from. The guy's unkempt mop of straw blonde hair and tanned skin pointed to loads of time in the sun. He certainly didn't look like a native to the rain and gloom of Seattle – or Ireland for that matter.

Drew pulled her to him, his little turn now completely forgotten. "I'd like you to meet an old friend of mine. Phoebe Ray, meet Lance McCabe."

The guy smiled a gorgeous smile and immediately kissed her cheek. It was nice to meet a normal-sized man she didn't have to crane her neck to look at.

"Please to meet you, Phoebe." He flashed that lovely smile again and his warm hazel eyes laughed along with them. The whole place was eye candy central, but this guy was a looker that emanated real warmth.

"You too. How do you two know each other?"

"Lance has his own band too," Drew explained. "We were in a band together a few years back."

"A long time ago," Lance added playfully. "We were teenagers and really bad."

The two men laughed and recalled a gig they'd once played, to three teenagers and a dog.

"I didn't know you'd lived in California?" Phoebe said, feeling a pang of hurt with no time to analyze why.

A little of the humor fell from Drew's face. "I've lived all over," he said, studying her.

It occurred to her then how little she really knew him.

The silence was clearly uncomfortable to the onlookers as someone coughed and Lance broke it. "Hey, you'd better meet my mate." And he pulled a girl into his body and the conversation. "Everybody, this is Lily."

Phoebe was transfixed by the sister least like the rest. The bone structure and the frame was the same, but she had tight black corkscrew curls bouncing out in all directions that barely touched her shoulder. Her skin was covered in the same markings that came out on her own skin when she was wet. Her eyes were a bright violet shade she'd never seen apart from with contact lenses. Above all, what struck her was that there was nothing girly about her at all. Everything was masculine and boy-like. From her vest top showing off muscled sinewy shoulders and arms, to the fit of her jeans tucked into men's boots left open and untied.

The girl just nodded.

"Hello," Phoebe said, a little unsure of this one.

Lance put his arms around the girl's shoulder and she looked up at him with complete adoration. "OK, babe," he said, then turned to Phoebe. "She said, you're beautiful and asked what instrument you play? She can't talk," he tacked on. As if it was only the afterthought of someone who was totally used to it.

Phoebe fell in with the connection to Darres and her mother. It made her feel a little more at ease with the girl. It appeared that it was a common trait in the family for them not to be able to speak aloud. "I don't get the question. I don't play an instrument," she said, a little puzzled.

Lance looked at Lily to make sure she'd heard. Then he looked back. "Oh don't worry. It's just that all the sisters are musical in some way. Lily is a bad-ass drummer." He crushed her to him and grinned as if he was the proudest boyfriend in the world.

Drew was smiling and nodding too.

"Sorry, I rode ponies as a kid and did my damnedest not to practice my piano. I just draw and take pictures … Camera ones!" she blurted lamely, to all the blank, unreadable faces.

Again, the girl looked at Lance. He raised his eyebrows and shrugged.

"Mind saying it to me?" she said, starting to feel a little exasperated.

Dante stepped forward with perfect timing. "Come, Phoebe, you must be tired." And he began to guide her by the elbow.

She dragged her feet, eying Lily, still waiting for her answer.

Then Lily's voice came to her mind in a loud blast. *I said you appear to be the silver spoon sister!*

Phoebe stopped and frowned, trying to work out exactly what she meant by that.

Dante rolled his eyes. "For fuck's sake," he muttered under his breath.

"What's that supposed to mean?" She'd pulled out of

Dante's grasp now and was facing Lily square on. "Are you trying to say I was spoiled or something?"

Lily shrugged. *If the cap fits.*

Phoebe's eyes went wide in shock. How dare this girl judge her when she didn't know a thing about her? Before she knew it, Dante had renewed his grip and Drew and Lance were pushing her in the direction of the corridor. "You have no idea about me. You don't even know me," she was shouting over her shoulder.

Rage seared through her such as she hadn't felt in a very long while as she was literally dragged away.

CHAPTER 10

Phoebe was led down a long corridor cut into the rock with dim lighting in alcoves, until they reached a line of doors to their right. After they passed a few Dante stopped at one and pushed it open. "This is your room. Settle in, and I'll send someone for you in about an hour to explain a few things."

She was still fuming and went to walk past him without looking or engaging with him in any way.

Dante put out his hand to stall her for a moment and waited for her to reluctantly meet his eyes. "Try not to be angry. None of your sisters had it easy, okay? You were all hidden in the world. We'll talk later." He finished with that knockout smile of his.

She nodded eventually and he removed his arm barring the way. "You have a temper like my wife." He touched her on the shoulder and winked at Drew.

They both watched him walk away with Lance in the direction they came from and she and Drew entered the room in silence.

The room was lovely – there was a large bed with what

looked an expensive counterpane that matched the chaise longue and dainty chair in the corners, all in the softest pale lemon. Two doors led from the room. Phoebe peered inside; one was to a small bathroom and the other to a walk-in wardrobe. It was like an expensive hotel room except it had no windows.

Their bags were already there and she collapsed heavily on the huge bed, exhausted. Drew opened his bag and then walked into the bathroom. She surveyed the tastefully decorated room. All the frilly silk reminded her of a French chateau.

Drew came back out of the bathroom and sat down next to her. Phoebe waited for him to speak but he didn't say anything. *What could he really say?* If she was honest, he didn't know her much more than the rest of them back there. They'd spent no more than a few hours together if you counted it all up.

After a few minutes she felt herself calm down and took a glance at him. He was looking around the room. When he realized she was watching him he looked at her and grinned. "Do you think there's a mini-bar?"

It broke the atmosphere instantly and she burst out laughing.

Drew pulled her to him until she scrambled awkwardly onto his lap. It felt good to snuggle into him with her head next his shoulder and his arms wrapped tightly behind her back. The air left her in a long exhale of relief. "They don't know me, Drew … none of them do." Then she pulled away to look into his lovely blue grey eyes. "We don't really know each other either." It was a scary thought.

Suddenly she longed for the security of Connor. He knew her. He knew everything. Then she hardened when she reminded herself that he was with them. He hadn't really been on her side at all.

Drew's hand came up and he rubbed the side of her cheek with his thumb, startling her back to reality. "Hey! I'm here, aren't I? Doesn't that count for something?"

She wriggled round so she straddled his legs to face him squarely. "But why though, Drew. I don't get it?"

It was her turn to touch his face when he frowned. "I'm a weirdo English girl who's nothing but trouble, and you, you're, you know …you."

He smiled weakly as if defeated and she didn't know the half of it. "You kind of left an impression, you know? No one ever ran out on me before," he finished with a small blast of laughter. "You never know, we might be more alike than you think."

More than a little puzzled, she didn't want to push it. The night they'd spent together was now a blur, although the steaminess of it still punched her in the gut whenever it came to mind. She swallowed, suddenly realizing that perhaps her reaction here was a little extreme – that maybe she was jetlagged and a little overwrought. It certainly was none of Drew's fault.

"I haven't been able to stop thinking about that night," Drew said, mirroring her thoughts perfectly.

She threaded her hands into his long, curly dark brown hair. They were alone and out of earshot for the first time since. Her eyes became riveted to his lips.

He seemed to know and began drawing her to him slowly. "Didn't you find it a little strange?" she asked. Her heart was thumping, half expecting him to come to his senses.

"I like strange," he said in a husky whisper, as her mouth was so close she could feel his warm breath against her. "Strange is fucking hot!"

That was it, and she closed the small gap so her lips brushed the soft cushions of his. It felt beautiful and remained closed but ignited everything. Then Drew tightened his grip around her and parted his lips slightly to gently tantalize with his tongue. Something inside her moved and welcomed him. Her mouth immediately opened and she met his tongue with hers. Though, what started off as gentle and sweet soon became a need to taste and feel him urgently.

As the kiss deepened and their tongues swirled together her hips began to move against his. She shuffled and unfurled her legs either side of his so she could wrap them around his back. The only thing separating their bodies now rhythmically moving together was their jeans.

The dead weight she'd felt the last time began to bear down heavily in her chest. The points of her teeth suddenly made their presence felt by pushing painfully against her lower lip. Something was happening to her again. She was changing but she was just too darn steamed up. Despite an almost unbearable need to devour him whole, she pulled back.

He was breathing as heavily as her when he opened his eyes and stilled. It was probably only a moment but was a pause nonetheless. In that small amount of time he was assessing her – taking in her changes. But instead of putting her away from him, he rubbed his thumb across her mouth to touch the sharp point of her tooth. The sensation shot from the tip and ran molten straight down to her groin. They were as sensitive as fingertips. Still he didn't move, but stared deeply into her eyes as if studying them.

Unable to stand it any longer, she said, "What?" *Was that it? Was she just a curiosity to him?*

"Fuck! Your eyes," he said on a breath. "I thought I dreamt them." Then he pulled her into the most searing of kisses.

It wasn't what she expected and before she could relax into him fully, there was a knock at the door.

"Ignore it," he said, renewing his grip and moving her

onto her back in one move. Pushing his hips so tightly against hers the friction against her core made her gasp.

"The king requests your presence in the study, now!" the voice said from the other side of the door.

Phoebe put her forehead against Drew's but her body was still undulating with his. God, she needed his jeans gone. "We must go."

Drew's lips were next to hers while their bodies moved together. "Do you want to?"

Ahh! "No!" But she rolled him off her and sprang to her feet.

After a moment of gathering himself together, Drew slowly sat up.

"I don't want anyone to come and find us," she said, by way of explanation. It was partly true, but was more to do with the growing evil inside her that would escape if she continued. Her eyes stayed on him but were tinged orange and her body hunched over with the discomfort in her chest.

Drew got up, walked over and pulled her into his body. "Shh," he said, stroking his hand down her back. "Don't be scared. I know you won't hurt me."

Phoebe felt bowled over by his complete understanding of her and pulled back to look into his eyes. "Won't I?"

He touched the side of her face with his hand and ran a thumb along her cheekbone. "This is what they were talking about, that's all it is. Believe me, that kind of hurt I can deal with."

Maybe he was right, but he couldn't know for sure. *Bloody hell!* She didn't even know for sure. It made her wonder what kind of hurt he'd suffered that meant he wasn't scared of her.

The moment that followed was thick and heavy with unspoken meaning as they seemed to assess each other, until another, louder, knock made them jump.

"You must come to the study!" came through the door again.

Phoebe looked from the door back into Drew's eyes. Her vision was clearer with returning 3D color.

"You okay to go now?" he asked, understanding perfectly.

She swallowed and nodded. The way he continued to look after her despite seeing her change deepened something within her.

PHOEBE AND DREW took the two seats offered. The study was above ground in the conventional part of the castle and was dusty, old and lined with shelves of books.

Dante was seated behind the desk and regarded them closely. Then, after whispering something in Dante's ear, Alfonzo sat in an armchair to the left of him.

Dante cleared his throat. "Right, I'll get straight to the point so you can get some rest. I understand from Alfonzo that a few things have already been explained to you, so what I want to do here is explain to you who you are, where you fit in, and why your trip here is so important."

Phoebe glanced at Drew, who took her hand in support. Butterflies tickled her stomach. If only they would get on with it so they could get back to the privacy of their room. This thing between them – whatever it was – felt like the only real thing happening to her at the moment. All this other stuff felt like it was meant for someone else.

"Your descendants came from a planet called Atlas." Dante continued, "they came here ten thousand years ago and formed an underwater colony called Murrtaine. Your mother and sister, Isla, live there with her family," he explained.

"When they came out of the ocean and began to mix with humans Atlantis was built. But a few years later our people came back to this planet and became concerned at the new alliance with humans. We still have that alliance but it's shaky. We have strong traditions and also a great power that came with us from our old world. Our ancestors decided that the risk was too great and so they destroyed Atlantis and cut off Murrtaine completely. That was when the legend of the Soul Breathers was born." He flashed his knock-out grin at her.

Phoebe felt her cheeks go red with embarrassment.

Dante bobbed his head, appearing to read her mind. "Where do you fit in? Well, the legend says, in the time of the end, a prince will marry a Murr princess, five daughters will be born, and many sons to the five royal families. Then a great amount of fighting will break out between them, instability with the world's governments, and the weather on this planet will begin to become extreme as our power destabilizes. Well, to cut a very long story short, this has all happened." He smiled beautifully at her again. "You are one of those five princesses, Phoebe, all hidden in the world for the good of the Atlantean state. That is until such a time that suitors begin to approach you or it becomes too dangerous. Looks like we found you just in time," he finished with a warm smile.

Phoebe sat and listened to everything he said with a certain detachment. She'd kind of reached saturation point. After all, she'd just come from a room where she'd almost put her teeth into a man who drove her crazy. "Look, suppose I believe you."

The king inclined his head. "It's all true."

"Okay, well, why am I here; what do you want?"

Dante laughed in that easy way she was getting used to. "Right to the point. I like that. Okay, I'll lay it on the line for yer; you are one of the five Soul Breathers. That isn't just a name, it's what you do."

Phoebe subconsciously rubbed her chest and the king nodded.

"That's right. You feel it. It's a natural part of life for us. Have you shared it with him?" He tipped his head in Drew's direction.

Phoebe swallowed hard at the thought that he seemed to know so much about her, but was still curious why he hadn't mentioned the teeth and the blood. She decided to keep that to herself for the time being. "No, I don't think so," and she looked at Drew for confirmation.

Dante laughed. "Don't worry, you'd know. You'd definitely know," he said directly to Drew. "That's good, that's good," he repeated, thinking aloud. "Now, here's the thing. What you feel in you," and he pointed to her hand still resting against her chest, "holds power. That's why you were in danger in Seattle and why you were brought here."

He paused so what he said could sink in but, in all honesty, it didn't make any sense. Unless she was different to the others, hers was connected in some weird way to sex. That didn't sound right at all.

Again, he seemed to read her perfectly. "Look, I have three of your sisters already pledged to me, and another pledged to a prince who is loyal to me. When you were taken, did you pledge to another prince?"

All she could do was stare at him. "Taken?" She looked at Drew, startled. No one had ever mentioned that as a possibility to her. To her knowledge she'd suffered some kind of episode and lost a month somewhere. "I don't understand what you mean?"

"A thorough investigation is under way to get to the bottom of that, Phoebe. Don't worry, we will find out."

The thought terrified her and she looked at Drew again anxiously.

"She has no memory of that time," Drew explained.

Dante sighed and continued to regard her closely as if assessing her. Then he leant over to Alfonzo and whispered in hushed tones. He sat back in his chair and continued to make up his mind about something.

Phoebe looked between the two men. "Please, can someone tell me what's going on?"

"After you've had some rest, the families will assemble in the great hall. You will be tested and, if you're willing, I would ask that you pledge your allegiance to me. Then you'll be free to be with yer man here, if you wish it," he finished, smiling at Drew.

Phoebe narrowed her eyes and looked across at Drew. He shifted in his chair uncomfortably. "What do you mean, tested?"

Dante smiled kindly. "Just a small ceremony. Your mother and sisters will be with you. Just get into the sea beyond the window so all the witnesses can see and the test is complete."

She couldn't think of anything more scary. "But I can't swim!" The water was so deep. The thought was terrifying.

"You have to understand that it is natural to you to breathe the water. All your sisters can do it. You just have to have a little faith. It'll all be okay...then I would ask that you do a small exchange ceremony with me to show your allegiance, and it will all be over."

"I'm sorry, I didn't understand a word you just said." Everything appeared to be moving along too fast and she got the impression it was deliberate. She didn't know any of these people an hour ago and now this guy was expecting her to swim in deep water and do some wacky ceremonial stuff that she knew nothing about.

Alfonzo sat forward, sensing her indecision about the whole thing. "Listen to me carefully, Phoebe. You are a hybrid princess hidden in a hostile human world. We have a shaky truce with its inhabitants. The only hope is that we have a strong kingdom to hold our own with them. Dante is trying to do this," and he held out his arm to gesture next to him. "He can only do that with the power and allegiance of all five Sirens." Then he sat back in his chair and watched her closely.

It was all too much. Her life before had been a whirl of drinking, going out, travelling around and taking pictures. The biggest worry was getting a pimple when she came across a cute boy. Her eyes inevitably fell on Drew.

"Your life before has gone," Dante said softly.

When she looked back at him his face was filled with regret. "I wish I could say, you can go on and have a normal life, but that would be a lie. If not me, you must align with someone ... because if the humans get you, your life won't be worth living." His eyes drifted off to a dark place for a moment, and she wondered what it was he wasn't saying.

"One day soon, Phoebe, our ancestors will return. We need to be strong and the humans know this. Everything rests with you," Alfonzo said. "What you choose to do makes you the most important person alive right now."

Her eyes widened in fear and she realized she was squeezing the life out of Drew's hand. There was literally no one who could help her here. "Can I sleep on it?" she said, heart pounding, facing Dante again.

"Sure," he said, smiling, but she got from his expression that it was academic and there really wasn't a lot of choice. "Oh, I almost forgot." Dante reached into the drawer of his desk. "These are for you," he said, handing three glass vials of a clear liquid to Drew.

"What is it?" Drew said, taking them cautiously.

"Drink one now, then another in the morning, and twelve hours after that. You'll need it," Dante said, flashing an amused glance Phoebe's way. "Without it, she'll kill you."

Then, giving them no more time for questions, he ended the meeting abruptly. "Go! Get some sleep."

PHOEBE AND DREW walked silently back to their room and were brought up sharp to find Lance and Lily sitting on the bed waiting for them.

Phoebe sagged. She was dog-tired and really couldn't be doing with anymore hassle today. Drew gave her a quick smile in apology, then his attention was taken by Lance who immediately got up, clapped hands with him and kissed her on the cheek. "Just wanted to catch you before you went to sleep. We'll get straight out of your hair."

She smiled weakly and flashed a cautionary look at Lily.

"You just came from Dante?"

Drew nodded.

"They gave you the speech?"

Drew rubbed his eyes. "I guess so."

Lance looked directly at her. "It's hard – God, I hated it," he said, shaking his head. "I just wanted to say that it's harder for us men than you. It's kinda natural for you."

Can you swim?

Phoebe's eyes went wide at the girl sitting on her bed. It was the first time she'd spoken since their spat. Everyone seemed to be able to use the weird telepathy round here.

Once you get in the water with Dante, you will be able to do it too. You can actually do it already, you just don't know how.

Phoebe just shrugged. "Well I hope that goes for swimming, because I can't actually swim."

There was no sympathy on the girl's face. *Well I learned when someone tried to drown me as a kid. Once you know, it's like riding a bike.* The tomboy-looking girl continued to look at her unapologetically.

Phoebe was waiting for the punchline of a joke but it

never came. The thought horrified her. Then she remembered her comment from their meeting earlier. It made her
think a little differently about it. Perhaps in being hidden in
the world she'd been a bit luckier than the others. "Will they
hold me under?"

*They didn't me – but then they didn't have to. I think they may
have to for a minute until you get over the fear.*

"It's barbaric, I know, but there's a lot of stuff I don't fully
understand that's necessary," Lance said.

"Are you … you know?" she said.

Drew laughed, "Fuck, no he's not!"

Phoebe looked at Drew and wondered what was so
funny.

Lance laughed a little. "No, I'm not. I was adopted into an
Atalntean family, and …" He glanced at Drew with an
eyebrow up. "I'm something different entirely."

Drew looked puzzled but didn't question him further.
Then he got serious. "You're joking, right? About holding her
under water?"

"No," Lance said. Lily shook her head at the same time.

There was a stunned silence for a moment, until Phoebe
eventually said, "What did they mean about the allegiance bit.
Is that under water?"

"Yes," Lance said, looking straight at her. Then his eyes
went really strange for a moment.

Phoebe couldn't be sure if tiredness was making her see
things that weren't there, but she could've sworn his eyes had
gold glitter in them. Then it disappeared to the warm hazel
they were before.

"You okay?" he said, walking towards her and touching
her on the shoulder.

Drew came to steady her as if she'd swayed.

"I'm fine, I'm fine," she said, but couldn't keep the frown
away from her face as she stared at Lance. There was some-

thing so deeply familiar and unsettling in what she'd just seen. It was probably just exhaustion, but everything went completely out of kilter for a few moments.

No one's meant to tell you about the pledging stuff. It has to be totally your own decision. Nothing is supposed to sway you.

"What decision?" she said, starting to feel a little alarmed.

Lance looked over his shoulder at Lily still sitting on the bed, now cross-legged. "I think we should tell her."

"Tell me what," both she and Drew said together.

Then his eyes washed over in that gold glittery stuff completely and went again. It was so obvious, but when she looked at Drew he didn't appear to have seen it.

"What's in you …" He pointed a finger towards the center of her chest, "When you get near a man you want, it comes out and goes into him." Then he grinned at Drew. "It's awesome, man. I envy you feeling that for the first time." Then he faced Phoebe. "But the one you do it with first takes your power. They call it First Breath. That's why the king wants it."

Phoebe was confused and looked at Lily for some sort of confirmation. She just tipped her head and shrugged. *It's true.*

"But if I've never known I've had it, I won't miss it, will I?"

"Listen to me," Lance said, now deadly serious. "How can I say it so you'll understand. It's hard if you've never done it."

Phoebe flashed a look at Drew, bracing herself for the teeth and blood thing, but it never came.

Instead, Lance went and sat on the bed, picked up Lily's hand and looked into her eyes. "It's like nothing you've ever experienced before. It's the blending of spirits. The joining of two people – love, you know? It's the deepest bond you'll ever have with another person and it's for life. There's no breaking it, and you'll get sick if you don't nurture it."

Phoebe looked at Drew and when he looked back she

could tell he was as confused as she was. "Are you talking about marriage?"

Lance let out a long sigh and nodded.

Drew stood up straighter and she could tell he wasn't happy.

"They'll say it is in name only, but it's what it is."

Lily picked up his hand and kissed it. It was obviously something that affected them deeply as a couple.

"You did this?" Phoebe said a little more loudly than she intended.

"No, but I would have had I not already given my power unknowingly to someone else. Cesaré; no doubt you'll meet him. He's the king's right-hand man and loyal to him, but it boiled down to the same thing. I bound him to me first, before my true mate. She looked lovingly into Lance's eyes again.

There was something so deep that passed between them, it felt as though she and Drew were intruding.

"I'm sorry," she found herself saying before she realized.

"It's fucked up!" Drew said, making her head snap around to him. She had never heard him angry before. "They can't do this to people, can they?"

Lance stood with Lily, still holding her hand. "They can and they will. It's the Atlantean way."

"You just take all this?" Drew said, clearly exasperated with his friend.

Lance touched him on the shoulder as he walked past to the door. "I'm a part of this world, Drew. And now you're with her, you're in it too."

The door closed behind them and Phoebe was left staring into Drew's eyes. They weren't happy. Not happy at all.

They were both subdued when Lance and Lily left them. Phoebe didn't want to broach the subject of why Drew seemed angry – mainly because they barely knew each other and it seemed too presumptuous to assume he was possessive of her already. It was more likely to be pride, which wasn't exactly easy to talk about. He just didn't like another guy stepping on his toes. It was awkward.

Drew sat on the bed to untie his boots.

"You want to talk about it?"

He looked up at her wearily through his eyebrows. "Let's just sleep, shall we?"

She sighed and nodded, partly relieved but feeling a little abandoned by him. A small hug of encouragement was all it required. She thought of Connor for the umpteenth time that day. The last twenty-four hours had been exhausting – both physically and emotionally.

After stripping down to her underwear, she slid into the bed facing him and wondered what he was thinking. His face was unreadable, as he seemed to study her across the pillow. A long moment passed. Just when she thought he'd open up, he cupped her face in his hand and said, "Sleep! It's a long day tomorrow." Then he turned away from her leaving her confused.

Hurt, and not completely sure what had happened to make everything her fault, she told herself he was as exhausted as she was and closed her eyes.

It felt like just a moment had passed when they were awoken by a gentle tapping on the door. Phoebe sat up and padded to the door and cracked it a little. A small dark woman smiled. "Excuse me, Your Highness, I have brought your robe and costume for the ceremony. A breakfast will be brought to your room in about twenty minutes. You are to assemble in the great hall in an hour."

Phoebe opened the door more widely and gingerly took the folded black items from her. "Thank you," she said, and closed the door.

Drew was just swinging his legs over the side of the bed. He reached to the bedside table and picked up another of those vials Dante had given him. Then, after his face contorted with the taste, he beckoned her over with his hands. "Come here."

He pulled her between his legs so his chin was in the center of her chest and he could look up at her. She threaded her hands into his long, dark curly hair making him look totally the rock star. It surprised her, as her hands ran over the smooth skin of his shoulders, that he had no other tattoos – just the winged angel on his back. It was rare for a musician.

She moved his heavy curls behind an ear to find a line of piercings – a heavy tungsten hoop and four smaller ones up the cartilage of his ear. A quick check of the other showed it was the same.

"You like them?" he asked, his voice still a little raspy from sleep.

She nodded. "I'm surprised you don't have many tattoos?"

He shrugged and shifted uncomfortably. "Haven't found a strong enough reason to have my own yet."

His choice of words totally threw her for a minute.

Then he shrugged it off with, "It was kind of frowned on where I come from…standard issue," he said, gesturing his thumb over his shoulder.

It sparked a thousand questions desperate to be answered but his eyes glazed over and he disappeared somewhere in his memories. It didn't seem a good place either. The tension in his brow as she smoothed it over with her thumb told her that, so she kept quiet.

Drew came back to the present and tightened his grip around her backside. He nuzzled into her breasts and drew in a long breath. "You smell good."

Just that small gesture ramped up her temperature and the weight appeared from nowhere in her chest. But as soon as it arrived it only reminded her of her predicament – of what she had to do in less than an hour. "I have to get ready," she said, pointing half-heartedly at the pile of clothes she'd placed next to him on the bed.

Drew stood up slowly to his full height but didn't release her. He gazed down into her eyes. His long hair swung down and covered both their shoulders. He grazed a finger from the side of her temple and along her lips. "There!" he said, making her jump when his finger brushed the very tip of her canine tooth slowly descending.

When her eyes tracked back up to his they were tinged with orange and the edges of her vision had gone. All she could see was a tiny slither that held his face watching her in awe.

"I have to go and do that thing in a minute," she said, but his mouth was slowly coming closer to meet hers.

"You mean, get married," he said, in a whisper.

"I suppose," she said, breathing heavily next to his mouth. All it was going to take was one kiss. That was all.

His mouth closed over hers, his tongue searching and probing, hot and wet. Her eyes closed and she accepted immediately, groaning and pulling him more tightly to her. "We don't have time." But he was already lifting her by the backside, turning and throwing her down on the bed and landing on top of her. "Someone will be here in a minute."

He was pulling her t-shirt over her head and unclipping her bra adeptly with one hand.

"Drew!" she gasped. "Please!"

He was taking her nipple into his mouth. "Do you want me to stop," he was saying between nips.

Her teeth now made closing her mouth impossible. There was no way she could come out of the room like this. "No … I don't want you to stop." Her voice was low and completely unlike her. "Drew, I can't stop. I can't help myself!"

He smiled against her skin and drew hard at the side of her breast and goaded her on. Something in her reared up hard and burst out. It was her but it wasn't. More accurately, it was as though she was two people. The one on the surface and one that had been repressed her whole life.

Drew laughed as she threw him over onto his back. "Whoa!" It was nothing about humor and all about lust.

She pounced on him, ripped his boxers from him and placed him at her core. Within seconds she was riding him with abandon with him writhing beneath her. Nothing could get through to her now. Her vision was just a small slit and all she could see was Drew straining and throwing his head back to expose his beautiful throat. The veins so tantalizingly close to the surface –blood pulsing in time with his heartbeat that was getting louder and louder in her ears.

She couldn't explain how this felt. It was animal and primal and she had no control. All she knew for sure was that it was a claiming. He was hers, and as she rose and fell mercilessly on top of him, she was willing it, demanding it, and he was completely in the power of her body, which at that moment was infinitely stronger than his.

Now he was totally dominated, she felt an unfurling of heat in the pit of her stomach. The core of her was clenching while his length continued to stroke the inner most part of her. Then it flashed sending out a tidal wave of ecstasy throughout her whole body. What started slowly sped to a whiplash of utter pleasure. Then her mouth came down hard and struck his neck, sucking in huge pulls while she ground herself onto him and he pulsated within her. His initial gasp of her name disappeared into a long groan. His orgasm wracked through his whole body and her domination was complete. He gave himself over totally to pleasure and submitted his life force to her without a care to how much she took. It was completely foolhardy as she had no control and could have easily drained him if it weren't that the weight in her chest was now so painful there was no ignoring it.

It wanted out but there was no way she could release Drew's neck. Her senses were returning and the systems in her brain began to turn back on, but instinct still rode her hard. So when Drew's arms came around her softly the weight moved and began its ascent. It rose slowly like bubbles at first. Tickling and bouncing along the walls of her chest to her esophagus, into her throat until it reached her mouth.

She did the only logical thing she could do. Instead of drawing blood into her mouth she let whatever it was flow from her into the wound. Except when she began there was no filtering it or slowing it down. The pressure valve was off and it flew.

Drew jolted as if he'd been electrocuted. He became stiff and his body bowed beneath her. Every sinew strained.

It was out of her in a matter of about three seconds, and she closed the wound by pinching her lips together hard. Just to make sure, she replaced the pressure with her fingers pushing it closed.

Phoebe sat back on her knees sharply. She was shocked at the ferocity of what just happened. There was no control in what she'd done. She could have killed him. However, his body writhed, bowing and arching every so often when another wave of sensation washed over him.

It went on for several minutes until he eventually stilled. Easing herself off him, she lay beside him willing him to say something – anything, but his face was red and his eyes were bloodshot and hollow. "I'm sorry."

Drew managed a small smile. "Shh! Don't apologize. "I think I know what the king meant now. Wow!" he said, still in a husky whisper. His eyes fluttered and were slowly closing. "I don't think I'll make it to your wedding. I…" And he trailed off.

Phoebe clambered up on her knees and put her ear to his chest. *Thank God.* His heartbeat was strong and clear although a little out of rhythm.

The door knocked again. "Ten minutes, Your Highness."

Bloody hell. This stupid ceremony was the last thing she needed after what just happened. She looked around the room in panic. The only thing she could think of was to hurriedly get ready and get the whole thing over with. When the knock came again, she'd showered and was just tying the sash around the black robe that covered the black swimsuit. Everything fitted her perfectly.

Drew was fast asleep. She'd listened to his chest several times just to make sure. A small smile played on her lips when she reminded herself that she'd worn him out.

Still smiling, she yanked the door open and hitched a breath in surprise to see Connor standing there. Showered and dressed, with moisture still clinging to the ends of his overlong hair, he smiled his beautiful, insecure smile "Ready?" he said.

In that moment all the angst that had gone before was forgotten and she flung her arms around his neck. His strong, big brotherly arms came around her – the only ones that could make everything better.

"Hey, you okay?" he said in concern.

"Where have you been?" she breathed into his chest.

"I'm sorry, I didn't realize. I was giving you space, and …" His voice trailed off making her pull apart to look at him.

"And what?" Her heart was thumping knowing she wasn't going to like whatever it was.

Connor touched the side of her face gently. "Bringing you here means my job is kind of over." Her expression quickly turned from horror to rage.

"So I was right. It was all just a job to you." She went to pull out of his grip.

"No you don't!" He yanked her back to stand in front of him like the naughty child she always was.

The chronic feeling of déjà vu only compounded her feelings of betrayal.

Infuriatingly, he was fighting not to smile. "I am a Protector, Phoebe. We are born into this job. Most never have the opportunity to serve, but I was lucky – really lucky, in that your family placed me with you."

"Why?" she said, wiping her tears away angrily.

Connor pulled a handkerchief from his pocket and dabbed them more gently. "Because you're special. I've always known it." He pulled her back into his arms, which she allowed reluctantly. "Even though you'll be married today, I want you to know I'll always be your Protector and I'll always be here for you."

After a moment she pulled away with a sniff and nodded. "Okay. Does that mean you have to do as I say?" she said, looking down at her fingers.

He laughed. "I guess so."

"Right then, no shagging my friends!" She marched past him in the direction of the great hall.

"You're such a brat!" His laughter echoed behind her.

Dante was the first person to see and greet her when she entered the room. It was morning but the room was still dark and lit up like it was Christmas, with twinkling lights everywhere.

Lance and Lily smiled when they saw her from across the room.

"Ah, Phoebe, I want you to meet your brothers."

As she neared, two beautiful men stepped forward. One was a little taller than the other but both had the most glorious coffee skin and pale green eyes. They were completely striking to look at and, also, far darker than her and her sisters.

One took a step closer and kissed her on the cheek. "Hi, I'm Luca. We share a father but not a mother, if you're wondering," and he winked as he stepped back.

The taller one came forward. "Dino!" he said and did the same with a huge grin showing off the whitest teeth.

She looked from one to the other smiling widely. They were adorable and she couldn't help but like them instantly.

Dante led her away by the elbow and whispered, "Where's Drew?"

"We agreed it was probably best that he wasn't here," she said, trying to keep the pink flush from her cheeks.

"Very wise." The twinkle in his eye made her seriously wonder if he knew the real reason.

However, it was soon forgotten as they continued to circulate the room. Everyone was there that she'd met the day before, but they were standing with groups of people Dante introduced as delegations from the royal families.

First they came to her sister Lacy and the huge man, Keenan. "You remember Keenan," Dante said. "This is his family and the one your sister, Lacy, married into. They are the Santalinis … Marius, Drago, Louis," he said, pointing to each of Keenan's brothers one by one.

All words she might say became lost as she shook hands with the biggest, toughest men she'd ever seen.

"They are the soldiers of the race," Dante explained.

Lacy smiled at her kindly as if she knew exactly how overwhelming it all could be.

They continued on with their tour of the room.

Next they came to Lily and Lance. "Lance and Lily you've met." The king then shook hands warmly with a beautiful blonde man with long curly hair, stubble and startlingly blue eyes. "This is Ches. Cesaré is a great friend, and his family, the Florianna. This is the family your sister Lily married into."

Her eyes went to Lily in confusion, who made it worse by putting her arm around Lance's waist. *You don't always get it right first time.*

Phoebe then understood. Lily must be the one sister who didn't marry the king.

Dante smiled. "Yeah, you got it. She's with Lance, but bonded to Cesaré, who is aligned with me."

Phoebe rubbed her head. "I think so." She wondered if bonded meant married?

The next group they came to she had to crane her neck to look at. They were at least a foot taller than her, still with the remnants of stripes showing on their pale skin. They either had very pale blonde or black hair and all had large black or dark brown soulless eyes.

"You've met Isla and her husband, Darres. This is the Borge family. They come from the city of Murrtaine." Dante raised his eyebrows so she could join the dots.

Her eyes went wide when she made the connection. These were the pure bloods – the ones who lived permanently under water. A beautiful blond man took a step towards her and leaned forward as if to kiss her. Instead of going for her cheek, he put his forehead to hers. The movement shocked her and was the weirdest sensation, but she felt a warm, comfortable tingle. *Welcome, Phoebe, I am Vionne.*

When he pulled away the corners of his mouth were turning upwards into a strange smile. It looked like something he'd practised more for her benefit than his own.

He inclined his head. *You are very insightful, Your Highness. May I introduce my brothers, Dax and Caan. Alas, our brother Axyl is permanently based in our colony, Murrla in Antarctica and couldn't be here today.*

The information she was learning was fascinating but also overwhelming as there was so much to take in. The last person was an older-looking gentleman who put her in mind of a fairy-tale courtier. His grey hair skimmed his shoulders, and his small beard and dancing eyes only backed that up as he bent over her hand and kissed it.

His sing-songy voice added to the illusion when he welcomed her. "Phoebe, today is a great day for the Atlantean nation. We welcome you."

"This is the Duke Ormond Delissi – the representative from the Dubonnetti, my family." Dante smiled with more than a little mischief in his eyes.

Hers widened in understanding. The same eyes, the same beautiful smile; the man could be none other than the king's father. However, she somehow got the impression that it wasn't as simple as all that.

"Record that the Siren, Parthenope Riadne Teles Bonaci, is to be tested this day, and married to the king in accordance with all Atlantean rights and tradition," Delissi was saying as a man scribbled on a clipboard next to him.

They were now right next to the fountain that glowed a magical blue. She guessed there must be some kind of underwater lighting to make it glow that color. Naomi, her mother, stood up from her seat on the edge. *My beautiful girl, are you ready?*

No, I'm not, she suddenly realized, and scanned the room for a friendly face or someone she really knew, but there were so many people they were just empty faces; blank, unfeeling strangers.

Her mother was now holding her hand and the other girls, her sisters, were surrounding her. *Please don't be afraid, Phoebe. We are all here and we will stay with you until the test is complete.*

"Seriously, I can't swim," Phoebe said, now looking around her frantically in the hope she would spot Connor or Drew.

Her sisters were removing their robes. Each one was so similar – not exceptionally tall, similar frame, beautiful but individual and so different in their characters.

Spokes to a wheel, her mother answered for her, smiling. *Not great in stature, but all necessary to make up the strength of the whole.*

Phoebe frowned, processing what she meant, while a maid began helping her out of her own robe.

Dante appeared stripped down to plain navy blue shorts, showing off a surprisingly muscular and trim body. However what completely amazed her was the number of tattoos. He was completely covered in them. It immediately made her compare it to Drew's almost completely clear skin; just the mysterious one on his back.

"It's the Atlantean way," he said, answering her unspoken question with a wink.

She got the idea that, even if he had not been Atlantean, he probably would have had them anyway. He was totally a man of contradictions.

Lacy came behind her and took her hand. "We'll be with you every step of the way. I couldn't swim before either."

Phoebe searched her kind face and gave a small nod. "Thank you,"

"It's time," Dante said.

Delissi nodded.

His scribe scribbled.

The room hushed to such quiet that you could clearly hear the slosh of the water as she, her mother and Lacy stepped over the fountain wall into the chilly water.

"You see the dark part?" Lacy said.

Phoebe nodded, unable to speak, her heart was thumping so hard.

"That is the tunnel. We're going to step into it and swim out to the sea," she finished, pointing at the huge window to their left.

Phoebe looked over her shoulder.

"Isla and Lily will follow – they're great swimmers, so don't worry. Then Dante will come out last of all."

Her mother gave her hand a squeeze.

Phoebe nodded feeling wooden and tense, it was now or never.

"Now!" Lacy said.

The three of them stepped out over the edge and plunged down into the neon blue waters.

CHAPTER 12

Phoebe was still holding her breath as she was pulled along the jagged rock tunnel, out to the deep water. They kept moving until they reached the thick, flat expanse that must have been the window.

With Naomi and Lacy holding each hand tightly, Dante swam in closely and held each side of her face. *Stop holding your breath now, Phoebe. You must let the water in.*

No! She began to struggle, trying to pull her hands from her mother and sister's grasp, but they held on fast.

You're just prolonging it. Look at me.

Her eyes darted wildly as panic set in.

Look. At. Me! Dante said in a strong mental blast.

There was something so powerfully authoritative about it that it stopped her thrashing and her eyes immediately locked with his. The strength in his mental voice and an overwhelming feeling of calm grounded her. *Listen to me; I wouldn't let anything happen to you, you are too precious, too important. You understand?*

She nodded.

You are a Soul Breather. The answer is in the title. Get it?

She nodded again.

Now trust me. Close your eyes and gradually let the water in.

After one last, searching look into his face she did exactly as he asked. Except the moment the salt water began to trickle into her lungs it burnt, making her want to expel it and cough. *No*, she shouted, and pulled, pushed and kicked wildly.

Her hands were still held in a vice-like grip. Someone grabbed an ankle, and then the other. It seemed to go on forever – her head shaking from side to side with her silent screams. Until eventually, the lungful of air she'd taken upon leaving the hall began to run out. There was nothing else she could do but give in. This was it – death – the final numbing ending that she'd never envisaged for herself. There was warmth, then she was floating and time stood still.

The next thing she knew, her brains were rattling in her skull. The blissful, safe warmth she felt was smashed by her last memories of panic and suffocation. For a moment her heart pounded as the feelings returned and she thrashed again.

Someone was saying soothing words, "It's OK … you're breathing."

She should be dead. She'd drowned. And yet she was blinking and aware she was being shaken.

Phoebe opened her eyes and found she wasn't in floaty heaven, but still under water. Five people were all staring down at her with huge grins on their faces – including her mother, who just looked plain weird.

Feel behind your ears, Dante said, pointing.

She put her hand to the soft skin of her scar that had been there ever since she could remember. Except now, when her fingers ran across it, there were bubbles and an opening resembling a small mouth on either side of her head. *Oh my god!*

Gills! Dante explained. *We must complete the ceremony.* But there was no amusement in his face now as he took her hand and she faced him squarely.

I will replenish my bond with Lacy and Isla, then it's your turn.

For some reason, her eyes found Lily's.

I have no bond with Lily. That's for Cesaré, Dante explained. Then he brought her chin back round to look at him again. *When our bond is complete, you will find psychic speech comes easier.*

OK, she honestly couldn't see how though.

First Dante beckoned Lacy.

She swam up to him easily, placed her hands on his shoulders and his circled her waist. Phoebe was entranced when Dante slanted his mouth over hers and they appeared to kiss. Except it was obvious this was no mere kiss when Lacy's upper body began to glow. A ball of light grew and rotated white and orange. It rose and before she could see what happened, the two of them became completely illuminated in a warm haze. It was gentle, didn't appear to be painful and lasted a full couple of minutes. Then they floated apart.

Phoebe looked around her to see if that was it, and someone would go and wake them, but they came around, gathered themselves and went straight back and did it again. They held the position until both their bodies were surrounded by a soft, glowing halo. It was fascinating.

Briefly she tore her eyes away to glance at the flat black rock that she knew was the window, and wondered what Keenan was making of this.

This time, when they parted, the pair simply hung in the water until her mother, Naomi, swam to her sister's side and gently pulled her out of the way. Then she appeared to wake up from whatever trance she was in and smiled at her mother.

Next it was Isla's turn. She repeated the process in exactly the same way. It was intriguing.

Lily had appeared at her elbow. *Now it's your turn,* and she gave her a little push. *Don't overthink it,* she said, as Phoebe moved away from her and in the direction of Dante who trod water and, she had to admit, looked pretty magnificent.

He seemed to have grown in height. His skin had lightened and was now covered completely in dark grey stripes, and his hair fanned out to frame his handsome tribal-striped face. When she neared him she glanced around her, and they were all the same – except her mother's skin had a blue-grey tinge and her stripes were darker than everybody else's. They all moved gracefully in the water with their hair swaying and waving around their faces.

Dante's hand came down on her shoulder bringing her attention back to him. *Look down,* he said, dipping his eyes for her to follow his line of vision.

Copying him, she got exactly what he was driving at. She was identical to them; every marking identifying her as part of the same tribe. It wasn't that she'd never seen it, but it had no meaning before. It had always been hidden, and treated as something to be ashamed of. That was until now. Today she felt a curious sense of elation.

He brought her chin back up to look at him. *Don't be scared. You see...you're one of us.* Despite the evidence, it was still overwhelming. Because if they were telling her the truth about this, then she guessed everything else must be true too.

You've never done this, what we're about to do?

She shook her head.

It seemed to be the right answer, as he looked a little relieved. *Then let us begin.* Dante pulled her into his body. They were so close, she expected to feel warmth, but his skin was as cold as hers. When Drew was this close he was warm and inviting. Then the truth struck her; that it only went to prove how human he was in comparison.

Slowly, the king drew her closer, smiling.

Oh heck!

Still smiling, he closed his mouth over hers. *I cannot tell you what to do as it is a test. You can't kill me as I'm too strong, but it's a test nonetheless.* The psychic words weren't making a lot of sense, she was so nervous. She waited with her heart pounding, expecting something to happen but it didn't.

Dante began to move his mouth over hers. *Relax.*

She tried her best to but it was impossible when he pulled her body even tighter into his. This didn't feel like a test, but more like a prelude to sex with someone she had zero feelings for.

Please, Phoebe, don't be afraid. He drew back slightly to look deeply into her eyes. *This is a marriage; it's bound to feel strange. But I won't touch you, I promise. The power of the bonding comes from deep inside of you. Think about it.*

Phoebe continued to search his face. Something deeply within her was urging her on. Perhaps it was instinct, she wasn't sure. It seemed to be speaking to her, soothing her, telling her it was okay, that no harm could come. It was just physical.

Whatever it was, it seemed to be working. When Dante's mouth covered hers again she moved her lips with his. The process was erotic and began to reach something deep down. By the time his tongue probed her mouth apart and began to swirl with hers, it became clear. Everything started to make sense. It felt sexy because it was meant to. This whole thing was supposed to happen between partners. The fact that she was doing it with a complete stranger, in front of God knew how many witnesses, seemed beside the point. She challenged any girl not to be affected. All this king was asking for was the very thing that had flowed from her that afternoon when she'd been having the sex of her life with Drew. Maybe it wasn't an evil force at all, but more an electric current for pleasure.

The kiss built and the weight stirred in her chest. It still gave her misgivings. Not only was she glad the sister genuinely married to him wasn't watching, but she was changing. Every one there was stripy and breathing the water, but she hadn't seen one of them change into something like her. Their eyes seemed to widen to allow for more light, while hers narrowed to thin slits like a predator.

A stroke of his tongue sent a tingle into the teeth that were already straining to descend.

Then she wasn't sure what happened exactly. Dante nipped her lip, or altered his stance. An image of Drew writhing beneath her slammed into her mind. Her teeth shot into her mouth like the fall of a guillotine, pinning Dante's tongue. The taste of copper compounded thoughts of Drew submitting and needing her, and that lit a fuse. The memory hit her of Drew's arms tightening around her at exactly the moment Dante did the same. Dante jolted in shock but didn't pull apart. The weight rose sharply and burnt where it touched. Whatever it was hurtled out of her mouth and into the king she held in a vice-like grip. For a long few moments they were melded together. There was no prising them apart.

Despite the initial shock of her bite, Dante must have been incredibly strong, because he took every last particle. There were no shudders, spasms or convulsions. His eyes just closed, he absorbed whatever it was into him and his arms remained gentle holding her.

Phoebe watched enraptured until he opened his eyes and smiled. *My turn.* She was unsure exactly what happened after that. She was certain he didn't move or do a single thing. There were stars, a white light and a slam that hit her head and square in the stomach. Then everything went black.

Her heart was beating all over the place until it found its rhythm again. The tips of her fingers and toes tingled. She still couldn't see anything but floated in the void a while listening to indiscernible voices. They seemed to echo all around her head. Maybe this was the psychic speech they were all going on about.

What happened? a female said.

Not sure. It was Dante.

Did you complete the exchange immediately?

No, I didn't get the chance before she passed out.

What is it, do you think? The voice became clearer as belonging to Naomi. *Is she ill – too weak for this? You are so strong now.*

I don't think so.

Then she felt a finger prize back her lip.

What's the matter?

They've gone.

Not able to bear him telling everyone something she'd sought to hide her whole life, she stirred.

She's awake!

Hey! Dante said. *You okay?*

Phoebe nodded, not sure what happened any more than they were.

Should we take her in and complete the ceremony another time? her mother said, hanging on to Dante's arm as if to hold him back.

Her sisters stood a little way off, regarding her curiously.

I think we should continue if she is feeling up to it. Dante looked deeply into her eyes. *Do you feel up to it?*

What little confidence she had definitely wavered. Doing it to him had somehow short-circuited her brain, and now the process had to go the other way around. She glanced nervously at the others treading water a little way off and wondered how much they had seen.

Dante kneaded the tops of her arms to bring her attention back to him. *Listen to me, Phoebe. I am speaking directly to you. No one else can hear, okay?*

Her heart thudded as she looked up at him and waited.

I want you to answer me honestly.

Phoebe nodded.

You drink blood?

No! she lied and looked away from him.

He studied her for a long moment as if he was deciding whether he believed her or not. *Atlantean blood is very strong is all, and mine is stronger than most. You understand? The power in it is too strong for you. So, for your own good, it's inadvisable to try it with anyone. Are you able to continue?*

Guilt at her lie pricked her cheeks, she was glad the water hid it. However, he hadn't mentioned her teeth, or the change in her eyes. Perhaps it wasn't such a big deal here. Mainly because of that, and even though she was unsure, she agreed with a small nod. She figured they'd only bring her back another time so she wanted it over with.

Now smiling and with a small nod in reply, Dante slanted his mouth over hers. He held her firmly to him, but there was no kissing this time, just pure functionality. It sobered her a little to think that he'd only done it to coax the thing out of her and it had worked. It hurt a little.

There wasn't time to dwell. A tingling sensation began to creep into her mouth. It travelled to the back of her throat and down into her lungs. All the way it heated and prickled. For a moment she thought she'd have to cough but she didn't get the chance. Whatever it was felt like it was boring a hole through the center of her chest, spinning faster and faster.

Her eyes opened. Dante was glowing in white luminescent mist. Then her insides exploded.

There were colors rushing past, sounds like music playing backwards and pictures of people she'd never known. Then came the feelings; passion, love, kindness, longing. A girl's face flashed, and she somehow instinctively knew these were the feelings Dante had for someone. It was the sister she hadn't met – the queen. Finally, as her heart began to beat more slowly and settled back to its rhythm, came a cozy warmth. It reminded her of how she felt about Connor – brotherly. It was Dante's feelings for her and it filled her with awe.

*Hey, we have a fainter...*filtered through with laughter. *Wake up, darlin'.*

Her eyes flickered open after passing out for a second time. She looked into Dante's smiling eyes, slightly embarrassed. *Thank you, Phoebe. You gave me a great gift.* Then his grin widened to his knockout smile. *Your man is very lucky.*

Phoebe couldn't help smiling, even though he was hinting at knowing some of her innermost thoughts – which were a little raunchy.

He winked, proving her point and making her blush. Judging by what she'd just learned, he was a complete rogue and a real handful. Secretly, she wished her sister luck with him.

His laugher rang through her head. *Come, it is over. Let's go back inside.*

The party swam back through the tunnel and scrambled up through the hole in the center of the fountain. Each of them leaned over and quietly coughed the water out of their lungs. Phoebe watched and copied, a little less lady-like. She thought she'd vomit all over everyone, she coughed and spluttered so much.

Someone shoved a glass into her eye line. She took it without thinking and took large sips. It was warm and soothing. The others stepped out over the fountain wall one by one and took a large neatly folded towel from two servants standing with piles of them in their arms. The guests were all shaking Dante's hand and kissing Naomi's cheek in congratulations, as if it was them that had accomplished something that day.

Phoebe stumbled to stand in the shallows of the fountain and noticed Dante already walking away. *Hey!* He didn't respond. She went to call out but he continued walking, rubbing his head with a towel as he went off with several men she couldn't remember the names of. Nothing came out except a raspy croak and she held her hand to her throat until the searing pain passed.

Keenan lovingly wrapped Lacy up in a towel, Lance kissed Lily tenderly doing the same. Isla was waving goodbye and, with Darres' hand tightly in hers, stepped back over the wall and disappeared back into the fountain's depths. Everyone was with someone. Everyone appeared to be loved.

Then her eyes found his: *Drew.* For a moment all her anxiety floated away, but his eyes were heavy lidded and he turned and walked away.

Here, my child, let me help you. Still distracted by Drew's departure, she looked into the doe eyes of her mother. She was dabbing the water from her face and caring for her as she imagined mums did with small children at the beach.

All she kept thinking was, she'd been up close and personal with a hot Atlantean male. *How much had Drew seen?*

CHAPTER 13

$\mathcal{D}$ante showered, changed and called an impromptu meeting in his study above ground. Duke Delissi, Sebastian, Alfonzo, Cesaré Florianna – all his trusted advisors – trooped into the room looking a little puzzled as to why they'd been summoned. The day had been a resounding success. With the identification and marriage of the last Siren, strength and stability seemed within sight for the first time. Now all the sisters were accounted for and mated with the right people, the new government could now flourish and prepare for Atlas' return.

Everything should be rosy.

Dante waited for everyone to settle and become silent before he spoke. "Forgive my voice, it hasn't yet properly returned."

At that moment a maid entered and brought him a steaming mug of hot honey and lemon. "Thank you."

"Is today not a joyous day, Your Highness?" Cesaré asked, clearly bewildered.

Dante conceded with a dip of his head.

"But I can't help notice that the whole council is not here."

The others murmured their agreement.

"What is concerning you, Your Highness? All seemed to go well and in accordance with the laws and traditions," his father, Duke Delissi said.

"Indeed it did," Dante said, not sure exactly how to say what he couldn't fathom himself.

"Yet something still troubles you." Alfonzo said. He narrowed his eyes. "Has her power been pledged to another?"

Everyone shuffled uncomfortably at that. It was an outcome that could be potentially disastrous to the kingdom.

The door knocked and his human advisor and tutor Max entered. He apologized for being late and took a seat.

"In all honesty, I can't be sure. She is powerful," he assured them. "But after the debacle of the sea witches pretending to be Tia's sisters, I have to be extremely careful."

"I think you can be assured of her authenticity, Dante," the duke said. "I have traced her roots, and all tallies with her original placement by the Santalini family as a small child."

Dante sighed and nodded slowly, but he wasn't happy. It was true, Delissi would have left no stone unturned in proving who she was, so much depended on it. However, this one was so much more than the others. There was a powerful darkness in her and not the ray of sunshine that her name would suggest. "I don't know how exactly to explain it. I was expecting the day and instead I got the night," was what immediately sprung to mind. He looked around at the faces surrounding him, flummoxed.

The others frowned and looked at each other in confusion.

"You suspect foul play?" Cesaré said, with bitterness. He himself had been the victim of a plot that almost cost the kingdom and his life. "Isla was an authentic Siren and still my ring was tampered with."

That was true. "I don't know, it's more than that." He looked around at all the faces hanging on his every word.

"What is troubling you?" Sebastian said.

Dante smiled at the aging gentleman who he'd always relied on for his calming, fatherly influence – the complete opposite to his own fiery nature.

"When we were in the water, she went through certain changes."

"It is her nature to change," Delissi said.

"This was different. Her eyes…and she …she drew blood."

There were several murmurs as everyone shifted uncomfortably and sat back in their chairs.

"Was it accidental?" Max said, trying to put a voice of reason into proceedings. He was well versed in the laws against the consumption of blood. They all were.

Everyone accepted it as part of life for the Santalini royal family, but for anyone else it was strictly breaking the law. It was punishable by death. It created strong bonds that undermined the king's power, especially if it went on with any of his wives. He simply couldn't allow it. "Possibly," Dante said, with a bob of his head. It was easily done.

"Was that the reason for her loss of consciousness?"

Dante nodded. "I think so. My blood is very pure and has the power of three already."

It made sense and they muttered their agreement.

"I think, in the circumstances, it can be overlooked." Delissi said. "You just must be careful not to complete the blood bond. As long as the exchange of breath went without a hitch, I can see no problem."

That part went well but Dante's mind wasn't at ease. He hadn't forgotten Lacy's disappearance and the use of Isla. All to make Cesaré think she was his to get close to him and steal his kingdom. Both instances had one common theme: Malleven Mancini, Cesaré's first cousin and powerful alchemist, who would stop at nothing to overthrow him and take the crown for himself. "I want to know everything Malleven was doing the month Phoebe Ray was missing. I want to know what he had for breakfast and when he went to bed at night, and with whom."

Delissi bowed his head.

Cesaré's face visibly darkened in hatred. "You suspect he has been at work here?"

He looked each of his advisers in the eye one by one. "We must suspect everyone and everything so as not to be taken off guard. Someone not only took Phoebe Ray but they returned her as if nothing happened. That to me says something far more sinister and far beyond what the humans would do."

All the men nodded and accepted the truth in that.

He looked straight at Max. "You must scour the books, human and Atlantean. Look for legends of Sirens where one was different to the rest and find out why." If anyone could find out what he was dealing with, it was Max.

"It would help if I knew *what* was different about her, sire?"

"She has fangs!"

PHOEBE MANAGED to assure her mother she was okay and went back to her room. When she slipped inside, Drew was sitting on the bed with his head in his hands. He let them drop and watched her cautiously walk towards the bed and sit next to him. His collar was pulled up high, but she could just see a small dressing on his neck.

"Did someone help you with that?"

"Lance." His voice was flat and unreadable.

"Did he ask you how …?"

"He knew how!" Drew snapped.

"I'm sorry," Phoebe blurted, not sure how she could make this all better. "I don't know what to do." Everything had got so weird and out of control. She couldn't be sure what exactly she'd done wrong anymore. "Was it the marriage, or you know …" she trailed off, pointing at the wound on his neck.

Drew huffed and got up and paced the room. When he stopped and glared at her his face was red and hot. "This is just a part of it," he said, gesturing to his neck. "I'm out here in fuck knows where, with a girl that not only got married an hour ago, but was kissing and moving on him like they needed a room."

Phoebe felt her own cheeks flush. It sounded terrible.

"But you know what the worst thing is?"

She shook her head and swallowed.

"I'm changing. Whatever it is you do to me in the sack, it's fucking changing ME! I'm all over the fucking place."

With the worst possible timing there was a knock at the door.

Drew let his hands fall to his sides and looked at the ceiling. Phoebe didn't dare move a muscle. With the loudest sigh, he strode to the door and snatched it open. "Someone for you!" he said under his breath. Shaking his head, he pushed past Connor and out of the door.

Connor walked in, glancing back over his shoulder in confusion. "Everything okay?" he said, sitting down next to her.

Phoebe turned into his chest and sobbed.

DANTE WENT to walk back through the great hall when he stopped short. The new guy, Drew, was standing close to the large window lost in the hypnotic quality of the sea. He'd done the same thing himself countless times when he needed to think.

He came up behind him. "Got a minute?"

The mass of long curls swung round and the guy looked at him with contempt. It was a look he'd seen many times. It was the kind he got when he'd trod on someone's toes with their mate – except this guy was a human. Maybe this kind of aggressive jealousy wasn't unique to his race. "Take a seat."

Drew turned but hesitated.

"It will only take a minute." Dante sat down heavily, feeling worn out by the day already.

The guy shifted a chair around opposite him then sat and waited with his eyebrows raised in a question.

Dante almost laughed. The guy simply had no idea what he'd got himself into. However, experience had taught him that no one should be underestimated, and very often people were not what they seemed. "Thank you."

Drew dipped his head in acknowledgement, which only made him grin. Drew remained deadpan. "What do you want? I mean, you got what you want – we should be okay to leave, right?"

"There's no rush. When Phoebe comes to terms with who she is, learns what she needs to know and we are sure she has adequate protection, she can leave. You can leave any time you wish."

Drew's eyes narrowed and he sat back in his chair. The upturned collar moved and Dante saw his neck, clearly confirming what he already suspected. "Accident?" he said, pointing to his neck.

Drew adjusted his collar. "Yeah, shaving." But the attitude shifted to one of discomfort.

Dante's heart sank. He already had a human – not only bonded to his wife but also addicted to Atlantean blood. He didn't need another. Blood was highly addictive and taken so seriously it was punishable by death. Although he didn't want to come down heavy-handed here. The guy was an unknown quantity and he needed information. This Siren had something dark within her and was not like her sisters at all. "She drinks from you?"

Drew covered his neck again and attempted to look nonchalant.

"I'm not your enemy, Drew. I, above all people, know what you're dealing with – what it is to love a Siren. They are passionate and unpredictable. And what they give you…well, it's indescribable."

He paused to allow his words to sink in.

Drew didn't speak but he was listening closely.

"But the payoff for all that pleasure is that she never gets to live her own life. She really belongs to the state."

"To you, you mean," Drew cut in.

Dante bobbed his head. "Kinda. I am the head of state."

Drew let out a mirthless blast of air.

Dante decided to change tack. "You know Lance?"

"Yeah, I haven't seen him for around a year. We jammed together for a while."

"He found it difficult at first, but he settled into our world."

Drew started to rise from his chair. "It doesn't suit everyone."

Dante nodded, accepting his point. Drew started to walk away from him but paused when he spoke. "You're free to go any time, Drew. I myself will okay it, but you need to be aware that you are now connected to this race whether you like it or not. Your connection to Phoebe will be known to all intelligence-gathering agencies. You will be at risk of capture and torture. But the most important thing of all is that your abandonment leaves her by law to the crown."

As expected, that snippet of news made Drew turn

around to face him. "Are you saying what I think you're saying?

"I'm saying that now we have a full bond, for her own safety and that of the kingdom I will have to claim her."

Drew stood so long with his eyes narrowed that he honestly didn't know if the guy would jump him, but he said eventually, "I'm not going anywhere."

Dante stood and went to leave for his apartments. "Glad to see you've come to the right decision." He felt the guy's eyes on him all the way out the room, knowing full well he'd manipulated the outcome. There was no other option. If he had some kind of bond with her already, then separation could kill both of them. And there was something else nagging at him. The last Siren might be a mystery, but this guy wasn't all that he seemed either.

CHAPTER 14

Phoebe had cried for ages, held by Connor just like he'd done a hundred times before. He was her rock, her safe place, the one person in the world who really knew her and she could be totally honest with.

He put her away from him eventually and came back with a handful of tissue for her nose. "Here, snot isn't a good look."

She half laughed and took it from him giving a good loud blow. "Sorry," she said, laughing again. Blowing your nose like a trumpet wasn't sexy either.

"What's up, Phoebes … why were you two rowing?"

Phoebe crossed her legs and began tearing little pieces of tissue off in her lap. She wasn't sure how to put it, not entirely sure she understood it herself. "You know how I'm different, you know change and all that?" She took a cautious glance at Connor who was frowning.

"He rejected you?" he said, looking angrier by the minute.

"No, no, that's not it. It's me, Connor. I think I'm just too weird, too weird for anyone."

Before Connor could say any more, the door opened and

Drew came back in without knocking. He halted immediately as if he hadn't expected Connor to still be there. Connor slowly stood and the atmosphere went decidedly frosty.

Connor walked right up in front of Drew, clearly trying to intimidate him. Neither man stepped off.

"No, Connor, please," she said, jumping to her feet. "We just need some time to sort things out, okay?"

After a full moment more of glaring into Drew's eyes, Connor moved towards the door. "You know where I am if you need me." His eyes were still very much on Drew as a warning. Then, after a last glare, he left.

Drew blinked slowly without comment. Then he focused and walked towards her slowly till he stood toe to toe with her.

Craning her neck, she looked up and matched his glare. "Where did you go?" It came out more breathily than she'd have liked and her vision was already becoming tinged with orange. Her heart hammered with the effort of trying to hold back the change that seemed to happen involuntarily around him these days. It was the last thing she needed, when she wanted to convince him that she could do normal.

He didn't answer, just searched her face with those beautiful dark-lashed ice blue eyes. So she steered him back to the reason he'd left earlier. "I wasn't expecting you at the ceremony. When did you get there?"

"When he put his mouth on you." His gaze didn't waver despite the obvious raw jealousy.

Even though it was a blokey Neanderthal reaction, it made her heart flutter. It was a reaction she'd never had before – from anyone. He waited, as if gauging her response. Then he took a step closer into her space, backing her up to the bed where she fell backwards. In the next moment he was on top of her, pinning her arms to either side of her ears. "Do you want him?"

Her breaths became very shallow and her vision tunneled completely. She tried to pull half-heartedly free of his grip but he held her fast.

"Answer me!" He lunged and bit down her neck and rotated his hips.

"No!"

"No, what?" But he was loosening his grip on her hands as he moved down her body, which responded as if he'd turned on a switch.

"I don't want him," came out as a rasp as her canine teeth punched out through her gums.

With her vision now slithers of light, he hovered over her taking it all in. For an agonizing moment she was fully exposed. Then he plunged and kissed her ferociously, the two of them acting like a pair of foxes rolling over and over, almost falling off the bed. As soon as they'd pulled off each other's clothes she sunk her teeth into the soft part of his shoulder. Just that feeling alone sent her into the stratosphere.

Drew slowed down and she released her hold. Licking her lips, she watched as he hovered over her again. Blood spatters now covered his face. It must have transferred to him from her mouth or she'd nicked him as they kissed. "What did you give him?" His eyes remained fixed on her lips.

"My breath," she answered, simply – not sure he'd understand. *God,* she barely understood it herself.

"And that's the bond?" With that, his hips began moving again. "Give it to me, then," he said, coaxing her, pushing against her slowly and really beginning to move. For a moment, Phoebe's eyes fluttered closed, and she gave herself over to feeling every micro-movement. Until the strength in his kiss brought her conscious thought back to him.

It was understandable. If she could give herself to a complete stranger in that way, then surely she could do it with Drew – a man she'd known only a short time, but was becoming embedded deeply in more ways than one. She sighed as he penetrated her to prove a point.

"Please," he reminded her breathily from next to her cheek.

His anger had turned to vulnerability and was impossible to resist. He was utterly beautiful. She nipped at his cheek till her mouth found his. Her now fully distended fangs made closing it impossible.

Drew seemed oblivious to them and kissed her deeply, open-mouthed. It was not a pretty movie-like kiss; it was a devouring hunger that consumed them both. The one thing that grounded her was the painful weight building in her chest. She needed to do this – they both needed it. They were moving together, building themselves. Her mouth filled with blood. She wasn't sure whose and then she knew what she had to do.

The familiar steam rose from her chest, just as it had done with Dante. Except this time, instead of breathing, when her mouth was full she pulled back and sunk her teeth deeply into Drew's neck.

Now there was absolutely no going back. The chest pain only built again. With every pull of his blood, she left something of herself behind. It felt the right thing to do – like a payment. Blood for breath. Soul for soul. They couldn't get any deeper, or closer connection.

Blood was everywhere. They were covered in it as they rolled over and took the sheets with them. They wrapped their glowing bodies in red, like a single cocoon, well timed, as the door burst open.

. . .

THE GUARDS STEPPED BACK and Dante stood on the threshold. Getting involved between couples wasn't his style at all, but the noise coming from this room couldn't be ignored – especially as it was cut from solid rock.

Connor had alerted him as he believed Drew was angry, which wasn't unusual in partners after a bonding ceremony. As they'd neared the room, it sounded more like they were killing each other.

One of his Santalini guards kicked open the door after finding it locked. And this was the sight that greeted him. In all his life, (and he'd seen some shit), he'd never seen anything like this. The two lovers turned to him in surprise, still intertwined, in the midst of a scene like an ER after a car crash.

Their wild eyes stunned him into inactivity. He was utterly shocked. Of course he knew blood-drinking went on – particularly in the Santalini family, who formed part of his guard – it was necessary for them and only allowed at certain times. For the most part, it was outlawed within his race but it still went on. His own best friend had developed a habit. Never in his born days had he imagined anything as feral as what was right in front of him. "Get dressed. NOW!"

Then he turned to his guard, Reeve, next to him. "Get them apart before she drains him." The last thing he needed was an international incident where a royal Siren killed a human like this. His enemies would have a field day.

Reeve hesitated, as shocked as he was. "Then what should I do with them?"

Dante turned and went to walk from the room. "Have a doctor sent here for him and a maid come and clear up. And she ..." Dante looked into those terrifying, almost reptilian eyes, "She can go to the basement."

With that, he left, sick to his stomach. If by some stroke of luck Drew was still alive by morning, he'd want some answers.

Just when he thought things were going his way, and his kingdom secure, something like this blindsided him. To cap it all, after months apart, Tia had sent word she was coming home and he'd have to break some news that would be devastating to her.

CHAPTER 15

The Duke Ormond Delissi was a high-ranking prince of the Dubonnetti house and no stranger to the White House. He was also a well-respected ambassador for the Atlantean nation and a permanent fixture in D.C. However, even though he'd been building a close working relationship with the president of the United States, a summons to speak with him informally was still very rare.

He was a little nervous as it meant something. They'd met a few times privately where the president had questioned him about Atlantean history and ancestry to get a better understanding of his people. He seemed genuinely fascinated. Not surprising, he guessed. Few got the opportunity to question aliens directly about their home planet – even presidents.

Delissi liked and respected the man who'd come up through the ranks of politics through cleverness and hard work. Much like him. He seemed to help where he could, even though his hands were often tied with bureaucracy and he walked a tight line.

That had been the case when the Siren, Tia Storm, had been captured by the authorities. It had been the president himself who'd made sure she could be rescued. He had also signed the mandate for the Siren, Isla Snow, to be released to the Florianna family after spending eight long years kept in an American facility working for them.

The doors were closed quietly behind him by a secret serviceman and he approached the president still working behind his desk in the small study. He still had no idea why he'd been called.

The president stood up and smiled as soon as he noticed him. He reached out and shook his hand firmly, his smile was genuine and his aura friendly. There appeared to be no nerves about the man. A good sign.

"Sit, my friend," the president said, indicating a comfy high-backed chair just away from the desk to his right. Delissi mentally noted that it was a strategy to make him feel at ease and not a subordinate in an interview situation.

"Thank you, Mr President," Delissi said, taking the chair offered.

"Can I get you anything? My wife made lemonade today with the children. Or something stronger, maybe?" he said with an eyebrow up.

Delissi smiled. "Lemonade would be wonderful."

The president poured some of the cloudy liquid from a glass jug and pushed it towards him. "I expect you're wondering why I brought you here at such a late hour?"

Delissi took a sip of the drink and bobbed his head. "A little," he admitted. "Although it was a pleasant surprise. It has been a while."

The president smiled warmly. "It has ..." He frowned and paused briefly. "The young ladies... They arrived safely home?"

Delissi inclined his head at the reference to the Sirens' release, knowing full well that the president would have this information already. "They are safely with their husbands and doing well. Both have children now." Delissi never lost an opportunity to portray the royal family as humanlike and as personal as possible. He wanted them considered as real people to those at Washington who very often made decisions based on prejudice and fear.

The president smiled and understood perfectly. "That's just wonderful. Which brings me nicely to the reason why I brought you here."

Delissi's heart rate rose slightly in anticipation.

"You know that I value your opinion and your mediation between our two peoples. What you have taught me has been invaluable to my understanding. It has always been my aim to ensure that we can inhabit this planet side by side peacefully."

His heart rate rose higher still. He had no idea where he was going with this. "What is it, Mr President? Whatever is in my power I will do."

The president nodded. "I know." He took a deep breath and then looked around the room as if he was searching for the right way to phrase something. Then he let out a deep sigh. "The head of the agency met with me earlier today. He said two of his agents had been approached by some guy who clearly knew exactly who they were and said he was a representative from some old holy order." He looked down at something scribbled on a piece of paper. "I can't give you this name right now." Then he folded it up and put it in his pocket.

Delissi let out a small snort of derision.

The president mirrored the reaction. "Yeah, that's what I first thought."

Neither men were particularly religious or had any time for fanaticism of any kind.

"But what he said was disturbing and very definitely of interest to you. I'm afraid I can't ignore it or keep it to myself in the interest of national security."

Delissi put down his glass and straightened in his chair. "What is it?"

"He said he could give the government the exact coordinates of Murrtaine. He also said he had access to more than one Siren."

Delissi's heart stalled. Normally a straight-talking man given to very little emotion, he couldn't hide his astonishment. It was the last thing he was expecting. His feelers were everywhere. It was untenable that something like this had gone under his radar.

"The reason I brought you here is, if what the guy says is correct, I won't be able to stop them going in."

Delissi let out a ragged breath and pushed his fingers through his hair. He understood perfectly. Atlanteans were the richest and most powerful on earth and Murrtaine was its source of power. They'd denied its existence, but humans in the know had searched for it for millennia. The balance of power was always tipped in their favor and the humans hated and distrusted that. If there were a chance to get at their rumored power source, then they would take it. Then no one, not even the president, could stop that.

"What does this madman want?" Men seldom give information for nothing.

The president shrugged. "That's just it. He said nothing. He says he is a patriot and a man of god. All he wanted was the destruction of the alien city for the good of mankind... what I was most curious about was how he knew anything about it at all."

Delissi was shaken. The president was right. Most men on the street knew nothing of the Atlanteans at all, let alone their below sea-level city that, up until recently, had no interaction with the outside world for centuries.

"There is a chance he is some kind of mad-man, but if he can come up with these coordinates the navy will go in and the rest of the world will never know it existed. It will be explained as something as simple as nuclear testing."

"And the murder of thousands of males, females and children living peacefully undetected for millennia will be completely unknown and unpunished." Delissi clenched his fists. The injustice of it was unbearable. "What do you suggest we do?"

"Nothing yet. It could still be some kind of hoax. I'll let you know as soon as he contacts us again."

Delissi's head was reeling. He swallowed hard and nodded. "Thank you, Mr President."

"It might be as well to start some contingency plans."

The president started to close his files, so Delissi took his cue and went to stand. "There's just one more thing."

He relaxed back into his chair. Information such as this rarely came without a price. Now he would hear it. "Time to stab our swords in the sand," he said sardonically. The president was well aware the Atlanteans needed friends at this time. "Ask your question, Mr President, and I will answer it as honestly as I can."

The president tipped his head in thanks. "Your king prospers?'

"He does."

"He has his council now. Is it full?"

The question had finally come and it was the right one, because even if the president knew of the fifth Siren, a full council meant she had been accounted for, prophecy fulfilled and their ancestors from their home planet would return. He knew his stuff.

Delissi deliberated a few moments. All Sirens were now accounted for but the last one was believed unbound and unmarried.

However, the glint in the president's eye said he knew more. Delissi knew he'd done him a huge service in sharing what he knew. Today was a test of sorts; a test of their trust and friendship. He had to think quickly and carefully. How he answered now affected everything. In a snap decision he opted for honesty. He hadn't got where he was today from being a poor judge of character. "Mr President, the council has not yet been filled."

The president's face didn't falter. "You are still searching for the last one?"

After the briefest pause, Delissi finally said, "We located the last one in the last few days. She was recently tested."

For a moment the president looked relieved. Then he nodded as if he was pleased, which was a little curious given what he'd just told him and what it meant. "In Seattle," the president said as a statement not a question.

The president already knew.

It hit him then how much the president had held back.

"We located her and lost her again a few weeks back. She simply upped and disappeared." The president smiled. "But you have her now," he finished with a smile.

Delissi nodded, now wary where he was going with this.

"I think I may be able to help you with that too. We found where she was. We were about to go in and they simply put her back. It was baffling."

Delissi regarded the president for a long moment. They had both showed great courage and put enormous trust in each other. If either's people were to come out of this unscathed, they needed to work together. The president stood, took his hand out of his pocket and held it out to him. When Atlas returned both peoples were in danger. This was way beyond silly power games, this was survival and the president understood.

Delissi stood and reached out and took the hand. After a warm handshake he was left with a folded piece of paper.

CHAPTER 16

*D*ante sat in his study with all his advisors into the small hours of the night. "I've never seen anything like it. Is it like that for you?" he said, directly to Keenan. He was married to Phoebe's sister and a prince of the Santalini family.

"Noooo," Keenan said on an exhale, shaking his head. "Nothing like that."

Dante wasn't sure why but he found that comforting.

"Where is she now?" Sebastian, Phoebe's father, asked.

"I've put her in the small holding tank in the basement. In all honesty, I didn't know what else to do with her."

Most of them understood and nodded.

"All divining rings change in her presence, I guessed it wouldn't hurt to see how she holds up to a night under water."

They'd talked and talked; no one seemed to have an answer to why she physically changed like she did.

All the Sirens had human worldly names as well as Atlantean ones that held meaning, both connected to the weather and, to an extent, their characters. Tia Storm, Lacy

Rain, Isla Snow. Lilian Gale and then there was Phoebe Ray. It was baffling. Everything pointed towards sunshine and light, which made sense when she completed everything for the kingdom. Instead he was met by the bride of Dracula with eyes that looked like she'd been dragged from the pits of hell. Nothing could be more dark or opposite to the name, Ray. She was the last of the five Sirens and everything pivoted on her, yet nothing fit. Nothing at all.

Dante looked around at his men, sitting in the armchairs and sofa of the small study. The mood was somber. Debate continued in hushed tones with the gravity of the situation etched on their faces. The initial euphoria of locating the last Siren had disappeared to be replaced by uncertainty. None of them saw this coming. The walls were lined with thousands of priceless books crammed with knowledge, compounding his conviction that the answer must be somewhere. Nothing in their world happened by accident. Everything appeared engineered for an outcome – even if it wasn't apparent what it was at first. Somewhere it would have been foretold. Someone somewhere must know.

Wearily, Dante turned to Max, his trusted human expert in Atlantean antiquities. He'd seen his worth and headhunted him from the British government at the very beginning of his reign. "I want you to get onto this, Max. Scour everything you can find on the last generation and the end of days' prophecy." He'd come through for him on a number of occasions; he hoped to God he would this time. Nothing in the whole of Earth's history had been more important.

LIGHT PENETRATED Drew's eyes like an icepick, making him blink and look away.

He's waking up, a female voice said.

Suddenly remembering where he was, Drew went to sit up.

Hands gently pushed him back down. The pain hammering around his skull made him submit. He was as weak as tissue paper.

A nurse pushed a small beaker and a glass of water into his eye line. "Here, take these …they're for your head."

Drew looked up at the kindly female face he guessed was a nurse and took them from her. Anything to get rid of the headache from hell. He knocked both tablets back with a large glug of water. Then a tidal wave of nausea washed over him, making him lie flat again.

Lance took a step closer.

"What time is it? Where is she?" Drew said, not giving Lance chance to speak.

Lance looked a little uncomfortable at the girl, Lily, standing a little way off.

"Tell me!"

"It's morning and she's fine," Lance said, holding his hands up to reassure him. "They just took her to the basement … I think to double-check on some things. She almost killed you."

Drew ignored the last remark. It was a risk they all took being with a Siren. "What things, Lance? You're making me nervous." He leaned up on his elbows to get up, but had to wait for his head to catch up with the rest of him.

"Stuff … ya know. She's not like the others."

"What stuff. What's in the basement?"

Lance looked to Lily again, in some kind of silent conversation. "Cells…and a holding tank."

Drew stared at him, taking a long moment to fall in with what he meant. Then, ignoring the pain and an overwhelming urge to throw up, he swung his legs over the bed in an attempt to get up. Lance immediately came to help. "You're too weak."

Drew glared at him as he struggled to stand up.

His vision went to zilch and then orange blobs floated all over the place so he thought he was going to pass out. In the end all he could do was squint at Lance with a small slither of light, his head hurt so badly. "Take me to her." His voice sounded deep and weird in his anger.

Lance's eyes widened in surprise, but he guessed he'd made his point when he started handing him his clothes.

Drew's hand instinctively went to the large square of dressing at his neck. It felt tight and itchy. He looked cautiously at Lance and Lily, but they appeared not to have noticed and busied themselves with helping him dress. Then he stumbled out of the room to find Phoebe.

It was dark and smelled damp when they stepped out of the service lift that went down to the catacombs that formed the basement. They followed a row of doors Drew guessed were cells, until they came out into a wider room containing a large tank of water. It reminded him of a magician's prop for an escape routine or something. There were several men there he vaguely recognized from before, all staring at the contents of the tank.

"You're alive," Dante said, half jokingly, although his expression changed from mild surprise to curiosity.

Drew's head pain had subsided but was replaced by a weird tingling sensation. He stumbled a step. Lance grabbed his arm to steady him but he glared back at the king. Somehow he knew it was Dante doing something.

Dante smiled, proving he was right.

Drew glared at him. He didn't give a shit about him being king. He wasn't *his* king. The guy was meddling with his personal life; coming between him and Phoebe and causing trouble. He had no right to confine him, or Phoebe for that matter.

Something moved in the murky waters of the tank. *Phoebe?* He hadn't noticed at first as she was huddled in the corner. As he stepped closer she moved towards the glass and he saw the chains. "What the fuck!" he spat at Dante. Then he vaulted up the small iron steps to the side.

Two guards stepped forward but Dante signaled for them to leave him. "You'll need the key!"

Drew paused and turned at the top. The guard threw him a bunch. He caught them and jumped down into the tank with a sharp intake of breath. Water definitely wasn't his thing. *He came from Seattle.* But he managed to dive long enough to undo the manacle attached to her wrist and ankle. Then he pushed her up to the surface where the two guards helped him hoist her out of the tank.

When he jumped down next to her she was bent over at the waist spewing the water from her lungs. All he could do was hold back her sopping hair, rub her back and scowl at Dante. "What's wrong with you people. Have you lost your mind?"

Dante laughed sardonically. "And nothing else strikes you as a little strange about the last twenty-four hours?"

Drew continued to scowl. He didn't want to get into what he considered private. "You could have fucking killed her."

"Believe me, she wouldn't be here if I thought there was any real risk."

Phoebe straightened up and Drew could not ignore what he saw. Her skin was very grey making her orange narrowed eyes stand out even more, but the thing that amazed him most of all was that every inch of her was covered in black zebra-like stripes – even her face. *Drew,* she said directly to him, like a plea. All he could do was stand there and gawk at her. Even when he'd seen her in the sea she hadn't appeared as striking as this. He simply couldn't drag his eyes away.

"It's really nothing to be afraid of, Drew," Dante was saying, but his eyes were riveted on hers. The whole thing with her had been wildly exciting and definitely off the chart sexy, but it wasn't really until this point that it hit him that she really was not human. And she knew it. Despite every-thing, this was the first time she was utterly exposed to him and he'd given it his full attention. Here was the truth standing right in front of him, impossible to ignore or put to the back of his mind.

Still distracted he looked back at Dante who was taking a small dark blue velvet pouch from his pocket. "What's that?" he asked.

"It's just a test," Dante said, removing his large turquoise ring and passing it to one of his guards to hold for him. "For me." Then he took from the pouch what looked like an iden-tical ring except it was white. He turned it in his fingers until he found what he was looking for and pressed it. A long, sharp pin shot out from the side.

"What are you gonna do with that?" he said, a little uneasily.

"Watch." Then Dante put it on the same finger the other had come from and pushed it on hard. "These rings are forged from the power source that came with us from Atlas. All princes have one. A virgin ring is always white, as it is for the wearer most days," he said with a small bob of his head. "But it needs royal blood to work."

Drew couldn't believe what he was seeing. Dante had stabbed himself in the most painful soft part between the knuckles with the ring. However, before he could say a word something started happening around the stone.

Blood dripped onto the floor and smoke started to

surround it a little like dry ice. The ring seemed to take on the color of the blood.

Drew glanced around him at the men gathered there. Sebastian and Alfonzo were watching closely, in fact despite a few murmurs, everyone was.

"Watch!" Dante said again, holding out his hand and smiling as if it was a wondrous thing. "It becomes part of the wearer."

The ring was changing again, settling on exactly the same color as the one before – turquoise. He frowned. "What does that mean?" It made no sense to go through that to end up where you started.

Good question. A ring will always turn this color in the presence of a Siren – except in certain circumstances. Then he narrowed his eyes on him. *One of which is in the presence of a Siren's most compatible mate. On that rare occasion it will turn deepest purple.*

Drew's eyes widened. *Did he say that in his head?*

Dante smiled. *Welcome to the bond.*

Drew was stunned for a moment while his meaning sunk in. He'd witnessed what Phoebe had done to Dante in the sea and what they did last night had been nothing like that.

"I don't mean to freak you out, Drew, I'll switch to speech. This is the reality of life with a Siren, and why I have to be so cautious." Then he shook out the last of the contents of the velvet pouch into the palm of his hand. It was another ring. "I was going to come and find you later anyway. As you're here … This test is for you."

Drew took it from him, warily, and scratched his head. His eyes tracked to Phoebe's, which had returned to normal now; a beautiful shade of light hazel. But they were sad – no, more than that, they were resigned. She hadn't attempted a single word because she had no explanation, or excuses. His heart broke when he understood. The feelings from her were washing over him and he felt them all. She expected him to leave and abandon her to all this.

"It's the bond," Dante said quietly again.

Drew was forced to look back at him in annoyance. "Are you listening in my fucking head?"

"It's hard to understand, I know. Being with a Siren will give you the wildest pleasure, but also comes at a price. The first you already know: you'll be hunted and your life will be at risk and never your own, but the hardest thing is the bond." Dante narrowed his eyes as if there was something else – something he couldn't quite get a handle on. "I'm not sure where the blood thing fits into all this yet, but you would have been aware when she breathed for you."

The pause was left for him to answer. He guessed what he meant. Something had definitely passed between them last night. The kissing, her searing bite, but no breathing, he would have known it for sure. Although, at the time, there had been no time to analyze it. The sex had been mind-blowing and he'd become carried away.

If he were really honest, he'd begun to feel different ever since that first night at the party. He was changing and he knew it, but it wasn't just physical, he was sensing things too. Like just then; he knew exactly what she was feeling and he didn't know how that was possible. All he could do was nod in answer to Dante's question. It all seemed too private, too personal to say out loud.

"You're right, it is," Dante said, airing his thoughts yet again. Except now he was frowning. If he were sifting through his thoughts then he would know all of them, and yet he continued to say, "The breath makes you feel all those things. It's her life force. For an Atlantean it is the greatest gift. The gift of self. You will never feel closer to a living person after that. Of course, we can return it and humans can not."

Drew couldn't understand why he continued to harp on the breath which he was sure never passed between them and ignore the blood, which very definitely did. He glanced at Phoebe and she was watching him closely, still waiting for him to bolt. Instead he picked up her hand and a wave of her relief flooded over him.

It floored him and he looked back at Dante, amazed. He might be wrong about how he got there, but he was right about how he felt. Then he got what Dante was driving at. "And you feel it too?"

Dante inclined his head. "I have a two-way bond because of the ceremony you witnessed yesterday."

Anger rose up at the reminder, but Dante put up his hand. *For fuck's sake,* he even felt that.

"Hold yer horses. You feel what she feels. Think about it. Accept it down into you as it was meant to be taken. Think! You know she doesn't feel for me like that."

Drew frowned. His hand went to the center of his chest while he worked through what he meant. She was there. He could feel her. His eyes shot back to Dante's when he understood.

Dante was nodding. "It's for the state, man. That's all it is. I have a connection with all except Lily. That means I can keep them safe."

Drew stared at him trying to take it all in.

"The privacy thing is annoying, I know, but it's a small price to pay for their safety."

It was kind of making sense. *As long as he keeps his distance.* "So that's it. That's all I have to worry about?"

Dante frowned but seemed slightly amused, then let out a blast of laughter as if he couldn't believe his ears. "It's enough for now, I guess."

"And this?" Drew said, holding up the ring as a reminder.

"That's your test."

"What does it test?"

"Well, for starters, it hasn't burnt you. The metal comes from our home planet and normally burns the skin of humans. Are you human, Drew?"

The question sounded so ridiculous he almost laughed. He was completely taken aback by it. "Yeah, I guess."

"You don't know?"

Drew laughed on a breath of disbelief. "It's something I've never had to consider before."

"You know your roots?" Then Dante looked at Lance, who'd hung back a bit with Lily watching the whole thing. "Some of us have been surprised by what we've found."

Lance shifted a little uncomfortably.

It was definitely a question for Lance later. "I know my roots," was all he replied in the end. Dante knew enough already with what was going on in his head. There was no way he was going to spill his guts up about what happened to him as a child.

Dante studied him for a long moment, as if deciding whether to push it. Then he motioned him on with his hand. "Go on then. Your turn."

Drew looked down at the ring he'd forgotten all about. He examined it, found the small button and pushed it releasing the pin. It looked nasty, but he guessed this was some test of manhood too. He couldn't wimp out because of a bit of pain. He held it at the tip of the middle finger of his right hand

You don't have to, Phoebe said in his head and laying her hand gently over his.

It made him pause and search her face. He shouldn't be surprised. Of course she could do it too.

He wasn't sure if she could hear his thoughts, but he hoped she understood that he *did* have too. It wasn't just a macho thing. Even he understood that it was an unanswered question that needed answering.

"It has to be the left," Dante reminded him.

Phoebe pulled her hand away and he frowned and swapped hands. He wasn't sure what difference it could possibly make. Especially when Dante said; "It has to draw blood, is all. It's a kind of blood test."

Drew looked straight into Phoebe's eyes. The stripes on her face had subsided but it was filled with concern. She smiled but looked so sad. All he wanted to do was hold her. *Whatever happens, it's OK,* she said straight to his head.

"Aren't you at least curious, Phoebe? A purple ring could mean a partner hand picked by fate," Dante said with eyebrows raised.

Her eyes moved to Dante distracted only for a moment. Then she returned them to Drew. *Whatever happens,* she repeated.

Her unspoken words soothed him. *Guess there was a plus side to all this.* He quickly scanned the room at all the rapt faces, then he pushed it down onto his finger.

It was only when all eyes went to his hand and he felt it tingle that he looked at it himself. It was doing exactly as it had done before. First it went red, then it changed again.

He frowned at all the outraged, shocked faces not understanding at all. "What does it mean when it goes this color?"

He held up his hand so the blood rivulets ran down his arm, but every eye remained glued to the purple ring.

CHAPTER 17

$\mathcal{D}$ante dismissed everyone else to the comfort of their rooms but remained with Max, Sebastian, Alfonzo and Cesaré.

"How can it be?" Cesaré said, as soon as they were alone.

Dante was staring into the middle distance when he shook his head. "I have no idea." Then he turned his full attention to Max. "Check all the archives, Max. Leave no stone unturned on this. After the last time, we must know what we are dealing with."

"We already have one human prince," Cesaré reminded him. "The tomes say nothing about a second wild card."

"I don't believe that is what's going on here," Dante said, not wanting to go too far into his concerns just yet. He was as confounded as the rest of them.

"I will also speak with Darl in Murrtaine. They may be able to turn up something older than we have here." He couldn't shake the niggling feeling that this was more to do with Phoebe than Drew. "I want you to look for anything on the very last Siren. One like nothing ever seen before. A dark Siren."

Dante remembered and touched Sebastian on the shoulder. All this must be hard on him. After all, this was his daughter being taken into question, but if anyone could turn up something it was Darl, Lord Advocate of the underwater City of Murrtaine.

He eyed them all shrewdly. "I want you all on this. Stick to the facts: We have a Siren …"

"Are you positive?" Cesaré cut in.

It was a reasonable question from him. Not so long ago, he had been shamed and humiliated when his own cousin, Malleven Mancini, had cheated him out of his place as head of the Florianna family by tampering with his divining ring.

Dante gave his shoulder a squeeze. "There is no doubt of that here, Cesaré. But I get where you're coming from, and we must not forget that she has a month of unaccounted for time."

Cesaré's face went to thunder. "You think he's got to this one too?"

Dante shook his head wearily. "It's always a possibility. The fact is, we can't know at this stage. What we do know is that physically she appears to change more than the others, and it doesn't seem to be water dependent."

"And she is vampiric," Alfonzo added. "That is a complication that shouldn't be taken lightly."

Dante understood perfectly. Drinking blood by anyone other than the Santalini was punishable by death. He'd narrowly avoided that shit storm already with his best friend Jay. However, if it was a Siren that the kingdom sorely needed? He nodded wearily in understanding.

Alfonzo observed him knowingly. "For the moment, let us concentrate on what we can find out. I'll send a nurse to take a blood sample from Drew."

Dante let out a long sigh. It was a good place to start.

· · ·

DREW TOOK Phoebe's hand and returned to their room. They wordlessly each took a shower and got back into the changed, newly made bed. The lamp was on low to give them just enough light to see facing each other.

Everything about her looked totally normal now. A pink blush on her cheeks instead of grey stripes, warm autumn eyes instead of slashed orange and beautiful, even teeth just visible between her parted lips.

The weird thing was, he was starting to love her both ways. Her deep red hair, freckles and perfect bone structure gave her a rare purity he'd never seen before. Then when she changed – possibly with extreme emotion – she was dark, wild and dangerous. That he found madly addictive. When he really analyzed it, he couldn't understand what she saw in someone as mundane as him – a poor northwest musician, from poor beginnings and going nowhere fast.

Why didn't you go when you could? she said, straight to his mind.

It still amazed him that she could do that. He cupped the side of her face in his hand. "I was thinking the same thing. Can't you feel it?" Everything she felt was now so embedded in his heart.

Phoebe shook her head and a tear escaped her eye.

Drew snatched her to him and hugged her while the sobs vibrated into his shoulder. "Don't cry. It's probably because I'm human." He put her away from him so he could look into her face.

She tried a smile. "I'm a freak, Drew." Her face went to crumple again. "Even in this world, I'm a freak."

He shook her gently. "Stop, no. Please don't cry, Phoebes. I'm here, okay? I'm not going anywhere." His heart broke for her and he recognized the time had finally come to face up. If they had any kind of future he needed to open up and lay himself bare to prove he was invested in her. "I'm a freak too…I am. I hide it but really I'm a fraud."

Phoebe wasn't listening and went to put her head down and under the covers but he pushed her chin up with his hand. "Look at me. Didn't you hear what I said?"

She reluctantly opened her eyes and he wiped her tears on the pad of his thumb. "Listen to me, okay. You think I'm this popular rock musician dude, but I came from a group home."

She looked at him bewildered.

"It's somewhere they stick orphans or unwanted kids." Now he'd got her attention he relaxed and revisited those awful times he usually tried not to think about. It seemed so long ago.

He ran his finger along her cheekbone. "I got sick – real sick. But I got adopted into a cool family," he added more cheerfully. This was about gaining trust not pity. He didn't tell her about the bad dreams of deprivation and endless training and drills. Everything had gotten so hazy he wasn't sure what was real any more. "They had money and got me the best care. It meant several operations, bone marrow transplants, shit like that."

She was searching his face, doing the math, as if she was seeing him for the first time. He hadn't really gone into specifics but it was a big deal for him to tell anyone and he knew she got that. "Music was the one thing I had that got me through, you know? When I was sick I could write and when I was well I could play. Then, as I grew up, it was kinda my golden ticket straight to the cool crowd. The rest you know."

She smiled a little at that.

"What I'm saying, in a way, is that I am feeling you."

Phoebe swallowed hard and frowned. "What, you understand what I feel?"

Drew shook his head. "No, yes, no. What I mean is, I feel the same about you."

She looked amazed, as if she hadn't expected it in a million years. That just made her all the more adorable to him. There was a long moment while they just stared at each other and processed what it meant. Drew was in no doubt when he closed the gap to kiss her. For the first time in his life he had something real that he couldn't run away from. At that moment he was sure he'd never want to.

If Drew was attractive to Phoebe before then he'd just gone up to a whole other level. It wasn't exactly what he said but what it meant. He trusted her enough to tell her something that made him feel vulnerable.

It did make a whole lot of sense. The limp blamed on an old injury, trips to his doctor – all hidden to keep up his carefree musician façade. Except it wasn't a façade. There was no way he was a fraud even if that was what he thought he was. Her heart swelled with pride for him. He'd managed to claw his way out of the most horrendous circumstances at such a young age and turned it into something not only positive, but the envy of all his peers. Not to mention all the hundreds of broken hearts she was sure he'd left in his wake.

When she felt herself dissolve into the sweetest kiss of her life, she knew she was in love. There were no secrets, nothing to hide. She'd never felt closer to a living soul.

They lay in bed dozing for most of the day until a knocking at the door made them blink awake and check the time. 5pm.

Neither of them could be bothered to get up and answer it. They were both drained. Now they were speaking openly about stuff, they decided that their lethargy was to do with the giving and taking of blood. And, the night before, they'd done a shit load. They were both kind of in the dark here.

"Come on, guys!" Lance's voice came from the other side of the door. "It's me and Lily."

Drew hauled himself out of bed, threw the latch on the patched-up door and let them in. Lance hugged him briefly and put a hand up to Phoebe, propped up in the bed. "Sorry, we didn't realize …" Then he paused while Drew eased back under the sheets next to Phoebe, making no apology. "We're wasted."

Lance and Lily had one of those internal conversations which he ended with, "They probably know."

"Know what?" both he and Phoebe said together.

Lance pointed to the large dressing on Drew's neck. "A large part of why they are watching you so closely is that."

Drew couldn't help putting his hand to his neck. It was still itchy and sore. "This?"

Lance pulled Lily up against him as if for comfort. "It's illegal … serious shit."

Drew swapped a look with Phoebe, who snuggled into his chest. It seemed ridiculous to expect them to stop just like that. They weren't hurting anyone and it had become such a fundamental part of their lovemaking.

Lance nodded to Lily again, then said; "You have the Sirens bond now. You can't get closer than that."

Drew's brain was fried, not sure how much more weird he could take in one day. Everyone was talking about the bond, but for him and Phoebe, blood *was* the bond. He was beginning to lose patience. "What brings you here, Lance?" he said, in an attempt to steer the conversation away from it.

"The king knows we're friends from before – he was asking me a whole bunch of questions. Thought you should know."

It wasn't surprising. He'd felt under scrutiny since he got there.

"So he sent me to tell you that there will be a celebration tomorrow. The whole Atlantean world will be there – those who matter, anyway. It's to witness that Phoebe's here and all five are accounted for and pledged to him. It's a big deal for him as king."

Drew sunk down into the bed, not able to think about it now. His brain was so sluggish it didn't want to work.

"It's huge, Drew." Then his eyes rested on his hand that was above the sheets and he pointed. "So's that." And he held up his left hand with an identical purple ring on it.

It didn't seem that big a deal. So they'd pulled the same shit on Lance.

"I'm the wild card prophecy and there's only one. There can't be two most compatible humans. What they're trying to find out is what that makes you."

Drew looked into Phoebe's eyes, staring at him to gauge his reaction to all this. He smiled when she shrugged. They were good and tight. That was all that mattered. "Thanks for the heads up, man," he said, smiling at Lance and wanting to be alone again fast. "Just let us know what we gotta do for tomorrow. Right now we gotta sleep."

As they walked towards the door, Lily spoke telepathically for the first time so they could both hear. *They reckon our sister, the queen, comes back at some point tomorrow. Then the shit'll hit the fan.*

Phoebe snuggled into him further, making no comment and Drew was glad. He wasn't allowing anymore stuff to get in their heads right now. He simply put a hand up in thanks and Lily and Lance left them alone.

.   .   .

THE NEXT MORNING Phoebe reluctantly got out of bed when breakfast was delivered. However something had shifted between them. They were closer somehow. Everything felt easier, as if a new understanding had been reached. No deep conversation was needed. They just ate and savored the glorious, close companionship.

Soon after that, dressers and tailors came, forcing Drew out of bed too. They were pricked, pulled, pushed and measured, until they left in a whirlwind and returned a few hours later with a gown of deepest green velvet and a navy blue formal suit and tie for Drew.

The dress went perfectly with her red hair and pale freckled skin. The effect was dramatic and she found it highly amusing at how aptly vampish it made her feel.

When Drew returned from the bathroom after fixing his tie, Phoebe giggled, not able to imagine her rock star in something like that. Drew picked her up and threw her on the bed, tickling her until he flopped on top of her breathless. She gazed up at his handsome face while he brushed the tendrils of hair from hers.

"Lance is right about one thing, Phoebes. They don't trust us together." Her heart rate spiked as his eyes immediately dropped to her mouth, which responded with a tingling in her canines. "I got that impression too."

Drew closed the distance between their mouths and kissed her slowly. It would have been easy to get lost in his kiss and give way to the all-consuming urge to make love all day. "We'd better get ready," she managed eventually. "But I think, after today, we should slip away. We don't belong here." The day had shown her clearly that they didn't need anyone else.

· · ·

DREW NODDED SOLEMNLY. Her viewing the two of them as a team against the rest of the world was the biggest gift she could have ever given him. Any kind of deep connection with anyone had been hard up until then. It moved him so deeply emotion rode him hard.

If she saw, she hid it well. In the next moment, she wriggled out from under him, scrambled off the bed and held out her hand. He smiled wickedly. Using it to hoist himself up, he allowed her to lead him to the bathroom.

Inside, Phoebe took him to the basin where a large mirror hung from waist to ceiling. Then she arranged him behind her so he could look over her head. It felt good being head and shoulders taller than her. It brought out the protective side of him.

"You see?"

Drew was already distracted pulling the soft curls of her hair back with his finger so he could kiss down her neck. It felt so powerful feeling her pleasure as well as his own. Tingling waves of desire went outward from the touch of his mouth right down to her core. He felt like a master magician, but she would not be sidetracked. "No look, Drew," she said, shuffling to get his attention back on the mirror.

With low eyes he straightened, did what she wanted and looked in the mirror.

It was so clear to see. They were perfect for each other. His dark curly hair that went way past his shoulders was so similar to hers in red. His larger, taller body perfectly shadowed her smaller one. Similar high cheekbones accentuating perfectly shaped eyes of autumn mirroring a winter sky.

He got it. She wanted him to see how alike they really were, whatever his origins, and he loved her all the more for it. His arms snaked around her waist and he pulled her tighter into him. She remained rigid, as if there was something more.

Drew gave in and relaxed back to stand up straight. His eyes grazed over the two of them again. Despite the wishful thinking he was under no illusion. He rested his hands on her shoulders. "I am human, Phoebes. I know what I am. I had so many tests as a kid."

As the words slipped out, it still amazed him how at ease the two of them had become. It still felt an odd thing to say and he blasted red. She didn't seem to pick up on it. Instead, she turned in his arms and pulled him down into a kiss. Her eyes zeroed down to orange slits. That was all it took and he was all over her. His hand went between her legs and she groaned into his fingers. Smoothly slipping beneath the layers of clothing they found soft hot skin. Not able to wait any longer, he flipped her around, anchored her hands to either side of the basin and fed himself into her slowly.

They both gasped.

This time, as he stroked in and out of her, he had a perfect view. It was like a scene from a gothic horror film. The dress made for a vampire tilted forward, allowing him a perfect view of the rounds of her breasts, and his long hair cascaded over her like some olden times prince in an oil painting. One hand held her hip and the other smoothed over her back and slid the zip down so the dress fell away.

Drew reached forward, turned on the cold tap to cup water in his hands and trickled it down the center of her back. Phoebe gasped and renewed her grip on the sink. It was like a miracle in front of his eyes. The stripes came to the surface everywhere the water touched. He repeated the process again and again, spreading the water all over her, whilst watching in the mirror. His thrusts became wilder, until he was driving into her like a machine. Her gasps became louder as if he were taking her breath. It was the ownership and mastery of a mesmerizing striped creature whose other worldly eyes drove him insane with a thirst for more of her.

When the thought arrived it came with about one second of guilt. Nothing would stop what he needed to do. He leaned forward, kissed over her writhing back and put his wrist under her so it brushed temptingly against her mouth. He didn't wait long. She struck hard and fast, the sensation so strong he was forced to remain still and grip her other shoulder with his free hand. "Phoebes," he gasped into her hair. From then he was lost.

His free hand travelled, caressing downward, kneading her breasts, until it nestled safely between her legs. She was so wet.

His now slick fingers circled the small nub. Responding and eager to have him there, she circled her hips into his hand.

It felt too soon when she released his wrist and he murmured his disappointment. It felt like they were both so close. Instead, she pushed up from the sink, grabbed a chunk of his hair, and pulled his mouth to hers over her shoulder.

It was then that the breath everyone seemed so mad about left her like a bolt of steam. There was no time to react, just to accept it. Every last bit.

A tidal wave, a sizzling white light, some kind of quake, went through him from the skin on his lips out to his limbs, fingers and toes, until it exploded in his chest.

He wasn't sure if he shouted or stopped breathing but he sagged and almost fell over in his ecstasy. He had no other conscious feeling other than the sensations that rode him in those few moments. Time literally stood still.

He felt soft arms snake around his backside to steady him and at that point it was game over. He rippled and pulsed inside her over and over. His knees buckled several times and he only realized their mouths were still joined when she pulled hers away from his. Then instinct took over and all he could do was grip the soft part of her shoulder with his teeth.

He was breathing noisily through them, against her skin, hissing in and out. His eyes were still tightly closed. It felt so satisfying to be sunk this deeply and so right to feel his teeth in her flesh at the same time. It felt so good. It was perfect.

Gradually their bodies stopped moving and her hands shifted from holding the back of his thighs to resting lightly on his arms gripped around her waist.

Drew finally started to blink and focus back on the room. He was still leaning heavily across her back. Her cheek was pressed hard against the porcelain of the sink. He wasn't sure how she'd held the two of them up.

"Drew…Drew," she whispered, like she'd been attempting to wake him for a while. "Release them slowly, don't tear."

His mind was so sluggish he didn't really follow what she'd said, but he released his mouth from her shoulder.

"Lick them closed."

He did as she asked, in a daze. Eventually he felt steady enough to gently lift her from the waist to stand up with him, and they returned to the position they started, facing the mirror.

He couldn't believe what was in front of him. It wasn't just the blood smeared over both of their faces.

"You see, you're just like me," she said in a husky whisper.

His eyes dropped to hers, orange and narrowed like a wild animal, teeth keeping her bloodied swollen lips apart. It was just for a moment, as he couldn't take his eyes away from his own face—a perfect copy of hers. Feral eyes, bloodied mouth dripping onto his chin and aching teeth that receded slowly back into his skull.

There was just one thought going around his head while he remained glued to his reflection. *She was catching.*

CHAPTER 18

*P*hoebe wasn't sure if it was the blood they'd both taken or just the madness of the last forty-eight hours, but the party that evening felt wild and moved through her consciousness like a dream.

Their pupils were now so dilated they had to wear sunglasses for fear someone would think they'd taken drugs or, worse still, guess correctly. However, it couldn't hide their flushed faces and slow responses; as if they'd drunk a couple of bottles of wine.

They stuck close to Lance and Lily, who remained cautious and watchful while they escorted them into the great hall. Somehow they'd managed to shower and salvage their beautiful evening clothes. They'd been discarded in a heap out of harm's way and meant they didn't look halfway decent.

All of them paused at the top of the marble staircase taking in the spectacle before them. Loud and exhilarating, it bombarded them, much the same as walking into the wildest Ibiza nightclub. The room that was once like a fairy grotto had been transformed into the most exotic, exclusive after party in the world.

Phoebe clung more tightly to Drew as they descended the steps and inched through the crowds of gorgeous-looking people. She had no idea where that amount of people had come from at such short notice--every size, shape and color, speaking all manner of different languages and every one of them beautiful. Dressed as if they were at the Oscars, Phoebe couldn't help feeling that it was all a little bit too perfect, and something was a bit weird about them all.

Drew turned and kissed her forehead, sensing her unease. "Come on, it's okay," he said, at her ear.

The small act of caring totally sent butterflies to her stomach and helped her relax. They were in this together. Nodding, she squeezed his hand and continued on through the crowds. Lance and Lily were now smiling and greeting strangers.

Phoebe kept telling herself that these weren't normal people and it still blew her mind. To think that they were all descendants from another planet and, though she didn't know a single one of them, they were all here to celebrate her arrival. Even in the thick of it there was no way to be unobtrusive. All eyes went to her and everyone clapped as they cut a pathway through the crowd.

Phoebe couldn't cling to Drew anymore tightly. He, on the other hand, was used to crowds and adulation. He just moved through as if it was nothing less than he deserved and she loved that about him.

Lance got them a drink from the large bar that seemed to have come alive to the left of the huge marble staircase.

"Hey, stranger," came from directly behind her.

She'd know the deep Irish accent anywhere. *Connor!* She spun and grabbed him around his neck.

"You okay? You're quite the A-lister tonight," he said,

pulling apart. After the briefest pause, he nodded at Drew, but was already looking at her puzzled. "What's with the sunglasses? Are you getting into your new celebrity character?" he said, finishing with a smile.

Phoebe grinned a little nervously and hoped he didn't notice the embarrassed blush entering her cheeks. "Something like that." It felt bad not to tell him the truth and confide in him, but he was still frosty towards Drew and her world had suddenly got very grown up. She didn't feel like she could tell him everything anymore. A wave of sadness washed over her and she kissed him on the cheek. She'd just outgrown him. He looked even more puzzled, but what was happening to her was huge and exciting and she was a big girl now. There was no way she would risk telling him and him getting all serious, doing the big brother act and spoiling it.

Lance saved them by giving them each a drink, shook Connor's hand and said, "We'd better mingle a bit." It felt disloyal when they moved off leaving Connor standing at the bar. She looked over her shoulder at him watching them until the crowd blocked him out.

The rest of the room passed in a blur of kisses, introductions and handshakes. Weirdly, there was no sign of Dante, but her father and uncle appeared and did all the necessary introductions until, eventually, they too got distracted and the four of them got left to it.

"Follow me," Lance said, tipping his head in the direction of the opposite end of the hall.

Phoebe longed to find a good spot to relax and escape all the inquisitive eyes but there was standing room only. Each of the delightful-looking alcoves, scattered with cushions, appeared to be full. Even Atlanteans appeared to have VIPs. Her dark glasses allowed her to stare at all the interesting people laughing, drinking and kissing in them. It reminded her of a film about the Romans she'd once seen.

Eventually, they reached the furthest corner. It wasn't far from a specifically erected stage for the band and had a great view of the sea window that stretched out from one side of the huge room to the other.

"Here!" Lance shouted. "I've reserved this one."

Phoebe squealed with delight. Drew must have felt it too because he squeezed her to him. The large, empty alcove had low, soothing lighting; just enough to see, but not enough to ruin the chilled ambience. Red and orange gauze curtains were draped from a single point from its ceiling like a tent and large, matching sumptuous cushions were scattered all around the floor. It was cordoned off just for them. It was an ingenious idea. They could remain at the party, but feel in their own little world.

A large guard pulled the dark red cord away from the wall and nodded once at Lance, then spoke into an ear-com like the secret service. They all silently followed Lance into the small space and immediately dissolved into the sea of cushions, rolling around and giggling like a bunch of kids. She wasn't sure what possessed them, just that it felt like they'd made a great escape.

Soon a waiter came, carrying a small table to nestle in the middle of the cushions, and a maid with a bucket of champagne and four glasses.

Lance shrugged when she and Drew looked at him, amazed at the full VIP treatment. Neither of them were used to any of it yet.

"With His Majesty's compliments," the waiter said, immediately solving the puzzle of who'd sent it.

Phoebe crawled into Drew's lap. "This is amazing," she shouted over the din. It was turning out to be the perfect evening. He agreed and kissed her.

Then he leaned closer to Lance. "Thanks, man. This is so cool."

"None of this is me, brah, its Dante. It's a who's who of the Atlantean world tonight, and they're all celebrating you, Phoebe," he said, smiling at her. "You're the star!"

She smiled back at him and decided he looked more like a surfer than a rock star. "Thanks for getting this little hideaway for us."

Lance laughed and hugged Lily tightly to him. "Don't mention it. Thought you could do with the privacy."

"You have no idea," Drew said, tipping down his glasses so that Lance could see his eyes that went from being dilated like saucers to the thin slits they'd discovered earlier.

Lance and Lily's eyes went wide; they frowned at each other and had to take a second look. "What's the matter with your eyes, Drew?"

Drew shrugged, put his glasses back in place and pulled Phoebe with him to lounge back into the cushions. "Pour the bubbles," he said absently, kissing her forehead and pointing at the champagne.

Lance was still looking at him, a little troubled, but he did as he asked. Phoebe watched his reaction closely. He seemed to let it go. Relieved, she relaxed when they followed and flopped back into the pillows and people-watched the maddest party of their lives.

As jugglers entered the room on stilts, Phoebe's heart hitched in her chest. This was actually her life. Everything had suddenly got so exciting.

THE BOTTLE WAS SOON drunk and another arrived. Gradually the drapes got pulled around until the party was merely silhouettes behind them.

Two shadows appeared. "Anyone home?" a strong American accent said.

"Hey!" Lance laughed and jumped to his feet, almost falling over all the arms and legs sprawled everywhere.

Phoebe and Drew immediately sat up while Lance pulled the two men inside.

Lance hugged them both. Phoebe glanced up at Drew, a little unsure. A smile crept across his face. "Remember this dude?" Lance said, pointing at Drew.

Recognition lit up the guys' faces and Drew was on his feet shaking their hands. He clearly knew both of them. Phoebe slowly followed, uncertain of the newcomers and a little unsteady on her feet. She blamed the cushions, although it was more likely to do with the champagne she'd been drinking.

"Phoebe, this is my brother, Nathan, and my good friend and drummer, River. Guys, this is Lily's sister."

Both their eyes went wide with interest and they both kissed her cheek. Any awkwardness went when they spotted Lily, who'd hung back a little. It seemed her default position.

The men were having none of it and picked her up into chest-crushing hugs and noisy kissing of her cheeks. Lily squirmed but allowed it with a huge smile until they plonked her down onto her feet.

Eventually they simmered down and all reclined in the cushions again. "What are you doing here, man?" Nathan said. "You are absolutely the last person I would have expected here."

Drew grinned. "Me too. The place is madness."

They all laughed. Phoebe was enjoying watching Drew interact with his friends. It was good to learn more about him. Apart from the little bit he'd recently told her, she knew absolutely nothing.

"We played together for a while in LA," River explained.

"Then he up and disappeared to play with some hot-shot Seattle band and we haven't seen him since."

Drew put a hand up. "Apologies, but you have to follow the muse, you know."

They all laughed again.

"Seriously, though. Are you Atlantean?"

"He's fairly tall," River said, nodding as if it was a possibility.

"No. Are you?" Drew said.

Phoebe looked at him, puzzled. He sounded almost curt, like it was a sore subject. Lance and Lily exchanged a look too.

"Yeah, pretty much. All the guys we hang with have the blood, you know? We're Protectors."

Phoebe's ears pricked at that. It was the word that had been used for Connor. "Can you explain what a Protector is?"

Nathan smiled in surprise. It was as though he hadn't expected her to speak. Maybe they thought she couldn't because of Lily. "Sure, it's an honor handed down in certain Atlantean families. We're given these." He pulled out a pendant with a green stone on it very similar to the one Connor had. "And we're told that if we ever find a Siren we have to look after her for her whole life." He looked at Lily and winked and she grinned back, punching him in the shoulder playfully. "Some need it more than others," he said, rubbing the shoulder where she'd punched.

There was clearly a great deal of affection there and it was lovely to see, but all it did was make her feel terrible about Connor.

He'd been her only friend since she was a little girl. He hadn't bumped into her by chance, but he'd looked after her just the same. Then, as soon as she'd found out what he was, she'd pushed him away.

Suddenly, the need to speak to him became unbearable and she bounded to her feet.

"What is it?" Drew said, trying to get up as well.

Phoebe rummaged through the cushions to find her shoes. "No, it's okay. Stay here. I'm just going to find Connor. I won't be long."

He was looking a little bewildered, but she stroked his cheek and kissed him. Then she disappeared out through the curtain into the thick of the crowd.

Partygoers turned and smiled as she walked. It felt more like she had something weird about her than being a celebrity and she didn't like it at all. She just wanted to lose herself and blend in. It was all so suffocating and there were so many people that she thought she'd have to turn back. Then she breathed in relief. Connor was chatting at the bar with a small group of men she hadn't seen before. He was always so chilled. She should have guessed that was where he would be.

The crowd parted easily so she could reach him; it was as if they weren't allowed to touch her. There he was. A wash of warmth mixed with relief swept over her when she came up alongside him and linked her arm through his.

He stood up from his perch, clearly surprised to see her, but his face quickly transformed into his reassuring smile. "Hey," he said, kissing her cheek. "Wanna drink?"

"Water," she answered, but was immediately distracted by the three men he was in conversation with.

Connor ordered another round and put his arm around her shoulders. "This is Jay, Phoebes."

Phoebe locked eyes for a moment with probably the most beautiful man she'd ever seen. As he bent to kiss her cheek she got a waft of the most gorgeous smell. He completely put her off balance and all that came out of her mouth was, "Are you Atlantean?"

His face only got better with his smile, if that were possible, and he tipped his head. "No, pure human. Sorry," he said, his face looking regretful.

Wishing she could rewind the stupid comment, she spluttered out an apology. "No … sorry. Silly me … it's fine. Honestly. I'm just getting used to all this," she blabbered on and on.

He laughed. "Understandable," he said, tipping his head in her direction. "I'm like an honorary Protector. But these are the real deal." He pulled the two other men into the conversation. One looked like an off-duty soldier, with strawberry-blond crew-cut hair, and the other, a little older, greying but obviously in his prime. They both smiled. "I'm Cash and this is Sean," he said in a thick American accent. "We're your sister's Protectors."

"The one that's away," Connor added by way of explanation.

"We'll leave you two to chat," Jay said, with a wink.

Connor passed her a glass of water. "Shouldn't you be attending to your fans?" he said with a teasing smile.

There were still people staring at her then whispering to the person they were with, but she could ignore it standing with Connor, nuzzled into his chest. It was partly to shut out the prying eyes but mostly to get some comfort from his lovely, familiar smell. "I'm sorry," she said, pulling away to look into his kind brown eyes.

He threaded an arm around her waist and said quietly next to her ear, "What for?"

She shrugged. "You know, stuff … being an arse."

Connor threw his head back and laughed. "You're always an arse."

Giggling she rolled into his chest and he hugged her playfully. "No seriously, Connor," she said, pulling away a little again to look at him.

This time he waited for her to speak, his face straight and his eyes soulful as if he knew she had something to get off her chest.

"I just wanted to tell you that I know what you are now. I know what you did for me." A tear escaped from the corner of her eye and she wiped it on the back of her hand. "Shit!" she said, noticing the mascara stripe. "Do I have eyes like a panda?"

Connor just smiled, shaking his head a little. Because that was what he always did. He always listened and he was always there for her. "I wanted to apologize for being a brat when you've given up so much to be there for me." When she really thought about it, it blew her mind. "You were just a boy, really, Connor."

His smile grew and he gave her a hug. "It was never just a job … call it more a vocation."

Her head fit snugly into the crook of his shoulder and chest. "But you lived away from your family to be with me and they treated you like a servant." *Oh my god!* She wasn't even sure if the family she'd been brought up with were even Atlantean.

"Shh," Connor said, bringing her around to stand right in front of him like he used to when she was small. "Right, you listen to me, I'll only say it the once. I loved working with the horses for your family."

"But they weren't my…" She went to dip her eyes from him but he brought them back to him with a small shake.

"That's just it, Phoebes, I was never working for that family, but your real family here. I've always known what you were, and who I am. And I saw my family regularly. It was a huge honor for them that I had realized my life's destiny. It so rarely happens. Doing that job…looking after you, made me and my family very happy." His eyes held hers and she searched his face for a long moment after he finished speaking. Then all she could do was fall into his chest and sob.

Maybe it was the wine or the blood; she wasn't exactly sure. Probably that she had no idea who or what she was any more. But the one constant in her life had been this man, and she would always love him for it.

Something else now had the crowd's attention.

The king had arrived.

It was her cue. "I'd better get back to Drew." She went to walk away, letting her hand run the length of Connor's arm till he held her hand.

"Be careful," he said, nodding knowingly.

Her hand reluctantly let go of his and she was already moving away, but she continued to look into his eyes. "I'm fine," she mouthed.

"Don't trust too easy," was the last thing she heard as she was swamped by the crowd. It was much harder to move through as they no longer seemed interested in what she was doing; they now had the king as an object of interest.

Phoebe didn't mind, it was a welcome distraction. She guessed she'd been gone a while and went straight back to their alcove. She pulled back the thin curtain and let out a breath of relief. There were Drew, Lance and Lily, lying on the cushions each with a snake-like pipe attached to one of those North African hubbly-bubbly things and giggling like a bunch of kids.

"There she is," Drew said, letting go of the pipe from his mouth. He moved over and patted the place next to him. "Come and try, Phoebes."

She took the place next to him and was given the tube coming from the bulbous metal vase.

"Pull on it slowly, babe," Drew said. "Then relax."

Phoebe had no idea where they managed to get the thing

from, but she decided to give it a go. What was one more new thing to try?

At first it felt and sounded like making bubbles in a drink. Then the smoke hit the back of her throat.

"Hold it for a moment if you can," Drew said. The sunglasses were gone and his eyelids were heavy and seductive. "We put a little something in of our own."

She frowned, troubled by that revelation. But how could she argue with that sexy, mischievous look? So she did as he suggested. Instantly, coughs racked her till her eyes streamed and she wanted to be sick.

Drew rubbed her back and pulled her back with him to lie against the pillows. "You'll get used to it."

Every limb felt like a lead weight. Her heart was beating out of her chest and yet she couldn't move. Her lips were tingling and her eyelids could barely open as she lay with her head on Drew's chest with his heartbeat reliably bumping her cheek.

His deep laugher rumbled underneath her. "You wan'another hit?"

The pipe appeared in her eye line.

She could barely move her head to shake it. He laughed again and kissed the top of her head.

The atmosphere felt heavy and thick, even though the curtains remained partially open to the party beyond. Everything seemed to have slowed down to a much more manageable pace. Joss sticks burned in little holders in the wall giving off a spicy scent. It felt like they were floating on a life raft drifting aimlessly here and there and, the weird thing was, the lack of conversation meant that all of them were feeling the same thing. Time stood still in their little alcove haven. Phoebe wasn't sure whether hours or minutes had passed when Drew passed her a fresh glass of champagne. He helped her sit up to take it.

Thankfully, the hubbly bubbly had been pushed to the side and replaced with an ice bucket. Lance and Lily had moved in closer and were sitting opposite them.

Phoebe was only half listening to the conversation between Lance and Drew. Lance was explaining how he'd been adopted into an Atlantean family and met Lily in California or something.

Phoebe was more interested in Lily, who was now close enough that she couldn't help studying her. She was the most intriguing of the sisters she'd met so far.

Her hair was so dark and curly that she would never have picked her out as her sister. And the stripes faintly visible on her arms and shoulders made her wonder how else she was different to her – like her teeth, for instance.

God, your thoughts are so rambling ... and loud.

Phoebe's eyes widened when Lily turned her face to her and her lips hadn't moved. It freaked her out. She wished people wouldn't do that.

Lily peeled back her lips so she could see all her front teeth in answer to her question. Initially embarrassed, Phoebe reached out her hand to feel if her canines were sharp like hers.

The two men had gone quiet. Distracted from their conversation they were watching and the atmosphere was suddenly charged.

Phoebe ran a tentative finger all along the top row of Lily's teeth. "They don't come down at all?" It was fascinating that she could even bear for them to be touched. If it were the other way around, it would feel like someone twanging a wire to Phoebe's brain.

The urge came from nowhere.

One minute she was staring into her sister's eyes, the next she was closing the distance between them. However, Lily didn't pull away. Instead, she remained still while Phoebe brushed her lips with hers.

The familiar ache tingled through her gums, and her canines descended a little. It felt reckless, but it seemed important to know how different to the other sisters she was. It also tested Lily's reaction to her own narrowed eyes and slightly elongated teeth.

There was a moment where the two girls just studied each other. Lily's features remained the same. Phoebe tested and moved in closer again. Maybe it was the blood, the champagne, or the sheer wildness of the moment, but the weight appeared in her chest and it seemed right to let a little free. She began to let a small flow into Lily's mouth.

Her eyes flickered shut.

One word echoed through Phoebe's head as the flow of her essence went into her sister: *Malleven.*

It was unfamiliar and she had no idea what it meant or which of them it came from. The world seemed to retreat so that it was just the two of them. Her stream of breath petered to nothing but, instead of ending it there, her sister gently cupped her face with her hands and repeated the process.

What followed was a mixture of pictures and feelings – a jumble of snapshots in time. It wasn't exactly Lily's life story as she was too drunk for much of it to make sense, but the answer to the word Malleven came through loud and clear. He was her husband.

It was shocking given how clear her feelings were for Lance. However, she wasn't without feelings for this guy either. He was strong, mysterious and very powerful. There was a connection with this guy to her sisters Lacy and Isla, too. One Lily wasn't too happy about. *Distrust. Annoyance.* Even a little anger over their relationship with this man. She wished she could sift the thoughts with a clearer head so they made more sense. From what she could gather, no one liked him because he was a powerful prince they blamed for Lacy's abduction.

Skepticism.

Lily didn't believe it. *No, she didn't want to.*

And Isla had rejected him as her most compatible mate. It was followed by an image of a beautiful dark male drowning, almost dead. *Malleven.* This was the guy.

Lily didn't trust Isla at all. She blamed her for almost killing a man she had great fondness for.

Phoebe had to admit he was fascinating and she wished she could find out more, but the stream of consciousness ended abruptly. In only a few minutes she had absorbed her sister's innermost feelings, until her skin glowed like she'd been plugged into the mains.

It was an immensely pleasurable process, even with her sister. She longed to go back over it. There was something so compelling about the whole thing. As if it lured her. It conjured feelings; warm, erotic and growing strangely familiar. It was the oddest thing.

One thing that hit her like a thunderbolt was that the strength of the Sirens' bond was undeniably powerful. She totally got it now. You could literally learn everything about a person.

Lily had finished and they remained still. Their eyes locked while both absorbed the download of information. Briefly, it occurred to her what incriminating information she had given away. Feeling suddenly weird, she shook herself out of the spell and became aware of her surroundings.

"Fuck!"

Phoebe and Lily turned their heads to find the table had been moved and their two men were opened-mouthed and riveted by what they were doing. She was also aware that her face was transformed and on full view.

"I've never seen anything like that," Lance said, more to himself than any one.

"Come here," Phoebe said.

The two men looked at each other until Drew nodded and Lance moved closer.

"Do you trust me?" She looked each of them in the eye, finishing with Lily.

Yes.

The two men nodded eagerly. It made her smile that they assumed it had sexual connotations.

Phoebe held out a hand to Lily. "Give me your arm."

After a small frown of confusion, Lily offered it to her, wrist up.

Phoebe clasped it gently and slowly brought it to her mouth. Their eyes locked. Lily's were moist, waiting for what she assumed would be a kiss.

Everything was orange and honed into a small slash of vision. Her lips parted, her teeth extended to their full length and, in a split second, she struck, scoring Lily's delicate skin.

She held it tightly to stop the flow of blood already oozing through her fingers. Her eyes zeroed to Lance's. "Here!" she said.

He looked immobilized by shock. "Now!"

Lance shuffled nearer on the cushions until he was kneeling next to the two of them.

Phoebe brought up Lily's arm and put her hand gently behind Lance's neck to guide them together. Despite the blood, neither seemed scared, mainly dubious. Their mind already on what Phoebe was clearly suggesting.

When Lance's lips finally touched Phoebe's fingers concealing the wound, she pulled them away and Lance covered it completely with his mouth. It was a mesmerizing sight. Something she and Drew had done many times now, but she had never seen any one else do.

She edged closer to Drew who put a possessive arm around her waist. Both of them couldn't take their eyes off the couple in front of them.

Lance's eyes remained shut and, even in the dim glow from the lanterns, the warm flush in his skin could be clearly seen. He released Lily's arm, gasped, then leaned back on his knees, laughing with his head back. The blood from his mouth ran down his cheeks to his neck and shoulders.

There was something so erotic and primal about it.

Phoebe moved out from Drew's arm and crawled back towards Lance.

Lily's eyes were on hers, waiting for what she would do next. "Your turn." Then she grabbed a chunk of Lance's over-long sun-bleached hair, pushed his head to the side revealing his throat, and struck fast and precisely.

It wasn't so deep that it gushed. Just dripping enough to show Lily what she was meant to do. "It's okay, it's natural for us. You've just not been given the equipment to do it."

Lily moved closer, a little hesitantly at first. Then her lips sealed over the wound at Lance's neck and he threw his head back and gasped, totally submitting to the bite.

To an outsider, it did look a little depraved, but she and Drew found it only brought them closer. It added something to their lovemaking. In a world of bonds made in name of the state, at least this was something they didn't have to share with anyone else. They were aliens and this felt right – maybe primitive, but natural all the same.

When she looked into Drew's face, she knew he was feeling the same thing. She read no jealousy there. His low-lidded eyes raked over the whole scene, taking in every moment like an erotic show. Then he gestured for her to come to him with his hands.

His eyes were now as feral as her own when she crawled up his body so they were face to face. She yelped in surprise when he grabbed her and threw her onto her back and clamped to her neck as Lily was still doing with Lance.

What surprised her more and made her instantly dissolve was the sharp sting of the skin breaking. Her arms snaked around him and she pulled him tight, groaning with the sensation of being at the mercy of his bite. A bite she never knew he had.

The four of them became intoxicated with a new drug and they couldn't get enough.

CHAPTER 19

The four of them were now a blind, drunk mess, rolling and messing around in the cushions. The hubbly bubbly was dry and the ice in the champagne bucket melted.

The music stopped abruptly and everyone started clapping in the main room beyond the shield of the curtain. "Lance…where's Lance?" came loudly from a microphone.

"Shit!" Lance said. "I'm supposed to go on stage."

Drew barked with laughter at the state of him. He could barely scramble to his feet. "Like old times, man."

Lance was shaking his head in such an exaggerated way that it made them all laugh.

"Here," Phoebe said, dipping the ice bucket towel into the water inside and passing it to Lance. "You'd better wipe your face."

He looked blankly at her for a moment until he got her drift and gratefully took the towel from her hand. They all looked the same with daubs and smears of blood all over their faces. It was probably on their clothes too if they could see in proper light.

When Lance had finished, Phoebe dabbed her own and Drew's faces and passed the cloth to Lily

"Lance! Come out here and show us all what you're made of." It was the king.

Shit! After smoothing down his t-shirt and a little worse for wear, Lance emerged from their alcove, with the three of them behind, to whoops and claps from the crowd.

They gave him a little push in the direction of the stage, already set up with the members of his band, and he seemed to pull it together enough to make his way through the cheering hordes.

"Please welcome, everyone, all the way from California, Lance McCabe and his band Leviathan." Dante backed away clapping as Lance, surprisingly lithe, hopped up onto the stage, arranged his mic on the stand and put his guitar over his head.

The cheers were deafening.

Phoebe stood a little way back with Drew and Lily, clapping and whistling along with everyone else. It had grown into the best night ever. They all started nodding the minute the band struck their first note. It was a thundering anthem that carried the crowd. Soon smart phones were popping up in the air to film it as if they were at a rock concert. It was exactly what it felt like; a merry-go-round of sight, sound, blurred faces and colors. Lance's band became the soundtrack to an amazing dream that only the four of them were having.

They moved seamlessly into two more numbers. Lance held it together, only stumbling on his feet a few times. Phoebe guessed you got good at that type of thing if you did it enough, and rock musicians would definitely practice a lot.

She looked up at Drew nodding his head and smiling, clearly enjoying himself, and gave him a squeeze. His arm went around her shoulders and he kissed the top of her head.

It off balanced him slightly and she had to steady him. They were all so wasted; she had no idea how Lance was managing to do this. The thought only made her laugh. Here she was at her own presentation to the elite of the Atlantean world, completely out of her head.

The band hit the last few bars in the song and Drew punched the air with his free arm. Lance went to the mic wiping away the sweat from his face on a towel and appeared to be scanning the crowd. "I'd like to call my beautiful life partner up here … where is she?" Everyone clapped. Drew nudged Lily in the direction of the stage. It was amazing how at ease they felt with each other after just one evening. She guessed the evening had revealed a lot and they were definitely no longer strangers.

Smiling but a little reluctant, Lily made her way towards the stage.

"And also an old friend of mine, who I know is here tonight. Drew, where are you?" He put his hand above his eyes to try and see better.

Phoebe looked up and grinned at Drew. "Do your stuff!" she said into his ear.

His face dropped immediately, realizing he had to get it together, and quick. Then he took a deep breath and moved away from her in Lance's direction. The crowd saw and immediately started to clap. "Say hi to Drew, everyone. Great guy, great musician and soon to be brother-in-law, kinda," he finished with a shrug.

The crowd loved it and clapped and cheered wildly.

Lance's band mate, River, moved off the stool to allow Lily behind the drums. Then he picked up a spare guitar propped on a stand. Drew stepped up onto the stage and was handed another. There was a brief conversation between him and Lance where they decided what they would play and then Lance shouted it to the rest of the band. Lily tapped her sticks together and Lance shouted, "One, two, three, four." Then they came in with their first note. It was a cover version of the old Incubus song, "Wish you were here".

The crowd loved it.

Phoebe wobbled unsteadily on her feet and looked around her. Everyone was having a fantastic time. Despite her foggy brain, which felt a good five minutes behind the rest of her, she was too. Her heart swelled with pride at her man, so at ease on the stage. That was when she realized it for the first time. *Her man*, and he was brilliant. In fact, the whole band were world class. Even her sister, behind the drums, was a natural.

They went on to do another number that Phoebe recognized as one of Drew's and then one she didn't know, she guessed was the band's. All the while Drew and Lance were swigging champagne straight from the bottle at every opportunity.

The two had been slaughtered before they even went on so, after beginning their fourth song, they were slow-eyed, swaying and now looking really the worse for wear. When Phoebe thought about the last few hours, it was a wonder Drew was still standing.

Thankfully, the band was carrying them so their antics of crashing into things and falling over just looked really rock 'n' roll. Lily was hammering away on the drums and Nathan was playing his guitar solo into a frenzy. It all served to whip the crowd up into their communal mayhem, with some climbing onto the stage and diving back into the crowd.

Phoebe giggled at the madness. It reminded her of a school prom gone out of control with Santalini guardsmen trying to stop those attempting to join the band, younger ones starting a mosh pit in the center of the room and party-goers falling into the fountain.

Phoebe's hand went to her mouth. This was, without

doubt, the wildest, most way-out party she'd ever been to in her life.

At that point Lance spun round, lost his balance and fell into Lily's drum kit and knocked her off her stool. The crowd loved it and jumped into the air screaming.

Phoebe stood, open-mouthed, and watched as Drew took his guitar over his head, swung it around and smashed it down into the huge Marshall amplifier. Dry ice was seeping out from the back of the stage making the whole thing seem staged like a music video.

The crowd was going wild.

The music stopped abruptly as it had all turned to chaos. Nathan stood laughing with River swigging his beer and pointing at the madness. Drew was rolling around with Lance on the floor in a schoolboy-like wrestle while Lily scrambled out from her pile of drums on her hands and knees.

Everything had got so out of control that guards began to swamp the place from every doorway. But the more serious things got, the more hysterically funny Phoebe thought it became.

The two princes, Keenan and Cesaré, leapt up onto the stage, pushed back party-goers and tried to pull Drew and Lance apart. Guardsmen were trying to calm the crowd, which had broken into several pockets of minor squabbles. People were herded and couldn't help treading on and bumping into each other. In fact, it was all starting to resemble a western bar brawl when she noticed Connor, Jay and his friends rushing into the fray as well.

Phoebe wanted to cheer Connor on and whooped with delight. Drew and Lance were hauled and shook to their feet, but they were hopeless, unable to be sensible, giggling and having to hold each other up. She couldn't stop herself laughing. It would go down as one of the maddest, funniest, most bizarre nights of her life. However, the party was very definitely over. The place seemed to calm down and guests were escorted out of every exit, lift and staircase. She had no idea what the time was, but it was very late.

The king was now on the stage and he didn't look happy. Jay, Connor, Cash and Sean soon joined him and helped Keenan and Cesaré keep Drew and Lance and the rest of the band from breaking into skirmishes with the guards.

The next moment the great hall was almost empty and Phoebe stood, a lonely figure who hadn't moved from the spot. She was joined by her two other sisters, Lacy and Isla.

"Shit, girl, you are all in so much trouble!" Lacy said, shaking her head.

Isla giggled. "Yeah, we thought we were bad."

Phoebe looked at them, only vaguely listening. It was just starting to register what the ramifications of this would be.

CHAPTER 20

The great hall was now completely empty of party-goers. Servants were sweeping and mopping the floors and pushing furniture back into its usual place. The haven of their little alcove was stripped of its curtains and a polished wood chest put in place of the cushions.

Dante walked towards their sorry group, flanked by Jay and Cesaré. He stopped right in front of them and he was fuming.

Phoebe immediately dropped her eyes to the floor. Astonishingly, his anger seemed directed at her. She wanted to say it wasn't all her and, in fact, it was Lance and Drew who were the main instigators, but it felt too much like being in trouble at school as it was.

When she chanced another look he was still staring at her, enraged. She was forced to say; "What?"

"Fuckin' what? That's all you have to say?"

Drew tried to get in between them, but his reflexes were way off and Jay put out an arm to stop him before he could intervene.

Dante's voice was low and even. He'd always seemed so

upbeat before. Okay, they'd kind of gotten a little out of control but everyone had seemed to have a great time. She just didn't get it. So when he said, "Why are you fuckin' with my kingdom, Phoebe?" she was gobsmacked.

It was late and she was drunk, but she was sure she would have picked up on anything as uncool as that.

"I've got a shit storm brewing, here … We're bound, Phoebe, I know what you've been doing all fuckin' night."

Her eyes went wide – well as wide as they could. "I don't know …"

"Yes you do. Look at the state of you." Then he turned to the two men, tutted and shook his head at Lance. "Take him and Lily to their room," he said over his shoulder to Cesaré.

Cesaré nodded and lightly steered Lance and Lily in the direction of the bedrooms.

Then Dante went toe to toe with Drew, who was almost as tall as him. "Blood is a crime here," he whispered menacingly. "And I don't care what color your ring is, you are expendable, remember that."

Phoebe couldn't believe her ears.

"Now get out of my sight, the pair of you."

DANTE WAS in a state of exhaustion when he met with his advisers early the next morning. He sat drinking coffee after only a couple of hours' sleep.

Alfonzo, Sebastian, Cesaré, Keenan, Jay and Max sat in his study expecting something of him after the debacle of the previous night and he had nothing. Everything had gone around and around in his head but it all kept on coming back to one thing; *sabotage*.

"Shouldn't the Borge be here for this?" Keenan said, drawing attention the fact that Darres Borge, the Siren, Isla's husband, had not been summoned, even though he sat on the council. Neither had his brother, Vionne, who would be Lord Advocate of Murrtaine one day.

Dante shot him a look that would slice like a knife. "This isn't a council meeting. After last night, I'm not sure there is a council any more."

Everyone looked uneasily at each other.

"All eyes are on us at the moment. With a fifth Siren the humans will do anything to destabilize us and, with the first hint of trouble, Murrtaine will cut itself off. I can't let that happen."

"You must be seen to be strong, Your Highness. You speak the truth but you need Darres and Vionne Borge on side," Alfonzo said, only vocalizing what he'd gone over and over in his head a thousand times.

Dante slammed his cup down on its saucer angrily, snapping the dainty little handle off. Then he stood up and began to pace the room while he thought. The others waited expectantly.

"This blood thing, it's like a cancer; and it needs to be treated like one." His eyes went to his oldest friend in the world, Jay, and flicked away at the steady, unapologetic stare.

Thank fuck he was due to be married any day now.

After another lap of the room, he stopped in front of Jay again. "I didn't just bring you here for the celebration. You all need to know that Tia is returning later tonight with our children." There it was, the smallest flicker of emotion behind Jay's eyes and then it was gone. The pain he saw was gratifying. The one man Dante knew better than himself couldn't hide the fact he was still in love with his wife. It must surely hurt to know that the reason she'd been away in Murrtaine for so long wasn't just to get her away from him, but to have more of his children. She and Jay shared only one, and that was a miracle.

"It is a good thing to have your wife by your side at such

dangerous times, Dante," Alfonzo said, bringing his focus back to the room. "The important thing now is to show the world we have a strong royal family and council." Alfonzo was right. It didn't sit well with him to leave his wife any longer with a male who could quite easily be a rival for the crown.

Dante let go of his locked gaze with Jay and continued walking slowly around the room. If the rest of the royals smelt the slightest hint of weakness, everything he'd built over the past couple of years would descend into chaos. The princes would see the Sirens as fair game and attempt to obtain them for themselves.

"There is no doubt as to the authenticity of the Siren; Phoebe Ray," Sebastian, her father, said. "Why would she jeopardize her own future?"

He had a point. Despite sensing absolutely no duplicity through the bond, he wasn't getting much else either, and that was unusual. With the bond, the other person should be emotionally an open book. He sensed her power and her sensuality. Heaven knew she clung to the human, Drew. But it was as if there was a barrier, like a force field around her emotions.

"What human intelligence do you have?" he said, pointing at his chief advisor, Alfonzo. "I spoke to Delissi a few hours ago, and he assures us that the humans know very little about Phoebe yet, but it's only a matter of time. He thinks they are twitchy and on high alert anyway, and doesn't think it will take much for them to launch some kind of offensive." The placement of his biological father at the heart of Washington was crucial to their security. He only hoped that he could trust him with the lives of his loved ones. There had been times when he wasn't sure he could count on it.

Alfonzo nodded as if it was to be expected. "There are several factions active at the moment. The Magi, we know, continue to align themselves around Malleven. Despite Cesaré heading the Florianna royal family, we must never forget that he is legally married to Lily and will always pose a threat to you.

There is another couple of ancient orders, one of which has been very prominent of late. Over the centuries their numbers have declined until they were just small, inconsequential pockets. But one particularly has been recruiting heavily over the past twenty years and can no longer be ignored."

"Who are they?" Dante said, narrowing his eyes.

"Perhaps Max is better to take over from here," Alfonzo said, gesturing with his hand to the wiry, elderly human who was an authority on all things ancient surrounding the Atlantean nation.

Max pushed up the small wire spectacles higher on his nose. "They are a mystic pre-Christian order called Scythians, Your Highness. Their doctrine differs from the peaceful teachings of Jesus Christ and is more in keeping with the fire and brimstone of older, more warlike gods. Often referred to in history as the fearless Warrior Knights."

"They struck terror in common and royal Atlanteans alike, often draining their captives of blood to use in their debauched rituals," Alfonzo added.

Max nodded in agreement. "They abhor the Atlantean race and make sure they recruit only from the human Germanic gene pool and are taken young. Early records speak of abductions of young boys from families as early as the third century, forced into a harsh life of prayer and servitude."

"They get away with that nowadays?" Dante said, shaking his head.

"Over the last few years, we believe they prey on the

vulnerable – street kids and those without the backing of a family," Alfonzo added.

"Is there any truth to the blood thing?" Dante asked. It was no great surprise. Atlantean blood had been sought by many over the years, for the power surge, as a health tonic or simply as an aphrodisiac.

Alfonzo shrugged and deferred to Max. "It is unclear whether they still have a preoccupation with it. Blood is so much easier to obtain these days without killing for it."

"You have to understand these people are fanatics, Your Highness," Alfonzo said. "They believe implicitly in the eradication of the Atlantean race by any means necessary."

Dante disliked them already. Extremism in any form made him sick to his stomach. If he were to choose any religion, it would be the one the Atlasians brought with them. Passed down the female line, and from the little he knew, teaching only peace and harmony. Some called them the Arawans or the way of the five moons. There was no direct translation as their native language was in mental pictures and feelings and not the spoken word. That was much more in tune with his laid-back personality. He had no time at all for fanatical bollocks. "Are they a real threat?" It seemed unlikely, as they hadn't appeared on his radar before.

Alfonzo bobbed his head. "We should not underestimate them. They hate our race with a passion, and see us as the Nephilim – spoken of in the Old Testament as the giant progeny of fallen angels who'd fornicated with the daughters of the earth."

Dante smiled. "Now that could be based in truth." He continued walking the room. That was all well and good but it didn't explain what was going on under his own roof. "Here's the thing that I just can't work out; Phoebe Ray is an authentic Siren. She has great power, I could feel it, but I don't think much passed to me in the bonding process. I know little of what she thinks and almost nothing of what she feels."

Sebastian went to protest but Dante silenced him with a raised hand. "I know she's your daughter, but I think we have to start to fear the worst – that she has been compromised in some way. Either through another unknown bond that I just don't feel, or we are dealing with something we've never come across."

"Her unaccounted time?" Alfonzo said.

Dante nodded. "The lost month." She had simply disappeared from the surface of the earth. There had been no witnesses nor any leads and Alfonzo had all his best agents on it. Not even his father in Washington had come up with a thing. "A legitimate prince would have claimed her and either presented her at court for a seat on the council--"

"Or announced his own bid," Alfonzo finished for him.

Dante nodded and continued to pace. The Santalini royal family placed the royal Sirens in the world at separate locations at birth. There they were left until such an age where they could reach womanhood in relative safety. Their only interaction with the Atlantean world was with Protectors that came into their lives or were placed there as in Phoebe's case. Too much surveillance and it could be deemed as tampering with the fates. Or the very thing meant to protect them could be the beacon for a Siren to be easily identified and abducted. It was the most likely scenario in this case. "But who?" Dante said, thinking aloud.

"What of the boy, Drew." Despite the purple of his ring identifying him as a true mate, all his blood tests came up as human with absolutely no markers at all. In fact, it was rare to have absolutely no Atlantean at all in the mix.

Dante stopped pacing and frowned. *It was rare.* Not more than a moment ago they'd been discussing the recruitment of pure-blooded boys. *Coincidence?* He didn't think so.

"We're all ignoring a massive detail here," Cesaré said, drawing everyone's attention to him. He stared at them all, amazed. "Aren't we going to address the elephant in the room? Was I the only one who saw the state of their eyes last night?" He paused and looked at everyone in turn. "If the guy is so human, why were his eyes like that? Why do we have a growing, totally unprecedented, preoccupation with blood at court?"

Dante shot a glance at Jay but didn't open his mouth. He didn't need to.

Jay leant forward with his elbows on his knees and spoke up for the first time. "Atlantean blood is a powerful thing. It could be something as simple as plain addiction." His eyes flashed back to Dante.

The two had been so close throughout their lives. It was the closest thing to a confession he was ever going to get from Jay. How he wished he could embrace his friend right then, but the chasm between them was now so wide, he wasn't sure it could ever be crossed – especially now he was to be married into another Atlantean family. Ruby Santalini was waiting impatiently in the wings and with Tia coming home he was grateful for it. However, it was yet another thing to stand between them. From that day he would be part of a family with their own set of values, politics and agenda. So even though he knew there was more to it both with Jay and with the newbies, he appreciated an apology of sorts for Jay's behavior over the last few months. With a lump in his throat, he merely nodded and moved on. "Maybe …but I think we are dealing with more than we know here." He pointed to Max. "Have the blood tests redone. Don't just do one. Have them done daily for comparisons.

Max nodded. "Yes, Your Highness."

"And look for everything you can get on the last Siren. I want no surprises like the last time." Then he looked at

Sebastian and Alfonzo, his oldest advisors. "Gather every bit of intelligence you can get your hands on from the humans – every government, every religious sect, however small. Check the lesser royal family branches for their activities at the time Phoebe went missing." They both bowed their heads.

"What will you do?" Cesaré asked.

"Me?" In all honesty, he wasn't sure. Tia's homecoming was like an ache in his chest. He couldn't get beyond thinking about that. Then it came to him like a bolt of inspiration – a revelation. Any strong king and great nation throughout history had one. And it was the perfect answer to Atlas. "I'm going to revive our religion."

Everyone stared at him open-mouthed, and clearly thought he'd lost his mind. Then Alfonzo narrowed his eyes and smiled. "As usual, Your Highness has great foresight."

DANTE DECIDED to leave the four troublemakers to stew. They were told they were all under arrest and confined to their rooms and checked regularly for any further wrongdoing. Then he shut himself in his library and surrounded himself with his books. Max had taught him to read them, as the language dated back to Atlantis itself and was no longer spoken.

It was very revealing.

The histories of the five families could be traced back there. The Santalinis – the vampires – had always been close to the crown because of their strength. The Florianna – the Alchemists – had wielded magic and were always feared because of it. Then there was the Borge – the Murrs and the ones with the purest blood. It seemed they were always the most hostile to the crown, believing it belonged to them because of their untainted ancestry.

Dante looked up for a moment. *Could that be the case here?* Darres Borge was married to Isla and had a seat on the council, and he counted his elder brother Vionne as one of his closest friends. He shook the thought away and continued reading. It bothered him though. Maybe he had been a little too trusting.

Then he got to the tome he'd been searching for. It was leather bound in what was once probably white, now a dingy yellow and browned at the edges. It was still beautiful, about four inches thick with gilded pages. Embossed on the front cover was the blue home planet of Atlas orbited by five pearl-like moons. *The Arawan.* He whispered. Even their name sounded magical. He carefully crackled open the book with his white gloved hands – the pages so old and delicate only the select few could ever touch its pages or read its contents.

Max had thought he'd died and gone to heaven when he'd first clapped eyes on the Bonaci private library. The contents were among the oldest in the world and beyond price. The calligraphy was hand-inked in arcs and swirls similar to the ones tattooed all over his body, and were intermingled with the most beautiful colored symbols and pictures.

For a moment, Dante didn't know what possessed him. He was filled with the most overwhelming lifting of his spirits. It was as though he'd come home to find the most beautiful sunny valley of grass and flowers in front of him. Somehow he knew what he must do.

He slipped the white glove from his hand and paused for a moment, hovering above one of the large pages. The symbol was one of a planet overlaid with an eye, simply drawn in bold black curlicues. Slowly, he lowered his hand to the paper.

The minute his hand made contact with the page, he jolted. A power so great surged through him and gripped his heart. Picture after picture flashed before his eyes and his soul was taken on a journey. It felt like a birth of a baby. Beginning with soothing warm waters travelling through blackness and then out into a wonderful light. But the light was of every color, whirling around until they became clear and in focus. It was the world – the Earth, but perfect. Utopia. Everywhere as far as the eye could see were mountains, green pastures, flowers. The birds were singing, animals grazing. A small child was rolling and tumbling with a full-sized lioness but was unharmed. What took his breath away was the absolute abundance of peace.

Then, as quickly as it came, the image went. The world went dark and he felt thrown back into the room.

Dante was left gasping for breath, unable to believe what just happened. He flopped into a chair, racking his brains for sense in what he'd seen. Somehow he knew that the vision had only been intended for a very select few – perhaps for the priesthood. *Or kings*, he whispered.

As his heart rate began to go back to normal, everything was solidifying in his mind and making perfect sense. The images weren't of a person's birth, they were of a journey – his people's journey – the one they'd made here to Earth. It had begun on Atlas, a watery planet. They'd travelled across the blackness of the universe to land on the planet that looked like a jewel in the night sky. It was a birth of sorts, one of a new nation.

The five moons were the five Sirens. Each was different to the other with their orbits around the Earth. He hurriedly turned to the last page. It clearly depicted the last days. There were the moons around a great shaft of light – the Orb. Symbols depicting the weather patterns came from each of them – all except one – the one that had grown dark. It was tucked behind Earth's moon, unable to feel the sun's rays.

Dante's mind raced. *A dark moon ... A dark goddess*. Then it came to him like a lightning strike: the one that should shine the brightest was hidden from view – The Night Goddess.

His hand went to his mouth when the enormity of the information he'd seen hit him. The book didn't just foretell the past, it revealed to him a possible future. It had given him a glimpse of what the world could be if he followed the path.

The Night Goddess's power was hidden but could be brought into the light at the time when the Earth needed it the most. It was entirely possible that the Atlanteans coming to earth heralded a new order where a troubled world could be changed to one of beauty and peace.

His heart hitched in his chest. That was it, and he knew it with every fiber of his being. *That was the secret truth of the five moons.* No one except him on Earth understood it. He knew the right path.

CHAPTER 21

*D*ante wasn't sure how long he'd been sitting there meditating on what he'd learned. With no more than a couple of hours sleep after the party, he must have been there all day as night was approaching again. He pinched the bridge of his nose when there was a knock at the door. "Come in."

Marius, the eldest of the Santilini brothers, and Keenan, Dante's brother-in-law, entered.

"Take a seat," Dante said, and looked at his watch. Tia would be arriving back from Murrtaine in a few hours and he wanted to be rested when he saw her.

His heart leapt. It had been almost a year since he'd seen her. What he'd kept to himself was she'd given birth to two more children. At that moment, as weary as he was, all he could think of was burying himself inside her and making everything disappear. If only he didn't have constant shit to deal with. Then maybe they could disappear for a holiday, but there was no chance of that.

He smiled weakly at the two brothers as they settled in seats in front of him. They belonged to the family most strongly aligned with the throne – the very one Jay was about to marry into. However, when his wife Tia had last been in their home in New York, trusted in their safekeeping, she was treated abysmally. The repercussions of which were still reverberating.

For a lot of reasons his marriage had been stormy. Although at this point he'd been completely backed into a corner. Her relationship with Jay and his preoccupation with blood meant he was forced to act in order not to look weak. It had broken his heart, but he was forced to put her away from him, giving Jay his last chance with her. Instead, as contrary as ever, she didn't go back to Jay. While at the Santalini mansion and while Jay was already distracted with Ruby – his soon-to-be wife, the head of the family had assumed wrongly that Tia was completely out of favor. She was ignored, verbally abused and humiliated in front of the whole of the extended family. Of course she had made it a hundred times worse by losing her temper and attempting to assault the old guy for it. The whole thing had been a nightmare from all sides. It had been a large part of why he was glad to have her out of the way while he sorted it out. Although after what he'd learned this afternoon, he wasn't even sure that Murrtaine was a safe place for her any more. Which brought him back to the reason the two were sitting in front of him. "Vionne has sent word that Tia and the children are on their way home."

The two men nodded. "We are aware, Your Highness," Marius said. "Our men have their orders to be ready."

"After the shit storm that went down with her at your home, I have a huge problem."

"My uncle understands that he made a huge mistake, Your Highness. Such an oversight will never happen again. I give you my word on my honor as a Santalini soldier," Marius finished, thudding his fist to his chest.

"I view Tia as one of my closest friends; I would never see any harm come to her," Keenan said. "If it weren't for Lacy being shot …"

Dante put up a hand to silence him, got up from his chair and walked around to their side of the desk. "Look, here's the thing. I know you're good men and Lacy was at deaths door 'n' all," he said, rubbing his forehead and leaning against the edge of his desk. "But what you don't understand is, Tia has lost all faith in you as her guard. The whole point of you as a family is to guard the royal family and the queen doesn't trust you."

The two men looked at each other and Marius shook his head. It would be a massive blow to his family if they lost their exalted position with the throne.

Dante wasn't daft. He wanted the Santilinis on side. After all, they were the only ones qualified for the job, and so far, hadn't used their position to gain power. He had enough to deal with keeping an eye on the crafty Florianna and his own family, the downright hostile Dubonnettis. Now he wasn't sure he could even trust the Murrs; he couldn't afford to lose the support of his guard. It was a real problem. "The last conversation I had with Tia, she asked for her Murr guard to stick with her on dry land as well."

"That is foolhardy. They can't function as well on land and would be weak," Marius said, exasperated.

Dante held up a silencing hand. "I said the same thing. The last thing I want is to give the Murrs any ideas that their influence is growing."

Marius relaxed back into his chair, relieved.

"She's insisted on Cesaré and his family instead."

"She what?" both Keenan and Marius said together.

"I know, but what am I to do? She doesn't trust you any more…" He walked back around his desk and sat back down. "Look, I'm tired. Let me renew my bond with her so I can think clearly. Stay close, but don't be obvious. As far as I'm concerned, you're her guard. Let me humor her for a while until she sees sense."

The two men relaxed a little. It seemed to satisfy them. They would understand that he had been without his wife and energy of their bond for the best part of a year and, without it, even with his royal blood and the strength of her sisters, he grew weaker.

"Does she know about Jay?" Keenan asked.

Dante let out a long sigh and nodded. "We speak telepathically daily. I couldn't let her come back without softening the blow."

Keenan nodded with a sad understanding but looked skeptical. He couldn't blame him. He'd witnessed the hopeless triangle he Jay and Tia were caught in being bonded together. They'd been on the same merry-go-round for years now. "It'll be different this time," he said, voicing what was on Keenan's mind.

He raised his eyebrows, not believing it for a second. "You think Jay marrying will change that?"

Dante narrowed his eyes. Keenan's allegiance had always been to Jay. They'd become firm friends and were about to get even closer when he married. "The Murrs have developed a new medication. Jay has had it for weeks now. He will not need to replenish his bond with Tia, and he won't become ill. It seems to be working."

Both Keenan and Marius looked surprised but not unhappy with the information. It meant that Jay had not spoken a word about it. That didn't surprise him. Jay had always kept most things to himself, and it gratified him a little that Jay and Keenan weren't that close to confide in him something like that.

He relented a little. They were good men. "Bear with me a little while. Let me settle again with my family, and I'll see that the Santalinis have their proper place. I have some news that I haven't spoken to anyone yet."

The two men looked at each other, perhaps communicating telepathically. He wasn't sure whether they had the gift. "I am a father again."

Keenan grinned. "Really?"

Marius bobbed his head but he was smiling as well. "There had been rumors as to why she went away, but we thought … well, that's great news."

"Boy, girl?" Keenan said.

"Two boys!" Dante said, his heart swelling with pride and he hadn't even met them yet. "Roman and Zander. They'll be here in a couple of hours."

Marius put his hands on his knees and stood up, looking a lot happier than when they came in, and Keenan followed. "We'll leave you to your preparations. Congratulations, Your Highness. We'll continue as her guard, but I'll give orders to be unseen."

Dante smiled, and put a shaking hand through his hair. Tia couldn't come home quick enough. And yet he was nervous.

Tia would come home to find Jay openly in a relationship with another woman. That had never happened before, and he had no idea how she'd react. The bond between them had at last been broken and there was nothing holding them together.

However, the castle was still full. Many had stayed over after the party. Even though Jay was no longer joined to Tia, he had every right to be at court as he grew up within the Dubonnetti royal family, was father to a royal child and a new member of the Santalini guard. There was no more softening the blow to Tia. She would come home to be hit with it all and, without doubt, be hurt.

Dante knew she loved him deeply. There was no hiding

feelings through the bond. Although that meant he knew how she felt about Jay. The man she'd met long before him and would always make him insecure with her. Despite being a strong man and a king, somewhere deep inside, he always felt second best.

He took a deep breath and shook away the sappy thoughts. The guard had stood down as her guard and that included Jay. It was slightly gratifying to have Jay on the back foot.

It made him chuckle at what a thorn in the side Tia was. She'd actually refused point blank to be guarded by any of the Santalinis. And when he'd refused her request to be guarded by the Murrs, she'd insisted on being trained by her Protector Sean in hand-to hand combat.

He wiped the amusement away from his face. It wasn't that bad an idea. After all, her sister Isla was a bad-ass martial artist and government-trained assassin. It was probably one demand he could indulge.

The door knocked again.

He had one last task before he got some rest. "Enter."

Cesaré and his brother Sandro of the Florianna royal family entered and were seated. Then he got straight to the point and explained what he'd told the Santalinis – minus the part about them secretly guarding in the background.

It wasn't something he was particularly proud of, tricking the men into thinking their family had a shot at taking the honorable guard position with the royal family, but he couldn't afford to tell them yet.

The two brothers looked at each other, amazed.

"What am I to do when my queen refuses them as her guard?"

Both men bowed their heads. "Of course, Your Highness," Sandro said.

Cesaré continued to look at him questioningly, as if he was already looking for the catch.

It made Dante smile. He really did like the guy he'd taken as his right-hand man in his government. But he had to play a long, clever game. Jay and the Santalini family needed slapping down a peg, to know their place and not get too bigheaded. Even though he had grown to respect and like Cesaré as a man, he was still a Florianna. They were powerful and known as the mystics and often the mercenaries of the race. The bottom line he was balancing so carefully was that each family was as ambitious as the next, and he had to keep them happy enough to throw in their lot with him, but down enough that they felt they needed him. It was an exhausting job.

"Can you afford to alienate them?" Cesaré said, speaking what was on Dante's mind.

It was a good question. "I don't want any family on my council to think they have any more precedence over another." It wasn't a lie, and he was sure Cesaré knew exactly what he was talking about.

"The Murrs grow cocky too, with the amount of time Your Highnesses' family spends there."

Dante looked at Sandro for a long moment after his comment. He was right, of course, and it confirmed that there were grumblings between the other Atlantean families. He inclined his head. "It is difficult with the close connection with the queen's family." The sisters were half Murr. "But I realize that the Florianna have felt on the fringes for a while and I would like to remedy that by bringing them closer to the crown.

Both men in front of him smiled. Sandro, with open awe and amazement, Cesaré a little more reserved and tinged with embarrassment. The family had suffered enough because of the traitorous actions of their cousin, Malleven Mancini. They'd been humiliated on two counts; first Malleven's tampering with Cesaré's ring, disgracing him as a cheat, and second when Isla rejected Malleven and therefore the Florianna royal family, both instances in front of the whole Atlantean world. Something like that was hard to come back from. Redemption had come in the unlikely package of Lily, who'd saved him from drowning. She'd breathed for him in ignorance, transferring her power to him, but in doing so saved Cesaré's life in more ways than one that day.

So, Cesaré aside, the family could not be trusted any more than the others. "You two particularly will be Tia's personal guard. She will also have her Protectors, Cash and Sean."

"What about Jay?" Cesaré asked.

"Let me worry about Jay. He has a wedding to plan."

The two men would have heard the rumors. The relation-ship he'd shared with the queen had been no secret. He knew everyone was expecting Tia to royally kick off when she returned, and Jay to break his engagement. It was under-standable, but it was something Dante would not allow this time. He now had four children to think about, and Jay's behavior had become erratic and unpredictable of late. Marriage was the safest place for him to be right now.

"Have they named the day?" Sandro asked.

"It's in two weeks."

Both men looked surprised. He guessed they never thought it would really happen. "This is a great opportunity for your family, gentlemen."

They understood perfectly. This was a chance for them to oust the Santilini and become closest to the king. It was what he wanted them to think. It was what he wanted all the fami-lies to think. "If you'll excuse me, I need to rest before Tia arrives back."

They both stood and shook his hand, Cesaré a little longer than his brother. He was doing that weird thing the Florianna always did, trying to sweep his brain.

Dante raised an eyebrow. *Sincere enough?* he said telepathically.

Cesaré grinned and bobbed his head. "Old habits die hard, Your Highness."

Dante laughed, Cesaré was fast becoming one of his closest friends.

"Ah, one last thing," Cesaré said. "What do you want us to do about Ruby Santalini? She arrived at the castle recently. Is she to attend the queen's homecoming, or should she be told to keep out of the way?"

Dante pinched his nose again, then rubbed the back of his stiff neck. There seemed little point prolonging the meeting with Jay's fiancé. "No," he said wearily. "Let her come."

The two Florianna brothers bowed and left the room.

He needed sleep now more than ever. Shit was about to get very real.

CHAPTER 22

*W*hile the troublemakers were allowed to cool off and Dante decided what to do about them, everyone else had gathered in the great hall to welcome Tia and the children home. It was a collection of friends, family and dignitaries summoned to witness the growth of the royal family. It wasn't just to satisfy tradition, it was to show the Atlantean world that Dante and Tia were strong and could offer the nation stability.

Dante stood tensely with every nerve ending prickling, while everyone else chatted easily. The familiar weight in his chest ached as if she were standing right next to him.

She was nearby.

He excused himself with a touch to Sean's arm, and walked briskly over to the fountain in the center of the room. Conversations soon hushed as people cottoned on and began to wander over as well.

It took a few hushed minutes until the water in the center began to bubble as something approached.

First to breach the water were two of Vionne's Lieutenants. Both had white-blonde hair and wide, unblinking coal-black eyes. They pulled themselves up into the shallows and effortlessly released the water out of their lungs.

Dante knew they were sent ahead as a safety precaution and would be speaking to Vionne telepathically the whole time. *Welcome,* Dante said, switching to projected speech. *Is everything okay?*

One of them looked vacant for a moment. *All is well. The journey passed safely.*

They come, the other said, reaching down into the darkest part of the fountain.

Vionne's blonde hair and huge, muscled, striped body came next. He didn't stop to greet Dante, but reached straight back beneath the water and carefully hauled a female arm, then body, until she gracefully stood on two feet.

Just one word; *'Tia',* came out on a breath.

She smiled beautifully back at him, but he knew those huge dark pupils were unseeing out of the water. She just felt him as he did her. A wash of warmth flooded over him through the bond, even though it was weak. The hollows in her eyes reminded him that it was as necessary for her to renew it as it was for him.

Before he could approach, Xavier and Alexia escaped their nanny and ran to her.

Dante's heart ached at the sight of them reunited. Her hands felt both of their faces, hugging them to her, feeling how they'd grown. They were now looking the human equivalent of around seven years old when, in reality, they weren't more than three. Even her regret at missing the last year was palpable through the bond.

With a hand on Xavier's shoulder she bent away from him and efficiently expelled her lungs. Alexia passed her a drink, then Xavier a towel.

Dante approached slowly with the flutter of nerves at seeing her again. Without a word, he grabbed a towel from a servant with a huge pile next to him and wrapped it around Tia's shoulders. Then lifted both children, one in each arm and kissed their round cheeks noisily. It had been a few days since he'd had a chance to be with the children himself. "Ahh," he growled, almost crushing the life out of them. "They've missed you so much!" Then he said more softly, looking straight at her, "I've missed you."

They giggled as he turned the laden moment into tickles and raspberries blown into the crook of their neck.

We missed you too, Daddy, Alexia projected.

"We'll do something all together," he said, feeling guilt and the weight of responsibility.

The children were taken from his arms; he had no idea by whom. Right then he could think of only one thing and here she finally was. After almost a year she was right in front of him. As beautiful a vision as she ever was. Her hair had now grown, and her magnificent stripes merely accentuated every contour and curve of her. Five children hadn't spoiled her figure one bit – if anything she'd just become a whole lot more womanly.

Suddenly conscious of the whole assembly quiet and watching, he realized he'd left her standing and immediately reached to help her out of the fountain.

Wait! she projected, and turned back to the water where two more children were handed up to her. She turned with one resting on each hip.

Dante's eyes misted over as emotion gripped him for a second. He reined it back shakily. "Tia, they're beautiful. You're beautiful." He could no longer help himself, and stepped over the wall of the fountain to wrap the three of them in his arms. He kissed each of the beautiful boys. Both had the characteristic black curls to their shoulders that glistened with wetness, and wide light green eyes and palest grey stripes that he knew would grow darker with age. He buried his face in Tia's neck to breathe in her scent and to camouflage the emotion that he was just about keeping a lid on. *I love you.*

Before he knew it someone had relieved her of the children, and her arms wound tightly around him. Everyone began to clap and he swore the moment was up there with one of the happiest of his life. He came up from her neck to look into her eyes, and her hand moved to cup the side of his cheek. *Are they what you hoped for?* she projected, searching his face.

He shook his head slightly, not believing that she could ever doubt it. *It's the best gift a man could hope for.* Then he locked lips with hers in front of the whole assembly, not helping release a small burst of his breath, which she returned. It had been so long, and they needed it badly. However, he soon became aware that all eyes were on them and pulled apart before they got too carried away. Then he held out a hand towards one of his servants. "The queen's eye drops," he said.

He was handed another towel, which he wrapped around her, then a tiny bottle that she hadn't needed for almost a year. "Here, tip back," he said. "Let me help you to see."

Tia tilted her head back. Dante looked lovingly into her ruined irises. They were now permanently stretched beyond capacity from long spells under water to accommodate more light. The moss green they once were was barely visible. He squeezed three drops into each eye, then hugged her into his chest. They would sting, and he didn't want her to rub and damage the delicate eye surface.

He watched those assembled over her head. Some were chatting, a few were cooing over the children who wriggled to get down and run around, but most were watching him with sympathy and understanding. It made him feel vulnerable and open. They were witnesses to a reunion they should have had in private, but as the royal family it was impossible.

Tia began to stir in his arms.

He held the tops of her arms and put her away from him slightly. And there she was, breathtakingly beautiful with the deepest green eyes he'd ever seen on anyone. "Hey," he said.

"Hey, handsome!"

Dante laughed with happiness and relief. It was always a worry that one day her sight would no longer return. Satisfied she was okay, he stepped back over the fountain with a protective arm around her where she was given a soothing drink. The throat was always sore after spells of breathing water when it was replaced by air.

Vionne placed a large hand on his shoulder. *Congratulations, Your Highness. The Orb has blessed you with four beautiful children.*

Dante looked up into the dark coal-like eyes of the Murr who stood at least another six inches taller than him. *Thank you.* He wanted to gauge this huge male that would be Lord Advocate of Murrtaine one day and an incredibly influential man. *But I have five children,* he said, reminding him that he classed Jay's boy as one of his own.

Vionne bowed his head. *Forgive me the oversight, Your Highness. You are truly blessed.*

Our mother moons have certainly looked kindly on me, he slipped in and walked away. Vionne would not have missed his meaning. The Orb very definitely was the power behind the fates, but the way was the Five Moons and he would know that– except he wouldn't expect him to. It gratified him when he felt his eyes burning holes in his back while he thought about it.

After that he worked the room, picking up his children as he went. All the while his eyes strayed to Tia, longing to get her on her own. First, she was crushed by Sean and Cash, her

Protectors, and then welcomed by each of the families, who'd formed a line, to greet her one by one.

He could see she was lingering and putting off reaching the last in the line as long as possible. There stood the group of large men in red and black uniforms, the family that included Jay.

Tia! he projected.

She was hugging and talking to Sean again instead of moving on.

Dante linked her arm through his, forcing her to release him. "Come," he said, smiling but firm.

Sean kissed her on the cheek. "We'll start training tomorrow."

She mouthed a *thank you*, then looked up at Dante. For a moment he saw how hopelessly lost she was. This was impossibly hard for her. Today she wasn't saying hello, but goodbye to the person she'd been obsessed with from the moment of meeting – Jay. There were no words he could offer other than, *Ready?*

She let out a ragged breath and nodded.

CHAPTER 23

To the casual observer Jay looked as cool ever, but inside his heart was beating wildly. There she was standing in the fountain with the skimpiest gossamer-like outfit that barely concealed her. Even her ruined eyes were fathomless pools that he could get totally lost in. He tried not to notice the emotional reunion between his best friend and their beautiful family, and shuffled from foot to foot with his hands in his pockets.

"OK?" Keenan said in his ear.

He nodded and flashed his eyes to him briefly. It was the international look for "don't go there".

Keenan raised his eyebrows and tipped his head indicating to remember his sister standing on the other side of him. Jay shot Ruby a furtive glance and she was watching him closely. Of course, today was as hard for her as it was for him – harder maybe.

At a time when he and Tia had reached an all-time-low, he had struck up a thing with Ruby Santalini (because he didn't do relationships). It was way before Dante had ordered him to marry. Then, as she was already there, it just seemed the natural thing to do. She was Atlantean and from a good family. If he had to marry, then it might as well be her. She was stunningly beautiful. All raven hair and 1950s' curves. Any man would give his right arm to be with her. Her insecurities where Tia was concerned were not without grounds. She would never be completely out of his system.

Jay picked up her hand and gave it a squeeze. She shouldn't have come here really. He'd wanted to break the news to Tia gently. But he kind of understood Ruby turning up, needing to make her presence felt and marking her territory. She was no pushover, which he kind of liked in a way.

However, when he glanced back at Tia now slowly making her way down the line of well-wishers, he knew she lived up to her name: Storm – wild and volatile, to say the least.

Maybe he should have made his excuses and stayed away and let Dante break the details to her, but he was already part of the Santalini, Bonaci and Dubonnetti royal families, so even without being engaged to Ruby, he should be here as a Santalini soldier if nothing else. The truth was he needed to satisfy the thing that had eaten him alive since she'd left. Stuff in his life had got out of control and he needed to say he was sorry. This was his attempt to tie up loose ends and get closure.

Ruby snaked her arm through his, enjoying his small display of affection – no doubt making the most of it so everyone could see.

Tia's laughter brought his eyes back on her progression down the line. Sean had his arms around her whispering something. For a moment, he wished Ruby wasn't there. He missed being one of Tia's Protectors. Sean and Cash were still his friends, but it wasn't the same. They were very much a part of the Bonaci, and he now had to concentrate on the

Santalini who had taken him in as their own. It felt like there was now a clear divide.

Sensing his mind wandering from her, Ruby hugged into him more tightly, and he kissed the top of her head. He never thought he could entertain another woman, but this one had managed to somehow inveigle herself into his emotions.

Gradually, over the months, bit-by-bit, they had become closer. She was beyond hot, and she readily gave him her vein, which set her apart instantly. It seemed perfect – a hot woman and one who was a part of the only royal family where blood was legal. It was a no-brainer. He had a habit, and she had become tangled up as a part of it.

Jay's eyes drifted back to Tia. She was so close to them now. It was weird, despite his heart racing with nerves; the old tingle of the bond was not there. *The tablets.* They were definitely working. Before, after spending this much time without her, he would have been beyond tired. This close to her, his body would have ached with a need for her so deep, it would have been just like a thirsting man in sight of a river. Now all he needed to do was apologize then move on with his life.

With a deep breath he stood up straighter. He shook off Ruby's arm from his but kept hold of her hand. It was enough to satisfy her need to be part of this, but not too much that it was rubbing Tia's nose in it.

Dante was steering Tia and moving her closer as if she was stalling. A pang of pain hit his chest.

The nearer she got, the more his heart was in his mouth. Dante wanted this over with and he couldn't blame him. Tia wouldn't take this well. The two men hadn't spoken properly for months, but nothing would ultimately change how they felt for each other. They were angry, but a brotherly love like theirs wasn't easily broken. Theirs had been under more strain than most, so that counted for something. Not many men could have stayed friends when they both loved the same woman.

Tia was now with Lacy, the other side of Keenan. The two women hugged tightly. They were the closest of all the sisters. All she reserved for Keenan was a curt nod.

It was quite shocking, as Keenan adored her. It showed she was definitely bearing a grudge against the Santalinis. Finally she came to a stop right in front of him.

The room hushed. For a long moment, neither spoke. As if the two of them needed a minute to map any changes to each other's faces.

"Tia," Jay said, eventually.

Instead of being angry she seemed lost for a moment and murmured, "Jay."

"Welcome home," he said, trying to smile. Then, conscious of the chasm of silence, he quickly pulled Ruby into his body. "There is someone I want you to meet." His hand rested on her shoulder. "This is Ruby…my fiancé." The word sounded so wrong and alien on his tongue, but he'd finally said aloud what he'd scarcely admitted to himself; he was getting married and it wasn't to Tia.

Dante put a protective arm around her shoulders. He knew how hard this was for her. He would feel it through the bond. Instead of feeling jealous, it just made Jay respect the guy even more, if that were possible. His love was so deep for this woman that he was allowing her this goodbye.

Jay was forced to swallow down a lump.

Tia looked up into Dante's eyes and he appeared to steady her. Then she turned back to face Ruby and Jay braced himself for whatever fury was to follow.

"It's nice to finally meet you, Ruby." Her voice was still gravelly from the water, making it sound heartbreakingly emotional.

The whole room seemed to let out a collective breath as if

everyone was expecting something – something that definitely didn't happen. In fact, as Jay allowed his body to slowly relax, it was kind of an anticlimax. There were no silly games with Tia. She was passionate and unpredictable and could never hide how she felt. It was one of the things he loved about her. The whole thing just unnerved him, both for her behavior and his reaction to it. It had never struck him that one of the main aspects of their relationship was drama, and it would be something to be missed. It was baffling.

Then as if to save him, his son, JJ, came running up to his mother after waking from his nap. He was the same age as Dante's elder two but, having more human DNA, looked younger by a couple of years. "Mummy!" he squealed, slamming into Tia's legs.

After one last meaningful moment, her face transformed to delight and she bent down and scooped the boy up in her arms. Kisses and tickles followed while she swung him around.

Then everything in the room seemed to slow down like a hand stopping a record disk.

Jay watched with growing horror as Ruby reached out with both hands to relieve Tia of JJ.

"Come, JJ, Mama's busy."

Jay didn't even have time to react before Ruby shot back, sharply rubbing and opening and closing her fingers as if she'd touched something hot.

Her eyes went to his in confusion. "My hands," she said, holding them up for him to see.

Jay frowned. They were covered in blisters.

He looked sharply at Tia, but she was oblivious. She hadn't seen a thing.

What captured his attention was the look in the aquamarine of his son's eyes. His angelic stare was on Ruby like he wished she were dead.

Then, a moment later, Tia whisked him around and said, "Can I keep JJ tonight?… I haven't seen him in so long," she said, plonking a noisy kiss on his chubby cheek. "I'd love for him to get to know his new brothers."

For a moment Jay was stunned. Nothing was making any sense. Disturbed and unable to work out what just happened, he looked at Dante vacantly. He didn't appear to have noticed anything either and just raised his eyebrows, leaving the decision up to him.

Still distracted, he said, "OK, I'll collect him tomorrow."

"Thank you, Jay," Tia said, kissing JJ again and again as if she couldn't believe he was real.

There weren't many things in life that threw him, but today was definitely one of them. Something had clearly happened between JJ and Ruby. The look he'd seen in his son's eyes alone was enough to set off alarm bells. Isla had already told him his son had strong mental powers. There was no doubt in his mind that Ruby's hands were injured due to him. Thankfully, he appeared to be the only one to see it. For that reason, he watched Dante lead his new family from the hall, and his little son JJ with them.

It was then the price he'd paid for Dubonnetti's warning of his real identity hit him. When he was at his happiest with Tia and it looked as if he would have a family of his own, the father of the Dubonnetti sons had told him of the Darkly Begotten prophecy. At first he'd dismissed it, but pretty soon he couldn't. There was something cold, dark and destructive in him, and he knew Dubonnetti was right. Any chance of happiness with Tia was shattered. If the prophecy came true, he would destroy Dante and his kingdom and Tia would despise him for it. There would be no happy ever after for him. Once it had sunk in he resolved to distance himself for the good of all concerned. It didn't make it easier to watch though. That little family – dysfunctional though it may be, was his a few months ago. Now he was excluded. *He'd excluded himself.*

THE NEXT DAY, Jay turned up at around one o'clock in the afternoon with his composure completely recovered. A servant showed him in to find Dante in the above ground library. It was still amusing to see the Dante who partied harder than anyone he knew, sitting working hard at his desk wearing small half glasses like a professor.

He looked up and put his papers aside as he walked in. "Jay," he said, simply. Gone were the shows of affection that he wasn't big on, but still.

"Dante," he replied.

They looked at each other as if taking in any changes that may have happened in the last twenty-four hours. Both looked decidedly better. Except Dante's would have been a refuel from Tia's breath, and his? Well his had been a fix from Ruby's vein he'd had not more than an hour ago. It seemed he couldn't get enough of that woman these days.

An uncomfortable silence dragged on so long, Jay was forced to hurry things along. "Where is he?"

Dante raised his eyebrows and began to stand. "Come, I'll take you to him. He's playing with the others in the grounds."

Jay followed him out of the room and down the dusty oak-lined hallway, back out the way he came. He could have kicked himself that he didn't look there first and save himself this awkward meeting.

They walked around to the side of the old castle to a perfectly mown lawn set idyllically in a circle of trees that had probably stood for hundreds of years. They found them all on a large rug, a picture of domestic bliss. Alexia was kneeling plaiting JJ's shoulder-length hair and Tia and the others were all lying on their stomachs coloring in with crayons.

He wasn't sure how long he stood there observing, but when he flashed a glance at Dante, he was watching him closely. That was it; he couldn't stand it a moment longer. "JJ! It's time to go."

JJ's happiness at seeing him evaporated into a frown. "But Lexie is doing my hair."

Tia sat up. "Can't he stay a little longer, Jay?"

"He looks pretty settled there, you sure you don't want to leave him?"

"No! I want him with me, Dant." It came out more sharply than he intended. He wasn't entirely sure what was pissing him off about the situation and, frankly, he didn't care. He just needed to get the hell away. He took a moment to gather himself so he didn't come across angry to JJ. "We're leaving for New York. We need to get to the airport."

Tia stood up and began putting a few things in a bag. JJ started to cry.

Jay flashed an angry look at Dante. He hated scenes and, most of all, he hated coming over as the bad guy to his son. And it was his fault.

Dante bent, picked JJ up and threw him in the air. It got him out of his whining immediately. Tia touched his cheek and said something in the boy's head as he nodded, looking a little placated. Then Dante kissed him and passed him over to Jay. "Lexie dotes on him. She'll miss him."

Jay was already turning in the direction of the large gravel area in front of the castle.

Dante caught up and walked alongside him to the waiting car. The engine was already running with a Santalini guard at the wheel.

"Jay!" Dante said from behind him, as he strapped JJ into a car seat.

When he was safely harnessed, Jay stood up and turned to Dante, who looked a mixture of confusion and annoyance. He wasn't going to wait around for the famous Dante temper. "He's mine, Dante. I want him with me."

Whatever Dante had wanted to say went unsaid. The guy just looked noticeably stunned. Jay cursed, walked around the car and got in the other side, furious with guilt.

JJ was waving and straining to keep Dante in sight as the car wheels crunched away on the shingle. "Bye, Daddy. Bye," he said, over and over.

Jay closed his eyes and felt an absolute shit. Dante and JJ loved each other.

Then he took a breath and pushed the sentimental thoughts to the back of his mind. As difficult as it was, the situation couldn't be helped. JJ needed to get used to Ruby and their new family. Things had to change. It was no good putting himself and JJ through this. It wasn't good for anyone.

The car purred slowly along the winding country lanes and his eyes fell on his son. JJ was watching the trees and fields flow past sullenly.

"We're going on the big soldiers' plane in a minute," he said, in an attempt to get him to forget leaving the castle behind.

Rather than clapping and bouncing with joy, as he was expecting, JJ just turned his head and said, "Mama told me to give you a message."

Surprised, Jay raised his eyebrows. "Oh yeah, what did she say?"

He screwed up his cute little face as if he was trying to get the words exactly right. "She said, 'Don't forget, Dante, now you've got the Santa weenies.'"

Jay would have burst out laughing at the pronunciation if he hadn't been so adorably cute and serious. The guard glanced over his shoulder at him, almost cracking a smile. JJ's stern face made him immediately school his features. "I won't, mate."

JJ seemed fine after that, but it left Jay with a mountain of emotions – most of which he didn't want to feel. His life had changed beyond measure. He had his own hotel, he still ran the Bonaci family business, but he worked more at home. Now he was classed as a fully fledged Santalini, which meant he was a soldier. It made him feel good in a world that increasingly made him feel hollow. It agreed with that violent side of him that he always kept tempered by pushing himself in business and hard physical exercise.

That didn't leave much time left for his old friend. He guessed that was life. People just grew apart.

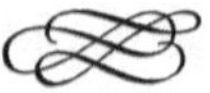

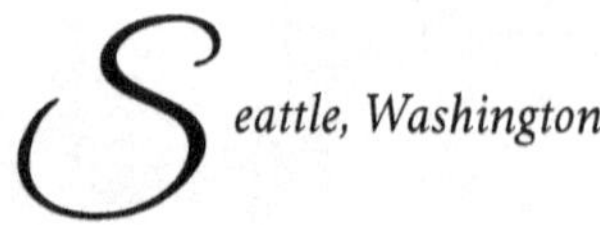

eattle, Washington

"Lord Croll," Seville said with a theatrical bow. "Forgive my interruption but I have excellent news."

Croll gestured with his arm. "Please sit, Seville … what is on your mind?"

Seville sat in the chair indicated and could barely contain his excitement. His pupils were large, giving him a maniacal look to match the flame tattoo slashing the side of his neck. "The boys, sire, our plan has worked … we have been successful."

Croll went to take a sip of his drink and stopped before it met his lips. "One has been captured?"

Seville shifted slightly in irritation. "No, that isn't it exactly …"

"That is the objective, isn't it? A Siren we can control to bring about the downfall of the demon spawn?" Croll had lost patience. A great deal of money had been spent.

Powerful palms had been greased, people silenced and much blood had been shed. All in the search for royal Atlantean blood of the purest bloodline. It had been eight long years since the boys had been sent into the world and so far nothing had bore fruit. Always dead ends and false alarms.

"One of our dormant interns has become active."

Croll became weary. "Seville, please. Say exactly what is happening."

"One of our boys is in very close proximity to a Siren – perhaps more than one."

"You are sure this time?" Croll narrowed his eyes.

"We were alerted a few weeks ago right here in Seattle. We called him in and now we are absolutely sure."

"So, you had a Siren in your sights and you didn't bring her in?"

"We needed to be sure there was a deep bond between them."

Croll shifted his stance impatiently. "This has something to do with that boy, doesn't it? It hasn't gone unnoticed, the favor you have placed on him. Always the same one."

Seville looked like he'd been physically struck. Of course he was right. "You've gone soft and strayed from the path, Seville. You grow weak. You are relieved of your post in this."

Seville jumped to his feet. "Please, Lord Croll. I've worked tirelessly and I'm so close. I promise you, if what I've planned succeeds, one Siren will be nothing compared to the power that could be ours."

"Where are they now?"

In Ireland, sire, at the ancestral home of the Bonaci."

Croll stilled mid-sip. Then he put his cup down on the table. "You are absolutely sure of this?"

"Yes sire, absolutely sure."

A slow smile spread across Croll's face. They knew the

Dubonnetti son had been crowned king, had married into the Bonaci and held court there. "The boy is there?"

Seville nodded animatedly again. "Right at the heart of Atlantean government.

"Then it is time to wake our sleeper."

SEVILLE LEFT Croll to make the last collection of blood from his contact. The deal had been in three lots with three payments. That way its authenticity could be tested and its effects prolonged. It had to be from the same donor. Two IV doses over the last year had already been given. This would be the last. He told himself it was given to his boy because he was his best operative. The truth was he saw him as his apprentice. One any master could be proud of. If any of the boys could succeed it would be this one.

Seville was Scythian through and through in his calling to rid the earth of the Atlanteans, but where Croll was a purist determined to stick to the old ways, he wasn't adverse to move with the times, sleep with the enemy or make deals with outsiders. It was the end result that mattered. Croll could never understand that. He'd made deals with the Americans and bargains with Atlantean princes. The times where they worked alone were long gone. Scratching a few backs was a necessary part of life to get the desired outcome.

MARCO WAS SITTING on a bar stool in a downtown Seattle bar sipping a cold beer. He'd been working on his acting career again, mainly to get away from his domineering father and his preoccupation with Jay. It made him sick to his stomach. He was no fan of Dante's, but Jay was a lowborn human bastard and had no place at such a level in Atlantean society. He'd always thought it. He was chuckling at the thought of Jay marrying his cast-off when his contact walked in. "Ah, Seville. Take a seat," Marco said, indicating the spare stool next to him. Then he ordered him some plain water and sat and smiled. Despite his everyday clothes, he still had the air of a monk about him – something Marco would never understand. Any religion seemed a ridiculous pastime for fools. Still, this fool was pretty handy for him right now.

"You have the supply?" Seville said.

Marco tipped his head. "You have the assurance?"

Seville bowed his head.

"It's in the car."

Seville was already getting down from his stool. "Then let's walk."

Marco looked around him and followed him out of the bar. He led the way to his car, parked a little down the block. When they reached it, he opened the boot, shifted some stuff around and put the black cool bag into Seville's hands and held on to it. "The assurance."

Seville reached into his pocket, not breaking eye contact. "You are absolutely sure it is from the purest bloodline?"

Marco nodded. "Now there is a king, contact with the Murrs is getting easier for all of us. It wasn't hard to gain access. Trade opens up every day."

"And royal?"

"I have been assured that it is."

Seville placed into Marco's spare hand the only thing that would convince him that he was telling the truth – His uncle's Dubonnetti ring. It was distinguishable as the Duke Delissi's to anyone that knew him. "He said you would understand its significance."

Marco absently let go of the bag and turned the ring in his fingers. It was hard to believe that his ambassador uncle was turning against his own son who was king, to help him in this. He supposed it was for the good of the nation and his eldest half brother was making a pig's ear of it.

He nodded. "Good … what happens now?"

"We obtain our Siren. You get the kingdom and the Americans get a share in an unrivaled power source—"

"And my uncle?" Marco still didn't understand. "What does he get?"

"Forgive me. Atlantean politics is not my forte. I suspect with such a bargaining chip he will have greater power for himself with the most powerful human government in the world. Knowledge is currency in today's world, is it not?" Then Seville narrowed his eyes. "He's from your own family, isn't he? I know family is important to Atlanteans. Perhaps he seeks to continue to push forward his own."

Marco frowned, but haltingly accepted the explanation even though it didn't completely make sense. Maybe he expected Dante to fail. That figured. Plus, Seville didn't know Dante was Delissi's son. Still he nodded with a sigh. He'd gone out on his own on this one and it did feel reassuring to have his uncle's backing.

CHAPTER 25

*D*rew cracked his eyes open by a few millimeters and had no idea where he was. He tried to sit up but was sure his head had split open. For a moment his hand went to his mouth, afraid of vomiting right there on the bed.

He scanned the room. "What the fuck?" Flashes of the night before came in a blur. Parts made him cringe but nothing that he could think of that warranted a spell in the cooler. It had been a messy night with some blanks. He clutched his head and threw his legs round to put his feet flat on the floor to steady him. It was a cell. There was no other way to describe it – worse than that, a dungeon, with bars in the door and everything. "Hey!" he shouted, standing clumsily and shuffling to the door to put his mouth at the bars. "Hey, let me out! Phoebe! Lance!"

One of the massive guards came up into his eye line and there was a crunch of keys. The door opened and the guy said, "Out!"

"Where's Phoebe?"

The guard moved him out of the room roughly by the

arm and closed the door. "Come with me. Make a move and I'll cuff you."

Drew blinked, not sure he'd heard right. His mouth was dry, his eyes sore, and his brain felt like someone was pelting metal against his skull, but he fell in step with him figuring it was more likely to lead to answers. "Where's Phoebe, she okay?"

The guard nodded but didn't make eye contact with him once. More snippets of the night before came to him but nothing more outrageous than some of the gigs he'd played. It didn't make sense. Something was badly wrong and it wasn't just the fact he'd been transported back to the middle ages. The whole thing reeked of déjà vu, which was unsettling, as he'd never been here in his life.

They stepped into the lift. "Are we still at the castle?"

The guard just nodded.

It put his mind at ease a bit. The lift went upwards and he began to feel Phoebe nearby. It struck him as strange that he knew she wasn't far away.

The doors opened and they stepped out into the above ground part of the house and stopped just outside of the study. The guard knocked, the door opened and another guard walked out with someone looking as bedraggled and unwashed as him. "Lance!" But before he could get any closer, the guard grabbed his arm. The other one pulled Lance along, arms clasped behind his back. He looked over his shoulder at him with bruised, bloodshot eyes and his straw-like hair all over the place. "Who are you, man?"

Lance's words stung him for a second, so much so the guard had to roughly nudge him into the room. *What had he missed?* Drew tried to turn back to ask him what he meant, but the guard slammed the door. He whirled around expecting Dante but found Alfonzo sitting alone in the chair he usually occupied. "Take a seat," he said, indicating with his hand the vacant chair placed a few feet away from the desk.

"What's going on?" he said, racking his brains and still coming up with nothing. He sat slowly and the guard relaxed back against the wall behind him. He faced Alfonzo. "What is this, where's Phoebe?"

Alfonzo inclined his head and said calmly, "She is in her room sleeping off a very large hangover, I suspect. Do you not remember the events of last night?"

Drew put a shaky hand to his forehead. "Parts," he said honestly. "Do you mind explaining what all this is about?"

Alfonzo slowly stood and leaned forward with his knuckles on the desk. "Do not jerk me around, boy. I've lived a very long time. I have full authority here in the king's absence. You will tell me who you are working for."

Drew's eyes widened in shock. "Are you for real?"

Before Alfonzo could answer, there was a knock at the door. "Come."

A uniformed nurse came in and put a little box on the desk. She proceeded to open it and take out a syringe. "What the fuck?" Drew went to get up out of the chair but rough hands on his shoulders shoved him right back down. Everything was taking on an awful horror film-like quality. Faces morphed into people he didn't recognize and voices sounded very far away.

"It's just a simple blood test so we can monitor any abnormalities."

"Abnormalities?" Drew repeated.

The guard held him still while the nurse stabbed his arm strategically and he watched, heart pumping, as she filled four vials of blood. A plaster neatly covered the pinprick and, before he knew what was happening, a second jab was smacked against the side of his upper arm and clear liquid pushed into it fast.

"What?" he looked at Alfonzo, who'd relaxed back into his chair.

"Just something to relax you," he said, in his usual calm, sing-songy Italian accent. "Just a few more questions and you can go to your room and sleep it off."

Drew wanted to demand to see Dante, but his limbs began to weigh a ton and he just didn't have the strength to move. His eyelids lowered to thin slits. "Don't let him sleep," echoed from somewhere.

The guard roughly shook him. "Wake up!" He opened his eyes but everything felt too slow and far away.

"What is your real name?" Alfonzo said. At least he thought it was him.

Drew's head rolled forward and the guard roughly pulled it back by his hair. "Answer the question."

"Drew," he said, irritated. "Drew Stone." He attempted to stand and gave up quickly when nothing coordinated.

"Who sent you here?"

"You did." That sounded really funny and he began to giggle. He did, it was true. When he looked at the guard his face remained hard and unreadable.

Alfonzo shifted impatiently. "Okay, I'll rephrase. What is your plan?"

"Get my stuff and get the hell out," he said, making a lazy gesture with his thumb over his shoulder. "Hey, my headache's gone. I just realized. Good stuff, thanks man." He nodded sloe-eyed and smiling like a stoner.

Alfonzo looked at the guard and things happened in a blur. The next thing he knew, the guard had his throat in some death grip, which he batted away lightning fast. He was up on his feet bouncing forward and with his hands up like Jackie Chan. The guard came at him and threw several punches, all of which he managed to dodge. He kicked once, in the guard's gut, and the second up around the side of the head. It made him stumble but he quickly righted himself.

Drew staggered as his head swam with whatever they'd shot into him, but the fog was clearing with the sharp spike in adrenalin. He became conscious of his hands still up to protect his face and studied them as if he were seeing them for the first time.

Alfonzo quickly took charge of the lull. "Now we get somewhere. Please sit, Drew. A couple more questions and you can go."

Drew slowly sat back down, bewildered. It had happened so fast and he had no idea where it came from. He'd never fought in his life before. His face must have said it all because Alfonzo simply carried on as if nothing had happened. Instead, he turned the computer monitor around on his desk and hit a button. "Watch!"

Drew's eyes reluctantly went to the screen. The noise was loud and indiscernible – a party –last night's party. He could see himself on stage with Lance falling over and knocking mic stands and drums everywhere. There were angry shouts with small fights in the crowd. Then the stage was swarmed with the huge guards and a few of the men he recognized. It was then his jaw dropped open. Four guards were trying to grab him and he was fighting them all. As uncoordinated as he was, he was punching, kicking, whirling and landing blows. Instruments were grabbed and stabbed with like weapons until the camera lens zoomed in and Alfonzo froze the shot. It was of his face. Eyes like slits and a snarling mouth with two razor-sharp teeth.

Alfonzo ended the show and the screen went blank.

Drew stared at it for a full minute afterwards.

"You put four of my guards in the castle infirmary last night."

Drew went to open his mouth but he had nothing. "Listen

... I ..." A long moment of silence followed where he was at a complete loss.

"Let me be quite frank with you, Drew. You are human and yet your ring is purple. You came into the life of our Siren, and that never happens by accident. And yet you flout our laws encouraging everyone to blood lust around you right under the king's nose. What do you hope to achieve by this?"

Drew was still reeling. He locked stares with Alfonzo. Everything he said was true. A few days ago he was an ordinary Seattle guy, playing a few shows and hanging with friends. He shook his head. "I have no idea." His voice sounded choked when he said, "I was just an ordinary guy."

"Was?" Alfonzo repeated.

Drew swallowed hard. "Who am I?"

After a long, loaded moment, Alfonzo nodded once at the guard and, with absolutely no answers, he was dismissed.

CHAPTER 26

The wedding was to be held at one of the Santalinis' many homes in Italy, at Lake Como. Now Tia was back they wanted no delays in sealing the deal for their family, not allowing any time for second thoughts on the groom's part – a plan Dante agreed with whole-heartedly.

Dante knew it was going to be hard for Tia and so he set about showering her with every distraction and hedonistic pleasure he could think of. It was working. He'd never seen her so settled and content when they arrived at his villa, directly overlooking the lake. As king and queen they would be expected to attend a Santalini wedding, so there was absolutely no getting out of it.

There was one proviso. Dante stipulated that under the circumstances they would attend the simple service, retreat in the afternoon and come back much later in the evening. It would enable Dante to whisk Tia away if it all got too much, and remind her in those few hours while the children napped why she'd chosen him as her mate.

Everything was going smoothly until a letter was delivered addressed not to him but to Tia herself, with the

Santalini seal. They were drinking their morning coffee on the shady terrace when it arrived. It would have been a simple thing to make her uncomfortable and force her to open it in front of him, but he made his excuses and left her to her privacy. It wasn't easy as her trepidation prickled through the bond. They both knew whom it was from.

Dante returned an agonizing half hour later to find her in exactly the same place staring off into the distance, neither seeing nor taking in the beautiful view. The card was still in her hand and the envelope crumpled in her lap.

He touched her shoulder gently as he sat in the wicker chair next to her. "Tia."

Sadness hung heavy on her like a huge cloak. After a long, achingly tense moment she turned her head and gave him a weak smile. "He's asked me to do a small DJ set."

Dante relaxed and picked up her hand. If she'd been expecting Jay to write some heartfelt apology or explanation then she didn't know him at all. Although it didn't mean he didn't care. They'd drifted apart, but the one thing Dante knew for sure was that Jay did love her; he barely admitted stuff like that to himself. It would have simply been Jay's way of including her in a day that was always going to be devastating. It was actually a great kindness in the circumstances.

She let out a small blast of breath as if the request was the last thing she was expecting. "I kind of hoped ..."

Dante smiled regretfully. He understood all too well the burden she carried. Of loving them both, of wanting to say how gutted she felt and not wanting to hurt him by saying it. The bond said it all anyway.

He reached out a hand and caught a tear on his finger before it rolled down her cheek. "Don't beat yourself up." The look she gave him held all the pain she felt inside and she completely crumpled. He caught her before she hit the floor and scooped her into his arms holding her through the racking sobs. It went on for several minutes. There were no words worth saying. He just radiated warmth, love and security through their bond and allowed her to relax into his arms while he buried his nose in her hair. When at last it slowed to a shudder now and then he asked, "Will you do it?"

After a moment she nodded into his chest and he kissed the top of her head. Heartbreak for the three of them was inevitable. It couldn't be helped. Explanations weren't Jay's style and to let her know that he himself had ordered Jay to marry wouldn't solve anything. Jay had chosen his own partner and in this dangerous world it would keep him alive a little longer.

In Jay's defense, her DJing was a good idea, albeit an insensitive one. It would keep her busy doing the thing she loved and her mind off what was going on around her. And she was less likely to kick off with that volatile temper of hers.

Shaking off mixed feelings of sadness and guilt, he reminded himself that after tomorrow Jay would be safely married off and Tia would be totally his.

THE NEXT DAY the house was bedlam with everyone rushing this way and that. Even royal families were late when there were four children and themselves to get ready.

Dante was helping the maid pull black jackets on the struggling boys who'd much rather be out playing in the sunshine. Instead they must finish dressing in their smart black suits with the palest yellow waistcoats that matched the lemon in Alexia's perfect party dress.

It was a striking contrast. Dante thought it was a great idea of Tia's to wear one of the Dubonnetti colors. He wore a finely tailored black suit with white shirt finished with a lemon cravat. Sunglasses held back his hair and the only thing that gave him away as king was the customary gold pin in his lapel with the Dubonnetti yellow and blue banner.

Standing up straight, he turned to face the sweeping staircase when, one by one, the boys stopped struggling.

Tia stood at the top, a vision in the sunlight.

Dante watched spellbound as she slowly descended the stairs. He simply couldn't take his eyes off her. He knew she was going to make some kind of a statement today, but he was expecting the usual defiance and row that would inevitably follow. It was their pattern and one he didn't mind nearly as much as he should, as it was always a prelude to mad, passionate lovemaking.

Instead he followed every floating movement as she glided down in the silk lemon dress that kissed her curves and revealed the outside of each thigh. The slash was high enough to see the Duboonetti crest tattoo that covered her left hip.

As hot as that made him, he dragged his eyes to her intricately woven hair piled on top of her head leaving tendrils deliberately falling like a Greek goddess. Black ribbons criss-crossed her arms and the length of her legs all the way down to her feet. There were no sky-scraper heels, but simple flat black gladiator sandals. The realization of what she'd done began to creep over him.

It *was* the outfit of a goddess, but not just anyone. It was a goddess of the five moons from Atlantis replicated in every detail.

When she reached him he took her hand and turned it above her head so that she twirled in front of him. She was breathtaking.

The old religion was his latest obsession. At the beginning it was just to set him apart as a good king to his people. After what he'd learned he knew there was a higher wisdom in it and that it held great importance should their ancestors return. "How did you learn of this?" he said, when she stopped in front of him with her apprehensive large green eyes locked with his.

"I had to pass the long months too," she said, stepping into him and reaching up to touch the side of his face. "The Murrs still practice it. And I'm drawn to anything that teaches me about my family and my husband." Her lids lowered with an unmistakable invitation.

Dante kissed her ardently in the midst of everyone. Love and a searing desire to rip off the dress were only curbed because of the children present.

"You know it is an honor gown?" he whispered at her ear.

Tia pulled back to look into his eyes again. Something had changed between them again. Everything felt deeper, closer and hotter, if that was even possible. "I wanted to show everyone today that I'm happily married to you."

It was a moment he wished he could bottle for eternity – her eyes brimming with emotion, sincere and honest, and his heart thumping almost out of his ribcage. "It is a stroke of genius, Tia." And it was as far as public relations for the royal family was concerned, but he knew it was so much more. It was a declaration of love.

For a split second, he wondered if things would have been different if Jay was never to marry. He shook that thought away and decided to take the gesture for exactly what it was – a gift to him, and he thought he couldn't love her any more. He pulled her in close to hide the emotion riding him hard. "I am always proud of you, Tia, but this …" His voice trailed off before she could hear the wobble in it. "You look stunning." Then he wiped his eyes hurriedly and stooped down to grab the smallest of his boys. "And my lovely children. Look how smart they look."

Zander wriggled to get down immediately as he was already too hot. Dante laughed, allowed him down and ruffled his hair. When he thought about how far he'd come in his life – from lonely drifter, drinking and escaping with no more purpose than getting into scrapes with Jay – to this; his own beautiful loved ones looking to him for direction. *Him.* He couldn't be more proud of his family at that moment. Being a king didn't even come into it.

CHAPTER 27

$\mathcal{T}$ia stood with her beautifully turned out family under a specially erected silk canopy in the gardens of the Santalini villa. Beautiful white-linen-covered chairs were arranged in rows with an aisle, set a little way off, so they were away from the madness. Even in the heat of the day, all the children stood impeccably behaved as the guests congregated and trooped down the aisle in a constant procession to find their seats. That was all except little JJ. He was somewhere with his father's new family. It would seem that Jay was determined to break her heart one way or another today.

Something was happening.

He was coming.

Through all the commotion of cheering and clapping, she found JJ's little face at exactly the same time as he found her. He looked sullen and hot, with his cheeks bright red against the white of his shirt and his long curls had been cut off into a miniature version of Jay's hair.

Before anyone could stop him, he broke ranks and ran top speed to where they were standing. It was the final heartbreak when his brothers and sister group hugged him as if they hadn't seen him for a year. The children let him go and he stood in line between Xavier and Alexia. Tia put her hand to her mouth when he looked each way at his brothers' clothes and down at his red jacket and saw he was different. He took it off, crumpled it and threw it on the floor. Xavier put a protective arm around him in solidarity. She never knew a heart could break and swell with pride at the same time.

Tia looked up at Dante standing next to her. He'd watched the whole thing too. His face said he felt for the little boy as much as she did, but today there was nothing to be done. His father was getting married and he had to be a major part of it.

"JJ!" an unmistakable voice said, angrily.

Jay. Her heart leapt, then immediately sank. The next moment he was there in front of them – a slow-motion picture in the scarlet and black of the Santalini uniform. Surrounded in a cloud of the most beautiful cologne, he was freshly shaved and his hair was razor sharp, leaving it over-long on top to fall into one eye. Except he didn't appear to see her at all. He was focused on his son; that he'd disobeyed him and run off.

Tia didn't hear exactly what he said, but he was pointing at the crumpled jacket on the floor and JJ was bending sadly to pick it up and putting it back on. "But I want to stay here," he whined.

Jay was irritated by the boy's reluctance, she could tell. She guessed, with a heavy heart, this was the last place Jay wanted to be.

Tia felt Dante's calming hand on her back as he stooped down to JJ. "You're an important boy today. You have to be brave in front of all these people."

JJ huffed, looked down and nodded begrudgingly. "But I

don't want to wear the red jacket," he said tugging on it angrily. "I want a lellow one like Xav."

Dante laughed at his mispronunciation and hugged him. "Just for today," and he winked at the boy.

How she loved Dante and his infectious charm.

JJ seemed mollified, put his arm around Dante's neck and kissed his cheek. The simple act nearly brought her to tears.

Without looking at her, Jay put his hand out for JJ to take and pulled him with him to the front of the congregation.

Tia watched where he went for several minutes feeling a weird sense of emptiness. Nothing ever made sense where Jay was concerned. What could have possibly led them to this: his wedding day to another person, where he couldn't even acknowledge her or make eye contact.

Dante squeezed her hand, saving her from her tailspin. He looked down at her kindly as if he understood it all. Perhaps he did.

With a deep sigh she faced front again. Guests had come from around the globe, representing every branch of the five families. It was a big difference from her own to Dante, that had to be kept strictly hidden for fear one of them died, or the human factions got to know sooner than they should. This one was being shouted from the rooftops. The Santalinis wanted everyone to see how powerful they'd become to have the king's best friend closely aligned to their family – a man adopted as a son into three royal families. Dante was undoubtedly using it to advertise the stability of the crown and that his best friend was safely married off instead of causing trouble in the royal marital bed.

It wasn't long before it began to be obvious that she was causing quite a stir with what she was wearing. Those passing by whispered behind secretive hands and passed it along the rows to their friends that all looked over.

Tia looked defiantly ahead. She was used to causing a stir

– although usually for different reasons. She could guess the kind of things they were saying. Well, they could stick their opinions as far as she was concerned. Today she was here for her family and to make a statement, and she felt she'd accomplished it on both counts.

The music changed from background classical piano to the wedding march – the universal signal of the bride's arrival. A huge procession made its way down through the chairs. Ruby Santalini was at the head with her arm linked through her Uncle Andreas' – the one Tia detested.

Tia wasn't surprised to see the wedding dress was scarlet, dramatic, sleeveless and skimming her ample curves right to the floor. A triangle of blood-red roses were held in her hand and cascaded down to the floor. Her raven-black hair was coiled high on her head with a single tendril left hanging over one shoulder. *Scarlet for the harlot,* she whispered in her head. A little too loudly, it seemed as Dante chuckled next to her. She grinned up at him and he put a comforting arm around her shoulder.

The bride reached the front to where Jay waited in his ceremonial Santalini uniform. They were a stunning pair. His angelic gorgeousness contained in that strong intense body and she the exotic, dark beauty that made other women pale into insignificance around her. Tia swallowed down a lump. The woman was film star beautiful.

The two stepped into the gazebo adorned with white flowers and ribbons to the waiting minister chosen from the Catholic church to conduct the ceremony. She guessed weddings could be more conventional for non-Siren females – particularly if they married humans.

Everything was beautiful and planned to the minutest detail. If it wasn't for the fact that she and Dante had to attend out of duty she would never had put herself through this. *Jay was actually marrying another woman.*

The service went on for around twenty minutes then everyone clapped at the kiss that followed the words 'you may kiss your bride', and it was over. The boys were beginning to fidget next to them and she looked up at Dante for direction for whether it was too soon to go.

After a moment of studying her face he called one of the guards stationed next to them in Italian and whispered something in his ear when he came over. The guard nodded and indicated with his arm for them to step down from the dais and walk in the direction of the house.

As the boys ran ahead with Alexia, Dante gently put his arm in the small of her back and she felt a huge sense of relief. She hadn't realized how airless the place was until she felt the warm breeze and could breathe properly again.

Dante kissed the top of her head and projected, *You did well.*

Jay stood on the edge of the bleached stone terrace gazing out over the lake. His bow tie was left undone and his jacket slung over one shoulder. There couldn't be a better place on earth to hold a wedding. It was now dusk. The air had cooled down to a much more comfortable temperature. Twinkling lights, the scent of flowers and music from several places around the lake made him finally relax. Someone was playing lazy jazz on a piano somewhere behind him.

He felt a nudge. Keenan passed him another beer. "They came back then?"

Jay nodded and took the beer. Tia, Dante and their party had a table near the specially erected DJ's booth. Cash and Sean, Tia's Protectors and the kids were all seated in comfy sofas around them – all seeming perfectly happy, laughing and chatting animatedly.

Tia had just done an hour's set in the booth and even

played a few tunes she knew were his favorites. She was the only other person apart from Dante who knew what they were. "Yeah," he said absently. "On their best behavior."

"What is she wearing?" Keenan said.

Jay just shook his head. He had no idea. He was expecting her in holey, ripped jeans if he were honest.

Marius, Keenan's elder brother, joined them having overheard Keenan's question. "It is a high priestess's honor gown, from the sect of the Five Moons. It is a great compliment to the bride and the groom."

Jay raised his eyebrows and smiled. Tia would always do the unexpected.

"I would be taking more notice of the time Dante is now spending with Cesaré Florianna if I were you. The family openly guards the queen and grows far too much in influence." With those parting words, Marius left them.

Jay should have taken more notice but his attention was taken with Lacy pulling Tia up to dance on the decking set up as a dance floor. They were in their own little world, twirling, giggling and hugging, having had a little too much to drink.

Keenan was now sidetracked into a conversation with someone else so, with a deep breath, Jay made his way over to them. He hadn't said a word to Tia all day and knew he couldn't let the whole thing go by and not at least thank her for coming. Her arms were around her sister Lacy's neck when he gently tapped her shoulder.

Even with her back to him, she stiffened. Reluctantly, she let go of Lacy and turned to face him. It felt awkward. She looked everywhere else but in his eyes.

"I'll go get a drink," Lacy said.

Jay nodded and smiled in way of thanks.

Tia stood self-consciously playing with her fingers as she always did when she didn't know what to say.

"I've been trying to get a minute to talk to you since you got back," he said, adjusting his stance, trying to get her to look at him.

"Well here I am," she said, holding out her palms. At least she flashed him a glance then.

"Thank you for playing my favorite records and …" He suddenly felt uncomfortable, which was unlike him. "And for wearing the dress."

Another flash of her eyes and there was more than just the discomfort of talking to an ex-lover. There was anger and hurt in a second-long tempest she couldn't hide.

"You're welcome," she said, going to turn away.

He caught her arm. "Wait, Tia. I wanted to apologize.

She relaxed back to stand in front of him and finally looked him dead in the eye. "What for?"

The dull sadness in them made him pause for a moment. "For the last time we were together – for hitting you. I need to know … you forgive me."

Her eyes never wavered – except she suddenly looked so tired. "I forgave you a long time ago. You taught me a valuable lesson, Jay. I'll never do that again, so thank you."

Jay was momentarily stunned. It had been a terrible time. Dante had retired her as queen because of her relationship with him. He had only just opened up to how he felt about her, but instead of coming to him she had gone to Cash, her Protector. Lacy had been shot, by god knows who, and his own blood addiction had gone into free-fall. Everyone was flown to Santalini HQ and it was at that time he'd got particularly close to Ruby.

In all the uproar Jay hadn't realized that she'd been treated so poorly because of her new position. Everyone was so preoccupied with the shooting. Dante was also dealing with the situation with Cesaré and Lily and so she'd done what she always did when she was in pain; she cut herself.

Frankly, he'd snapped under the strain. She'd put herself and her Protectors in real danger, bleeding out in a houseful of vampires. So instead of coddling her, he'd put her over his knee and spanked her like a kid.

Turned out Dante had only put her away from him to save Jay's life. So he'd hit the roof and accused him of spite. Their friendship hadn't really recovered, maybe because there was an element of truth to it. He wasn't thinking straight at the time, that was for sure.

He couldn't help taking in her face for far too long. On the surface she was thanking him for stopping her from self-harm, or bleeding out in the company of vampires, but his instincts told him it was much more than that. It ran deep. He got the distinct impression that she'd learned to let him go and the unexpected pain that shot through him almost buckled his knees.

Tia went to walk away and paused. "I'm glad you've found someone, Jay." Then, without another word, she walked off through the crowded dance floor.

Jay watched her for a full minute after she left him. He was in the middle of his own wedding reception and felt as though his whole world had just fallen away. The scene he'd waited for – the screaming, the accusations, the passionate insults, simply never came. He was left cheated, bereft and utterly alone.

$\mathcal{D}$ante watched with curiosity the way Tia handled a private conversation with Jay and was pleased when she carried herself well. Despite Jay's hard exterior he knew he would have to speak to Tia at some time, he'd need closure. The only question was when and with how much damage. It was always going to be a flashpoint. Instead of it going the way he imagined, his friend looked sucker-punched. "Jay!" he called.

Jay turned towards him, still bleary-eyed as if he'd come out of a trance, when Dante walked over and pulled him into a hug. "Congrats, man," he said quietly at his ear. "I'm pleased for you."

He released him and Jay put his hands in his pockets, shuffled his feet and smiled a little unconvincingly.

"It works for you with Atlantean women," Dante said, trying to get him to grin.

His teasing got Jay to finally nod with a smile.

"Seriously though, Jay, whatever happens, you're still Dubonnetti. We're here for you, okay?"

There was a moment in Jay's eyes that was the old him –

the Jay he'd known from when they were kids. Then he sighed, nodded and pulled Dante into a back-slapping hug. Dante held him as long as was manly acceptable, kissed his cheek and let him go.

Jay walked away without another word.

THE PARTY WAS OVER and Jay was sitting with Keenan having a final nightcap before he went up to bed. He knew he was stalling. Arms came around his neck. "Are you coming to bed, husband?" Ruby finished planting a kiss to a neck that was already well scarred.

Jay tried not to stiffen. She loved him and she most certainly had something he needed, but he couldn't be doing with all the lovey-dovey shit.

Keenan watched him curiously, as if he'd given something away. After a challenging look, Jay pulled Ruby into his lap, kissed her and said, "Go and wait for me. I'll be up in a minute."

Her smile fell away for the briefest of moments while she absorbed the slap, then painted it back on just as quickly. "Don't be long then," she said, keeping his hand as she stood and walked away, holding it as long as she could. She was forced to let it go and continued to glance back over her shoulder until she was out of sight.

He was a callous bastard. A fact he knew only too well. Catching Keenan's gaze still on him, he said, "I'm sorry. She's your sister." It was a crap apology. He wasn't sure what he was apologizing for exactly. All he knew was she probably deserved better than his pathetic attempt at love.

Keenan scratched his head, messing up his over-long hair. "Your business, mate. I'm a Santalini, but I don't really know any of 'em more than you do really – least of all my sister.

My family's Lacy and, if it wasn't for all the Siren shit, I'd take her away so it was just us."

Jay smiled and nodded ruefully. He appreciated the sentiment. "I feel bad, Keen. I had to marry, and when your sister came along…"

"You thought it may as well be her," Keenan finished for him. "Don't beat yourself up. She knew what she was about." He narrowed his eyes and tilted his head to get a better look at Jay's neck. "She got her claws into you pretty good."

That signaled the end of the convo for Jay. He wasn't prepared to discuss the blood thing – not now. Everything was above board now he was married and a Santalini. No need to hide what he did with his wife – although it was only really encouraged during bloodings if they were betrothed as kids, or when they married. It was a link for safety and brought down their body temperatures during sex. Keenan had once told him they were given the special dispensation by the crown as food, as they'd been the first Atlanteans to leave the sea. He knew what he was doing was way off the scale, even for a Santalini, but that was his business. He knocked back his whisky and stood up. "I'll see you tomorrow."

Keenan just regarded him shrewdly and tilted his glass in salute.

Jay made his way up the large sweeping staircase to his bedroom where his new wife was waiting for him. On the way he turned things over and over in his head. Something had played on his mind tonight. Through all the back and forth with him and Dante and them both being dependent on Tia like some drug, Tia had never once asked for anything from him. Not ever. Today, after getting married to Ruby, when he'd signed the wedding certificate, it felt as though he'd signed his life away. It felt as though he was more trapped than he'd ever been.

He came to a standstill at his bedroom door with the heart of a condemned man instead of a newly married groom. He just couldn't shake it off. With his head hung low, he quietly opened the door and silently walked inside, hoping by some miracle Ruby had fallen asleep.

No such luck.

She was lying on the bed propped up on several white satin cushions. Her raven-black hair fanned out all over them. A deep-red lace camisole barely contained the lush roundness of her breasts. He had to admit she really was one hell of a woman. "You look beautiful."

Her eyes followed him like a cat as he walked past to the bathroom where he brushed his teeth and splashed cold water on his face. He grabbed the sides of the sink and stared at his weary, drunk reflection.

That was when he noticed the filled bath. It was scented and the surface of the water covered in red rose petals. Candles flickered around the sides waving in the breeze from the open shutters like an invitation.

Jay just stood staring at it, only coming to when he felt the snake of Ruby's arms around his waist and her cheek on the center of his back. "Get in, it should be the perfect temperature now."

He whirled around on her so fast she almost fell over. Instead, he caught her by the shoulders and made sure she was looking at his face. "How many times do I have to tell you, that

…" He pointed a finger angrily at the surface of the water, "is never going to happen between us." His attempt at not shouting sounded more like a strained whisper forced out through his teeth. He'd had more than a skinful to drink and had to keep reminding himself that none of this was her fault.

Instead of stomping off hurt she simply began to undo

the buttons of his shirt. She had patience; he'd give her that. When the cool air hit his bare chest, she picked up his hand and led him back to the bedroom.

Jay allowed it. There was no point in fighting it. Fatigue washed over him so strong that all he felt was a numb acceptance.

"I know what you need." Ruby gently pushed him down on the bed, climbing up his body as she went, making sure he was fully reclined against the cushions.

He settled back with every muscle slack and immobile, watching what she would do next. Apathy was slipping away to be replaced by a hardening of his cock and a searing thirst. If she didn't get a move on he swore he would bite out her neck without the help of fangs.

Ruby reached over into the drawer so her neck was tantalizingly close to his mouth. He took a deep breath and her scent hit his senses like a bolt. Then she pulled a penknife out of the bedside table and opened it in front of his eyes.

Any other human would have thought they were in trouble at this point. Instead, Jay rotated his hips.

She smiled lazily at him knowing she now had the power and he was a sucker for it. This was what drove him wild about her. His eyelids lowered when the blade came towards him. He wanted it; longed for it even. It was the only damned thing that made him feel anything at all these days.

She put the point next to his cheekbone and gently dragged it down the center of his face. The sharp sting should have made him angry that she was marking him up so obviously but it only served to turn his temperature up. Ruby knew it and laughed. Then put her tongue to the rivulet of blood that threatened to run down onto his chest and licked upwards in one long drag.

Every muscle in his athlete's body went taut with the strain, ready to snap.

"Do you want to drink from me?" she whispered next to his ear.

His breathing was harsh and ragged. "You know I do," came out, forced through gritted teeth.

Ruby leaned back on her knees putting her full weight over his rock-hard erection, turned the blade and made a small cut on the side of her neck. Then she crawled hand over hand until the cut was no more than an inch from his lips. "Drink!"

Jay closed his eyes and tried to take shallow breaths to hold onto his control. How he loathed this. He wasn't sure exactly what to call it, but he was out of control and he hated it. The smell of her was all over him, in his nostrils, in the air he breathed – total escape just there for the taking. However every time he took it, he always wished he hadn't. Like an addict giving in.

It was hopeless. Despite his internal struggle, his tongue met the stream of blood running down her neck and he took it back to his mouth where the taste exploded.

He groaned as the high-octane nectar hit his senses and started its race around his body.

Her answering whimper and brush of her breast against his bare chest were the last straw and he snapped. He lunged at her neck and bit down into it hard.

Ruby cried out and collapsed down onto him. His arms came around her like a straight jacket. She wasn't going anywhere.

After several huge pulls of blood and becoming possessed by its energy, he ripped off the flimsy material covering her body, opened his fly and sunk deeply into her.

She was crying out loudly while he pulled on her neck viciously. One hand held her head in a vice-like grip. The other held her down hard by the shoulder and his hips moved like a piston inside her. At that moment he owned her. The drug addict's illusion.

Jay went on mindlessly until she began to go limp and no longer cried out. The truth was he had no idea whether she'd come or not. In all honesty when the blood lust took hold he didn't care. He was that cold-hearted. Even though he was calming down, he still drew blood from her neck. Whether the thirst was quenched, or he was just able to handle it, he wasn't sure, but his brain began to come back to the room. It was the part he hated; the cold light of day. Remorse seeped into his bones, like a druggie's comedown. Shallow. Hollow. Empty.

The higher you go, the deeper you fall.

It was always the thoughts that followed that filled him with dread. Like he'd swapped one addiction for another. Except with Tia it was accidental and almost beautiful. Sex had never felt cheap and he'd certainly never regretted it. It had always been about sharing pleasure and everything about setting each other free.

With Ruby, everything about the woman trapped him. All she had to do was bleed. He was hopeless. It had got so bad that he wasn't even sure if he stopped the medication Dante gave him it would make any difference. He was becoming convinced that the blood thing with Ruby had become stronger than anything that went before with Tia. He despised that most of all. Tia was completely gone.

As his erection faded away, as it invariably did with such thoughts, he was reminded again of what a pure spirit Tia was – perhaps that's what the Sirens were. It was only the men around them that corrupted and debased them.

He hadn't realized that he'd finally let go of Ruby's neck and flopped back exhausted against the cushions. "Sorry, it's the alcohol," he lied.

She smiled and lay down gently next to him, then put a finger to his lips with a, "Shh…it's okay."

His eyes went to hers looking up at him with open adoration. Deep black pools it would be easy to lose his soul in – if he had one. It had long gone to hell.

"I love you," she whispered.

He let out a slow, exhausted breath. "I know you do." Final words of a sad, empty, utter bastard.

CHAPTER 29

*D*rew knocked, then quietly slipped into the bedroom he shared with Phoebe. She was laying flat on her back on the bed with a folded washcloth on her forehead. "I have the mother of all headaches," she said, barely moving her head to look at him.

His face softened immediately and smiled that she knew it was him. He approached the bed and sat as gently as he could next to her. She looked so small and fragile lying there. He leaned back on an elbow and trailed a finger down the side of her face and made circles around her eyes.

"Mm, that's nice," she whispered.

"Phoebes … shall we get out of here when you're feeling better?"

She went to sit up quickly, the compress fell off and she grabbed her head. "Shit!" She leaned up more slowly on an elbow. "Is everything okay?"

Drew had a moment where he warred with himself about telling her about the meeting with Alfonzo, but decided against it. He needed to process it himself first. "Yeah, sure it is. I just want to get back to normal life, don't you?"

She pulled him to her and hugged him tightly. "As long as I'm with you."

He kissed her and looked over her shoulder into the middle distance. Something had shifted in his heart and was the only thing that made sense. "I love you, Phoebe," he said, quietly into her hair.

When she pulled back to look at him her eyes were wet with tears. "Really?" she said, cupping his cheek in her hand. He nodded. Whatever else happened, whoever or whatever he was, that was the one thing he knew. He moved in and gave her the gentlest of kisses. Then he pulled back the blanket so the two of them could snuggle down together. "Let's sleep," he said. "Then we'll work it out."

JAY IMMERSED himself in a few days of hedonistic honeymoon. He was in one of the most beautiful settings on earth, with an outrageously sexy woman who kept him supplied with blood, sex and, when that wasn't enough, plenty of Jack Daniel's. Most men would have thought they'd died and gone to heaven. He could have blocked life out indefinitely if allowed, except his vital organs would have probably given out and he knew the summons would inevitably come.

Tia was the first person he came across in the hallway of the Dubonnetti villa. They almost bumped into each other as she hurried through still wet from the pool. A towel was tied around her hips and stripes licked around all the curves barely contained by the triangles of her green bikini. "Ooops, sorry," she said as she almost went straight into him. Then her face fell in shock at who it was.

He steadied her and couldn't help but stroke a thumb over the back of her wrist. He smiled a little. It was good to see her. He leant in to plant the softest of kisses to her cheek.

Her wonderful smell hit him immediately and he stayed there a moment too long.

Tia took a step back. "You smell different."

Jay just bobbed his head. He understood Atlantean women now. They had much more heightened senses than humans. It was very hard to get anything past them. Ruby would be all over him or, more precisely, her blood.

He looked intently into her troubled eyes and still held her arm.

Her eyes darted looking for an opportunity to get away.

"Tia, I ..." He wasn't sure what he wanted to say even. He guessed he just wanted to explain, so maybe it took some of the sting out of the fact that he'd married someone else. But every sentence that formed in his mind just felt lame and inadequate.

"You're married!" she said, curtly, and pulled her arm out of his hand.

It made him smile. "So are you." A fact that had been the case for most of their relationship.

She scowled at him. "You chose yours."

"So did you ... eventually," he finished with his eyebrows raised in question.

Tia didn't respond but stomped off down the corridor. Despite her exit, her anger strangely cheered him up. It was much more common ground for him than the flat acceptance she'd shown him at the wedding.

He refocused on the reason for his visit and went in search of Dante.

Dante was sitting alone in a shady part of the garden reading a document of some sort. He looked older, more serious and a far cry from the wild child Jay used to hang out with twenty-four seven. "Take a seat," he said, looking over his glasses and indicating to one of the many comfy garden chairs arranged around him. His mobile phone rang and he pressed it to mute.

Jay sat and crossed his ankle over his knee and waited.

Dante put his papers away from him, studied him for a long moment and smiled.

"What?" Jay looked out over the pool and back again, willing him to get on with it. Being around Dante and the children made him feel all kinds of uncomfortable and he wanted to get away as soon as possible.

"You look good," Dante said, with a slightly mocking smile.

Jay just tipped his head to acknowledge the compliment.

"Come on, Jay. Admit it, Ruby is a good fit for you."

"What do you want, Dante?" he said a little harshly. Somehow he didn't much feel like chatting today. It felt as though the two of them had grown out of all that.

Dante sighed, pushed his glasses up on top of his head and held the hair out of his eyes. Then he pinched the bridge of his nose. "Okay, Jay, I'll be straight with you. Tia's refusal to be guarded by the Santalinis is unworkable."

Jay sat up straighter, much more able to deal with a less personal kind of conversation. "I thought it was all for show. Marius said …"

Dante nodded. "And that's true; the Florianna guys are capable but they are not soldiers. They haven't got the same clout with the humans, if you get my meaning. Plus, I need to sort out the mess with her sister. I can't take my eye off that any longer. I need peace of mind, Jay."

Jay nodded. He understood perfectly. The government agencies were used to seeing the Santalini guards as soldiers. Not only did the Florianna not have the same presence but also it showed there was some kind of instability within the ranks and could signal a weakness. "So what do you want from me?"

"It needs to be put right, Jay."

And you think I'm the one to do that?" He raised his eyebrows and shook his head.

"You and Keenan need to make friends with Tia again. Once you've done that, the rest is easy."

Jay put his hand to his forehead. Surely he wasn't pushing them together again. Not after everything that had happened.

THE FOLLOWING day Phoebe was feeling more like herself. The castle that had started off as intriguing was now quickly feeling like an elaborate prison. Learning that Drew had been put in a cell overnight helped her see that he was right. They needed to escape. She felt no affinity to these people – particularly when most of her so-called family had sodded off halfway around the world without telling her.

Drew had spent the night with her and they'd just finished packing when there was a knock at the door. "Shit!" she said, staring at Drew for a long moment. He quickly opened the bathroom door, shoved their bags in and nodded.

"Come in," she said, in an unnatural squeaky voice.

She sagged in relief when she saw Connor's friendly face.

"Are you decent?" he said with a grin.

She rolled her eyes and motioned her arm for him to come in.

He came in, nodded to Drew and sat next to her on the bed. "Hear you've been out of action," he said.

Phoebe felt a bit like when he'd told her off as a little girl. "Just a hangover, stupid. Did you know they put Drew and Lance in the dungeons overnight?"

Connor looked between them and nodded. "I did know." Then looked at Phoebe with that serious steely stare of his.

"It was just a bit of fun that got out of hand. They need to lighten up. I don't even know who they think they are," she said, in the same whiny voice she reserved for family.

Connor laughed on a single blast and rested his eyes on Drew, who stood up a little straighter. "Is that what you call it?" Then he picked up her hand and shuffled a little closer. "Whatever it was, you managed to trash your entry into the Atlantean world. You couldn't have made a worse impression if you'd bombed the place. Thirty people were injured – some seriously." Then he looked sideways at Drew who dropped into the armchair next to the bed. "It looked like anarchy to those who'd like to see Dante's kingdom fall, and there are quite a few."

"It wasn't like that," Drew said, cutting in.

Connor shrugged, let go of Phoebe's hand and turned his body to face him. "You have to understand we Atlanteans are a nation allowed to rule ourselves because of shaky treaties made with governments centuries ago. Some are made for trade and financial reasons, but most are made because they fear us. If they get even a whiff that all is not well, they'll swarm in and take every last cent and every pile of bricks and laugh while they do it."

Phoebe got up and flopped into Drew's lap with an arm around his neck. "We had no idea about any of that though, Connor."

Connor's stare was still fixed on Drew. "Don't you?"

Phoebe saw what he was doing and waved a hand in his eye line. "Hey, it wasn't just Drew you know, it was Lance as well. Why isn't he getting all this agro?"

"Lance has been questioned, but we know about him and where he comes from. No one seems to know a lot about you, Drew. Where do *you* come from?"

Phoebe looked between them and Drew narrowed his eyes making her suddenly nervous. "There's nothing to know," he said flatly.

"If you hurt her you'll have to go through me."

"Connor!" Phoebe's mouth dropped open. "Apologize."

"No, it's okay," Drew said, arranging her more comfortably on his lap so he could sit forward. "Look, I get it, I do. You're like the brother figure 'n'all. I don't know what's going on here, but I can tell you I would never hurt her. That I know for sure."

Phoebe had an overwhelming urge to kiss him right there in front of Connor, instead she settled for looking at Connor defiantly.

He nodded once and slowly stood up.

Phoebe scrambled off Drew so she could follow too.

"Good. Then you need to pack. The king is moving the court. He'll meet us there after something he's sorting out." He reached out a hand to Drew, who took it. They held it a moment too long and stood a little too close for any real warmth. "Remember who she is," Connor said. Then said something in Drew's ear only he could hear. He kissed her on the cheek. "I'm here if you need me." He cast one more warning glance at Drew and left the room.

"What did he say?"

"Nothin'… he's watching me is all."

CHAPTER 30

$\mathcal{A}$lmost immediately, Dante moved his court to Malta leaving Alfonzo to watch over the troublemakers. It was supposedly the cradle of civilization, being one of the possible historic sites for Atlantis, but Jay suspected that his talks with the Maltese prime minister were more to do with it. Either could have been true. They all owned property and even the royal family names could be traced there.

In Dante's inimitable style, he'd wasted no time in putting his plan into action with collusion and trickery. On a bright sunny morning that promised to be a scorching day, he saw to it that Jay, Keenan and Tia set out on a trip around the islands on his yacht.

Tia had been promised a day out diving with her sister, but when she got there, all she found was Keenan and Jay. Then, before she could hop back onto the quay, the boat moved off. Without saying more than a cursory hello, she soon got as far away as possible, perching on the bow of the boat looking out to sea.

Keenan raised his eyebrows to Jay while they sipped beer in the shade. "Gonna be a long day."

Jay nodded. He guessed Keenan was wishing Lacy was there. He envied their unbreakable bond but, looking at the lonely figure at the bow, he thought it was for the best that they did what they'd came to do and went back to their partners ASAP.

"Just how exactly are you supposed to clear the air?" Keenan went on. He was looking at him straight in the eye like he knew what Dante was like and didn't actually want to believe it. He'd witnessed the weird relationship between the three of them over and over. There was no need to spell it out and he just gave him a sardonic look with a sigh.

"Fucking serious?"

Jay leaned his elbows on his knees and watched as Tia stared out to sea while the boat cut effortlessly through the water. "That's not the right question here, Keen."

Right then his eyes were fixed on Tia's tanned, smooth profile and lithe body, easily visible through the sheerest sarong. She looked the loneliest, most unreachable person in the world. An overwhelming feeling of sadness washed over him. He guessed he really did love her because on some level he didn't want to do what he'd been sent there to do.

Of course Dante had sent them out together now safely married—like some kind of test. It did make him analyze how he felt about Ruby where that was concerned. The truth was, he felt nothing. It was an eye opener. There were no qualms at all. None. Love and sex rarely went together for him. Neither had a bearing on the other in his mind and the same went for Tia and Ruby. They were completely separate.

Dante had even sent them out with Keenan as a chaperone. Which was bollocks. Jay wasn't buying that bullshit for a minute. Dante wanted Tia guarded by the Santalinis. He wanted it sorted and done quickly. Jay was the only one capable of getting it done by any means necessary. It was one of those tasks he set and then turned his back on the means.

Dante loved Tia, but he was also king of the most powerful race on earth. After the kingdom, Tia and those he loved, control came next on his list. Somehow, this whole day was all those things thrown together. It was sick but true and only someone close to Dante would ever understand it.

Keenan was still waiting for him to elaborate. "What's the right question then?"

"What's his angle? Dante's always several moves ahead."

Keenan frowned while his words sank in. "Fuck," he said, simply, and shook his head. "I will never understand that guy. I thought he loved her."

"He does." Jay took a deep breath. "But he loves me, his kingdom…ah, he's a complete nutter." He let out a blast of mirthless laughter. There was no point in explaining it all to Keenan. "Lets get this over with … Tia!"

She didn't even fully turn her head, just said, "what?" moodily over her shoulder.

"Have a drink … I need to talk to you."

Jay watched her slowly get up and make her way towards the tarp-covered section where they sat. He passed her a cold beer and she sat opposite him a few feet away, then shrugged for him to get on and say what he had to say.

"Do you know why we are all here?"

She shrugged again and shook her head lazily. "I guess he wants us all to make up and everything to go back to how it was before with the Santalinis?" She finished with a daggers look at Keenan that made him smile.

"Can't we do that, Tia?"

Her face hardened. "I don't trust you to have my back, Jay. Or you, Keenan," she tacked on.

"Come on," Keenan said, half laughing. You can't blame me for what happened. I wasn't even there. Lacy was fighting for her life."

"Tia …" Jay could see that she was becoming angry and

frustrated. "I promise you, we weren't aware that you were being treated like that." It was the truth. Even though he'd acted appallingly and lost his temper with her for cutting her own wrist, he really didn't know the extent of how badly she'd been treated at the Santalini, New York mansion.

Tia narrowed her eyes and spoke angrily through her teeth. "No you didn't. You were too fucking busy."

Jay blinked at the verbal lashing. She was right. He was being inducted into his new family and already getting close to Ruby, but she had pushed him away just after he'd finally opened up to how he felt about her. He caught the vicious comeback on his tongue before it flew.

Tia looked down into her lap while she picked at the label on her beer. "I never have to question Cash and Sean's loyalty, they are always there for me." Then she looked directly into Jay's eyes.

Suddenly it was as though they were alone and Keenan wasn't there. Neither of them cared. "You're acting like you're hurt, Tia?" He was shamelessly goading her, but there was only one way this conversation could go to get the necessary result.

The temperature literally dropped around them. Keenan shifted uncomfortably next to him.

"Just telling it like how it is," Tia said slowly and deliberately.

"Yeah? I'm all for the truth. So why is it exactly you are so hurt – not back then, at Santalini HQ, right here, right now? Tell me, I'd like to know?"

Tia's chest was rising and falling with her building anger and her eyes widening in shock. "You seem to know so much, you tell me?" she spat.

Jay smiled and went to stand.

Keenan followed and tried to steady him. "Jay, lighten up, eh?"

Jay shook him off; he was in his flow now. It was all bigger than him and needed to be said. "You're hurt because Dante has done what he always does and handed you to me on a plate!"

There was a moment of absolute stunned silence.

Tia stood, slowly, without meeting his eyes and pointed at him. "You can fuck off, Jay. This is old. You're married to someone else."

She gave him a flash of hurt eyes before she went to move away from him and he went in for the kill. "Dante doesn't seem to think it should make a difference." He picked up his beer and took a huge glug to wind her up another notch, then added, "and neither do I."

Her eyes widened with the further insult and she pushed him in the chest. "Keep the fuck away from me, Jay." She started to look panicky and flustered. "That's it, I'm going back."

Jay looked around them, seeing what she was thinking. You could still see land, but they were quite a way out. Tia began to take off her sarong and went to march off to the bow. "Tia, sit down," Jay said, trying to regain control of the situation.

She took no notice, stepped over the railing and dived straight into the sea. For a moment Jay put a hand to his forehead. That was unexpected. Then, with a deep breath, he put his beer in Keenan's hand. "Keep the boat on course." He unbuttoned his linen shirt. Put it down on the bench and ran and dived straight in after her.

TIA OPENED her lungs as soon as she submerged and started swimming with absolutely no sense of direction; except to put as much distance between her and the boat as possible.

However, even as angry as she was, she felt the splash as someone jumped in behind her.

She whirled around in the water and circled her arms to remain steady. Jay stopped and did the same. *What are you doing here; you'll get yourself killed?* She had no idea if the drugs he was taking blocked her mind-projected speech.

He looked like a model in an underwater fashion shoot with his boyish beauty and his hair swaying in the water. It still managed to catch the light and remain perfectly in place with razor-sharp precision. Bubbles escaped his full lips and his honey-tanned skin looked vampire pale. The black lettering of the tattoos that covered the whole of the top half of his body moved perfectly with muscle and sinew.

For a moment she just watched him, mesmerized. As a human she never got to see him like this. But he was holding his breath and would soon run out of air. He was foolish to come down here.

He came forward a little as if he didn't want to startle her.

Tia shook her head. This was madness and she pointed up to the surface.

Jay shook his head.

Don't be so stubborn. You need to breathe. But even if he could hear her thoughts, he certainly couldn't return it. She ventured closer and pointed upwards again.

He reached out and placed a hand on her shoulder. At first she thought she could take him with her to the surface, but instead he pulled her to him and put his lips on hers. It was the sweetest gentlest of brushes.

Her eyes remained open and his mouth moved over hers again. When she didn't shove him away, he pulled her in close.

He was so warm against her.

His hand gripped her backside and ground her to him.

It became clear that he wanted sex right there in the

water. It shocked and terrified her but excited her too. The idea was madness as she could so easily kill him – not to mention the shit-storm it would cause.

His arms came around her, encasing her in his body's warmth, doing his best to be gentle with her. Everything between them was always so rough and urgent and very definitely not in deep water.

She couldn't help but contrast the whole thing to Dante. He loved her and she knew that, but Jay had been right. Dante had pushed the two of them together, knowing full well that this could happen. It was a fact that did hurt her but troubled her too. When he did this there was always a reason far greater than they knew. The thought sobered her.

Jay's mouth moved down her neck in small nips. Her legs were already wound around him holding him tightly. It would be so easy to do what Dante wanted but the hurt returned suddenly like a firebrand, pinpointing the pain to the center of her chest

Jay had recently married, and she sure as hell knew he wasn't doing this for any lofty reason other than physical gratification to possibly prove to himself that he could still have her.

He must have felt her stiffen and he moved away but he still didn't attempt to go to the surface.

Go and breathe, you idiot!

He squeezed his eyes shut. Time was running out.

Tia groaned in frustration, grabbed him under the arms and hauled him upwards. They breached the surface together. Jay was limp in her arms. She looked around her frantically. The boat had gone but there was a small yellow sandstone island. A crop of rocks no bigger than a football field. With her arm around his chest she swam with him until the waves washed them both onto a smooth rocky table so she could get her footing and pull him onto it.

The waves washed in and out over him making him immediately cough the water out of his lungs. He rolled onto his knees spewing and coughing in painful hacks. Then she pulled him higher onto smooth drier rocks.

When he flopped down she screamed, "Are you fucking mad, you lunatic!" and she kicked him for making her shout when her own throat was so sore from breathing the water.

He rubbed his leg with an, "Ow!"

It broke the tension and she flopped down next to him exhausted.

CHAPTER 31

*J*ay and Tia crawled to the edge of a naturally made rock pool where they both collapsed away from the crashing waves. The water was shallow and warmed by the sun and the yellow rocks were smooth, making a comfortable resting place.

Air was like razorblades in Jay's throat from the salt water. He totally got now why the Sirens couldn't speak after breathing the water. It killed. He put his arm around her and pulled her to him so her head rested on his chest. "I wanted to feel what it was like, just once."

Tia was quiet for a long moment. "It was suicide," she croaked. She didn't look at him but continued to stare out to sea.

Jay watched an old brightly colored fishing boat chug by. Perhaps today had been his attempt to escape. Suddenly the weight of everything seemed just too heavy to bear. His whole life he'd been on top of things. Now everything seemed so out of his control and he hated it.

"You were right," she said.

Jay looked down into her eyes for the first time in ages.

"About what?" He'd talked so much bullshit lately it was hard to pinpoint when exactly she meant.

Tia sat up cross-legged to face him. He followed her lead and waited. She traced a finger along his forearm where the salt was drying over his tattoos in swirling white lines. "I was hurt … about a lot of things … You were right about Dante."

After another long silence, he picked up her hand, "It's hard for me too."

"Do you think it's a test?"

Jay shrugged. "Maybe, on some level." Despite what he'd said earlier to wind her up, he didn't want to be brutal. The truth was, he had no idea the depth of Dante's thinking in this. "He could be seeing how deep my feelings go for Ruby."

Tia frowned and picked up a small shell.

Jay watched her closely, warring with it all in her mind. She was so easy to read.

"And how deep are they?" she said, slowly meeting his eyes. There was so much sadness in them.

He wanted to remind her that she had most definitely chosen Dante – that they were king and queen and belonged together. That didn't really leave much room for him. Instead he just said, "I have to at least try to move on."

She gave him a small sad smile and nodded. "You hurt me, Jay. More than anyone."

Jay closed his eyes and breathed in deeply. "I know."

They were both silent for a few moments.

There was so much he held inside that he would never confide, like why he'd distanced himself in the first place, why he'd seemed hell-bent on this self-destructive course. But that would mean explaining the whole Darkly Begotten thing. As time had gone on he'd become convinced it was true. Like today, for instance, he could have simply said no. There was something inherently bad in him that made him hard and uncaring with the people he loved the most, but he did feel. He so badly wanted her to know that. It was like an epiphany really. He acknowledged for the first time in his life that he hurt too.

Jay looked around him at the beautiful cobalt sea. Small boats were putt-putting in all directions. They weren't that far out really. The small yellow Island of Rocks was the perfect place to take five and just contemplate stuff. It was the only time he'd been this alone with Tia in living memory.

His eyes rested back on her. She'd been watching him the whole time.

He smiled. They looked like any normal couple of young backpackers sitting chilling and soaking up the sun on the edge of a rock pool. If only they were, life would be so easy. Tia was literally the only person that ever made him feel like that. His worries seemed to just float away.

"What?" she said, grinning back at him. "I look a state?"

That made him laugh and he shook his head. "You think I'm that shallow?" He pushed his fingers through his salt-covered hair. "You wanna know what I was really thinking?"

She nodded, smiling. "It doesn't happen often."

They both laughed. He guessed he deserved that. He sobered, then looked her in the eye. "Back before all the shit happened at the Santalini mansion, why didn't you come to me after I told you I loved you?" She'd never actually answered that question properly. His cheeks blasted red and his chest felt like someone had pulled a gigantic plaster off the middle of it.

When his gaze fell on her again her eyes looked red and moist – probably from the salt water. "Shit." She blinked and a single tear cut a path through the dried salt on her face. "I'm so sorry, Jay."

He wanted to put up a hand to stop her and walk away, but today was about fronting up and mending things and, quite frankly, there was no place to go.

Instead, she continued, "Dante had just banished me to save you. The two of us had backed him into a corner, Jay. He thought someone would assassinate you for the good of the kingdom. I couldn't hurt him by running straight to you. I planned not to be with either of you."

Jay was watching her closely. She looked uncomfortable – probably remembering the brief reconciliation she'd had with Dante in the Santalini pool right before everything had kicked off. The look she gave him proved him right.

He let out a single blast of laughter. "How did that work out for you?"

"Not great," she said, still looking unsure.

It was strange. He wasn't angry with her any more. He reached out his hand and smoothed the track of her tears away with his thumb. "Dante thinks of us both as his you know." Jay cupped the side of her cheek a moment longer than he needed to and she shrank back from him.

"Where is your wife today, Jay?"

Jay sat back with his head on an angle as if he were seeing her for the first time. "What does she have to do with anything?" In all honesty she'd barely entered his head all day.

Tia uncrossed her legs and stretched them out in the pool. "Nothing. It's just that Dante shut me out today and he only usually does that when he sees his nymphs and he hasn't seen them in ages."

Jay looked at her for a full minute before he spoke. She was referring to the water-breathing girls Dante often saw for pleasure and consolation in the beginning when he and Tia had been together. He was trying to work out if she was being spiteful or if she had a genuine point. "Doesn't he do that when he knows you're with me?"

She leant back on her arms and looked at him seriously. "There are different levels of closed, Jay. How can I explain

..." She looked out to sea for a moment. "When I'm with you, it's kind of like me and Dante are in two adjoining hotel rooms. It has interconnecting doors, but they are both closed. Either of us can knock and the other answer fairly easily. It's a privacy thing."

Jay frowned. He understood but wasn't sure he liked it too much. He kind of wished he hadn't asked. "What's different about today?"

"When he's seen his nymphs in the past, I'm not sure if it's guilt, or to protect me, or what, but his presence isn't there at all."

"Like he's ignoring you?" Jay's mind was stuck on the creepy hotel doors analogy.

She shook her head solemnly. "No, Jay, the link has gone. He isn't in the hotel at all."

He stared at her a long moment after that, frowning. Then he shook his head and mirrored her position, leaning back on his hands. It hadn't even crossed his mind when he'd suggested the day out. *Ruby and Dante?* However he twisted and turned it over in his mind he just couldn't believe it. It might feel similar but Tia had to be wrong. Ruby was so into him; she was an open book like that. *And Dante?* It was true he hadn't been perfect with Tia in the past, but that was mainly because she wasn't with him half the time and he had to share her with him. It was kind of a strange set-up, but now? "No," he said, finally dismissing it. He hated to admit it but, "he has everything now, and Ruby wouldn't..." The insensitive words, because she loved him, went unsaid.

Tia shrugged and picked up a small shell to inspect it closely. "You seem bothered."

Jay shifted uncomfortably. He was bothered and irritated that she could tell. It made him examine his feelings and he hated that. "Do you have such little faith in Dante?"

The look she gave him then made him feel worse because

she wasn't annoyed at the dig he'd just given, she was more surprised – as if she was seeing something in him for the first time – Jealousy.

Was he jealous? Was it the thought of Ruby being with Dante, or was he just annoyed that this scenario hadn't entered his head and he'd been gullible?

"She is very beautiful, Jay."

She was, it was true, but as always, Tia amazed him. Dante was surrounded by beautiful women every day, and the one woman that he'd held on a pedestal from the moment he'd clapped eyes on her was Tia, and yet she still thought he could do this. He shook his head. "If that is what's happening, it's certainly not because of her looks." He was a little exasperated that she valued herself so little all the time.

Tia was scratching the soft sandstone with the shell and bobbed her head. "Yeah, he's always hatching some sort of plan. Not sure what it is. Still kind of makes a girl feel surplus to requirements."

Jay couldn't help smiling. That was the truth. Who could ever truly fathom the workings of Dante's mind? Today was a classic example of it; pushing the two of them together and knowing how they felt about each other, to do something crafty somewhere else and keep them both out of the way. That did have Dante all over it.

"Will you leave her if she has …you know"

"Fucked him, you mean," Jay said, a little short with her. He just shrugged. In all honesty he didn't know. He still had trouble believing it. Instead, he began to stand and held down his hand to her. "Come on, we'd better get to higher ground so Keenan can see us."

Tia was looking at him strangely as they both climbed the rocky incline. "Look, what do I know? She's probably at home doing wifey things."

He looked sideways at her to check if she was taking the piss. He grinned. "Yeah, what do you know?"

She punched him playfully in the top of his arm. "Hey! I can do wife stuff."

He just smiled and shook his head. Tia was probably the most undomesticated mother of five he'd ever come across. When they reached the top he pulled her down to sit with him again. "Honestly…I'm not bothered."

He felt Tia's eyes burning into him but he didn't look at her. It was too much of a raw admission of how much he still felt about her.

"Does Keenan know? She is his sister."

"He knows how it is with me and you."

There was stony silence for a few beats while Tia absorbed what he was saying to her. Life was absolute shit at times. *Why couldn't Jay have been this honest years ago?* "If you don't think about her, and it's not because she's Keenan's sister, why then?"

Jay pulled his knees up, rested his elbow on them and pushed his fingers through his hair. It was the body language of stress. A person didn't get to see Jay like that very often. His eyes closed and he rubbed his forehead over and over with his fingers. "What is it, Jay? Tell me." She knelt up and touched him gently on the arm. He was really worrying her now. She'd never seen him like this.

"She gives me blood, okay?" His eyes flashed at her angrily and he stood up and turned his back to her.

Tia didn't crowd him and just sat where she was. After a few moments she said, "We know that, Jay. We can smell it on you all the time."

He looked up as if for strength then turned around to face her. There was such pain etched on his face that her hand flew to her mouth. "I'm an addict, Tia. I can't stop." He held his forehead. "I'm trapped," came out barely a whisper.

She couldn't bear it any more and jumped to her feet and went to him. Pulling his hand away from his face, she wrapped her arms around him and hugged him tight. He relaxed into her and his head fell into the crook of her neck. His breaths were deep against her skin with emotion. It was ripping her heart open to see him broken like this. *Oh my god!* Kept repeating over and over in her head. He was the strongest man she'd ever known. In fact, he was known for his coolness.

She ran her fingers through his hair and whispered, "Shh."

Eventually she moved her mouth next to his cheek. "Don't worry, Jay, I'll …we'll help you," she amended. "We'll find a way."

It was inevitable that her mouth would find his and they would kiss. It was the deepest, most connected kiss they'd ever shared. It was passionate but not sexual. It felt like the seal of a deal or a promise. The fact was she'd loved the bones of him since the first time they'd met. There was no star-guided destiny between them or anything, just pure love that stood the test of time and, no matter how they treated each other or how far away they tried to get to ignore it, it was always there. In that moment it felt as though they just gave in and accepted it for what it was.

Tia wasn't sure how long they were there for. Time stood still until she felt herself lifted and carried back down the rocky path and away from visibility. Their mouths stayed joined until he gently placed her down on a smooth table of rock out of reach of the sea.

Jay reclined next to her and they lay facing each other while he pushed the drying tendrils of hair away from her face. There was a mixture of love and hopelessness in his eyes. He was breaking her heart to see him like this. It was better to see him happy and indifferent than this. This Jay she could lose by doing something reckless.

She went to say something, but he put a finger to her lips and shook his head. "No need to say anything. There's nothing left to say."

Tears brimmed over in her eyes again and she shuffled closer to kiss him. It was the softest of kisses, meant for love and comfort. With a deep sigh he crushed her to him and buried himself in her neck again. They lay for ages in the same position.

Tia daren't move for fear the magical moment of closeness would be broken. During the few years they'd known each other they'd had the hottest sex and she still found him wildly attractive, but this, what they'd shared today, topped it all. This was the closest she'd ever felt to him. "Maybe we can break the blood bond?"

Jay stiffened but didn't move for a long moment. Then he pulled apart to look into her face. A frown furrowed his brow. "What do you mean?"

She touched his lip with a finger. "If you have to be addicted to someone then I think it should be me."

He looked horrified for a moment. "The blood thing?"

She hastily shook her head at his misunderstanding. "No, no, of course not."

His face relaxed slightly, but he still looked worried.

"No, I meant maybe the only way you can be really free is to be bound to me."

Jay remained stunned for a moment. What she was suggesting was madness but, at the same time, perfect. She was offering, despite everything that had happened, to renew the Sirens' bond with him. It was lunacy but felt like a huge storm cloud slowly lifting.

It would mean coming off the medication that Dante insisted he take, but after months of anguish, the answer was so beautifully simple. He bent his head and gave her one tender kiss. "Are you sure you want to get on that roller coaster again?"

"I never got off," she whispered next to his mouth.

Then he grabbed her by the back of the hair, rolled on top of her and kissed her with everything he had.

CHAPTER 32

*A*fter the kiss that seared Tia like a hot brand, Jay let her breathe. Their bodies were moving together and she felt the familiar rise in temperature, but this was different. They'd reached a new understanding.

He wanted her and heaven knew she wanted him – she always would, but their life together had been a constant lurching from one catastrophe to another. His hips pressed dangerously into hers and the only thing between them was her bikini and his thin shorts that could be removed in an instant. However, despite what their bodies were telling them, they must get some kind of control from this point onwards if anything was to work between them.

Tia cupped his face and he stilled above her, his hips now moving in slow, tempting circles. He lowered his mouth so his breaths were next to her lips. Summoning enormous strength not to rush in, she managed to speak in whispers next to his skin. "Before we do this, I want to make a pact with you, Jay. One we mustn't break."

Jay leaned up on his elbows and searched her face, then

nodded. "Go on." His eyes were already focusing on her mouth again.

"If we do this, we have to be in control." She took a deep breath and continued shakily, "We join but only in spirit."

Jay frowned slightly as if he wasn't quite getting it.

"No sex, Jay." There, she'd said it.

His frown deepened. "Because of Ruby ... Dante ... you don't want it?" The words came out in the order they came to him and finished with a look bordering on horror.

Her hands smoothed into his hair. "No, no, Jay, it's not any of those things, I promise, but the fact that we can never be together is part of it, I won't lie." She averted her eyes for a moment while she gathered what she needed to say. "In order for this to work it has to be as regular as clockwork, right? We can't be pissing people off, Jay. We can't be getting spiteful and jealous when we go back to our partners. But, most of all, I want to be like we've been today, always." She paused to gauge his face. He was absorbing everything and without saying a word. It gave her a little confidence to continue. "I realized for the first time today that sex isn't the way to be intimate with you." His frown returned a little. "I want it, of course I do. I could hit the sack in a heartbeat, but for you it doesn't mean closeness. "I want what we had today for ever, Jay. And if we're strong enough to keep it that way, it can get stronger and it can last."

Jay seemed to really study her for ages, thinking deeply, until he eventually nodded. The look on his model beautiful face was nothing short of miraculous because his expression showed that he was genuinely impressed. Without saying one word he'd given her the biggest compliment he could have ever made. "I get to kiss you though, right?"

Her giggle released some of the pent-up tension. "Oh yeah, definitely kissing."

He put his head back and laughed loudly and when he looked back down at her there was no mistaking the love in his eyes. That moment would be etched in her memory for ever. The moment when she knew without any doubt that he loved her. "Shall we do it then?"

He nodded. "It's gonna kill me, but yeah."

His mouth moved down to hers and she pushed her tongue into it immediately. He drew it in sucking gently.

This was going to be harder than she thought. The act was so closely linked to arousal. She shuffled and tipped him over so she could be on top. Control was going to be everything.

Tia kissed him again, long and slow. "Are we agreed, then. You want to do this?"

"Yeah," he said simply. "No going back." His arms came around her back, their mouths joined and as their kiss deepened, her essence left her in one scorching hot stream that felt like it lasted a lifetime.

Jay felt the familiar warmth flooding every cell. He'd forgotten how good it felt. Like being exhausted and bathing in warm butter. Then, when it reached his heart and cocooned it in heat, his body bowed into the explosion of stars that followed and conscious thought was over. The groan that left him could be heard meters away and he couldn't make out whether the light he saw came from inside or the bright sunlight above them. He bucked and writhed for several minutes until the bone-deep need took hold of him.

It was easy to make promises when stone-cold sober and in control. It had been so long he'd forgotten the base primal part the Sirens' breath touched. The promise lasted in his head no more than a second. He bowed and flipped his body so fast Tia was under him before she knew what had happened.

If it weren't for the scream of "No!" to bring him back to his senses, his shorts would have been down, her bikini bottoms off, before another thought entered his head.

Instead he froze on his knees with his hands firmly gripping her hips. His eyes remained tightly shut while he took huge breaths.

"Please, Jay… remember what we said." The voice seemed strangled and sounded a long way off, but it was enough to make him take the time to get a hold on himself.

When he eventually opened his eyes it shocked him how much he'd lost it for a while. He had Tia so firmly under him she was literally on her shoulders upside down looking up at him. The fear on her face gradually relaxed until an unsure smile crept across it. "That's it. Put me down, Jay. It's okay. It's done." She was literally talking him down as if he was about to leap off a building.

He did as she asked, gently and slightly in shock.

THEY DIDN'T SAY anything for a long while. When Jay lowered Tia down she stood up, reached for his hand and led him back up the incline to high ground. Still a little wobbly on his legs, he followed in a state of bewilderment.

At the top she told him to sit and sat between his legs with her back to his chest looking out to sea. His arms crept around her waist and he rested his mouth on her shoulder and gently kissed it.

That perfect moment was bliss. Secure in the arms of the man she'd waited years to feel this safe with. It was right up there with the best in her whole life. It was now late afternoon and the surface of the sea looked littered with diamonds. She sighed with contentment. This place, at this time of day, was now her favorite in the world. Fairly close to the mainland, the glittering sea was busy with small fishing boats that waved from time to time. To passers by they were there for no other reason than a pair of lovers enjoying the view, but it was getting late and reality was slowly creeping in. "Are you okay?" she said, eventually.

Not only could she have killed him breathing for him while on his meds, with no booster of Elixir and no one nearby, but she had never refused sex with him and she wasn't sure how his ego would hold up to that. They hadn't discussed any implications "Will you stop taking your meds now?" she said, turning her head to look over her shoulder at him.

Jay was looking out to sea. His eyes were dilated despite the bright sunlight and looked dark and intense. He nodded and the arms around her waist tightened to pull her closer where he kissed her reverently on the mouth.

It was a perfect moment where all her cares evaporated. How she wished they could stay in their little oasis a while longer.

"Oi! I've been searching for you for ages!" came over a loud hailer.

They both turned sharply at the familiar distorted voice. The boat with Keenan at the wheel was a little way off from an inlet in the rocks.

Tia took in a huge lungful of air as if it was the last she'd get. Time was up. "Keenan's gonna hate us," she said, scrambling to her feet.

Jay beat her to it and helped her up. "He won't, I promise." Then he pulled her in close right in full view of the boat and kissed her one last time.

It was their last opportunity and she took it. When at last

she let him go, Keenan was dropping the ladder. "You'll have to swim from there!" he shouted. He either hadn't seen or wasn't bothered by the two of them at all. Still a little unsure, she hesitated.

Jay gripped the sides of her face. "Whatever happens now, I love you, okay?"

A huge lump was coming up in her throat but she nodded. He gave her one last squeeze and led her to the bottom of the hill and the smooth rocks that tapered into the sea.

The two of them swam the short distance and Jay helped her get her foot on the first rung and she climbed up with him following behind. Keenan passed them both a bottle of cold water which they glugged down fast. It had been a few hours and they were very dehydrated.

They both sat in the covered part opposite each other while Keenan steered them away from the tiny island. They hadn't taken their eyes off each other. Jay's skin had a healthy glow. A little too healthy she realized as he was a little burned. Her own skin prickled. *I love you*, she projected to see if he could still hear her. He grinned answering her unspoken question.

"I don't have to ask how things went, then?" Keenan said, holding the wheel and grinning from the small bridge.

Tia felt herself blast red and didn't answer.

"Not how you think," Jay said, still smiling.

"Does that mean I'm forgiven too?" he said over his shoulder. "I've had a nightmare day, you know. I was just starting to think I'd have to go back and tell him I'd lost you at sea."

Tia giggled and sighed. "Yes, you're forgiven," she said, rolling her eyes.

He laughed and winked at Jay, which she wasn't totally comfortable with.

"Thank god for that. Lacy's been giving me such grief."

With no idea what they would go back to, she curled up on the softly padded bench and watched Jay all the way until she fell asleep. Reality had to be faced some time and she wanted to block it out as long as she could.

CHAPTER 33

While Jay and Tia were out of the way, Dante hadn't been idle. Although, to the casual observer, that was exactly what it looked like. He reclined on his sumptuous day bed in the shade of his picturesque courtyard sipping a cold beer and listening to some ambient Tokio Myers. The children had gone with the nanny for their afternoon sleep, which gave him time to entertain the visitor he knew would show up. He looked at his watch and wondered how long he'd have to wait. His mind wandered to Tia and Jay. Today he'd severed the psychic link between them because of what he had to do. There was also a small part of him that considered it a test. Could either of them stay faithful to their partners when they were together – particularly as Jay was a newlywed and on his strong Murr medication? Keenan had been added to the mix to mend the Santalini rift but also to make life more difficult for them. If they managed to get together after all the obstacles, then there was no reason other than they were determined to do it.

A maid came out in her black dress and small white apron

and distracted him from his thoughts. "Mrs Gardiner to see you, Your Highness?" she said discreetly, in her beautiful Maltese-accented English.

The reason for Jay and Tia's day trip had arrived. He grinned. A little side bet with himself and another one of his hunches. Being proved right never got old. It was time to have some fun and see what she was made of.

The maid showed Ruby Santalini into the courtyard. It really was a beautiful place to receive guests. With shrubs, flowering bushes and shady lime trees lining the stone pathways and framing an archway with a perfect view of the sea, a gentle tinkle from the tiny fountain in its center broke the silence and made perfection complete.

Dante couldn't hide his amusement as the woman warily approached him. They'd met on social occasions, but she'd only really come onto his radar when it was rumored she was dating his brother, Marco. When she'd miraculously gone from his brother to Jay she'd suddenly become interesting. He raised his eyebrows at the whole visual package and pointed to a chair. "Have a seat, Ruby. What an unexpected pleasure."

Ruby perched uneasily on the edge of the seat, ankles tightly to the side in her shiny black heels. Dante took his time in appraising her, making her all kinds of uncomfortable. She definitely knew how to make the most of her banging-hot curves. Every part of her was put together with model-like precision. A scarlet sleeveless shirt cut to accentuate her breasts tucked into khaki Bermuda shorts, playful but also nipping in her small waist and hugging her shapely hips and backside. Her raven-black hair was scooped back into a ponytail in a matching scarlet scarf. Black shades finished off the film star look.

Dante smiled, lay on his side and propped up his head by leaning up on an elbow. The whole prim and proper act was highly amusing. Sex screamed from every pore. He couldn't help chuckling. "Drink?"

She visibly squirmed. "Just a little water, please."

Dante sat up, waved to the maid hovering in the doorway and tutted. "Nonsense, have some wine, I insist." He gave his order in fluent Maltese and she left them to fetch the wine.

Dante threw his legs over the edge of the bed to scrutinize Ruby closely. He loved making her uncomfortable. She had spoilt brat written all over her and was clearly used to getting her own way. She was also not used to being alone in the presence of someone higher in station and her body language was blaring how much she hated it.

The wine came and he poured a large glass of red and passed it to her. She pulled a face at the size of it that made him laugh. "Relax, Ruby...I won't bite." Then he winked.

Her eyes widened in shock, which made him laugh out loud. Then he sobered himself to ask the question he already knew. "So, Ruby, why are you here? Should you not be gallivanting around the shops while your man is away?" The uncomfortable expression on her face confirmed that she'd gravely underestimated him and now she'd arrived was way out of her depth.

He put on his most earnest face. "Let me help you a bit, shall I? I'm just guessing, but I'm thinking it's about Jay's trip on the yacht with Tia?"

She nodded shakily and sipped her drink. "How can you allow it?" she blurted.

Dante tried in vain to keep the amusement from his face and then frowned theatrically. "Why ever not?" While she squirmed, he leant over and picked up the bottle, topped up the drink she'd hardly drunk and then his own he was drinking at a rate. "Drink!" he prompted, and took a huge gulp so she was forced to do the same.

"Aren't you and Jay happy?" he said, mid-sip.

"Yes we are," she said vehemently. "It's just … well, she is," she faltered. "He still thinks about her, I'm sure of it." Then she took another huge gulp, as if she'd needed enormous courage to say what she'd just said.

Dante let the humor drain from his face. "Do you think my wife does not love me?"

"No, no, of course I'm not saying that. I just think they may be tempted…you know, if they spend too much time together."

He pretended to think deeply on what she'd said. "So you think I should keep a closer eye on them?" He pondered dramatically, then nodded sagely. "Come and sit up here with me, Ruby," he said, patting the bed next to him. He topped up their drinks again. "I can see we're gonna be friends."

She sat warily next to him and looked at her glass in fear. "No, please, Your Highness, I shouldn't." She was beginning to panic. Everything was definitely not going according to plan.

Dante, however, was having a whale of a time. He didn't want to dwell for a second on what Jay and Tia might be doing at that moment. Having put the bulk of a bottle in Ruby's glass he signed the maid to bring another one. "Nonsense, Ruby. You've done a great thing coming here to warn me. I insist you wait for Jay here and it'll either put our minds at rest, or we'll have it out with the pair of them." He clinked his glass with hers. "Drink!" he ordered and threw the last of his glass down his throat, indicating for her to do the same.

There was nothing she could do but obey.

He pressed a remote and some more chilled music came on and the new bottle came. "We'll drink this and swim."

She was already shaking her head as if it was the worst possible idea. "I don't have a swimsuit," she said, as if the idea had fallen from heaven to save the day.

Dante laughed. He couldn't help himself. She was acting like a frightened deer the huge lion was terrorizing before he ate her whole. She thought he was getting drunk. The wine dulled the edges, it was true, but in reality, he'd had almost a lifetime of practice and he'd become very good at acting drunk or sober – whatever suited best at the time. "We'll improvise," he said with a wink.

For a moment when he stood and held out his hand to Ruby, he allowed the bond to Tia to open. Everything seemed even and well and so he closed it down again. It was time to get a little more serious with the woman who'd managed to tame his closest friend – a feat not even Tia had managed.

After a nod of dismissal to the maid to give them privacy, he let his loose shirt fall from his shoulders and placed it on the bed. Then he smiled and held out his hand. There was nothing she could do but stand and put her hand in his. For a moment he looked into her mahogany eyes to see what kind of woman hid behind them. He had to admit, he was intrigued.

She swayed a little. He felt a little light-headed himself. The little girl lost look was disappearing and being replaced by a speculative one roaming over his many tattoos. He reached out a hand and pulled the toggle, setting free her long black hair. "You're very beautiful, Ruby," he said, touching her cheek gently. She really was, but so was a viper.

When she didn't protest, he began to unbutton her shirt. She took over with her shorts, stepped out of them and was left standing in her scarlet lace, two-piece underwear. "Quite fetching," he said, shaking his head in appreciation. "Like something from a magazine."

Any apprehension vanished as she glowed under his compliments. The jittery wronged wife was gradually replaced by the vamp he could imagine doing very bad things with. His heart quickened as he stalked so dangerously close he was talking into her hair. "Tell me, Ruby, do you breathe the water?" Her rib cage expanded against him in fear and excitement.

She shook her head manically. "No one has initiated me," she said, in a strangled whisper.

He grinned over her head. Life was just too easy at times. He'd expected it to take longer than a glass of wine. "The downside of taking a human husband."

She moved back slightly to challenge him in the eye. "Very few Atlantean men have the ability either, Your Highness."

He smiled with heavy-lidded eyes at the obvious come-on. She was starting a dangerous game with him. Instead it was she being played with like a toy by the cat.

Still breathing tantalizingly close to her cheek, he put her hand in his and turned and led her through an archway to the secluded tear-shaped pool. They descended the steps until they could wade into deeper water.

Dante made sure he took her to a depth that he could stand and she was forced to tread water. First rule of every Atlantean little girl: Never get into a stranger's pool.

As soon as he had her at a disadvantage, he pulled her to him a lot more roughly than she was expecting. He grabbed her behind so the only place her legs could go was around him, placing her embarrassingly over the top of his bulging shorts. Then she gasped when he pushed her into the side of the pool, pinning her there and kissing her fiercely.

The initial shock at the speed of his actions soon disappeared and she relaxed into the kiss.

He released her mouth but kept her trapped at the side while he caught his breath. The woman was a complete vixen, voluptuous and pliant around him. This was the real woman Jay had chosen and actually married. The one who

supposedly loved him. Well look where she was right now –
all but begging him for it.

He pulled her head back roughly to look into her dark
lust-filled eyes. She was his for the taking. For a moment he
questioned what he would do next. There was always a
reason for his actions, however reckless, even if he didn't
always know it right away. The question, as always, was the
price worth the risk he'd inevitably have to pay?

In a last-ditch attempt to hedge all his bets he allowed the
bond to Tia to open one last time. Wave after wave of
emotions hit him one by one. Love, anger, hurt, but over-
riding everything was a love so strong it could mean only
one thing – *Jay*. Despite the marriage and the medication, the
inevitable was happening. The bond was being renewed and
the severed pathway to Jay reopened. The jumble of feelings
weren't just Tia's but Jay's too.

He closed his eyes and disconnected from the bond again.
He'd long ago learned to stay was just too painful. Even
though he knew it would happen, it saddened him just the
same. However, now he could go on with what he intended
with cold detachment. He concentrated solely on the present
and what he had to do.

Ruby was still looking up at him questioningly,
wondering why he hesitated.

Dante frowned. In a rare moment of self-analysis he
wondered whether it was spite that had brought him to this;
where he ground this woman into the pool wall with his
hips. She was Jay's, after all, and his second choice after Tia.
It did hold a certain amount of excitement, he wouldn't lie.
He softened his approach and began a gentler trail of kisses
down the column of her neck. *No,* Jay's or not, in reality, he
had no interest in her at all.

She began to undulate her hips against him.

This woman had ties to the Dubonnettis, was once his

brother's and was right here with him now as soon as Jay's back was turned. She was either extremely clever or unbelievably stupid. "Are you still worried about Jay?" he asked in a whisper at her ear, almost willing her to stop him. It was her absolute last chance to come to her senses. A simmering anger was building in him that was turning into white-hot lust of which she was about to bear the brunt. "Last chance, Mrs Gardiner." He made sure he emphasized the surname.

"Not so much," she said, bowing her body tighter into his.

"Show me those cute little teeth," he said, passing a finger over her swollen full lips.

The sharp canines sat well amongst the others like neat little gravestones. "Do they come down?"

His knee was now tightly between her legs and she was rhythmically moving on it. "When I'm … excited," she said breathily.

He nodded. "I love a wild cat."

Her eyes glistened with interest at what he would do next.

He took her earlobe between his teeth, put her arms up around his neck and hoisted her up around his hips. She gasped and threw her head back at the friction against her.

Dante grabbed her hair tightly when he saw her fangs slowly descend to their full-inch long length. "I want you to come to me when you feel the need, okay? This need," he clarified with a rotation of his hips. He wanted no misunderstandings here.

Her eyes drifted shut as she whispered, "Yes, Your Highness."

He kissed her lightly, careful not to brush her razor-sharp fangs. Sensing his interest, she broke away to graze them in a hot scratch down his neck as she went. Then licked the smarting skin back up with the tip of her tongue.

He stopped her abruptly and yanked her head back by the

hair. "Behave!" he said. Then he softened a little. "Gently. My blood is a lot stronger than anything you know."

Instead of offending her she just licked her lips and nodded as if it was just a matter of time, which amused him. "I am somewhat an expert," she said, playfully, forgetting the prim and proper act. A single blast of laughter left him on a breath. She had no idea who she was messing with. *So she wanted to play,* and he slammed her forcefully against the side and with his lips next to her ear said, "If you're really good I might let you have a sip."

Her fangs descended involuntarily and her pupils expanded in anticipation. It was a reflex that Dante found fascinating. The longer he spent with Ruby Santalini the more he understood the hold she had on Jay. Despite trying to hide it abysmally, she was raw sex. That, with the mix of her sheer alienness, was what got him off. It wasn't such a revelation. He got it totally.

His hands roamed over Ruby's body, kneading her round buttocks and squeezing her ample breast under the tight wire of her bra. The fact she had it on made everything seem so deliciously wrong. His fingers found the smooth cleft through her panties and she groaned. Her fangs strained to their full length.

"Is this how you reel a man in?" he said, moving his shorts down and nudging the place where his fingers had just been.

Her legs came around and she began moving against him, willing him on.

Tia briefly entered his head. The living bond ached to join but he remembered what she was undoubtedly doing. It galvanized him in the moment. There was no backing out now, he told himself, as he tugged the red lace aside and pushed agonizingly slowly into her. She was going wild around him but he was determined to experience the feeling as slowly as possible. He was as hard as iron, so turned on, but there was still a small part holding him back. A tiny voice that kept telling him what he was doing was wrong on so many levels. But by the time he filled her completely, the word 'wrong' was morphing into 'bad', which made it infinitely more sexual. Then all restraint was lost as he began to move faster and harder and her cries echoed around the enclosed courtyard for the household to hear.

Before long her open mouth was against his neck and the whole idea seemed perfect for the purpose of bringing her there that day. "Just a sip," he whispered, as his breaths came into rhythm with his merciless thrusts.

There was no double-checking whether he was sure. She homed in and struck his carotid and drew. The huge suck nearly drained him of all willpower. The feeling was such an incendiary turn on, for a moment his knees buckled.

Strangely, the thing that anchored him was the feeling deep down that he recognized one thing. The bond had shifted. That meant, without dwelling on the whys and the wherefores, Tia and Jay had cemented their bond again. The day had been a success. Both objectives had been met.

Against Ruby's groans of satisfaction drawing out his life's blood, he became filled with a mixture of anger and elation. Everything had gone exactly to plan but sometimes – particularly where his wife and Jay were concerned, he'd love to be wrong – just once.

This brought his mind back to the wild-cat stuck to his neck. He quickly grabbed her hair and yanked, breaking the seal of her bite. "Close the wound," he ordered angrily. It wasn't so much to do with the volume she'd taken, but the strength in it. She would definitely pay a price for that. Although in that moment he couldn't care less. A beast now rode him as he did her, and he pounded his frustration into her. She was drunk and boneless and was his to command. At that moment he could have done anything. Instead he held her hair roughly and released himself inside her, caring for nothing except his release. It was a selfish physical act, but it also felt like an unburdening of his soul. In that small fragment of time, he wasn't a husband, a father or a king. He had no conscience. All that mattered was the end game, and only he knew what that was.

As he slowed, he'd been barely aware she was even there until she whispered at his neck, "You have the breath, breathe into me, and make me yours."

The moment had now passed, the objective reached and he couldn't wait to get away from her. She was a woman who had always got through life on temper tantrums and bombshell good looks. It was her pathetic attempt to gain some kind of power as she'd done with everyone before. But the day was his and she was now his bitch. "That's not for you, little vixen," he said, playing along and dismissing her with a peck on the cheek.

Dante pushed off from her in the water and her eyes followed him, looking decidedly sulky. It amused him. "Don't be angry, little Ruby. You're the first woman I've been with other than my wife in a long time."

It placated her slightly.

"Besides, you've had quite enough of my blood and I'm sure it will hit you shortly."

After a smirk like she didn't believe it for a second, her face dropped and went white and then a weird grey. She grabbed her mouth like she was about to be sick.

"Go!" he ordered, laughing. "I don't want spew in the pool." He continued to chuckle as she swam frantically to the shallow end, stumbled up the steps and ran into the house.

He leisurely swam, rewetting his hair. Then he got out, rubbed his face and hair on a towel and called for the maid to bring him a cold one. His limbs felt like lead weights as he flopped down on a sun lounger to dry off. It was late afternoon, Jay and Tia would be back soon and he felt hollow.

Dante put it down to the burden of leading a nation and took a huge swig of his beer. It would be interesting to see Jay's reaction when they returned – especially when he saw the state Ruby was in. That cheered him a little. Loud retching was coming from an upstairs window and made him laugh out loud, but there was little real humor in it. The shit-storm he'd created was about to begin.

CHAPTER 34

It was late in the afternoon when Jay, Tia and Keenan came through the archway to his part of the garden. Dante shifted in his day bed gauging their nervy solemn expressions. They were later than he expected. The severe heat was going from the sun, bringing with it a balmy evening. He ended his call with a local politician and gave them his full attention. The afternoon hadn't been all wine, women and sun.

They assembled some garden chairs in a semi-circle and sat around him. Jay released Tia's hand and Keenan was on high alert for trouble. Small things, but Dante didn't miss them.

"Ah, you're back," Dante said, staring straight into Tia's eyes, who stared back defiantly. He quirked a brow and looked back at the men. "Drink?"

Jay nodded and Keenan sighed, raising his eyebrows as if the whole world had gone mad.

They remained in silence until the maid brought each of them a beer.

"Nasty mark you have on your neck," Jay said. His face

was hard and his eyes held an accusation with a whole lot of 'I don't fucking believe it'.

Dante almost laughed but schooled his features. Tia stood, walked over to the bed and picked up Ruby's red shirt, holding it out in front of her.

Jay looked at what Tia held in her hands, then back at Dante. Keenan looked up for strength.

That was it. With the secret out he couldn't hold back his grin.

"Where is she?" Jay said, in a slow steady voice.

"She's probably sleeping off a king-size hangover on one of the beds." He chuckled at his own pun. Then he got serious at the reek of hypocrisy. "You renewed the bond," he said flatly, stating the obvious.

"Just like you wanted," Jay said, mimicking his tone.

Keenan twitched uncomfortably.

Dante switched his focus back on his wife. "Tell me, Tia, is it more painful when I am with Ruby or Jay? I kind of find it fascinating."

Her eyelids lowered into something resembling sheer hatred. Then she bundled up Ruby's clothes, threw them at his face and flounced off into the house. Jay looked at Keenan, who got the message and followed her leaving the two of them alone.

"Are you expecting me to believe, after all these years, that today was about petty jealousy?" Jay said, shaking his head.

Dante continued to play his dangerous game and narrowed his eyes, mocking him. "You don't think I'm capable of that?"

Jay let out a huff of disgust, lounged back with one leg crossed over the knee and stared at him in disbelief.

"So, you had a good day and you're back in the loop," Dante said a little more seriously.

Jay frowned. "I guess … I nearly drowned though."

"I can imagine."

Jay pointed at him. "Whatever you think, it's wrong." Then his eyes strayed towards the house and Dante followed his line of vision.

A bedraggled Ruby was waddling towards them, wrapped tightly in a towel. Tia stood arms folded on the doorstep with Keenan standing behind her. Dante couldn't help see the funny side of it.

Ruby looked sheepishly between him and Jay. Completely mortified, she quickly retrieved and put on her clothes.

Dante watched Jay's face. He was annoyed but more inconvenienced than hurt. It made him feel a little sorry for Ruby. "Don't be unkind, Jay. She's had a lot to drink." He laughed at his own joke.

When she was dressed, Jay flashed him one last angry look. "You didn't have to do that," and pushed Ruby moodily to get going and the two of them walked away.

"I really did," Dante stood and called after him.

Keenan followed and Tia joined him at his shoulder watching the three of them go out of the garden entrance. "Right, what the fuck are you playing at?" Tia said.

TIA WHIRLED AROUND ON HIM, so angry her whole body was shaking. His face was speculative; waiting and ready for her next move. "Is that it – is everything just a game to you?"

His face hardened and went completely blank. "You renewed the bond, Tia," he said flatly –his prepared excuse.

Rage seared through her. "Yes I renewed the bond, which is exactly what you wanted me to do. Why? We were happy. We had everything." With every word it cut deeper. She did love Jay, she always would, but she had chosen Dante. They'd had more children, and then he'd done something like this. He'd ripped out her heart. "You're a mad, sick bastard!" she screamed, and shoved him roughly in the chest. It was enough force to make him step backwards before he bowled into her personal space, grabbing her shoulders.

Tia was openly crying, battering him in the chest, all restraint gone. "Let me go!" she shrieked.

"Listen! Listen to me, Tia," Dante shouted.

She looked into his eyes still sniveling. "What are you gonna say, Dante…it was nothing? Jay's wife? That makes it better?" She ended with a shout.

Dante's anger was slowly rising to match hers. "It's not what you think."

He made it sound like she was getting hysterical over a little bit of lipstick on his clothes or something. The bastard had been completely caught out. It was a light bulb moment. "It's the Sea Witches all over again," she flung at him. It was gratifying to see her blow hit home. The reminder of their most serious break-up right at the very beginning of their marriage that he always said was the biggest mistake of his life. He'd put the kingdom above them then too; to marry four women he believed were her sisters. It had obliterated what they had and driven her straight to Jay.

Her face crumpled again. Jay had always been single then.

Dante frowned, looking genuinely hurt, and the comment uncalled for. "What? No, of course not."

His unwillingness to see what he'd done was the last straw and she fought to get out of his grip. In the end he tripped her, twisted and flung her onto the day bed where he could pin her down. She tried to not look into the angry eyes hovering just above her but he held her arms tightly either side of her head. Every time she went to look away he adjusted his position determined that she should look at him.

"Lets have this out, Tia. You think it's been fun for me watching you go off at every opportunity to fuck him?"

To use that argument was so unjust in their circumstances. Of course it was true, but not today. She stopped struggling and narrowed her eyes in contempt. "You engineered today, Dante, but you wanna know what? I. Did. Not. Have. Sex. Today. Got that into your skull?"

He smiled mirthlessly and shook his head as if he didn't believe it for a second.

"You want my memories, Dante?" she said spitefully. "You're always on about them." Then she let him have small chunks in fast spurts – her jumping in overboard to escape Jay and him following and nearly drowning. Her blowing breath into him with the feelings of such a strong love that they didn't need sex – they were just too close, their relationship too precious. She hoped they stung like hell. The only thing she left out was Jay's confession. She wouldn't betray him like that.

Dante looked as shocked as if she'd physically struck him.

"You see? No sex, asshole, now get off me." She began to struggle again.

It felt like he almost let her go but renewed his grip just in time. "First, I didn't invite Ruby here, she came of her own accord. I have my reasons, Tia. Ones I can't share with you – especially not now."

She tried to wriggle out of his grip. "No? Shame. 'Cause you royally fucked up today."

He roughly hefted her back under him. "Stop this, Tia. I had to do something, okay?"

"What? You had to ruin his marriage and ours?"

His grip loosened with that comment and she managed to escape his grip and scramble to her feet. He stood slowly and watched her snatch up her bag from the floor. "Where do you think you're going?"

"Away!" she snapped. "Anywhere. I can't do this any more with you." She marched right up to him, stared into his eyes and pointed at the side of his head. "You're a psycho, Dante, with all your games. I won't take it any more." And, as the tears fell again, she went to turn but he grabbed her at the last minute.

"Oh no you don't. You're mine and you're not going anywhere." His eyes were narrowed and his mouth set and deadly serious.

She whirled on him viciously. "That's where you're wrong – you *and* Jay. I don't belong to you. I'm mine. I belong to me!" she shouted. "And neither of you can do anything about that."

Dante seemed to lose steam after that and released his grip. Then she ran into the house to pack.

RUBY WAS SHOWN into Christian Dubonnetti's study, at his estate on the west coast of Ireland. Christian was the father the king had grown up with who'd taken Jay in as a small child and recently become an ally. With Jay finding out about her indiscretion, she'd taken off for a few days to regroup and get her head together. What she did next was so crucial; it was something she felt she couldn't plan on her own.

"Ah, my dear. Take a seat, I'll order some tea," Dubonnetti said, pulling a cord next to him. "I think congratulations are in order following your recent nuptials." He smiled, sat back in his creaky chair and steepled his fingers. "What brings you to my door at such a time?"

The maid walked in, placed the tea on his desk and left them to it. "Am I to assume that everything is going according to plan?" he said lightly, pouring tea into the dainty cup and pushing it towards her on the other side of his desk.

How she loathed and distrusted the old goat, but he had followed through on his promise. After years of being inconsequential in the Atlantean world, with his help she'd managed to bag herself *the* most eligible bachelor on the market. Now she'd messed up she found she had to be beholden to him again.

She sipped her tea angrily with shaky hands rattling the cup. "I think it may have backfired," she said, looking at him furiously.

Christian looked at her curiously over the rim of his glasses. "You married and have the king's best friend unable to resist you?"

Her eyebrows pulled together sulkily. "Yes."

"And you found a way into the king's bed?"

She huffed. It was all true. "You don't understand. Jay renewed his bond with her and then he found out what happened with me and the king." She shook her head bitterly. "I want to keep him, Christian. It's all ruined."

"Nonsense, nonsense," Christian clucked and moved around his desk to perch right in front of her. He looked down into her eyes. "You are a clever girl, you know that? No one could blame you for seizing your chances and running with them. You've managed to claw your way out of a family of sons and put yourself onto the world stage. That takes some doing."

She knew he was flattering her but it did act as a little balm to her damaged confidence right then. Everything he said was true. She looked up into his eyes feeling utterly hopeless. "Honestly, how can I compete with a love like that?"

Christian leaned forward and picked up her hand. "You listen to me, young lady. Jay Gardiner can't resist you. You are a beautiful woman and he needs you." His eyes glistened with meaning in his last few words. Jay did need blood; she'd known it a long time. It hurt to think that was all it was though.

Christian seemed to read her mind. "Don't sell yourself

short, Ruby. In entertaining the king, you have reminded Jay that you are a woman to be reckoned with."

She shrugged and supposed he could be right about that.

"Jay has a great darkness inside him and will be a challenge to hold, it's true, but I'm here to help you handle him," he finished, smiling at her kindly.

She gave him a small smile as he began to win her over, but it quickly dissolved. "What about the king?" He really was a lot cleverer than she thought.

Christian let go of her hand, threw his head back and laughed. "Never fear where he is concerned, my dear. He fell at the first hurdle we put in front of him," then his face became speculative, "Tell me, has he taken your blood yet?"

She shook her head. "No, but he allowed me his."

He nodded slowly, eyes darting, absorbing the information. "Good…good. You must keep up the good work."

"I don't get it, if we do weaken him, what then? I'm sorry, Christian, but no one will follow Marco. You're wasting your time."

He leaned forward again and pinched her cheek like a small child. "You are quite right, my clever girl." He sat back on the desk and looked at her shrewdly. "Keep going like you're going, and you could buy yourself a crown."

Her eyes narrowed, not understanding at all.

"Your husband is a strong businessman, aligned to three royal families and bonded with a Siren."

With everything he said, the furrows left her brow. He was right.

"And you, my dear, are married to him. And he can't live without you."

The penny finally dropped with what he was driving at. With his advice and her careful handling of Jay, "I could be queen!"

With their bags already packed, Drew and Phoebe went with everyone else in the household to answer the order to assemble in the great hall. They agreed they would go along with it until the opportunity arose to slip away.

Several guards, her sister, Isla, her big Murr husband, Lance and Lily were already there. Drew gripped her hand more tightly. Phoebe looked over at Lance and Lily a little nervously. They hadn't been together since the party. Lily smiled back and Lance nodded.

It didn't take long. Alfonzo breezed in with one of his guards, told everyone to pack for a long stay as the court was moving to Montana.

People began to disperse but Phoebe and Drew were in no hurry, they were ready to go. "What shall we do?" she whispered.

Drew frowned, then came to a quick decision. "Let's stick with the plan. We'll go along with them and go home from there. It's a whole lot nearer to Seattle."

Phoebe nodded. It made sense not to make waves until they had to.

Home. That felt a weird word to say. Where was that exactly? Not the place she grew up in, that was for sure. It hurt when she realized she had literally nowhere to go.

Drew seemed to understand, he hugged her to him and kissed the top of her head. "It'll be okay."

She turned when she felt him stiffen. Lance and Lily stood in front of them. For a long moment the two men locked eyes as if they were seeing each other for the first time. Lily seemed worried as she was looking between them. "What are you gonna do?" Lance asked, eventually.

"Looks like we're going on vacation," Drew said, with a smile that didn't quite reach his eyes.

"The two of you need to be careful. The king can take her away from you."

Phoebe couldn't believe it when Drew took a menacing step closer to Lance as if they would fight any minute. She pulled him back by the arm but he was fixated on Lance. "She dies if I leave her."

For a moment there was a stunned silence. Then Lance frowned and looked at Lily who shook her head. "How did you know that?"

Phoebe felt like her heart was in her throat as she looked between the two men. They were still staring at each other, but the vibe had changed from violence to confusion.

Drew tightened his grip on her hand and went to turn away but halted. "I don't know how I know that." Phoebe was forced to run next to him as he walked back to their room so fast.

DANTE HAD FINALLY GOT AWAY from some pretty intricate talks with the Maltese prime minister and was at last on his private jet to America. Some worrying information had been coming through from Delissi in Washington that couldn't be ignored. His personal life had gone into its usual tailspin with Tia having gone ahead, determined to punish him for what he'd done.

He had fucked up. Juggling too many plates, a man had to occasionally drop one. It couldn't have come at a worse time. He felt the noose of his enemies tightening around his neck more and more. Each one could be the end of him and all that he loved.

Moving the court to Montana would annoy Tia but it was a strategic move. He didn't feel that Ireland was a safe place any more. The navy was scouring the mid Atlantic looking for Murrtaine. That was nothing new but his biological father, Duke Ormond Delissi, had warned him that the American navy had been scrambled to specific coordinates. It remained to be seen if they were correct, but he wanted his family well away and time to plan for Murrtaine's inhabitants. Their camouflage technology should keep them safe for a while, but time was running out.

Then there was the human, Drew. He was the problem that kept going round and round in his head. They had their human member of the council in Lance. Drew's purple ring made no sense at all as far as the fates were concerned.

His plane landed in Billings and he made the long journey in one of several armored, blacked-out SUVs. People turned and watched them pass through the small towns, clearly wondering who the VIP was.

Dante was miles away in his thoughts. He had to save Murrtaine from the humans, Jay from himself and his own personal life from obliteration. He'd really hurt Tia and he had no idea how to make up for it. He was still astonished that they'd kept their hands off each other. His whole strategy with Ruby had been planned around them not managing to.

Cash welcomed him into his beautiful rustic home with a warm handshake. It was an easy place to relax and see what Tia loved about the place.

The house was like the set of a *Murder She Wrote* whodunnit. A moose head hung over the huge fireplace and a bear rug covered the floor between huge pieces of leather furniture. Everything was polished, wooden and supersized in comparison to home, but seemed right for a big country. "Where is she?" he said, immediately.

Cash smiled knowingly. Their tumultuous relationship was nothing new to him. "She's out back. I'll have someone take your things up to your room."

Dante walked to the stairs with his arm around the big man's shoulders. "Have you arranged what I asked?"

Cash nodded. "Sure thing. All set up."

"Grand. Everyone settled in?"

"Yeah, the new ones are quiet but they seem happy enough."

Dante knew the layout of the farm buildings fairly well. He'd been there often. The horses' barn was straight out of the back door through the kitchen, directly opposite. It was a huge, lofty place with great ventilation. The inquisitive noses of different colored horses poked their heads out of U-shaped grilles on either side as he walked through. Each one chewed contentedly on a mouthful of sweet-smelling hay. It didn't take him long to find Tia in the stable with her beloved palomino, Beau. He was stabled there permanently. A gift from her Protector Cash, who adored her as did all her Protectors. She'd managed to accumulate Protectors wherever she went, but Cash and Sean were the ones that had stuck with her from the beginning.

Dante came into the horse's partition as Tia was

grooming him. She didn't turn, although she would know he was near instantly through the bond. It was impossible not to as their spirits ran through each other's veins.

Her shoulders shuddered as she let out a ragged breath. He hated that he'd hurt her. "Where's Jay?"

Tia turned her head angrily. "How would I know? At home with his wife, probably."

It surprised him. "Just assumed he'd be here, is all."

"Are the kids with my mother?"

Dante shook his head. "They're inside. I'm not sure Murrtaine is a safe place for them any more." He didn't want to voice his growing distrust of the Murrs because of her mother, and just went with the obvious for now. "Delissi has warned of a growing presence of navy vessels in the Atlantic."

Tia stopped grooming and turned to look at him in surprise. "Could they find it?"

Dante shrugged. It was always a possibility. The whole city had been moved several times in history to keep from being found. However, the humans had made a lot of technical advancement since the last time. "It's safe for now."

She continued grooming but he entered the box-shaped stable, came closer and stilled her hand gently with his. "Can we get out of here tonight, just the two of us?"

She sighed, already shaking her head. "No, Dante. It's no good."

He pulled her into his chest, hugged her tightly and buried his nose in her hair. She would always be the woman he loved more than life itself. "Please, Tia. No strings, just allow me to explain."

She laughed derisively and pushed apart from him. "There ain't no way of talking yourself out of this one, Dante."

He laughed and touched her face gently. "Will you let me at least try?"

She rolled her eyes.

PHOEBE AND DREW followed the housekeeper to their rooms. The huge wooden staircase swept up two levels through the center of the barn-like living room, up to a landing with all the rooms in a single row. Phoebe peeked over the banister and could see the huge living space below.

The house was full of people. There seemed more guards than usual and all the sisters were there with their husbands and children. Phoebe looked at Drew and hoped he was thinking the same thing. It would be almost impossible to be alone. The housekeeper left them to freshen up and Drew quickly pulled her in close. "It could be a good thing," Drew said. "It might be easier to slip away."

Phoebe let out a sigh and rested her cheek on his chest. She really hoped he was right. There seemed to be a tension in the air and she wasn't sure it was just down to them. It made her wonder if there wasn't something more going on.

They showered and went down to a huge dinner prepared on a long table out on the porch. Everything seemed just like the cowboy films, right down to a triangle the cook chimed to signal the food was ready.

All the men dug in to the mountains of food. The sisters and husbands chatted, but the king and queen were notice-ably absent. The kids were soon bored and ran off to explore. She and Drew ate in silence, people watched and held hands under the table.

At the first opportunity they took themselves off to a swinging sofa at the far corner of the porch. It was a warm evening with only a slight chill in the air. Drew pulled a throw over them and they both snuggled down together and watched as children ran around and laughed until they were called in for bath time.

Drew kissed the top of her head and she snuggled into his chest. The place and the people were strange, but this felt like home to her. Lying there quietly with Drew, it occurred to her that she trusted him implicitly. She never had a single moment's doubt how he felt. *This was real love.*

The three remaining sisters and their partners chatted lazily with Cash at the table. Their husbands were affectionate and openly adored them. The dogs all sniffed around the floor for scraps making a chilled, peaceful scene. It felt like love was literally in the air tonight.

Drew seemed to get the same vibe and kissed her forehead. They still didn't speak; there just didn't seem a need.

"Where's Dante and Tia?" The big vampire, Keenan, said.

"There's a band playin' in town. I believe they've gone dancin'," the cowboy, Cash, said. "It'll do 'em good."

"Until Jay gets here," Keenan said, like a joke.

Lacy didn't seem to agree and thumped him if the, "Ow!" that followed was anything to go by.

Eventually people filtered off, some for a walk and others to bed. It had been a long, tiring day of travel. Soon her eyelids became heavy and she slowly drifted off in the warm cocoon Drew had made for her with her head laying comfortably in his lap.

CASH WANDERED over and passed Drew a brandy, moved a wooden armchair and turned it to face them. In any other circumstances he'd have felt a little uncomfortable in the spotlight of the older guy's gaze. Strangely, having Phoebe asleep like this while he drank and idly stroked her hair felt so natural. It was the most at ease he'd felt since leaving Seattle.

The cowboy seemed to be weighing him up. He knew he was what everyone liked to call a Protector for Tia, the queen. Mostly, where everyone fit into this new world was still a mystery to him. "Were you human when you came into all this, Cash?" he asked, breaking a long silence.

Cash laughed briefly but his eyebrows went up when he realized he was being serious. "It's kinda not how it works, Son." He continued to watch him with a frown. "Most Atlanteans' DNA is watered down, though – except maybe some of the royals, like the Murrs."

Drew nodded, taking it all in despite the cowboy missing the point of his question. There was something about the older man – an air about him that projected honesty and fairness. It gave him the confidence to maybe ask some proper questions for the first time.

"There are other humans among us. Lance for one. And some even hold high positions, like Jay," Cash said.

Drew smiled weakly. Feeling the odd one out didn't even cover it. How exactly did he put that his body was physically changing and he knew stuff he shouldn't even know?

Cash topped up his glass. "It's a strange old world, Drew, but when you find your place in it, you'll decide that it's a good one."

Drew let out a single blast of air with a derisive smile. "Strange, I'll give you that."

Cash was quiet studying him again. "What's on your mind, Son? I might be able to point you in the right direction."

Drew laughed bitterly. "Even if there's no going back?"

Cash nodded knowingly and sat back in his chair. "Yeah, there is that. Once you're in, there's no leaving." Then he pointed at Phoebe breathing softly in his lap. "Not now."

Drew frowned with exasperation. Leaving Phoebe was the last thing he wanted. He'd never been more certain of anything in his life. "You don't get it. This is not about leaving her. It's about me. It's like I don't know who I am any more. I'm doing stuff, thinking things I never have before."

Cash just nodded, listening carefully to what he was saying. Even if he was taking what he was saying figuratively, he wasn't passing judgment and he was grateful for that.

"I get that she's special, I even get that you're a different species, but why does Dante need to hold everything so tight. I spent time in the fucking dungeon couple a nights ago. I don't think I can deal with that kinda shit. He gets in our heads. Even dictates our fucking sex life."

Cash was smiling the angrier he got. Phoebe turned into him in his lap. "I get it, I get it," Cash said, still chuckling. "Seen it many times. You just need to understand this world."

Drew looked at him blankly, sure there was absolutely nothing he could say that could make him feel any different about things.

"Okay," the big man said. "Imagine this. You have this race of people that don't originate on this planet. They come here with their greater technology, their own legends and religions. They mix with human women and have children. They own most of the world's wealth, land and property. They manage to get into positions of power. They are like the biggest, toughest gang you'll ever meet and the humans, they start to resent it. They see us as the invaders that have taken everything and they wait for the opportunity to snatch it all back."

Drew really listened to what the cowboy was saying. It was the best explanation he'd had so far.

"And on top of all that, each of the heads of the families are waiting to take the power for themselves."

A couple of big Santalini guards walked past chatting and laughing. Drew raised his eyebrows and Cash understood instantly. "Appearances can be deceiving. There are some who would put a stable kingdom before personal gain. It's just a case of working out who those are."

"How do you feel about it? Are you behind Dante?"

Cash stretched out his legs and crossed them at the ankle. "He was a wild one when I first met him, mad as a box of frogs." He chuckled. "Some say he still is. But I'll tell ya, I never met anyone as dedicated to this race or his family." He nodded to himself. "Then there's the great power that came with us from the home planet, The Orb."

"The Orb?" It was the first time he'd heard it mentioned.

"Yeah," Cash continued, "no one knows where it is exactly. Some say it's buried beneath Murrtaine, but it's so powerful it controls the earth's weather. There are those that believe that some of its power is in all Atlanteans and is why they hold the wealth here – not sure I believe all that, but the humans sure do."

"So what you're saying is, Dante has to hold it all together?" If all that was true, then it was a job he didn't fancy doing. It made sense why he just wanted him and Phoebe to conform.

Cash laughed. "Kinda like catching rainwater in a rusty bucket."

"You can't make people do want they don't want to do."

Cash tipped his head in agreement. "That's for sure."

He seemed serious and lost to his thoughts for a moment. Drew got the feeling that he wasn't thinking about the trouble he had caused. "What is it?" Drew asked after a few moments.

Cash just shook his head as if the answer eluded him. "We're on a timeframe, Son," and he continued to shake his head. "Sometime soon our ancestors will come back and we'll all have to give an account of ourselves." He pointed at Drew. "You included. But the main responsibility will rest on Dante."

"Those that sent the pioneers from our home planet of Atlas, came back to check on them before. They weren't happy with what they found. Destroyed Atlantis and cut off Murrtaine until real recently. It's from that time the Siren prophecy was born. That same prophecy speaks of the 'end of days' and it's happening, boy, we all see it – even the humans. The Sirens' appearance triggers a list of events that has to happen: An increase in the amount of sons born to the families, extreme weather, war, unrest and hatred even between the humans."

"Like the Book of Revelation in the bible, kind of," Drew said. Not entirely sure how he knew that.

Cash narrowed his eyes, looking a little surprised himself. Then he tipped his head. "Sure … a lot of the old books say similar things; means there's truth in it. Ours says, when the last of the Sirens are found—" He gestured with his beer hand to Phoebe asleep in his lap. "They'll come back."

"What are you saying…the end of the world?"

Cash shrugged. "As we know it. Truth is, no one knows for sure. We know they punished us severely the last time for not following the rules. The humans sure as hell know it and they're shitting themselves. They're kinda low down in the pecking order, you know?" Cash said with a chuckle.

Drew nodded. "So we have to give an account for our behavior, like a day of reckoning?"

Cash tipped his head and chuckled. "And it don't look so good."

Drew took in a deep breath. It was scary and bizarre but it made sense. To think that there would inevitably be another alien visit felt like something out of a sci-fi film. "That's what's worrying you?"

Cash laughed on a single blast of air. "It should you too." His eyes dropped to Phoebe sleeping soundly. "Right now, being with a Siren will be your biggest challenge – particularly if you're not blood. And the king's situation is tougher than most."

Drew thought about what he'd heard about Dante's best friend, Jay, and Tia.

"Sometimes I think that's Dante's biggest threat right there," Cash said, assuming he was following his train of thought. Then he frowned as if an idea just came to him. "Have they tested your blood?"

Drew nodded. "At the beginning and they did it again after the ring." It was still there on his finger for everyone to see.

Phoebe stirred again in his lap and it seemed a good point to stop and go to bed. It was a whole other conversation that he didn't want to start now. It was getting late. "Let's go, sleepy," he whispered next to her ear.

Drew helped Phoebe to her feet and led her by the elbow as she shuffled along. He paused in the doorway and turned back to Cash watching them go. "They think I'm a mole," he said quietly.

"I know, Son. We'll figure it out."

Drew nodded and went inside, strangely feeling a little better.

CHAPTER 36

*D*ante led Tia into Buckin' Bill's Bar and Grill to loud music, hoots and clapping. He loved the place already. Brash and in your face rawness that made him feel alive. It wasn't often that he got away from responsibilities to be alone with Tia – even if she did have a face like a pinched arse.

There were Santalini guards around, but he ordered them well out of sight. Nothing was going to ruin the special night he had planned. A table had been reserved for them, but he decided to let the five-deep atmosphere at the bar help her loosen up before he took her there.

The trouble was she knew him too well. Her eyes narrowed when he passed her a beer and a sour mash chaser. "Don't start them tricks, mister," she said, knocking the chaser straight back.

He grinned and did the same. She could match him drink for drink and he loved that about her. He ordered two more each.

Pretty soon her foot was tapping and her eyelids were

lowering. It was all he could do to stop himself scooping her up and kissing her right there.

"Stay where you are, big guy, and don't get any funny ideas," she said, pointing her finger at him, making him laugh out loud.

"Can't I spend a little time with me wife, now?" he said in his thickest Irish accent.

Her face immediately dropped into a scowl. "Shame you didn't think about that when you sent me off so you could shag Jay's wife!"

"Ah come on, Tia!" And he pulled her to him.

She struggled a little but only half-heartedly. He took comfort from the thought that she wanted him to comfort her. "It was a mistake, but I had to do something."

She pushed away from him so she could look into his face. "What, just so you could make me have Santalini guards?"

He tipped his head. "It was part of the reason, but not all."

She was getting angry and went to push away completely but he stopped her. "Please, Tia, just hear me out and you can go on your way."

She huffed and looked up at him with a blank face like she doubted he could make a dent when her mind was made up. "Well go on then."

The music seemed louder and he didn't want to shout, so he called out another order to the bar man and led her to their table in a quieter corner.

"Well I'm listening."

Dante studied her angry, hurt face, not sure how much to tell her. He didn't want to blow his whole plan, but he was going to have to save the situation somehow having crossed a serious line with her. "You know how bad Jay's got over the last few months."

"So you thought sleeping with his wife would help him out? Good one!"

"That part I hadn't planned, I swear," he said, holding up his hands in surrender.

Tia rolled her eyes and started examining her nails as if she were bored.

"Listen, Tia, there's something very wrong with Jay. In all the years I've known him, he's never been this reckless. And as odd as this sounds, it's not you."

Dante detected something through the bond that pulled him up short. Where he would have expected jealousy, what came over in spades was guilt. There was something she wasn't telling him. He reached out a hand and held her chin so she had to look at him. "What is it?"

"I can't tell you, Dante. I made a promise. I can't break that kind of trust."

Dante pulled his hand away and studied her closely. It was killing him to not to find out what was discussed but he decided at this point it was good leverage. Instead he just nodded and felt her relax. "So Jay talked, you breathed for him – even though he is on strong medication, and you didn't have sex?" he said, in way of a recap.

Tia bobbed her head. "That's about the size of it."

After a long minute weighing up what to say and what not to say he decided to loosely base it on the truth. "I didn't know she'd come when you were out."

Tia narrowed her eyes about to launch into a tirade of abuse.

He held up a silencing hand. "But it was a fair guess that she would. She wanted an ally in keeping you and Jay apart, and I decided to do a little acting."

Tia scowled.

"Ah, you can't blame her. He is her husband after all."

Tia rolled her eyes. "Don't you dare start standing up for

her. And that doesn't explain how that got from chatting to shagging."

Dante laughed. "I admit I did get her drunk to gain her trust. Then I wanted to take her down a peg or two, so I got her in the pool … and the rest, you know about."

Tia tutted, having heard enough and went to get up. Dante caught her by the wrist. "Look, I haven't forced you to tell me what you and Jay have cooked up," he whispered. "But Ruby is very into me now and that gives me a certain amount of power over her."

Tia went to snatch her arm away, but there was something in his intense gaze. Something that seemed to link into what Jay had confided to her.

She slid back into her seat. "What are you saying?"

The look in his eyes went from mischievous, to serious, then to cautious all in a matter of seconds. "I mean I let her drink from me."

"Oh that." And she went to get up.

"Look, my blood is stronger than Jay's – stronger than most Atlanteans."

She slowly sunk into her chair again and narrowed her eyes. What he was trying to say to her was gradually sinking in. "And highly addictive," she finished for him.

He nodded somberly. "I'm not proud of it, Tia. You have to believe me."

"You never drank from her, did—?"

"No," he said, shaking his head vigorously. "Nooo. Nor would I."

She studied his face. It was a ludicrous excuse for a husband to give his wife when caught cheating. But from Dante, in this fucked-up world where they both lived, it rang true. In one day he'd managed to solve Jay's problem, well was on his way to, and in a way she would never have thought of. The idea of Dante crushing Ruby like a bug really appealed to her.

His lips began to curl at the corners as he seemed to read her mind. He held out a hand and stood up. "We have a couple of hours, let's spend it wisely," he said, with a smile that held so much regret she found herself standing and putting her hand in his.

She allowed him to lead her through the crowds of revelers as the steel guitars started playing a love song. When they reached the center of the dance floor he pulled her to him and just held her.

Tia felt the familiar flutterings in her chest and tried not to get caught up by him. She reminded herself over and over what an absolute scumbag he could be.

"Park it just for one evening, Tia. You can hate me again tomorrow," he said in her ear while gently moving with her. "One night is all I ask."

She laughed a little, more at his cheek than anything. Then she leant back a little to look into his eyes that held a softness in them tonight. "So you did it all for Jay?" She continued to watch him closely.

He bobbed his head. "Partly, and partly in curiosity ... I know what he sees in you," he said, allowing her to finish the train of thought with some of the old twinkle in his eye.

However, before she could get annoyed again he said, "And I'm not so sure she's working alone."

Before she could hitch in a breath in shock, he whirled her around and pulled her to him signaling the discussion was over. She wanted to question him further, but she knew it was useless. "Enough serious stuff," he said.

Instead she sighed into his chest and moved with him perfectly like they were made for each other which, of course, they were.

But as wonderful and sexy as he was, she couldn't help

wondering what was happening with Jay. Her heart pined for him.

Tia didn't say much on the way back to the ranch. It was late and they were tired. The guard had let Dante drive them back alone in their SUV, as long as they were escorted in the cars front and behind. It was only an old dirt road anyway. It gave them a little privacy at least.

They came to the pool made by the old creek, and Dante pulled into the side of the road and stopped. He picked up the two-way radio in the door panel and ordered the guards to go on a bit. They watched the cars disappear and both sat in silence as if they could see further than just a few feet. It was the place where Lacy was shot the previous year. Tia remembered it vividly with a shudder. She had been staying with Cash when Dante had sent her away. Jay, who thought she should have come to him, had come after her and Keenan and Lacy had joined them. It had turned into kind of a holiday for a while. They'd all been swimming in the pool on a hot day when a sniper took a shot at them. It was still unclear who the target was or who was responsible for it. After all, there would have been major repercussions should any one of them have died. The fact that Lacy had been hit kind of made it more likely to be humans. An Atlantean faction would have wanted her alive at all costs. It suited humans to kill or capture a Siren.

Tia looked over at Dante from the passenger seat and wondered if he was thinking the same thing. How close he came to losing it all. He was beautiful in the light from the dashboard. He was older and more serious than he used to be, but the devil was certainly still in him. He turned, smiling, in his seat and gazed intently back at her with those steely grey eyes of his alive with mischief. He had to be the hardest man in the world to resist – especially when he whispered, "Give me tonight, Tia."

An intense feeling of longing reached out to her through the bond. "Just tonight."

She closed her eyes and pretended to look out of the window, too black to see much of anything. "I can't," she whispered to herself.

Dante studied her for a minute and he knew she was in turmoil. It was a mixture of not wanting to keep getting hurt and some weird misguided loyalty to Jay who was probably working as they spoke to save his own marriage.

There was also a niggling tension in the bond. Something was brewing back at the ranch and they should really head back, but somehow, he knew that the nearer to that she got, the tougher her resolve would be. One lousy hour wouldn't make much difference to whatever shit was about to kick off. His whole bloody life was spent dealing with problems. He was an old hand at it.

Suddenly he felt unbelievably tired of it all. He closed his eyes for a long moment then looked over at Tia. She was looking down at her hands in her lap. "Then I'll make it easier for you."

Her eyes immediately went to his as if he was going to give her a break. However, he didn't feel charitable tonight. "I command you to get out of this car."

Tia let out a single blast of laughter thinking he was joking. After a few beats of gauging his unmovable expression, her eyes went wide with understanding. She unclipped her seatbelt and got out of the car.

After a moment composing himself – only too aware that he was improvising here – he got out and walked around to join her.

She was leaning back lazily against the car but her emotions were firing off like the National Grid.

He cupped the side of her face and rubbed a thumb along the cheekbones. "No need for guilt here, Tia. All this is my fault." He felt real sympathy for her as he moved in for the kiss. "Jay knows," he whispered softly against her lips.

Dante held both sides of her face and kissed her softly. Tears were falling gently down her cheek. "Come ... forget everything for a while." He picked up her hand and led her towards the creek.

CHAPTER 37

*P*hoebe had gone off to sleep as soon as her head hit the pillow. Drew got in the bed as weightlessly as possible but, despite it being late, sleep wasn't coming any time soon. After much tossing and turning, he gave up and lay looking up at the ceiling.

He mulled over the conversation he'd had with Cash. If he wasn't such a grounded, sane guy he could have dismissed the whole thing as madness. Although that and what he'd seen happening to himself over the last few weeks made everything start to click into place.

Then he thought about the shock he'd seen on Lance's face when he said he knew Phoebe would die if he left her. *How did he know that?* Maybe it was because he knew she loved him and would simply be broken-hearted. Deep down, he knew that wasn't it. Knowledge came to him from somewhere and he couldn't for the life of him pin point how.

It was troubling, because if it was true that Phoebe would die, he needed to find out more about it.

Now he was wide awake. He looked across at Phoebe and could hear the soft purr of her breathing.

Carefully, he slid out of bed, pulled on his jeans and baggy t-shirt, then he padded softly to the door and slipped out. He headed down to the kitchen in the hope of grabbing some milk or something to help him sleep. As soon as he arrived, he knew he wasn't the only one. The soft under-counter lighting was on and a female already had their head in the fridge.

She went to turn with a plate of something and yelped in surprise. "Oh! You made me jump!" she said, holding her chest.

"Sorry," he said, holding up a hand recognizing the girl as Lacy – the sister married to the big vampire, Keenan.

"Can't sleep too, eh?" she said, sitting at the island. "Help yourself. There's tons of food in the fridge."

Drew relaxed a little, went to the fridge and took out the carton of milk. Then he found a glass in one of the cupboards and sat down across from her.

"Cookie?" She pushed a jar over to him.

Drew marveled how someone could be so striking and similar to Phoebe in so many ways and yet be so different. Her hair was dark brunette where Phoebe's was a rich auburn red. Lacy's eyes were a ripe apple green, while Phoebe's were mixed with colors of autumn, which of course changed into the wild animal version he'd grown to love. He wondered whether Lacy changed like that? "Sorry, we haven't spoken much. You're Lacy, aren't you?"

She nodded with a huge mouthful of a doorstop sandwich she'd put together. "No worries. It's madness first of all, I get it." She held up her half-eaten sandwich. "You want one?"

He bobbed his head. "Sure, I can't sleep anyway."

She busied herself making another sandwich that started to resemble a Scooby snack. He put up a hand. "That's it, thanks."

Lacy slapped the top piece of bread on it and passed it across to him without a plate.

"Thanks," and he took a huge bite. There simply was no other way of tackling it.

"Worked up an appetite, huh?" she said, mouth full, nodding with a wink.

He laughed. "Not yet." They both laughed and ate in silence for a few moments.

"Have you been with your guy long?" he said, eventually.

"Since we were kids," she said, popping in the last of her sandwich.

He raised his eyebrows. That kind of history together surprised him. "I thought you all stumbled across your Protectors by accident."

"He's not my Protector – well, he is, like he over-protects me, but no, he's my prince, my most compatible. We're one of the lucky ones."

Drew nodded slowly trying to piece it together with all the other snippets of information he had. The old five prince, five sister thing, but, "Lucky?"

It started to make sense when she explained that if Phoebe wasn't with her prince then he was probably still out in the world and he wished he hadn't asked. It also explained the upset over his purple ring, which kind of said the opposite.

"Isla does too, but we know who he is and we don't really talk about him."

Drew nodded, none the wiser.

"And there's the whole Dante, Jay, Tia, thing," she added, as if everything was common knowledge.

He continued to nod, not wanting to get into all that. Quite honestly, he didn't really care about that shit. He got that it all seemed fucked up apart from her relationship with Keenan, and guessed that's what she meant by lucky. There was just one thing that burned inside him to know. "Does he drink your blood?" he asked, quickly before he could think better of it. Then put up his hands. "Sorry, that's none of my business."

She seemed to study him for a moment before she spoke. "It's illegal, you know, Drew," she said softly.

Her tone made him feel a little uncomfortable. "But he is a vampire and, you know, a Santalini?"

She bobbed her head and put down the cookie in her hand to get serious. "Listen, Drew. Santalinis have it in their nature. They developed it from way back. Some say it's because they were the first of the families to live on land and needed blood to survive. Nowadays it's done at puberty and marriage," she said, counting it off on her fingers. "But we have the bond. We don't need the blood thing…The whole breathing thing, well, it's way stronger than blood."

He guessed that was true if it was a two-way thing, which ruled him out.

"So is that what all the trouble is about? Have you two been doing it?" she said, eyes wide with scandal.

He laughed, taking another bite of his sandwich. It seemed the understatement of the century. "Oh yeah, we've been doing it."

"What?" she squealed. "You devil. Tell all. What's it like for a human?"

It seemed the most absurd comment he'd heard so far, but he felt carried along by her excitement. "Like the best drug ever," he said, laughing into his sandwich.

"What's going on in here?" a deep voice said from the doorway behind him.

Lacy's eyes went wide in warning. "Keenan!"

The vampire prowled in like a big cat in just his battered jeans.

"Just eating and chatting, baby," Lacy said, a little too merrily.

Drew shifted, wondering if he should be nervous too. The guy was twice his size in every direction.

"I heard," Keenan said, flatly.

The guy's hostility was palpable. Drew slid off his stool, quite willing to take the hint that snack time was over. "Lacy just kindly made me a sandwich." He turned his body slightly to Lacy. "Thank you, Lacy. Goodnight."

She smiled apologetically. "My pleasure. Night, Drew."

For some reason completely unknown to him, the vampire walked right up into his space and towered over him. "I don't know you and I don't like you, so you keep your distance from her. Are we clear?"

Lacy flashed around the island to get to them. "Keenan!" she hissed, hanging off his arm, trying to pull him backwards but he wouldn't budge.

Then Drew must have blacked out or something as Cash had him pinned to the counter and Cesaré, the king's right-hand man, was holding back Keenan who was bleeding from the mouth. Lacy stood between them very upset.

Just as he thought the night couldn't get any worse, Dante walked in with the girl he guessed was the other sister, looking like they'd just had a shower with water still dripping from their hair.

Cash released his grip on Drew slowly, like a school bully getting caught in the act. It was then he homed in on the blood on Cash's t-shirt and when he looked down it was all over his own chest.

"I had to split these two up," Cash said, in way of explanation.

Everything felt weird. He was violently shaking. His vision was coming and going so he had to keep shaking his head. The coppery tang made him run his tongue over his teeth and he felt his elongated fangs. *Shit!* The changes to his body he'd wanted to hide were now on full view for everyone to see. Then not much else registered as he dropped to the floor in body-bowing convulsions.

He could see the vampire standing over him in flashes of vision. "That's it, arsehole. Mine's supercharged. I hope it fucking kills you."

"He bit you?" a gravelly voice said.

"Yes he fucking bit me. Latched onto my neck like a ferret."

DANTE WATCHED as Drew dry-heaved and his eyes went up into his head. There was a lot of blood – far too much for the injury Keenan had. "You bit him back?"

Keenan glared at him with his hands on his hips. "Yes. For fuck's sake. Just a nick to get him to let go of me."

Dante exchanged a look with Cesaré who still had his arm across Keenan's chest. He was thinking the same thing. Yet another person linked to Drew through blood. "Everyone to bed!" he shouted. Suddenly he felt very weary. "I'll deal with this tomorrow." He looked at one of his guards. "Make sure Drew stays in his room."

Tia went to turn away to make for the stairs. *My room, Tia. It's not morning yet,* he projected.

She paused and nodded. The hush in the room meant the exchange didn't go unnoticed.

"GET UP! Get up! Everyone. They're gonna kill each other. Come on … outside!

It was Lacy's voice, running up and down the hallway, banging on all the doors. Phoebe's eyes cracked open to Drew facing her awake too.

"Get up!" With another loud rap at their door.

They both wordlessly slipped out of bed and pulled on the first t-shirt and jeans that came to hand. Drew held her hand and slowly opened the bedroom door. There appeared to be uproar right outside their door.

"Where?" a voice shouted.

"Out the back," Lacy said, already disappearing down the wooden staircase with Cash on her heals. Now all the doors were opening and everyone joined to follow. Drew looked at Phoebe and she nodded. This sounded like something they didn't want to miss. They half walked half jogged after the growing procession of people.

"Who's killing who?" someone said.

"Dante and Jay."

Phoebe wasn't even aware that Jay was there and assumed he must have arrived in the night.

They reached the kitchen and went out through the back door. A ring of people had already formed out in the back yard between the house and the barn.

Cash was trying to come between them, but it was like coming between two pit bulls. He was getting caught heavily in the crossfire, so satisfied himself with keeping the crowd back at a safe distance. Phoebe looked at Drew whose eyebrows went up as shocked as she was. No one around them seemed to be attempting to break it up.

They were stripped to the waist and barefoot in their jeans. Both were covered in the tattoos that Phoebe was getting used to seeing on the men. Dante was taller, leaner and looked far stronger. Jay, on the other hand, was smaller-framed but lightning-fast with some obvious fighting skills.

Phoebe looked around at the worried faces to see if she could spot Tia. She was dying to meet the girl who'd caused all this trouble but there was no sign of her. The whole thing had taken on the feel of a prizefight. Blow was exchanged for blow with bone-crunching accuracy. It was more disturbing, as they were supposed to be close friends and were literally tearing chunks off each other. No one was doing a thing about it. In fact the guards were now watching, shoulder to shoulder, as if it was a good sparring match.

Phoebe looked anxiously between the two men. The blows were taking their toll on their mouths and eyes, now swollen and bleeding. Blood trailed down from their noses in smeared lines across their chests. They rolled over and over in the dust so they became filthy and unrecognizable.

Drew squeezed her hand and she looked up into his eyes and understood right away.

AFTER FIFTEEN MINUTES of taking out a lifetime of frustration on each other, Dante and Jay were still on their feet but swaying. There was no winner today.

Cash handed Dante a towel and began herding everyone inside to give them some space. "Here," Dante said, after he dunked the towel in the water trough.

Jay sat heavily on a bench. "Thanks."

Just a couple of guards remained at a distance.

Dante sat on a pile of logs a few feet away, still breathing like he'd run a marathon.

"I think you broke my nose," Jay said, dabbing the blood tentatively underneath it with his elbows on his knees.

"What you doing here, Jay?"

Jay let an arm drop and looked at him deadpan. "You seriously asking that question? You fuck my wife and I get here and Tia's emotions are on the floor." Jay narrowed his eyes. "We agreed, Dant, right at the beginning that Tia had to choose for herself."

Dante bobbed his head, amused that it was still Tia at the forefront of Jay's mind. Then he flinched as another part of his body complained. "Yeah we did, but this is too far along. It's different."

Jay winced in pain as he tried to get up onto his feet. The arm around his middle indicated some cracked ribs.

"You didn't answer my question, Jay. Are you and Ruby okay?" As he said it he couldn't keep the smirk off his face.

Jay looked daggers at him but was forced to lean down with his hands on his knees and spit some blood. Instead he gave him the finger, which made Dante laugh and hiss in pain too.

Jay straightened up and began to shuffle towards the back door. Dante joined him shoulder to shoulder.

"This can't go on, Dante. You have to start talking."

Dante looked sideways at him. "Says the man who never says a word."

Jay sighed and tilted his head. "Both of us then."

As they reached the back door, Lacy nearly knocked them off their feet. "She's gone, I can't find her anywhere."

"Who?"

"Tia! She's gone!"

Dante locked eyes with Jay and the pair of them sagged.

Cash came up behind her and added quietly, "Drew and Phoebe have gone too."

CHAPTER 38

ia had known the moment that Jay bounded up the stairs to the room where Dante sat waiting for him that she had to go. There was no room for her in their relationship any more. Their fight had started immediately, smashing furniture, moving out onto the landing and down the stairs.

She didn't follow. They could kill each other for all she cared. Instead she punched clothes into a holdall, trying to think of a single place she could go.

Then she heard Lacy calling for everyone to come, swore under her breath and ignored it.

A commotion of doors slamming and feet clomping down the stairs followed, but she didn't get sucked in. She waited behind her door in case someone put their head in to check where she was, then she slipped out and ran down the stairs. Instead of turning right towards the kitchen she flew left out the front door to Cash's big old red pickup.

Tia started the engine with blood pumping and was about to screech away when the front door opened and the two new ones, Drew and Phoebe, ran out with armfuls of stuff obviously grabbed at the last minute.

They both stopped dead when they saw her.

She put her arm and her head out of the window. "You running?"

"Are you?" Phoebe snapped back.

For a split second the two girls assessed each other, assuming the obvious of who they must be.

"Get in." Tia wasn't sure it was a good idea at all. They knew nothing about each other, but the quicker they were away, the bigger start they had. She was kind of impressed that they'd figured out enough to run already.

They rushed around to the passenger side and scrambled into the messy back seat. Before she pulled away she said, "Ditch your phones," into the rear-view mirror. "Quickly!"

The newcomers looked at each other.

"Come on. They can track us with a phone."

An arm came past her head and the sound of two phones hitting the dirt followed. "Where to?" she said, pulling away.

"Seattle." Drew said.

DREW COULDN'T HELP FEELING a sense of elation the further away from the ranch they got. They headed straight for Seattle, only stopping for gas, bathroom breaks and snacks for the road. He made a couple of calls ahead to friends to warn them they were coming and they made it by nightfall.

Their old places weren't an option, so they clubbed together what little money they had, and booked into a mediocre hotel. It was a basic but clean single-story building that overlooked the car park. It had twin beds, a TV and a bathroom. By then they were all dog-tired so amenities weren't high on the list.

Food would be though and they couldn't use their credit

cards. "Won't they be able to find you with some weird sensory shit?" Drew asked.

"Not accurately and it gets weaker the further away we get."

Drew didn't ask any more and helped Phoebe pull a few things out of their bag. He continued to watch Tia though. He'd seen her grab her head a few times as if she was in pain. Maybe she wasn't telling them everything. He pulled Phoebe against his chest and kissed the top of her head. If Dante could use the link to get to Tia, then it meant he could get to Phoebe too.

Tia stuffed her holdall under one of the beds she'd claimed as her own and sat down heavily on it. "The worst thing we could do is pulse."

Drew and Phoebe looked at each other then over at her.

"You've never done it? Guess not," she said, pointing her finger. "It's something we do with music. Something happens and we release our power in a rhythmic sonic wave. I've seen it happen with Lacy when she dances and Isla when she's in the zone practicing her fighting katas. It's to do with the whole luring humans thing, they're suckers for it. But Dante can home in on it like a beacon. I've been caught out like that before."

"You've run away before?" Phoebe said.

Tia shrugged and lay back with her forearm across her eyes. "You could say that I've kind of made a career out of it."

"We'll get up early and get some food and somewhere more permanent to stay," Drew said, pulling the other single bed a little further away for privacy.

Tia raised her head at the scrape of furniture.

"I don't want your two men to fight over who gets to gut me first," Drew said, with a wry grin.

Tia chuffed a mirthless blast of laughter and relaxed back down.

Drew got in the bed so he was nearest to the door. Then he pulled Phoebe in next to him so her body lay half over his. There wasn't much maneuvering room in the bed. Still, he enjoyed the closeness. The need for this was growing daily.

Drew smoothed down her hair and looked over at Tia. She'd stripped off to her vest and panties and was lying face down with her arms folded for pillows watching him back.

He pulled Phoebe tighter into the crook of his neck and continued to stroke her hair.

The sharp sting of her teeth piercing his neck made him close his eyes for a second. When he opened them again Tia was watching with heavy-lidded eyes.

It was a few minutes before she made a comment. "Does it hurt?"

"No," he said simply. With no apology he allowed his eyes to close.

He heard the shuffle of covers and the creak of a bed and guessed Tia had turned the other way.

LIGHT FINGERS BRUSHED across Tia's shoulders. "Turn over," a voice whispered. A male voice but not Dante's. She was too groggy to protest.

The voice was familiar but she couldn't place it. The room was too dark making whoever it was into an inky black outline. With him came a darkness that felt as if he was seeping into her soul and there was nothing she could do. She was helpless.

A finger traced down her cheek, neck to the swell of her breasts. Cool air hit them as the vest was lifted up and over her head.

Suddenly she was raging hot. Everything felt strange and wrong but, for some reason, she couldn't stop it.

Dreaming...

Nothing had actually touched her but the feeling of hair falling in her face and dragging down over the bare skin of her body. She found she wanted more and arched her body up but nothing came.

There was no face and no touch and yet she instinctively knew whoever it was. "You must be willing…" came like a whisper on the airwaves and disappeared again.

"Yes," she groaned.

"When the time is right you will come to me."

She was writhing and turned her head to the side to reveal the column of her neck. Hot breath and then soft lips travelled it gently. Then, just as she began to feel a white-hot scratch, she shouted, "No!" and sat bolt upright.

Tia reached over and clicked on the bed-side lamp. She was breathing heavily and perspiring all over. Looking down at herself she realized she was still in her vest. Then she looked across at the two bodies asleep in a tangle of long hair, limbs and covers.

"Shit!" she said, dragging a hand across her damp brow. It felt so real.

She lay back down but kept her eye on the two sleeping across the way. The dream must have been triggered because of what she'd seen them doing just before she went to sleep. The bloke must have some serious magnetism. The whole thing had deeply disturbed her. Now she kind of got what Dante meant about him. He was dangerous.

Then she shook herself out of it. She was exhausted and overwrought. Little wonder she was having nightmares. The guy was sleeping blissfully unaware with his Siren, minding his own business.

DANTE PACED the ranch sitting room, frantic with worry, several hours after they'd all disappeared. He'd dispatched guards in all directions and sent some more to Billings Airport, but all his efforts came up empty.

Jay, Cash and Keenan watched him walk up and down. "I knew there was something about that one. If that fucker so much as touches…"

"I think this has more to do with us than him," Jay said.

Dante stopped in his tracks. "What, you think it's just coincidence that they all left at exactly the same time?"

Jay shrugged. "Yeah, I do. The CCTV out front clearly shows Tia out there first."

"I think the other two just hitched a ride. At least they're together," Cash reasoned.

Jay nodded.

"Nah, I'm not buying it." Dante said, resuming his pacing.

AFTER PHONING AHEAD, Drew took the two girls to his friend Glen's apartment in downtown Seattle. It was late afternoon and the small brownstone apartment block was bathed in the last, rare afternoon sunshine. "This must be it." Glen had explained that he'd moved there right after he and Phoebe had left. Tia pulled up to the curb.

They buzzed the intercom and climbed the two flights to the second floor. The guy opened up immediately and pulled Drew into one of those half-hug back pats all the guys seemed to do. "Hey, man, you're back. Hey, babe," he said to Phoebe. "Well hellooo, sugar." His head tilted and watched in exaggerated appreciation as he watched Tia follow Phoebe in through the door.

Drew ignored it. "Any one else at home?"

"Nah, just me," Glen said, still eying Tia up and down.

She looked disinterested, as if she was used to the reaction. It made Drew smile. "This is Phoebe's sister. She's staying with us for a few days."

His face brightened. "You single?"

Drew clicked his fingers to bring his focus back to him. "Why are you here? Why aren't you at the old apartment?"

It worked. Glen's face immediately got serious. "Had to, man. Right after you left some dudes came and smashed up the place. We barely managed to save the guitars."

Drew ran his fingers through his hair. It was all he needed. He was hoping to be able to get a few of his things. Phoebe looked up at him with big, worried eyes. They had barely any money and nowhere to go.

Glen waved them further down the corridor. "What I could save of your stuff I put in a bag in my room."

Drew slapped his friend on the back. It was something. "Can we stay a couple of days, Glen?"

He was already grinning at Tia. "Sure thing, what are bros for?"

Drew laughed and pulled her into the room with him and Phoebe. "She's with me."

Glen made a noise of frustration as Drew closed the door on him and he was left in the hall. "I thought Phoebe was with you?"

The girls giggled.

"That's right!" Drew called back. Then he winked at the girls. "That will give him something to think about."

Tia dropped her shoulder bag and sat heavily on the bed. "I need a phone, Drew."

After studying her for a moment he said, "I'll get you one … don't do anything stupid with it." Then he went in search of Glen's, came back and dumped it in her hands. "Be quick!"

She was.

"Sean? Come and get me … yes … Seattle … OK, I'll be ready."

Drew couldn't help feeling a little disappointed in her. He exchanged a look with Phoebe. "You going back?"

She shook her head. "He'll be here tomorrow. I'm going to one of my dad's places."

Drew wondered whether he would bring the cavalry with him but she said, "Don't worry, as long as I'm alright he won't drag me back."

There wasn't anything they could do today. They needed some rest. He pressed a button and turned a huge knob around to the right. The punching rhythm of the start of "Man in a Box", by Alice in Chains, began. "I say let's get wasted," he said, holding his arms wide in a question.

Both girls laughed and began bounding around the room to the music and playing air guitar on the bed.

Glen banged on the door. "Open up, I have beers."

"Come in!" they shouted.

He peered his head around the door as they all fell in a heap on the bed. "Holy shit! My kinda love!"

Everything was hysterically funny for a while. Like the valve on a pressure cooker released, until Drew was forced to crumple at the knee in pain.

"What's up?" Phoebe said, trying to see through his fingers at what he was clutching. "Your knee again?"

His face was screwed up in pain, but he managed to nod. "I thought they fixed it," Drew said, through gritted teeth. "You crazies have fucked it again," he said, half laughing, half wincing.

"I'll grab some ice," Phoebe said.

Tia and Glen tried to pull Drew up to a sitting position on the bed. Then Tia put a pillow under his knee and it started to feel better.

"You okay, man?" Glen said, shoving a can in his face.

Drew laughed despite the continued low-level ache. "Yeah. Gotta make sure I see my guy tomorrow."

Phoebe came back with a pack of frozen peas and put it straight on his knee, which made him jump in shock.

She was trying not to giggle.

"That's it! You have to give me pain relief now." And he grabbed her while she dissolved into fits of giggles. Then his eyes homed in on hers and took on a much more feral shade.

TIA DIDN'T MISS the look the two of them gave each other. It was the one where no one else existed. Her chest ached at her own situation. With them it seemed so much more animal and basic. She glanced at Glen, hoping he hadn't clocked the same thing. "Say, Glen, you're a musician? Are you any good?"

It did the trick as, after a brief frown, his face brightened at the lure of speaking about his obvious first love. A lively conversation followed and they lounged on the floor with vinyl record sleeves spread all around them. Her eyes flicked to the bed a few times and she noticed the lovebirds lying still on the bed with Drew's mouth to Phoebe's neck just below the hairline. Just a subtle rhythmic movement of his head to show it was anything other than a kiss.

Tia kept him talking and pulled out her MP3 player. "Got some old-school House and Garage on here," she said, waggling her eyebrows playfully to Glen.

He laughed. She liked him – a sucker for any kind of music. Before long, the trance-like House beats were booming through the walls. A hypnotic wave of sheer bliss went through the apartment. No one was immune. Like a shot of euphoria, everyone was soon jumping on the "one love" vibe; smoking, drinking and completely forgetting the hopeless predicament they were in.

A COUPLE OF HOURS LATER, the communal buzz began to wind down. Everyone was sprawled out somewhere. Tia was sorting CDs and Drew, now a lot better, lounged on a beanbag next to her. Phoebe was lying on her stomach on the edge of the bed in some conversation with Glen.

Tia found their dynamic fascinating. She did with all her sisters and their mates. Their eyes never strayed far from their partners. Then she frowned as she remembered just how far Dante's had strayed recently.

She squashed the sob that threatened to give her hurt away and focused on Drew. *What the hell was he?* He sure as hell didn't act like a human.

His eyes flickered over to Phoebe and it wasn't that he was jealous. It was as though he just enjoyed watching her. It was like a knife twisting in her heart. *Lucky girl*, to have devotion like that. "You're in love with her," she said, as a statement and not a question.

His gaze reluctantly moved from Phoebe to her. "I guess." He sifted through a few more CD cases. "I feel like I'm on limited time with her, though."

It was a strange thing for him to say. "Why? She obviously adores you. You look great together." And they did. There was no two ways about it.

"One of these days she's gonna meet that guy – you know, the one she's meant to be with and I won't be able to compete with that."

"That's bollocks, Drew, whatever any of them say, you've got the purple ring."

Drew held up his left hand slightly. He guessed he didn't believe in it much either.

"And anyway, look at my situation." She began laughing before she'd even finished her sentence at how ridiculous that sounded. "No seriously," she said, trying to school her features. "I love Jay even though I'm meant to be with Dante."

"Look how that worked out," Drew said, laughing,

making her laugh with him. "That's not a good argument, Tia."

As her laughter died away and she studied him, it was strange because he seemed so much more like Dante than Jay.

CHAPTER 39

It was nearly light when they all finally fell asleep. Then, in no time at all, Phoebe felt her shoulder gently shaken. "Phoebe … Phoebe. Come on, wake up. I need to go to the doc."

Phoebe cracked her eyes with a lot of effort to see Drew doing the same to Tia, who she realized was in the same bed as her.

"I need you to drive, Tia, my knee's killing me."

Phoebe snuggled down in the bed. "I don't need to come then." She drifted off again.

"Yes you do. We all stick together. If I've got to get up, so do you."

In ten minutes and without really waking up properly, Phoebe filed out the apartment with the others, leaving Glen enviably asleep on the sofa.

They pulled up right outside the medical center that Drew appeared to know well.

"I'm just nipping to that coffee place. Won't be two ticks. Anyone want anything?"

Phoebe just opened her mouth when Drew said, "No!" so

abruptly that it made her study him for a moment. "We'll all go after," he continued a little more calmly. "Please."

Phoebe frowned. Maybe his leg was hurting a whole lot more than he was letting on. He really didn't sound like himself this morning. He was always so laid back.

After throwing her a slightly exasperated look, Tia reluctantly agreed and slid out the driver's-side door.

Drew held the door while she got out the back. "I don't want you waiting for me on your own, that's all," he said, looking either side of him.

She smiled at his thoughtfulness and kissed him as soon as her feet hit the Tarmac.

"Arghh, come on," Tia said. "Sean will be here soon, and you thought the other two were moody."

Drew whispered "great" under his breath and Phoebe giggled. He was really limping now and she got under his arm to help support him while they made the short walk into the small practice surgery.

Inside it was bright clean and minimalist in design. A reception desk curved like a wave and there was grey padded seating around the other three walls. There was a gap for a corridor leading, she guessed, to the small examination rooms. They all flopped down into the chairs. The place was quiet. It didn't appear like anyone else was there.

A woman dressed in the standard smock uniform of a nurse breezed in from the corridor and asked, "Mr Stone?"

Drew got back up taking most of the weight on his good leg. "Yes."

Phoebe went to help and he held up his hand. "Won't be long," and he hobbled off down the corridor. "Thanks, Cara."

Phoebe looked at Tia who looked enquiringly back. It felt odd that he knew her name and she couldn't tell if she was just plain old jealous, or whether it was genuinely weird.

Then the nurse walked out from behind her desk, flipped

the latch on the front door and followed him down the corridor. "Did she just lock us in?" Phoebe said, a little panicked.

Tia seemed to dismiss it with a shrug and reached for a magazine. "Maybe they just opened up specially. It is Saturday."

Phoebe sighed uneasily and guessed she was right. She needed sleep. Everything was making her on edge today.

Tia slammed the magazine down, bored already and slipped her bag over her shoulder. "Come on, let's get some coffee over the road. He can't moan if we go together."

Phoebe looked down the corridor, a little uncertain. She did feel like death and they could bring him back one. In a snap decision she stood up and gestured for Tia to lead the way.

They walked quickly to the door and Tia flipped the latch. After a last check behind them, she snatched the door open and walked straight into the chest of an extremely tall, muscular guy. In fact, when Phoebe's mind got over the shock of seeing him there, he did seem kind of familiar. There were three of them, shoulder to shoulder, dressed completely in black. They gave off a weird aura but smelled absolutely amazing.

"Shit!" Tia said.

Phoebe put it down to getting up too quickly and the night before's alcohol, because she started to feel really strange.

Please go back inside, the one in the middle said. Except he didn't say it, his lips never moved.

SEAN THUMPED three times until a scruffy guy with a serious case of bedhead opened with a bleary, "Where's your key?"

Sean pushed him roughly aside and walked right in.

"What the fuck?" the guy said following him down the hall while he looked in all the rooms.

"Where is she?" Sean said, coming to a standstill but still scoping out the place.

"Who?"

Sean had no time for games and shoved him up against the wall roughly by the t-shirt. "Don't fuck with me and you won't get hurt. Tia and Phoebe, where are they?"

Glen's eyes were still wide with fear when he asked, "You her guy she's waitin' on?"

"Yes, I'm here to collect her. Where is she?" He relaxed his grip a little so the much smaller guy relaxed.

"They've all gone out. Drew was headin' to the medical center today."

"Where?"

"Corner of Leyton and Sunrise."

Sean was already on his mobile phone to Dante as he was making his exit.

"Hurry, Sean. She was pulsing all over the place last night like a fuckin' beacon." Sean shook his head as he left the apartment and Bedhead called, "Everything OK?"

Beer cans, records, CDs, all the evidence of a heavy night, that girl would never learn. A bit of music and alcohol and she just couldn't help herself. She'd announced to the world where she was.

PHOEBE AND TIA were forced to move back into the medical center and the huge men followed them in. They moved strangely and their faces had very little expression, which was unsettling. *Murrs,* Tia projected straight to her head.

One of the guys flipped the catch on the door again, except he did it with just a look.

We are so screwed, Phoebe thought back.

"It's Vionne, isn't it? I know you … I mean, we've met, haven't we? Is everything okay?" Phoebe was fully aware she was gabbling. Her brave act wasn't quite cutting it.

"Do you really want to piss Dante off, because he's on his way?" Tia butted in.

Phoebe nodded and glared back at the guys as equally unconvincing.

Relax, please. Take a seat, Highnesses.

They both sat cautiously and Phoebe glanced down the corridor to see if she could see anyone. She didn't want to call out and give Drew away. They may need him to have the element of surprise. If only he would hurry. There was just a radio playing some indiscernible tune in the distance. *Come on, Drew,* she prayed.

Your Protector has been detained. We have some time to talk.

Phoebe swallowed hard. She wasn't sure if it was from fear of what might be happening with Drew or the fact the guy seemed to know what she was thinking. Either way, things were looking really bad.

Tia held her hand and she calmed a little. Then a picture of Tia standing in a field shaking and pointing at her head flashed in her mind. She was trying madly not to show the shock she was feeling on her face. Somehow she knew that Tia touching her enabled her to flash the picture into her head.

It happened again.

Stop fucking thinking, idiot. Tia projected.

The Murr, Vionne, who seemed in charge looked down at his hands at a ring Phoebe recognized. It was the same as the ones all the princes wore and it was a striking turquoise color. *Can you move away from Phoebe please, Tia. Just for a moment.*

Phoebe grabbed onto her as she went to stand up. "It's okay, he's just testing to see if you're his...that's right, isn't it?" Tia said, looking straight at the guy, who inclined his head. "He wants to see if it goes purple and I might interfere with it."

One of the men walked with Tia to the furthest part of the surgery around fifty feet away. Phoebe refocused on Vionne's ring. *Please don't change, please don't change,* she found herself chanting over and over again.

The ring swirled in white smoke and, for a moment, she thought it would turn purple but it eventually stopped at a blood red.

He held up his arm so Tia could see. *What magic is this?*

Tia looked as baffled as he was – and Phoebe, sure as hell, stopped knowing what was going on weeks ago.

DREW LAY LOOKING at the cluster of bright circular lights above him. It occurred to him for the first time that it might be a little overkill for a bad knee. He tried to lift his head, then his arms but nothing would move.

"Lie very still, Drew, we won't keep you long."

He felt a small scratch in the crook of his arm and the world seemed to swirl around him. For a moment he remembered something – just the smallest flash – a tiny child on an operating table just like this one. This had happened many times. He'd been drugged but he could hear perfectly. His brain seemed alert, it was just his body that didn't seem connected.

Familiar men's voices were moving around the room. He felt heat in his knee and a tugging on it.

"Bring the girl through to the car out back," a voice said.

"But there's two of them," a female voice said.

Silence followed for quite a few beats. Then laughter. "Bring them both. You have been busy, Mr Stone."

Drew tried to move. Everything was feeling off now. He

needed to get the girls away from here but nothing budged. His vision was blurred and with the bite of nylon he realized he was restrained. Head, arms, chest, knees, ankles, he tested them all one by one.

"Is he awake?" Someone said. "He sure looks awake."

"It's a semi dreamlike state. He won't remember any of it."

"Now we have what we came for, what shall we do with him?"

Running footsteps came right into the room. "Trouble, you'd better come."

THE THUMPING of boots made all their heads switch round to the corridor. Four of the most undoctorly looking men were marching down the corridor toward them.

Phoebe was already on her feet and Tia ran over and dragged her nearer the door. The three Murrs stood in front of them like guard dogs.

The men approaching were big, but human big, like doormen or soldiers. The Murrs had a foot in height over them and wasted no time. The soldiers rushed them.

Tia was pulling her backwards. *Careful. Don't turn. Just move slowly.*

Phoebe did as she was told, unable to take her eyes off the strange fight in front of them. The men were throwing punches and kicks and anything they could get their hands on and the Murrs barely moved. It was the ultimate in economy of movement. Had the predicament not been so dire she would have loved to stay and watch the Murrs causing so much damage with a flick of the wrist and a mere look.

Now! Tia said. In a split second she turned, flicked the latch, and the two of them slid out of the front door into the brilliant sunshine of the street.

"Shit!" they said or thought collectively. Phoebe wasn't exactly sure which.

"Hi, Dax!" Tia said with a weak wave of her arm.

The Murr held out his arm in the direction of a blacked-out van parked at the curb. *Please come with us, Your Highnesses. It is not safe here. My brother will join us shortly.*

Phoebe guessed he was referring to one of the guys back inside. Everything had gone so Alice through the looking glass, he made it sound as though he'd popped to the shops.

Tia visibly sagged. "It's no use, come on."

Sean peered through a tiny piece of glass that wasn't frosted in the shop front. It looked like any other medical surgery kind of place except there were no people. He looked at his watch. 11.30 a.m. *Weird.* He didn't like the feel of it. Cash's old red pickup was right outside.

He looked left and right and spotted a service alley, then jogged in that direction to see if he could see more around the back. It followed the length of the building and came out to a Tarmacked area behind. He sprinted and stopped behind a large dumpster. *Shit.*

A blacked-out van waited with its engine running. Large military-looking guys were loading stuff up into it and filing back inside. This was no doctor's surgery. Something was gravely wrong. Sean jogged noiselessly closer, pulled his army-issue baseball cap low over his eyes and joined the back of the line. It was a reckless move to get inside, but he needed to act quickly. He kept his head down past a small kitchen and followed the sound of voices straight to an open doorway to the left.

He palmed his gun but kept it hidden in his jacket pocket and stood on the threshold of the room. A doctor in a white coat was helping Drew from the table. A woman in a white smock was the other side.

He coughed.

All three eyes went straight to him. Drew looked unsteady.

"Sorry we're closed," the woman said.

"Just came for my man here," Sean said, nodding in Drew's direction. "I don't think he should be driving."

The doctor and the woman exchanged a look, then he looked to someone out of vision behind the door. No doubt waiting to see what trouble Sean was about to bring. The doctor gave him a slight shake of the head. Another big guy came up behind him. Whatever this was, it was not your average checkup. After a very quick assessment he knew his chances of getting out were slim. "Ready, Drew?"

"Phoebe?" Drew said, but his speech was a little slurry.

Sean brazened it into the room, took the arm the woman had and held Drew's weight. "Come on, mate, let's get you home ... where's Phoebe and Tia, any idea?"

Drew looked into his face and wobbled as if he was confused, then tried to walk.

Sean steadied him. "No, they're not out there, mate." He looked at the faces around him, who looked at each other awkwardly.

"They were in the waiting room when I showed Mr Stone in," the woman said, looking really convincing.

Sean turned his head to the doctor, who shrugged, "The receptionist is correct."

Nothing was adding up. Whatever they were doing with Drew here, the girls were nowhere to be seen. He figured the best thing was get Drew out onto the street where he could get more sense out of him without anyone hearing. With a fake grin, "Girls, eh, sure we'll find 'em," and with a hand up in thanks, Sean hurriedly helped Drew out of the building,

going left this time and out the front door where the receptionist held it open for him.

Sean leant him against Cash's truck so he could think.
Drew pointed to a shop across the street. "Tia wanted coffee."
His speech was improving.

"Okay, mate. Stay here, I'll run across and ask whether
they've seen 'em."

He darted across the busy road and asked, but the girls all
said they hadn't seen anyone fitting the girl's description. He
acted relaxed and chatty. "What do you know about the
medical center across the street. I was thinking of signing
up?"

"Oh that's been closed for over a year, honey," a more
senior waitress said.

Another girl came and stood next to her looking through
the window to where he'd left Drew. "Funny, though. Saw
three real tall guys go in this morning – like huge. All dressed
in black with sunglasses. They had like the whitest hair.
Don't get many men like that round here."

Sean paid for two coffees and thanked the women. His
mind raced all the way back across the road.

Drew looked at him anxiously. He waved at his driver
parked a little way down the street. "Get anything you need
out of the truck."

"What's happening?"

"The center is a front. It's not been open for a year." Then,
without looking too deeply at the incomprehension on
Drew's face, he put his phone to his ear. "Problem. Murrs
have 'em."

CHAPTER 40

$\mathcal{D}$ante was no longer pussy-footing around. He summoned the whole court back to Ireland. There was only one place the Murrs would take them and Ireland was the nearest landmass. Americans in the waters or not, this could be an outright declaration of war of which he would fight using any means necessary.

A message was sent out to all the royal family heads to be on high alert. This was code red as far as their race was concerned. The only thing higher was DEFCON and that was reserved for the return, and he couldn't think of that right now.

Drew had been confined to his room. He wasn't sure where the boy fit into all this but there was a connection somehow.

Dante stood with his back to the huge window. Behind him the sea was serene and oblivious to the storm about to begin. His eyes rested on everyone, one by one, in front of him. "Cesaré, Keenan, Lance, Alfonzo." Each nodded gravely when he said their name. Jay was even there, bruised from their fight and standing to the side with Connor. "All who have aligned themselves to me," he said, sweeping an arm to include those who stood behind them. Cash, Sean, Keenan's crew and brothers. Many of the Florianna family, Tia's brothers, Dino and Luca, Sebastian and Naomi, Tia's mother and father. The only families not present were the Murrs and his own, Dubonnettis.

The fountain bubbled and splashed and a blonde head breached the surface. *Isla,* Dante thought, and breathed again. Two Santalini guards helped her out of the water.

She wasn't alone. Long black hair and huge striped body rose slowly out of the water after her. *Darres.*

Outraged, several guards rushed the fountain.

"Stop!" Dante shouted before anyone could get hurt. They stopped short as Darres stood, dripping, in just the thin, shimmering gauze that covered his lower half.

Dante walked calmly up to him and stood toe to toe, aware of his temporary physical weakness out of the water. "Guard the fountain. Make sure no one else comes up."

Darres' eyes never left his as he spoke. Dante was in no doubt of the strength of the man. He could probably kill any one of them in the room just with his mind and his allegiance could not be counted on. He was a lone wolf – brought up alone in the same American base that Isla, his mate, had spent time. *Are you here as a friend, Darres?* he said, straight to his mind.

The big Murr resembled a Native American in full war paint with his dramatic stripes and black hair to his waist. Isla put her arms around him protectively and his went easily across her small shoulders. *My allegiance is to my mate.*

Dante assessed him for a full minute through narrowed eyes and decided it was enough. "Very well, are you willing to act as mediator?"

Immediately, men crowded in shouting their objections.

"He cannot be trusted," Keenan's eldest brother, Marius, said.

Dante shifted his gaze to Isla, who he could feel was terrified. "Can you vouch for him?" he said softly. He had real affection for the small woman who outwardly appeared so delicate but could kill a man without thinking twice.

It was the only time the huge Murr took his eyes off him to look down into Isla's loving face. She spoke to Darres and not him when she held her throat and said, "My husband stands with me whatever happens."

The strength of their love was evident through the bond and he knew that she spoke the absolute truth. As long as Isla was with him he could count on the big Murr.

He quickly took his attention from them and addressed the crowd. "As you all know, Tia and Phoebe are missing. Judging by their last known whereabouts, I think it safe to assume they have been abducted."

There were several grumbles and murmurs from the onlookers. "Does the boy have something to do with it?" Someone shouted.

"Is he in league with the Murrs?"

Dante quieted everyone down with his hands. "Sean, tell everyone what you told me."

Sean came forward. "Drew wouldn't put Phoebe knowingly in danger and I don't think he has the contacts to be in with the Murrs. But I do know that the medical center was a smoke screen. What they were doing to him I don't know, but he was in pretty bad shape when I picked him up – like they'd drugged him or something."

"Who were they?" Dante said.

"Honestly, I have no idea, but they were human. It's my guess that Tia had forgotten herself and pulsed and given them away to other Atlanteans in the area."

Dante nodded. That woman would be the death of him.

He himself had felt her using her power the night before. The Murrs could simply have been first on the scene. "Were they Government, the ones with Drew?"

Sean shrugged, "Could be. They had some pretty trained men."

"A lot depends on what Drew can tell us."

Naomi came forward with Sebastian. "My wife has something to say to everyone."

Dante watched the Murr woman step forward calm and expressionless, but she was devoted to her husband and children. *Let me go with Darres to Murrtaine. They cannot hide them. It is such a small city and they cannot be held for long without our knowledge.*

Several of the Florianna gabbled their distrust in Italian. Cesaré was forced to calm his family down.

Please hear me, I am close to my cousin, Darl, Lord Advocate, and I know he doesn't want war. The Americans threaten Murrtaine as we speak. It is not in his interest to anger the king.

Everyone began speaking at once, but Dante remained quiet. He'd listened carefully to every word. What she said did make sense. The Murrs were not an aggressive people and seldom swung the first punch. He nodded at Naomi in reassurance and Sebastian led her off.

Drew had been awake for a while. The moment he put the fragments together of what had happened he was hit with a weight of guilt and loss such as he'd never had in his life. *He had removed Phoebe from safety.* It was his fault this had happened. Everyone here at the castle suspected his involvement, but what was killing him was the growing fear that there was more to this than even he knew. Shady dark snatches of memory were coming to him – whisperings in his mind of images of him fighting as a child. Being hungry and cold and sleeping on a bare mattress in a wooden dormitory. The children's home he believed he came from was morphing into a stark training camp and went against everything he thought he knew. As well as the winged angel tattoos all the boys wore on their backs legally far too young. When he really thought about it that part had never made any sense.

The monks had done it.

Monks? What school had monks in this century?

European voices. His knee. The doctor he'd seen over and over. And not just as an adult, which the memory of his knee injury first suggested. It was all so jumbled it felt like he was losing his mind.

Phoebe had trusted him blindly and now he didn't even trust himself. Before her, the only thing that had meant anything to him was his music, but that seemed an empty, shallow life now – one big round of drinking and partying, like a distraction where he was just passing time. Nothing felt real or of any substance. But Phoebe changed all that. She'd changed him mentally and physically and he would never be the same again. She was beautiful and rare and he had corrupted her.

He stood up from the bed with his mind made up. Snatching open the door he said to the guard, "Take me to Dante. I have something to say."

When he reached the great hall there were a lot of people all standing around in huddles. He scanned them all until he found Dante. He was standing with a group of Tia's Protectors – even Jay was there, who he'd been fighting only hours before.

He let out a blast of mirthless laughter. All Phoebe had was him, and he'd let her down.

A white light and a train hit him hard in the jaw. Next thing he knew, he was picking himself up from the floor.

Drew turned to see where the blow came from. *Correction*, she had Connor as well. Two guards were holding him back. The room hushed as people noticed him. Rubbing his jaw and allowing one good hit as probably deserved, he continued on aware Connor would probably hit him again and *that* he wouldn't take. Guards soon appeared either side of him. No one here trusted him. *Well, news flash*, neither did he.

"I need to talk to you privately," he said, coming to a standstill a few feet from Dante.

He just nodded, looked at Sean. "You, come with me." Then he looked across at Jay. "Make sure all lines of communication are kept open."

Jay nodded back.

He was too focused now to dwell on how truly weird that conversation was.

"Come with me," Dante said.

DANTE SETTLED in the chair behind the desk in his study. Drew sat opposite him, Alfonzo on a sofa to his right and Sean leant against the bookcase on his left. There was a long silence while he scrutinized Drew looking all kinds of uncomfortable. After a few moments Dante prompted him. "What do you need to say, Drew? I do have kind of a situation here. You didn't just manage to lose your own valuable Siren, but my wife too." He didn't raise his voice but his face remained hard.

For a second, misery was etched all over the boy's face then it transformed into anger. "You don't think I know that?" he shouted. "You don't think I love Phoebe every bit as much ..." He trailed off as emotion rode him hard. Then he bit it back. "Look, I know you haven't trusted me since I got here." He looked across at Sean. "The fact is, *I* no longer trust me."

It was a statement Dante wasn't expecting. "Go on."

"It was when you said that the place had been shut for a year," Drew said, directly to Sean. "When I know it definitely hasn't. I visited that clinic every couple of weeks for months." Then he shook his head as if it was fuzzy. "It may even have been years – if not there, somewhere. I hurt my knee ... at least I think I did. A bad fall, on stage ... you know?"

Dante nodded as if he was following along perfectly. "Do you have the doctor's name?"

Drew shook his head. "Dr Gilbert or something. The thing is ...what I'm trying to say is, I think I need to steer clear of Phoebe. When you find her. When she comes back ..." He looked at him with steely determination. "I don't want to hurt her."

Dante leaned forward in his chair to rest his elbows on the desk. "You think you would hurt her, Drew?"

"No," he said, shaking his head and running a shaking hand through the roots of his hair. "I wouldn't intentionally. It's just I got this feeling that this is somehow down to me." He let his hand drop into his lap and his face looked weary.

Dante sat back in his chair and let out a loud sigh, weighing him up. Then he looked over at Sean. "And there was no doubt it was Murrs?"

Sean shook his head but looked at Drew. "Unless some very pale basketball players decided to go into the same empty surgery?"

Dante didn't laugh, although it was pretty funny, and returned his attention to Drew. "I have many enemies."

"Sometimes they work together. It was probably that," Sean said.

Dante bobbed his head in agreement. "What do you want, Drew? Time is getting on."

"If I leave her. How do I do it so she doesn't die?"

Dante's eyes widened, and he looked over at Sean. It was the absolute last thing he was expecting. He smiled a little and settled back into his chair. "Don't let's be hasty. Let me think on it and we'll talk later."

Drew frowned and got up slowly when he realized he was being dismissed. He walked slowly to the door and reached for the handle.

"For what it's worth, Drew, I know you love her."

"Thank you," Drew said and left.

PHOEBE AND TIA were hurtling along in a blacked-out SUV so fast they didn't know how they weren't pulled over. There were two of the weird Murrs in the front, one either side of them and the one she recognized sitting in the chair facing the wrong way opposite to them. Very soon they were joined by another car to escort them in front and behind.

Phoebe shot a worried glance at Tia, who had clocked the same thing. *We're screwed,* Tia projected. What she didn't get was how anyone knew they were there.

"I thought you and Dante were friends, Vionne," Tia said, to the guy opposite them.

Phoebe guessed he wasn't bad-looking. His bone structure was good. And despite his huge size he seemed in proportion. But the Murrs had either the whitest or the blackest hair with eyes like huge pools which definitely set them apart as not human.

The corners of his mouth curled into a weird smile. *I am as much friends with your husband as anyone can be from a rival family. I have to first safeguard the kingdom.*

Phoebe was confused. "You two know each other? Where the hell's he taking us? We're heading towards the coast not Montana."

Forgive my rudeness, Phoebe. We have met. I am Vionne, Prince of Murrtaine. You were going to be abducted today by the order of Scythians. Vionne slowly moved his strange gaze to Tia. *They were not expecting you. It was as well we intercepted the situation. With two Sirens ...it would have been catastrophic to our race.*

Tia sat back in her seat moodily. "Oh cut the crap, Vionne. Who the hell are they, anyway?"

Phoebe felt rather than saw his amusement at the way Tia spoke to him, but then the temperature around them literally dropped.

"They are a religious order who kidnap little boys and turn them into killers, they want to destroy our race and they very definitely would have killed you."

Phoebe's heart froze and she shuddered at their narrow escape and, for a moment, Tia looked as shaken as she was, but then she appeared to shake it off. "If you butted in to save us, why aren't you calling Dante and taking us home? You know, Phoebe's only been underwater a couple of times."

Phoebe sat up straighter. "What do you mean? Where are we going?"

Tia narrowed her eyes, "Are you declaring war now you've got us?"

Phoebe was becoming more and more alarmed. She needed to find out if Drew was okay.

Vionne looked at her strangely. *Don't be frightened.* Then held up his left hand with the large ring they all seemed to have. It hadn't changed from the red color of before. *We merely want to keep you for your own safety.*

Tia shifted impatiently.

Vionne adjusted the ring on his finger as if he was puzzled by something. *This should at the very least be turquoise in your presence.*

Tia frowned. "I don't get it?"

The only time I have heard of this happening is when a prince is disqualified as a mate for some reason. It's extremely rare. Or because the natural order of things is being tampered with. Then he looked eerily straight at Phoebe, as if he was looking right into her soul. *The Orb safeguards order.*

"You don't need us kept prisoner in Murrtaine for that, Vionne."

He was still staring at Phoebe, making her want to blend right back into her seat. *Not prisoners, guests. You have abandoned your husband and your Protectors; I am offering you sanctuary out of human reach ... at least for the time being.*

On the surface it kind of made sense – except for the last bit. That worried her in that she was way over her head in a situation bigger than her. It didn't help because she had a strong feeling that he was worried. "What are you afraid of," she said, before she thought better of it.

His face kept eerily calm but the energy he exuded was thunderous. Phoebe felt for Tia's hand and she didn't object.

Things are changing. Can't you feel it?

Phoebe checked Tia's face and she was staring at him looking as uneasy as she felt.

For a moment he looked away and out of the smoky-tinted window. His thoughts were projected so quietly Phoebe strained to hear what he was saying. *We are pure Atlasian with no human blood to taint us. Your mother is one of us. Your sister married one of us..."*

It was as if they were listening to his internal monologue until Tia said, "What are you saying, Vionne?"

He turned back to them and they were hit by another wash of anger. "The Santalini are out of favor, we should be the ones who take their place. We should be at the king's right hand, not the Florianna."

Suddenly everything began to click into place. Phoebe

didn't need a degree in Atlantean politics to realize they were leverage.

Tia was trying to explain some history about Cesaré being bound by her sister Lily and deserving his place, or some crap like that, but it seemed beside the point.

Vionne's mind was closed off from reason. *I won't let your husband slowly sideline us because of his affection for a Florianna prince.*

Tia continued to try to talk him round, but Phoebe could tell she was wasting her breath. She was more worried about the speculative look in his eyes every time they rested on her. Although she had pledged to Dante, she was an unmarried Siren very much at the big guy's mercy.

CHAPTER 41

Things were moving fast in Washington. Ships were assembling frighteningly close to Murrtaine already. The last piece of intelligence that reached Delissi confirmed they were getting closer every day. That meant the person feeding them the coordinates was either teasing or didn't know them precisely yet. Either way, they were waiting for something.

Delissi was frustrated. He couldn't meet with the president, as it would compromise him. So he left with the snippet of information scribbled on the piece of paper at their last meeting. The person Phoebe Ray had spent her mysterious lost month with. Nothing had been said to Dante. He wanted to check it out for himself, given who it was. If it turned out to be true, it was going to cause problems. Huge ones.

In the Atlantean world something like this needed careful handling. The person was Atlantean and royal and had kept it quiet, which, now there was a king, was strictly against etiquette. They were well along into the last days and everything had a bearing.

Part of his responsibilities in Washington had been to work closely with scientists and meteorologists to monitor the earth's weather patterns and record temperatures and droughts that were on a steep rise. Not a good sign. The Orb was destabilizing.

It signaled the end of days and that outcomes in the fates were being tampered with. Someone was rigging the game and the Atlasians who'd written the prophecy ten thousand years ago knew that they would. In the time of the end princes would fight princes, tricking them out of what was rightfully theirs, convincing themselves that the end result justified the means. Their ancestors knew all this and scheduled a return to judge them. No one would go unpunished, just like before. Except this time the Atlantean race had grown and spread across the Earth. So however they were punished it would affect all life on this planet. There would be no more kingdoms and no more generations of Sirens to get it right. This was their last chance. It was a scary thought and couldn't be ignored.

Delissi had arranged to meet Malleven Mancini at his Manhattan apartment. It was conveniently not too far from Washington or Ireland should the need arise to depart urgently.

A Middle Eastern-looking guard, dressed in the black tunic of the Magi Brotherhood, showed him into the large darkened sitting room.

"My lord, Duke Ormond Delissi," he announced, bowed and left the room.

"Malleven," he said simply, spotting the object of his visit already pouring drinks at a large carved sideboard. He couldn't help respect the boy. Low born yet royal, from an obscure branch of the Florianna family, he'd made the most of his chances, graduated from Cambridge with honors and become a skilled alchemist. For an Atlantean that was no mean feat given the stiff competition. Then he'd quickly been recruited by the Magi Brotherhood, cementing his position where his blood ties could not.

"My lord, duke," Malleven said, passing him a glass of red.

Still, there was a darkness about the boy. He'd alienated himself from the king by being linked to the abduction of the Siren, Lacy Rain. It had been rash and foolhardy, for that Siren particularly had been betrothed and bonded to her mate from a baby. Then, instead of claiming his true mate, Isla Snow, he used his great expertise in alchemy to tamper with his first cousin, Cesaré's, ring to get close enough to take the crown. It had made an enemy of the king and his cousin in the process.

However, despite all that, he was legally married to the sister, Lilian Gale. Even though the human, Lance McCabe, was her mate. With her he'd been initiated to breathe the water and could not now be ignored on the Atlantean stage, despite how much the main players wanted it.

As he shook hands with Malleven, and took the drink offered, he decided it was his job not to have personal opinions, but to ensure protocol and the fates were served fairly and uninterrupted.

"I am honored that you took the time out to see me, given the current situation brewing in the Atlantic."

Delissi tipped his head accepting the compliment and not at all surprised how well informed Malleven was. He'd have contacts to rival his own. He sighed. "Yes, indeed. We live in dire times.

"Please sit," Malleven said, pointing to a soft leather armchair. Then he sat in one opposite with a waft of expensive cologne.

The man was always turned out and groomed to perfection. It was hard not to admire someone so young who was so fastidious about every aspect of their life. Even now, while he studied him, the boy sat relaxed and waiting, not feeling the need to talk to fill a silence.

Delissi could not help make comparisons to his own son; after all, this boy made no secret that he wanted the crown for himself. His son, Dante, was growing into a good statesman from a less than ideal start, but he was still given to moments of impulsiveness that made the families nervous. His time was taken constantly managing the troublesome Sirens and their mates – the worst being his true wife, Tia Storm, who refused to be tied down and couldn't make up her mind whether she wanted him or his best friend, Jay.

They all needed a firm hand, and this young man would have no qualms. He had an unwavering ruthlessness and drive. If the nation could get past his watered-down genes, he could be a ruler to rival Dante.

Still the boy waited for him to speak, not with trepidation but with an eerie air of confidence way beyond his years. It was a little unnerving. "I'll get straight to the point of my visit and keep you no longer," he said at last. "Does the name Phoebe Ray mean anything to you?"

He smiled but his eyes glistened. "Ah, the last of the sisters. Pledged to the king now, is she not?" he said in his melodic, Italian-accented English.

Delissi smoothed the fibers of his trousers on his crossed knee. "Are you saying you have not met this woman, Malleven?"

"That was not the question, my lord duke. Had you asked: Have we met? I would have answered yes, I have been given that great pleasure."

"And how did you come to meet?"

Malleven sat back in his chair as if he was searching his mind as to when exactly that was. "One of my brothers met her many years ago when she was just a child, then he bumped into her again only recently in Seattle. He came upon her by chance when she strayed into a poor neighbor-hood. He did the only wise thing in the circumstances; he brought her to me."

Delissi had to frown at that. The safest thing was to take her home. He didn't want to let fly with accusations, so he took a different tack. "Your brother...did he know who she was as a child?"

"He did not, but it was suspected, and her guard was increased without her knowledge. My brotherhood always seeks to be of service to our race. They stayed in the shadows and the families and human authorities remained in the dark so as not to interfere with the fates."

Delissi tipped his head in a show of deference. The Magi were clever. They had found their valuable bargaining chip and held her until such a time until she came into play. The exact time when a prince, i.e. Malleven, was inducted into the ranks. It was a masterstroke – a prince who already had links with several of the Sirens, one way or another.

Although he already knew the answer, he had to ask, "Why did you not defer and deliver her to the king when you realized she wasn't yours?" He pointed to the opaque divining ring on his left hand. He would have known instantly that she was not and would know exactly what was correct to do.

There was no backtracking or poor excuses. Instead, Malleven looked him directly and unapologetically in the eye. It was at this point he was sure Malleven knew he'd come armed with facts that he wanted clarified and not to fish. He felt the sweep of his scan several times, trying to glean hints of how much he knew. His mental blocks were far too strong. He was forced to read his aura and would, of course, find it direct and honest.

Malleven bowed his head slightly and said, "Ask me what

you need to know, lord duke, and I will answer you as honestly as I can."

Delissi wasted no more time prevaricating. "How long was Phoebe Ray with you?"

"One month."

"To what purpose did it serve to keep her that long and then just put her back?"

Malleven took a deep breath, rose and began to saunter slowly around the room. He seemed to be thinking deeply on how best to answer the question. He reached the sideboard, picked up the decanter and refreshed both their glasses. "In all honesty, I had no idea what I would do with her when she came to me. At first, I merely began to get to know her, but then she began to mean so much, I was loath to let her go."

It wasn't what Delissi was expecting. "Are you saying you married her?" The idea was outrageous.

Malleven knocked back his drink. "No...I hadn't forgotten I'm married to Lilian Gale." It was said bitterly with stiffness in his jaw, as he well knew marrying more than one Siren was a privilege reserved only for the king. "But she breathed for Cesaré first ..."

Cold realization began to creep up Delissi's spine when he knew where Malleven was going. The implications were enormous.

"But we became friends and in a short time we became lovers." Malleven's eyelids lowered for him to join the dots."

"You got in the water with her," Delissi finished flatly, not even looking at him.

"It was a simple thing. I already breathed the water."

Delissi still didn't look at him while he worked through what it all meant. "She breathed for you?"

"She did."

"And you were the first?"

"I was."

Delissi rolled his eyes to the ceiling. "So you have her power," he said as a statement of fact.

"I do," Malleven said, quietly.

This was the worst possible outcome at a truly critical time with the humans. It was a leadership challenge. He knew it. Malleven would settle for nothing less.

The king was bound to her and married legally, but Malleven held her power and that automatically qualified him for a seat on the council and full rights at court.

Then one small detail sprung out at him. "Why did Phoebe return with no knowledge of where she had been?"

Malleven bowed his head and sunk back into his chair with a poof when the air squashed out of it. "Forgive me when I say, old habits die hard. I temporarily masked her memories. When she sees me again they will return. I needed time to gather my thoughts and decide how I wanted to move forward with this. I knew she lived with her Protector who would recognize the danger of the situation and she would be taken to court. It just gave me the necessary breathing space."

Even though it was obvious what Malleven would decide, it sounded reasonable and made sense not to rush his hand. Malleven's track record had been poor and he'd managed to make an enemy out of just about everyone – particularly those on the council. He'd have his work cut out there winning them over. "I don't envy you. It won't be easy."

Malleven nodded. It was the first sign of weariness he'd ever seen in the man. "I am a marked man. It is what it is."

"Your claim will have to be substantiated."

Malleven nodded. "Of course."

"She is also bound to a human. One who bears a purple ring."

Malleven did give away a little surprise at that. Then he recovered quickly. "Even that cannot displace First Breath."

Delissi had to concede that. "Okay, give me some time. I will organize an audience at court when everyone is there for you to make your claim. There will be much opposition. You must be sure that Phoebe will back you up." He was reminding Malleven of the embarrassment he suffered when his own mate, Isla Snow, abandoned him during his test to drowning and took the prince Darres Borge as her mate instead. It had been a crushing blow.

Malleven's smile seemed bright though a little forced. "I am certain."

For a moment it did make him pause. He couldn't ignore the implications all this would have on his biological son, Dante. There was nothing for it; they would have to see it through to the end. If the fates wanted him as king then he would win. It was a belief he had to hold onto to do his job.

However, he had to hand it to this boy. He'd played a poor hand in life extremely well.

He patted his hands on his knees and rose to his feet. "Leave it with me. I will contact you in a few days. Be ready."

Malleven stood as well. He shook his hand with a strong, confident grip. "As always, I thank the stars for your fairness and impartiality, lord duke."

Deliss nodded at the compliment, but it did not sit easily with him. He walked slowly towards the door, then he stopped and turned. Everyone at court underestimated this young man but he did not. It was that that truly worried him. "I ask one favor."

Malleven touched his heart and his forehead in the way of a Magi promise.

"Whatever your long-term goal, I ask that you think first of our race and its survival. I say this to you as I would to Dante. The Atlasians *will* come and you will have to stand by your actions, as will Dante."

Malleven's eyes glistened knowing full well what Delissi

was driving at. If he intended to take the kingdom for himself, then he would take on the same weight of responsibility as Dante, and he didn't want to be found wanting for all their sakes. He simply bowed his head and said, "As always, my lord duke shows great foresight."

With a feeling of deep disquiet, Delissi left the apartment.

CHAPTER 42

$\mathcal{P}$hoebe and Tia stood looking out at a craggy area of coastline while the Murrs began unloading stuff out of the cars. *Can't we fight them or run for it?* Phoebe thought in the hope Tia was listening. She had no idea about the whole telepathic thing yet. The Murrs all laughed.

Phoebe blasted red and guessed they had all tuned in. "No point," Tia said, giving her hand a squeeze.

Listen to your sister, the one called Dax said, with a grin that looked almost human.

They were nudged to get walking to the shore's edge.

Wait! Vionne said, holding her back by the arm. *A little insurance.* Then he started to wrap some jelly-like string around her wrist, then his own. When she tried to prise her fingers underneath it was as though it had become welded to her skin. *Our technology. Don't fight it as it will tighten,* Vionne explained.

She looked across at Tia who remained free.

Tia won't go anywhere without you.

Tia scowled back at him.

They were led to the very edge of the rocks where the

waves boiled up a few feet beneath. Phoebe was terrified. They were expected to jump. It was very different to the small underwater tests she'd experienced for the breathing thing.

"Just breathe like you've done before," Tia said, coming up next to her.

"That's just it, I've barely done it."

Trust in us, Vionne said, with that weird, almost hypnotic, look again. *We would not see you hurt in any way.*

With her heart thumping she gave him the tinniest of nods. Then, before she knew what was happening, he picked her up and stepped straight off into the sea.

For a moment she was overcome by absolute panic. All she could see was white froth and taste the bitter salt, until everything calmed and Vionne appeared directly in front of her. *Just breathe slowly and normally, Phoebe. You are one of us. This is natural for you.*

It was hard to tell if it wasn't just due to lack of oxygen, but she began to feel better, then euphoric. The water entered her lungs and she kept her eyes on his. It felt like he was all around her, stroking and calming her, but no part of him physically touched her except to hold her hands. It was all just a feeling but somehow, she knew it emanated from him.

On land the Murrs looked strange and awkward, but down here in the environment they belonged there was no other word to describe them but magnificent. Covered in bold savage-like striped skin that seemed a more natural color in the water, the shades of their hair went with it perfectly. They were lean, muscly and then hitting her like a thunderbolt, hot. These guys were smoking hot.

Vionne smiled smugly inside. *How was she feeling this?* She heard his chuckle as he pulled her with him to the deeper water. They swam for only a short distance when a faint buzzing began to get a little louder until it became a gentle hum. A small craft hovered a few feet above the rocky seabed. When she neared, she could see that it was translucent with tiny colored lights pulsing in rhythm. It reminded her of a microscopic deep-sea organism she'd once seen on a wildlife program. The way in was underneath. Dax went through first. Then Vionne released their handcuff and pushed her up through what felt like a soft membrane in the floor. Another Murr pulled her up and straight onto her feet. She immediately started retching to expel the water. The more she tried, the more unpleasant it felt and the more the urge increased.

Hands touched either side of her shoulders and gripped them firmly. *Stop!* It was Vionne. She continued to struggle. *You're still submerged. Be calm.* He pulled her to him and put his forehead next to hers. The effect was instant. The stress just ebbed away until all she was aware of was just how close they were and how incredibly intimate the gesture was.

Vionne seemed to sense her discomfort and gradually put her away from him. She waved her hand in front of her face and looked at him in confusion. Then she went to speak but no noise came out. It was true. They were still under water. *But I can't feel it at all.*

Tia sat down moodily in her seat. *Yeah, yeah, seen it all before. Just Murr technology crap.*

Phoebe looked back at Vionne and found herself wanting to apologize for Tia's rudeness, which was just plain dumb considering they were being kidnapped. Again, he seemed to already understand just from her thought alone. It was unnerving.

The technology allows us to move when we are inside as freely as you do through air.

She looked around her. There were another two Murrs driving the little submarine and they nodded politely.

Allow me to introduce everyone properly. These are my lieu-tenants, my brothers, Dax and Caan and I am Vionne. We are sons of the Lord Advocate, Darl.

Phoebe looked at Tia for clarification.

More bloody princes, Tia said, looking at her nails, bored.

Again that weird chuckle. *Yes, Tia is correct. We are from the Borge family.* He bowed his head slightly.

Phoebe remembered him, but at the time she'd been too wrapped up in Drew and her new surroundings to give him much attention. She found herself liking him despite herself. He was handsome and strong and not a bit awkward now he was under the water. She guessed that twenty-four, seven, under water was like a constant resistance workout. No wonder they created special machines to make the water lighter when they were inside.

He laughed again.

She found herself studying his stripes, so vivid and jagged. Hers were so much more soft and sweeping around her contours. However the biggest difference seemed to be in his eyes. They were soullessly black and haunting with no whites at all. When Phoebe looked at Tia she was shocked to see hers were almost the same. They seemed to have grown to completely engulf the rest of her eyes.

Vionne shook his head. *Yours remain smaller,* to answer her unspoken question.

Oh, she smiled cautiously and he seemed to study her features closely to try to do the same. Laughter bubbled inside her at the strange face he was making trying to copy her. Tia looked at her as if she'd lost her mind.

Vionne shrugged. *I will perfect it.* Then he turned his head, distracted by one of his lieutenants, and Phoebe noticed the soft blondness of his hair that reached his shoulders in gentle curls.

Dax came over and dumped a piece of shimmering material in each of their hands. *You should put these on. Land clothes are no use to you down here.*

Phoebe held it up in front of her and examined it. It weighed nothing and she didn't believe that it would cover her at all.

It actually does. Tia said, now standing up next to her.

Phoebe's eyes strayed to Vionne again and saw the shimmering pants he had on that were a cross between a sarong and sheik of Bagdad trousers. *Like that?*

Kind of. You make a barrier for me and I'll change, then I'll do the same for you.

Phoebe did what Tia suggested and they were soon standing in very different but not half bad little mini dresses that had panties built in. They seemed to shimmer in pastel and silver like the underside of a seashell.

Despite the weirdness of his eyes, she didn't miss the visual sweep that Vionne gave her. It made her feel smug. She totally rocked the mermaid look, and for the first time she wasn't conscious of her markings, now on full view. She wondered if it was from the Murrs that she got the teeth and feral eyes. No one seemed to show them so far. Maybe it was because no one needed to.

Vionne approached her, cocking his head to the side. *How do you transform?*

Shit! She really had to stop thinking. The whole thing was getting on her nerves now. *Do you mind giving me some privacy?*

You have to practice mind blocks, Tia explained. *That's how the Murrs do it. Otherwise it's like constant mental diarrhea all the time. Except they don't like teaching us coz they like to ear wig, don't tcha, big ears!* She said, addressing Vionne directly.

After a very human-like shrug, he still waited for her to answer. Phoebe was beginning to realize there wasn't much that riled up Vionne.

Oh nothing special...you know, regular Siren changes.

He took an uncomfortable step closer. *Then why the avoidance – the quickening of the heart rate?* He touched the center of her forehead. *The fear.*

The moment her terror spiked her vision zeroed in and there it was for all of them to see. Then followed anger, which only made it worse.

Bingo! Tia said, coming closer.

Vionne just stared and his brothers joined him.

Phoebe wanted to run away but there was nowhere to go. However, instead of saying one word, Vionne just looked at his ring. As if her changing might make some kind of difference. It remained the same blood red color.

Preoccupied, he moved away to the front of the little marine craft and his brothers continued with whatever they were doing driving it.

Phoebe was left standing absolutely still in the middle while it hummed and zipped through the ocean.

CHAPTER 43

*D*ante stood facing the huge window out to sea without really seeing the beautiful underwater view. The children, sensing his preoccupation, were running wild all over the hall while his closest advisors chatted in the armchairs around him. Max, Sebastian, Alfonzo and Cesaré spoke in hushed tones but none of them came up with anything new.

He was vaguely aware of Jay's voice quickly taking charge of the children and sending them off to the kitchen for cookies. Then he felt a nudge at his arm and Jay passed him a scotch. He nodded in thanks and turned to see he'd brought Keenan with him. "Fellas," he said, and knocked back the drink in one.

"Any news?" Jay said.

Dante shook his head. "Naomi and Darres have gone to Murrtaine. The girls aren't there yet, but they said there's definitely something brewing."

Dante's hand shook slightly as he ran his fingers through his curly shoulder-length hair. "This is my fault," he said, so only Jay could hear. "I always have to push her to the limit."

Jay didn't argue but tipped his glass in salute and drank his drink. "There are two of them. They would still have had Phoebe."

Dante nodded with a sigh. "Why though, why now? Just when we need the Murrs' strength."

He turned sharply, sensing someone's approach. Cash and Sean descended the stairs from the lift chatting animatedly. "What is it?" Dante asked, immediately.

"We've found out a load of stuff about the doctor's surgery," Sean said.

"It was rented about a year ago by a company called Lieburgh Medicines owned by a holding company out of New England," Cash said.

"After more digging it turns out it's owned by some charitable religious organization calling themselves The Illuminated," Sean said.

Dante frowned. It was the first he'd heard of them. He looked to his college professor, Max. "Have you heard of them?"

Max looked a little disturbed when he said, "We have spoken of them before, sir. The only order I have come across ever considering themselves illuminated were the ancient war-like order of monks known as the Scythians from around 900_{BC}, but they went into obscurity around 200_{AD}."

Dante remembered the conversation. Everything fit them perfectly. He looked to Alfonzo, his closest advisor. "This sect?"

"Humans have recorded nothing in the last hundred years or so, however …"

"What?"

"This organization is on our watch list. They are a very closed order seeking the purest blood lines, but they are reputed to take children – young boys – to train as one of them."

"Lost boys," Dante echoed to himself, remembering their previous discussion perfectly.

There was a collective hush around the room while they all thought the same thing.

"Do you think they could have tampered with our boy, Drew, in some way?" Cash said for them all.

It seemed the most logical conclusion. Dante began to pace while he thought, racking his brains for the best way out of this. Time was running out.

"You could give the boy a blood test?" Cash said.

"It's been done," Dante said, with a dismissive wave of the hand.

"Has it been done lately?" Cash said. "Just that when he was with me, he asked what family I was from. Odd question from a human."

Dante stopped pacing and looked at him. It hadn't occurred to him that anything could change. Then his eyes tracked to Alfonso, who nodded. He would see to it.

"What's the connection between the Scythians and the Murrs?" Jay asked.

"Could be something or nothing," Dante said, resuming pacing. "We'll learn soon enough. The Murrs will contact us soon with their demands." It was a sobering thought. This was very much a hostage situation.

"I'll tell ya something though, Jay. The Scythians will pay now that they've fucked with me."

Jay nodded as if he expected nothing less. Then they waited.

.   .   .

AFTER THE INITIAL novelty of zipping along the ocean floor in what was basically a jelly bubble wore off, Phoebe dozed. Tia had curled up on a seat opposite her.

She wasn't sure how long she'd slept, but the men seemed to be communicating and getting quite busy with colored lights and images appearing in mid-air. *Think we're nearly there,* she projected to Tia, who stirred and unfurled to sit up.

The little craft had definitely slowed up considerably. Phoebe put her hands on the weird jelly wall and peered out. There wasn't much to see until the sheer size of what was looming hit her. *Bloody hell.*

Tia appeared at her shoulder to look as well. *I know. Mad, isn't it?*

There, as far as the eye could see, was a vast bubble that looked like a blue-green hue way into the horizon. Whatever it was was semi-circular and opaque, like a world within a world.

Some sort of docking was taking place. That wasn't strictly true, as with a flick of a switch her jaw dropped open.

Every time I see it I never get over it, Tia said from next to her. *Like abracadabra and there it is.*

A magical city seemed to just switch on through the glass of a snow globe. They were still moving forward slowly and she began to be able to discern buildings. All of them seemed to be made of glass of varying degrees of transparency and were in different shades of blue and green. Nothing had hard angles and seemed rounded off with smooth curves.

It's all to reflect light, Tia explained. *We are the only outsiders to have ever seen this.*

For a moment Phoebe felt completely overwhelmed. Of course she'd been told what she was and where she was from, but seeing all this somehow brought it home and it was breathtaking –almost worth being abducted.

One of the Murrs was counting.

We're going in. Tia said.

Then Phoebe understood as something engulfed the little craft and everything outside suddenly became brighter and clearer. Whatever their snow globe was made of it acted like a membrane and they'd just passed through.

There were walkways and roads with smaller vehicles like the one they were in. All zipping here there and everywhere like little bubbles with colored lights inside. Seaweeds and pretty corals were arranged as if they were planted to make small gardens. Small shoals of little neon fish swam overhead like flocks of birds. They continued on slowly, street after fascinating street, and everything was a grand designer's dream. It was beautiful.

They appeared to be slowing down to a stop. She hadn't felt him until he was right behind her. *Welcome to Murrtaine,* Vionne said.

When she turned around, he put out his arm. *Shall we?*

Phoebe looked at Tia, a little unsure.

We'd better get out, Tia said. *I'm starving.*

Phoebe watched in awe as Dax and Caan stood in the center of the craft and simply dropped through. Tia followed. Vionne was watching her with that intense look he had. *Someone will catch you. Don't be afraid.*

She nodded, closed her eyes and stepped onto the area where the others had disappeared. Within a second Dax's large arms were around her. But she needn't have worried. The water buoyancy was back and, for a moment, she had that awful feeling like she couldn't breathe again.

Her face was immediately cupped in large hands and a forehead put to hers. It was Vionne again. The intimacy of the move made her want to push him away but it really did work. A familiar feeling of peace came and she became calm and relaxed.

When Dax released her, she looked around and saw a

crowd of inquisitive eyes gathering. They seemed all different ages; men, women and some cute little children with next to nothing on. They wore the same shimmering material that glimmered different colors depending on the light. They were similar to Vionne and his brothers with varying paleness to their skin, some more bluish than others. All had the vivid stripes and deep soulless eyes.

Welcome, the Princess Phoebe. I'm hoping she loves Murrtaine enough to stay. She looked at Vionne briefly in alarm but was soon distracted by the weird clicking sounds the crowd were making. They sounded like a group of dolphins.

They're clapping, Tia said.

Phoebe saw no movement of hands, but she guessed it was impossible in the water. They did look kind of joyful and she smiled at them a little painfully, not knowing what else to do. *You're doing great.* Vionne projected next to her. He said his goodbyes to the crowd and led her by the elbow towards a group of buildings. Her unease was growing. Vionne was a charming escort but she wasn't here voluntarily and the way he was acting around her was way too personal and familiar. *Perhaps it's their way.*

He fancies you, idiot, Tia said from behind.

Shit, she really had to do something about the thinking thing.

Why? It's way too entertaining.

They neared the buildings of what must surely be a palace. There were several domes connected by tubular walkways and one huge dome in the middle with a pointy spire on top.

Phoebe wondered why they needed to be inside at all if everything was under water and inside the huge protective bubble that covered the city.

A group of guards swam past in unison, perfectly matched and timed as if they were parading the courtyard like soldiers. It was like a kind of gliding trooping of the color, except it was silent.

It was a very silent world.

When the soldiers saw their party, they stopped swimming and remained upright and bowed their heads in salute. The guards parted either side of them and they swam through to the doors of the palace.

They went into a vestibule. Vionne passed his hand over a reader on the wall and Phoebe fell clumsily onto her feet. The gravity had returned just like on the little sub. Vionne touched her shoulder to stop her coughing up again. *Still under water?* she asked.

He smiled a little. *You are learning our ways already.* Her discomfort returned.

The doors in front of them opened and they walked in as if they were walking through air. It really was remarkable. It didn't feel like they were moving through water at all.

Believe me, it never gets old, Tia said, mirroring her thoughts.

They continued to follow Vionne who said he would show them to their quarters to freshen up. That felt odd considering they were under water. Just how did a person freshen up down here?

You will be treated as the royal princesses you are, here. You may request anything...except of course, to leave.

It was the slap back to reality Phoebe needed. This wasn't a holiday.

They came to a halt in the most easterly part of the palace, to what seemed like their own dome. Vionne put his hand to the opaque wall. It shimmered into a gentle waterfall. He gestured with his arm for them to walk through.

Phoebe looked at Tia in shock. *Are the walls made of water?*

Everything is just atoms arranged in a different order, Vionne explained.

Tia walked straight through without a care. She wasn't so sure. Vionne held out his hand. *Come, we'll do it together.*

She took his hand a little shakily and took a huge step through the running water gripping him hard. However, just like that and they were through into the most beautiful spacious room. It was huge and reminded her of the set of a Fred Astaire musical.

Two rose-colored transparent beds in the shape of clamshells dominated the center of the impossibly shiny floor.

Go on, feel it, Tia projected with a nudge.

Phoebe cautiously went over and touched her hand against the milky fabric of the cover. It felt as smooth as liquid.

Don't ask me what it is. All I know is that all the soft furnishings are made from a kind of sea moss that's grown down here.

Phoebe looked over at Vionne in awe, who stood a little way off. He bowed his head slightly. *It has been a tiring day for you. I will leave you to settle in. You will find clothes in the dressing room,* and he pointed to what looked like a sheer wall.

Phoebe was too overwhelmed to question him further.

I'll come back later to show you around.

She smiled her thanks and he disappeared along with the waterfall so they were sealed in. For a moment sheer panic of claustrophobia came over her. They were trapped god knows how far down on the seabed.

Tia's hand gently rubbed her back. *It's weird but you'll get used to it. I spent months here through both of my pregnancies.*

Phoebe relaxed a little. That would explain why she could remain so cool about everything. *So that's how you know Vionne and his brothers?*

Mainly, yeah ... I don't know what he's thinking this time though. Her mind was already getting distracted as she spoke.

She was running her hand over the walls that rippled curiously like water.

Phoebe wandered over to follow what she was doing. They found an area with pretty pale pink and green lights and discovered they were control panels. In fact, any light they came across did something. One made the lighting dim, another sparked off some weird moaning sounds.

I think it's whales, Tia said, with her eyes heavenward thinking. *I need to get Vionne to pump round some decent tunes.*

Phoebe tried one that cleared a section of the wall to look out onto a delightful blue courtyard with sea anemones arranged in an intricate design. Then eventually they came across the light sequence that opened up another circular room as big as an average house. They discovered it was the dressing room. Rail upon rail of shimmering material lined its walls and a tiny pedestal with a clear vase and a single sea flower decorated the middle.

Phoebe turned around on the spot to take in the gorgeous place. Everything about Murrtaine was designed as if by some master architect and like nothing she'd ever seen before. It was clutter-free and all smooth rounded surfaces— a futuristic design heaven.

Tia pulled a dress off the rail and grinned. *Let's try some on.*

Phoebe giggled. Tia was really good company and took her mind off their situation. She nodded and pulled a garment off the rail for herself.

The material was whisper-thin and shimmered green one way and pink the other. She pulled it on over her head and the little dress she already had on. She soon realized you could get away with it because whatever it was made of was so thin and delicate. The material just kissed everywhere it touched. It was the ultimate in sexiness.

Tia was already doing her best impression of a catwalk

model, comically sashaying up and down in front of her. *Can't wear underwear with this,* she said, raising an eyebrow.

Phoebe guessed that was the idea. Everything just hugged and supported so gently that she was sure there was no need for anything as gaudy as a bra. It was dawning on her that this race of people utilized and worked with all the elements of nature and not against it.

They like, live in their swimsuits, Tia continued, holding up another garment against her. *But with style.* She touched a group of amber lights and a section of wall became as shiny as a mirror.

The place was utterly remarkable.

Could you ever see yourself living here, Phoebes?

She stalled mid-rummage and looked over at Tia as if she'd lost her mind. *No, never.* She couldn't imagine why Tia could even think such a thing. The place was pretty impressive, she had to admit. *I could never leave Drew.*

Tia shrugged, still distracted by a cute little dress she was holding against her. *Just curious, that's all. Because you know that's why Vionne brought you here, don't you? I was just brought along for the ride.*

Phoebe straightened and openly stared at her in horror. *I thought you didn't know what he was thinking? Anyway, I'm not a bit interested. I love Drew.*

Tia was now looking at her back view in the reflection. *Yeah...Dante's gonna go absolutely nuts. But, he's miles away, and Atlantean men can be pretty persuasive. Vionne is a big, hunky Murr. Kind of a triple threat. Hope you have a choice, Phoebes.*

Phoebe was still staring at her in utter shock. *You don't know that for sure.*

Well it's not me, I'm safely married off.

Oh my god. It explained everything. She was the very last of the unmarried Sirens.

CHAPTER 44

Another load of bloods was taken from Drew. Despite starting to feel a little like a lab rat, he wanted to cooperate in any way he could.

It worked, as Dante seemed satisfied that he wasn't knowingly involved with the capture of the girls. Although he was still heavily watched while they waited for the results from a trusted genetics lab somewhere in Ireland. He guessed they couldn't exactly use the Murrs' expertise at the moment, given the strained relations.

The time passed slowly for everyone, but particularly him. Something had happened to him in his past that somehow overshadowed everything. Yet he still couldn't pinpoint what it was. Overnight he'd lost his identity and had no idea who he really was.

He looked down at the big ring Dante had given him a while back. He wore it all the time now as a kind of symbol of Phoebe. Right then it was pearl white. Even that didn't make sense.

If it was true what they suspected and he was some kind of apprentice to some ancient order, then he should be one hundred percent human. It was a stipulation of theirs – supposedly. So he shouldn't even be able to touch the metal. Not only could he wear it, but it acted the same as with any Atlantean prince.

None of it made any difference though. Despite all that, he knew he was in love with Phoebe. It was the only thing he could be sure of. And because of that, he knew he had to make plans to go. Somehow he needed to get away to find out who he was, because even though they kept saying it was probably Tia who gave them away, something niggled inside him to make him believe it happened through him.

Until the opportunity arose and the blood results came back, he bided his time.

VIONNE APPROACHED his elderly father in the huge council room. Darl was Lord Advocate of Murrtaine and head of the large Borge Royal family. Vionne lived with the knowledge that he must take his place one day. Murrs lived long lives, but at almost six hundred and fifty, Darl was very much in his twilight years and his health was failing.

The assembled ministers left him and Vionne approached his father who sank wearily into a large carved quartz chair. He beckoned Vionne with his hand, *My son.*

Trouble? He recognized a war council when he saw one and was immediately concerned.

There is increased shipping traffic in our vicinity. We are on alert, his father explained.

Vionne frowned but came close and leaned over his father to touch his forehead with his. It was the gesture of intimacy between family members for Murrs. Through it they could impart feelings directly, making it a warm and pleasant experience. He sensed his father's disquiet. *Is it a serious threat, Father?* They had been on alert many times and he worried about his father taking on added stress.

Enough that we should be watchful, my son. Duke Ormond Delissi is in constant communication until the threat has passed.

Before Vionne could press him further, he batted his unsaid words away with a hand and changed the subject. *Give me happier news. I am told that through a human you were able to find your Siren.*

Vionne bowed his head. That was true, but he couldn't hide that it wasn't as easy as his father assumed.

She is not yours? His father looked surprised. *Your brother Darres was not a fated partner to his mate. He took the Florianna sister. There should be another sister for us.*

Vionne nodded his head. Everything his father said was the truth. *I feel an affinity to this Siren, but I fear something unforeseen has happened and corrupted the outcome in some way.*

Darl's eyes narrowed.

Vionne knew what his father wanted. It was something that could not be explained in clear thought. It had to be transmitted in the truly Murr way. He wasted no time and flashed an image of his left hand with his ring that had become blood-red in Phoebe's proximity. How he'd been alerted by his spies placed to monitor the Scythians – the sworn enemy of Atlantis. Then, instead of finding just the new Siren he was expecting, he found the queen, Tia Storm. Lastly, he projected the fight with the Scythians that followed and their escape.

The feelings he got back from his father were anger tinged with fear. It disturbed him more than anything. His father was a very brave man. *You abducted the king's Siren – the one of his heart?* Darl was furious with him.

Father, I couldn't simply leave her in the barbarian hands. Something isn't right here.

His father turned his head in exasperation. *The female*

runs at every opportunity. The correct thing to do was to contact the king immediately and return her.

You are right, Father, but the other sister, Phoebe Ray, is not like the others. I felt the best thing to do was keep them together until I had a chance to speak to you.

Darl relaxed a little. *Do you doubt her?*

Vionne shook his head. Even though his ring had changed to an unprecedented red, deep down he knew she was the real deal. *She transforms as all Atlanteans do, but with her emotions it continues into something else. Her eyes change into those of a sea serpent and her teeth resemble more the Santalini bloodline than her own.* He went on to project the mental picture of Phoebe transformed in all her terrifying glory.

Darl continued to stare at him for a long moment after he had finished. *Mention this to no one. You did the correct thing for the good of the race. However, the hotheaded Dubonnetti king will not think of it in the same way and will bring down his wrath upon us if we are not careful.*

Vionne pushed away from his father and began to pace. He knew he was right but something had to be done. *Every day that passes, they cut us out of government. Darres has no allegiance except to himself. This Siren has to be ours. We have no true representation, Father.*

Darl nodded, understanding his point perfectly. *You are a wise son. I forget sometimes that you are already a ruler in all but name.*

Vionne's anger evaporated and a wave of affection wafted over him from his father. *I only wish to serve you and my people.*

Darl seemed pleased with him but was still clearly troubled. *She has chosen a human in all this?*

Vionne nodded, admitting it didn't fit in with any ambition or master plan that he could see. *The humans are already represented with the fourth Siren, Lilian Gale.*

It was true. All the families were represented on the

council and had a say. The Sirens were Bonaci and so their father, Sebastian, and uncle, Alfonzo, sat for them. Tia Storm was married to the king and linked the Bonaci to the Dubonnettis, Lucy Rain linked them to the Santalinis through Keenan, Lilian Gale was with the human, Lance McCabe, but aligned herself to the Florianna through Cesaré by First Breath. He sat as the king's right hand – a highly exulted position. However, the Borge were linked through the mating of Isla Snow and Darres and couldn't be relied on. Darres was neither her most compatible nor her First Breath. She herself had chosen him, which was admirable, and in any other circumstances they would rejoice, but Darres was by nature a loner with no other loyalty than to Isla. It was understandable. Captured by the humans as a small boy, he'd spent his whole life in isolation away from his people. That didn't help the Murr people now though. They needed a strong voice.

There must be a true mating for the Borge. Then, of course, she could be for the Bonaci, Darl projected.

Vionne remained quiet, allowing his father to think aloud.

Darl made up his mind. *I believe you were correct in your thinking and your actions. The Bonaci are connected in the female line. It makes much more sense for the true mate to be an unrepresented family. Darres was chosen and most compatibles are paired at birth. This Siren must be for the Borge.*

Vionne looked down at his ring that rested in its default opaque white. *Then why is it red when I'm near her, Father?*

That was the question that stumped them both. Darl beckoned him close to touch foreheads and signal the end of the meeting. *We will allow some time to put the question to the Orb. In the meantime, I will get a message to Dante assuring him that the sisters are safe and in our care as our guests.*

Vionne knew Dante wouldn't believe it for a second, but

it would buy them some valuable time. Events were hurtling towards the end of days. The council was beginning to crumble, which couldn't come at a worse time now that the final Siren had been found. The return was imminent. Everyone could sense it. Putting a question like this to the Orb was risky. If foul play was detected it could rock this world off its axis, literally. He just had to have faith that they at least had done nothing wrong.

IT SEEMED like round after round of blood tests and questioning to Drew. Here he was waiting in Dante's study again. It was just Dante at his desk, him sitting in a stiff wooden chair opposite and a guard lurking somewhere behind him. "Do you have anything new from the bloods?" Drew said, completely expecting the answer to be yes.

Dante shook his head. "Not yet." Then he sat back in his chair and scrutinized him as he always did.

He was sick of it. Phoebe had been gone a couple of days and he needed action.

Dante cut through his thoughts. "What do you know of an organization known as The Illuminated Ones?"

Drew just stared at him blankly.

"Tell me more of the Scythians?"

Drew's patience snapped and he stood up, sharply scraping his chair. "Look, man, do what you have to do, I don't fuckin' care. Just cut all this bullshit and find Phoebe. Do you know where she is yet?"

The guard had stepped forward, but Dante stilled him with just a look.

"Sit down!" Dante said, without even raising his voice. "I know you're anxious and frustrated, I feel the same. I'm asking you if you know these people because they are the ones behind your medical checkups. You – if you know it or not – *are* connected to them in some way."

Drew closed his eyes and sunk slowly back down into his chair. Stricken didn't even cover it. "Who are they, what do they want?" he said, his voice cracked and broken. Right then he'd agree or sign anything if it would save Phoebe. "I thought you said the Murrs have her?" he said, bewildered, raising his eyes to Dante again.

Dante tipped his head. "And you'd be right – at least as far as we know. How far they are involved with the Scythians, we have no idea yet."

They were interrupted by a knock at the door. A Santalini guard opened it and entered with Sebastian, Phoebe's father. "Sorry to disturb, but we have news. Naomi has sent word that the girls have safely arrived in Murrtaine and are being cared for as Darl's personal guests."

Drew looked between them when Dante didn't immediately answer. "What does that mean? Who is Darl?"

Still a little preoccupied, Dante said to no one in particular. "They are safe. It means they are with my cousins, the Borge princes." Then he smiled at Drew as if his mind had come back to the room. "Darl is the ruler – their father. It was only a matter of time before they had to declare they had them."

"And now we wait," Sebastian said, nodding sagely.

"Wait for what?" Drew said, jumping up and then getting slammed back into his seat by the guard behind him.

The look that appeared on Dante's face was far worse than anger, it was apologetic. "For their demands."

Somehow that explanation wasn't cutting it and Drew thought he would go mad if someone didn't put him out of his misery.

"They will want a bigger stake in government," Sebastian explained kindly.

Drew looked blankly between them, wanting to smash his fists into something.

"They will make a bid for Phoebe as their Siren," Dante said, finally, closing his eyes as he delivered the blow. "We do need answers," Dante said to Sebastian.

"Yes," Sebastian nodded.

"Answers?" Two guards grabbed him either side, but he didn't feel them as he rose from the chair like an erupting volcano. "I will rip out the throat of anyone who dares touch her." He struggled and fought, not giving a shit that his vision had tunneled and his teeth bit into his own lip. He needed to kill something. And everyone else needed to get the fuck out of his way.

The guards held him firmly. His face had changed and all he could see was a thin strip down the center of his vision, the rest was a blur. But it was enough. Dante walked around his desk to stand in front of him. He searched his face in fascination. Then looked at Sebastian. Any embarrassment of being seen in his transformation was swallowed by his anger.

He guessed Dante handled weird well, as instead of railing or threatening him he just said calmly, "Vionne is a pure-bred prince from one of the strongest families. If his ring has divined her as a match …"

"You will have a fight on your hands," Sebastian finished for him.

Anger still rode him hard, but he listened. The guards didn't trust him enough to let go, but they loosened their grip slightly.

Dante was right. What chance did he have on his own against the might of a whole family? "Will you help me?" Drew said, but his voice was gravelly and quite unlike him.

After a moment of deliberation, Dante walked back around his desk and sat back down. "We still have some bargaining power. We can argue that you have the purple ring. On an Atlantean prince that would mean its wearer was her most compatible. If we could just solve the mystery of your blood. And they'd need witnesses if they want to make anything official. They have my wife which, if they don't handle correctly, is tantamount to a declaration of war."

Sebastian was nodding and agreeing with every word. "They will dispute the ring as a fraud. What do you suggest?"

Dante tapped his fingers on the desk while he thought. "We will insist on a Murr medical – if that's okay with you?" he said, tipping his head at Drew.

His teeth had receded and his vision was returning to normal when he shrugged and said, "I guess."

"They were getting you into that medical center for a reason, and we need to find out what that was. If anyone has the know-how to find out, it's the Murrs."

Drew shook his head in impatience. "Shouldn't we be storming the place to get her back or something? We're just wasting time."

Dante smiled a little. "There is no fighting the Murrs. That is not an option, not under water. If we find out who you are, and Phoebe has accepted you as hers, *and* if Vionne's ring has not declared her as his, then we have a shot at getting her back."

"And what of Tia?" Sebastian asked.

Dante's face darkened. "They need to do some serious explaining. The world's navies are assembling in the region above them. They will need us very soon."

Drew then understood how big all this was – like world stage stuff. All he cared about was Phoebe.

CHAPTER 45

The next day Drew was led back into Dante's study, now worryingly kitted out like an ER room. Except set up in the middle, instead of an operating table, was a huge space age chair, like something out of a sci-fi film. The Murrs, eager to do some damage limitation, had sent a medical team to the castle within hours of Dante's request.

"Take a seat," Dante said, indicating the chair in the middle looking more like something used for torture than healthcare.

Drew hesitated. "Seriously?"

Dante grinned, reading his mind. "Nail beds will remain intact, I promise."

Two of the tallest weirdest-looking guys dressed in floor-length white tunics and black steampunk goggles continued about their business twiddling knobs on machines and looking scientific. *Murrs*, he guessed. They both had a mop of impossibly white hair and moved like they glided rather than walked. Then, when they stopped to examine something, they remained impossibly still. Drew couldn't take his eyes off them.

Sebastian and Alfonzo sat on the small couch to watch and record proceedings. Another knock at the door and Cesaré entered and came and stood next to Dante.

The two Murrs waited, unnaturally frozen and looked at Dante, who nodded. "They're ready, Drew."

Drew sat in the chair and it immediately hissed and reclined like a dentist chair. His eyes darted and vision narrowed as he gripped the arms.

"Relax, man. The Murrs communicate telepathically, which makes them perfect to find out if you have anything in your subconscious. Hopefully their technology will project any lost memories onto this screen." He pointed to a large monitor on the far wall.

As the penny dropped and Drew realized what they wanted, his wrists, ankles and forehead were clamped and he was unable to move. His narrowed vision darted, tinged with red, and his teeth gnashed as the two strange men glided nearer. They stooped over him and appeared upside down from the angle he was laying. One moved his goggles up onto his head revealing his eyes. They were so dark and so deep they seemed disconnected like black discs.

The last normal thing he heard was the king telling him to relax and that no one wanted to hurt him, but he couldn't take his attention from the black discs hovering above him. The more he looked, the more depth they seemed to have and the more there seemed to be. There was a grey line in them swirling round and round beckoning him in. His heart rate began to slow and his struggles lessened until a wonderful warmth enveloped him. It felt like slipping into a warm bath on a freezing cold day. There was just no resisting the temptation to sink in and enjoy the feeling.

When he opened his eyes, he was surrounded by steam. It was over. The drips of water and the tiled walls filled him relief. He was in a bathroom. Perhaps he'd fallen asleep for a while. He sloshed the water up over his shoulders. The water was deep and covered in pink bubbles. *Pink?*

He picked some up in his hand. He'd never seen pink bubbles in a bath before. Then he scooped a handful of the water and brought it closer to his face.

Then he screamed.

"WHY AREN'T you doing this? You are capable of reading a man's mind," Cesaré said.

Dante shrugged and bobbed his head. It was true he could, but he did it with very little finesse not being that practiced; he didn't want to scramble the boy's brain. "I don't want to know what he had for breakfast, what I need has been buried very deep. This is a job for the professionals."

Their smiles died on their faces with the blood-curdling scream. Buzzers sounded and machines beeped.

One of the Murrs went to Drew's other side and began pumping his chest. The other released the clamp on his forehead and replaced it with his hands. Drew jumped as if he'd been given an electric shock. They continued to pump his chest. It was remarkable, as they seemed to be defibrillating him without a machine.

The next moment the buzzing stopped and the beeps went back to a gentle rhythm.

"What happened?" Dante asked one of the Murrs, who was administering some kind of shot into Drew's arm. Naomi had tried to retrieve memories from Lacy a while back and it was done with none of this fuss quite successfully.

His mental barriers are great. He has been taught. There are many layers to his psyche and they have been strengthened by blood corruption. More than a simple scan is needed.

Dante was silent. The whole room waited for him to say

something. Nothing was making any sense. "But he is human? The blood corruption comes from the Siren he is claimed by."

I can assure you that this being's mind has been locked down tightly and his genetic markers are not completely human.

Dante wished he had the blood tests back to check independently. He knew for certain that Phoebe had initiated the blood thing. His mind was in turmoil. He wanted answers but this opened up a whole new avenue. It made him question whether Phoebe was innocent in all this. Maybe he'd been looking in the wrong direction and it was her working against him. Her lost month came up again and yet every lead always came up a dead end.

There was nothing else that could be done. Despite the dangers, someone had to go into Drew's mind. He looked drowsy and subdued. "Can he handle it?" No one he'd witnessed had gone to pieces like that. Realizing there was little choice, he said, "Proceed."

The Murr stared at him for a long moment. *It would need the most skilled Mind Walker and done quickly while he is relaxed. It is our guess that he has suffered much psyche tampering. Layer after layer to hide their tracks. The Mind Walker should be someone capable, but someone he trusts, otherwise it could kill them both.*

Dante whispered to Cesaré to bring the other three sisters to the room urgently. Naomi was still in Murrtaine. Then he moved closer to the chair. "Drew...Drew! Can you hear me?"

Drew's head lolled toward him, but he smiled in recognition. "Hey, man, this is good stuff, you should try it."

Dante smiled along but went on quickly. "Listen, mate, someone needs to get into your head. It's all that can be done."

Drew's eyes were now wide and dilated. "Will it help Phoebe?"

Dante nodded. "We think so."

"Then do it." Drew swallowed and looked ahead of him, already preparing himself.

It struck Dante then how resigned Drew was. As if he was on a one-way mission to something anyway. He pushed on. "If you chose the one who does it, it's more likely to be successful."

The door opened and Cesaré returned with Lily, Lance, Lacy, Keenan and Isla in tow. The room suddenly felt very crowded.

Drew seemed oblivious. "Who? What does it matter? Just get the job done."

Lily stepped forward. *I know him the best.*

Dante considered it for a moment, then shook his head. "I have no bond with you, Lily. If anything happens, I couldn't help you."

"I am mentally the strongest," Isla said.

Dante nodded. She was the right choice, but Darres wasn't here. He'd accompanied Naomi to Murrtaine. There was no way he was going to be happy about it. His bond with her would mean he'd know right away and would likely high-tail it back there with murder on his mind.

The only other option was Lacy, and Keenan was already shaking his head. "Don't even think about it – not if you want a live subject," he said, tipping his head in Drew's direction.

That sealed it. Isla it was. She wasn't corrupted by blood bonds, had the strongest mental barriers he knew and had been taught to master level by Darres. He'd have to cross that explosive bridge when he came to it.

A chair was brought closer to Drew so Isla could sit next to him and make the necessary skin contact. She sat and put a gentle hand over his. Drew's eyes tracked to hers. They were strangers really so they were given a few moments to get comfortable with what was about to happen.

The Murrs got busy putting sticky pads on their temples and wrists. They were wireless with little green lights inside. When they were ready, one of the Murrs came close to their eye line and projected the pathway Isla should take.

Drew was warned of possible discomfort, but he nodded and said he understood. Then the Murr pumped something else into his arm and the lights dimmed.

"Try and relax as much as you can," Dante said.

"What if I hurt her?"

"We won't allow that, don't worry yourself."

Drew was unaware that he'd already primed Cesaré to go in if there were any signs of serious trouble. He knew Isla well, and as a Florianna, he was probably the most skilled here, except they didn't call it mind walking. To them it was plain mind control, hypnotism and spellbinding, but he was held back as the cavalry.

Drew stared upwards blankly and began to shake. Isla was just watching him.

"Isla?" Dante said.

"I haven't even gone in yet."

His shaking became more and more violent.

"Take it easy, man."

"Release him. I can handle it," Isla said.

Dante nodded at the Murrs. "Just head and one hand."

The clamps released. Then everything became a blur.

Drew's eyes went up inside his head and when they came down they were thin slices like a lizard. Fangs punched out from his gums and he moved faster than anyone could track and sunk them deeply into Isla's arm.

Everyone jumped forward at the same time but were stopped by a force around them. It was just visible like a bubble. Several of them tried to punch through but were left shaking out their hands in pain. "It's no use," Dante said. His heart was racing as Drew relaxed back into his lying position still holding Isla's wrist in his mouth.

After a few moments it was clear that he was just holding her there and Dante's heart began to slow down. "I think she's okay. He just seems to be making a direct link to her." *Like an animal,* he finished in his head.

As he said the words his heart sank. Isla's head fell forward as she lost consciousness.

"He's draining her!" Keenan shouted, and went to hit the barrier again.

"Let me go in," Cesaré said frantically.

Dante held up his hand. "No, he's just allowed her in." Nothing looked more feral, but somehow he knew that Drew wasn't hurting her.

It was miraculous. The more he relaxed, the more Drew seemed to know and the bubble vanished. Dante held up a warning hand again. "Don't touch them... Isla, can you hear me?"

"Yes," she said quietly.

"Where are you?"

"I'm in the tunnels of his mind."

Everyone seemed to let out a collective breath.

"That's good. What do you see?"

"It's like a maze in here. I've never seen anything like it."

Dante frowned, not sure how to tell her to proceed. Cesaré came forward, "May I?"

Dante held out his hand and he stepped back so Cesaré could take over.

"Hi Isla, it's me, Cesaré. Do you see a white light?"

"Yes! Yes I do, is that the way?"

Cesaré shook his head. "No." He closed his eyes to

concentrate. "You must go to the smallest, darkest avenue – the one you're least inclined to go."

Isla nodded and went quiet. "I've found it. It's so dark though. I'm scared."

Cesaré looked over his shoulder at Dante, asking silent permission. He nodded slowly. "Okay, Isla, that is Drew's subconscious. It is here we will find the answers."

Isla threw back her head and gasped for air making everyone jump, but Cesaré caught her gently with an arm around her back. "Isla?"

"It's okay. Something sucked me through. It took my breath away for a moment. I'm in."

Dante let out a ragged breath. This was intense. "Is it safe enough to continue, Ches?"

"I think so. I'm here, Isla, okay? You need to ask the questions from now on. He trusts you."

"Okay. I'm looking around."

There were a few moments of excruciating silence.

"I can see him with Phoebe. I'm seeing through his eyes … I can feel … He's biting her. He feels indescribable pleasure … he loves her."

Dante swallowed. It felt better to know that for sure. "We need her to go back to a particular place and time."

"You need to go back to the day of the medical center. Can you find that, Isla? Can you visualize in your own mind what you see?" Cesaré flashed his eyes at Dante, who nodded to one of the Murrs. Then the large monitor came to life. It was a perfect representation of the reception area of a medical center.

The technology was remarkable. The whole room now had access to what Isla was seeing in Drew's subconscious. It was moving forward as if she was holding a camera. These were memories as seen through Drew's eyes.

It panned around as if he was looking over his shoulder.

There was Phoebe and Tia sitting on the chairs in the waiting room. Phoebe gave him an unsure, worried little smile. Tia looked bored and picked up a magazine. It made Dante smile.

The view went into an examination room. Then they were looking up at the bright lights above. There was no sound.

Cesaré seemed to be thinking the same thing. "Can you tune in to what they are saying, Isla?"

Dante looked nervously at the screen. An injection was being administered. "Can you get any sound?" he asked the Murr.

The Murr technician waved an arm over a blue holographic panel.

"Set up the IV," came through loud and clear. A blood bag on an IV stand was pushed closer.

Dante was surprised that they were examining his knee. He'd thought that was a ruse. "What are they giving him?" Dante said, hoping someone in the room knew more than him.

Cesaré shook his head. "I have no idea. Blood and a sedative, probably. It would make him more suggestible."

It made sense.

"Elixir!" The doctor on the screen said, holding out a hand to an assistant.

The bottle came right up to the screen as Drew apparently drank down its contents. "Our elixir?" Dante asked.

"Most probably," Cesaré said. "How did they come by it?"

Then there seemed like some kind of commotion. Running heavy boots were just outside. Drew was struggling to sit up but he must have been very weak as the doctor was able to hold him down.

Dante was willing him up so he could find out what was going on. But the only way he could see was through Drew's eyes and he wasn't going anywhere, he was all over the place.

At least he knew for sure that the boy had no idea what had gone on.

There seemed a lot of activity. Echoey muffled noises, as they would have sounded to Drew. There was a heavy trudge of footsteps and Drew turned to face the hallway. He caught a glimpse of several men marching past. The view tilted as Drew tried to lift his head.

"Close it!" someone said, and the nurse pushed the door closed so Drew could no longer see. "Easy, Drew. Just a few more minutes and we'll be done."

Drew relaxed back down into the table. Crashes and shouts could be heard from the other room. "Finish up quickly."

The noise of Drew's elevated heart rate came over the speaker adding an eerie suspense to what they were listening to. It went on for an agonizing few moments until a soldier-looking guy came in and said they'd fought but the girls had gone.

"Who?" the doctor said, sounding furious.

The soldier described the three Murrs that Dante knew were his cousins.

"Load the van."

"What about him? Do you still want him disposed of?"

The doctor paused, then shook his head. It was at that point that Sean entered the room and the rest they knew. If the Murrs hadn't taken the girls at that point and possibly if Sean hadn't interrupted, then Drew would undoubtedly be dead.

"We are just finished," the doctor said with a fake smile. Then he released him and Sean took his weight and stumbled out with him.

It was frustrating because Dante ached to know what was

said after Drew left. "Go back further – back to the ranch. I want to see how Tia came to be with them."

In a single moment the image on the screen changed to the rough driveway at the front of Cash's place and his old red pick-up. Drew stopped running out of the front door with armfuls of stuff.

You running?" Tia said through the open car window.

"Are you?" Phoebe snapped back.

"Get in."

Drew ran over to the car and opened the door so Phoebe could get in. Then he followed and they all sped away.

Dante let out a long breath and shook his head. So the reason they were all together was that they had all used the fight as a distraction to get away. All three of them ran and just happened to choose the same moment.

He wished he could influence the screen and talk to the Tia in flight mode. But all of it was a memory of several days ago – a whisper, a residue in the back of Drew's mind.

Dante held up a hand to the Murr. They would learn nothing else useful from this era. They needed to go back in time, maybe even to when Drew was a boy.

The Murr understood and spoke telepathically to Isla. Groups of images flashed on the screen going back in time. Nothing seemed of any note until they started to resemble a boys' school. No, it was more than that; it was harsh and bleak, more like a military school, with fights, drills and whistles.

"There!" Dante shouted. "Back a bit … right there." A monk-like man was talking to him; except he looked like no holy man he'd ever met. The guy was built and covered in tattoos. He had two full sleeves visible from out of his cassock and images of flames licking up the sides of his neck. This guy was more like a fighting machine than a monk. "Tune in, I want to hear this guy."

"You will leave soon, Drew, and do the human race a great service," he was saying.

Young Drew looked so serious and focused, he answered with a simple nod.

"You and your fellow students will be sent to every corner of this country. You will not see anyone; you won't even remember where you are from."

Dante felt sorry for the poor boy on the screen as it became evident that he had grown up trained and indoctrinated in nothing more than a war camp. There had been no laughter, childish games or anything normal boys do. Life had been brutal and hard. Then his memories were tampered with and he was sent out into the world completely alone. Judging by the other boys, he put Drew at around thirteen years old. There was no clue where he came from prior to that. He could have been there years. They didn't have time to look and didn't need to. Drew was a sleeper – an operative that lay dormant until his objective was met. In his case it was Phoebe Ray. He'd been sent out into the world to find anything connected to their race. The sect's track record filled in the gaps. Their goal was to locate a Siren and ultimately the Holy Grail; the Orb – the center of all their power. That was what the Scythians wanted and it made sense. The bottom line was always power.

Dante held up a weary hand. "That's enough. Bring them both back."

Cesaré was immediately next to him. "Not yet. Find out where he went, what they were told, what their tactics were."

"No point. Nothing would have been said directly to him. It will all be riddles and codes. He found a Siren … mission accomplished."

Cesaré walked away, frustrated, obviously not satisfied. A Murr was giving Isla something to drink and the other was shining a light into Drew's half-open, unseeing eyes. Another shot was administered and Drew came back to the room.

He looked shocked and immediately released Isla's wrist as his fangs retracted. A Murr attended to the wounds and wrapped a light bandage around it.

Drew looked at her apologetically.

She smiled a little. Dante felt something pass between them like affection. He guessed the experience was kind of personal.

Then Drew's eyes moved to his. "Did it work?"

Dante nodded. "Kind of. You're off the hook." Then he turned to face Alfonzo, who was busy writing down the outcome. "Organize a meeting with Vionne. It's time to hear their terms."

CHAPTER 46

Prince Vionne would like to enter, a metallic woman's voice said.

Phoebe looked around.

That's the door ... Come in, Tia said.

Permission granted.

The area in the wall where they'd come in shimmered and changed into the cascading waterfall it was before and Vionne stepped through.

Phoebe thought it was so weird because he didn't look wet or even ruffled. It was, of course, because he was already under water.

Vionne bowed at the waist. *I see you have settled in. May I say how stunning you both look in our Murr clothes?*

Phoebe frowned and smiled a little. Despite what he said, his eyes remained on her with definite speculation. It made her increasingly uncomfortable.

Thankfully, Tia sensed it and prattled on as if she hadn't noticed. *Thanks, hun. You couldn't carry an ounce of fat in them.* She twisted to look at her backside.

God, yeah, can you imagine. Phoebe projected a little too loudly.

Vionne went on oblivious. *I thought I could give you a tour of the city?* His eyes looked directly into hers.

Phoebe went to pick up Tia's hand for her to come too, when he tilted his head and said, *Tia has spent long periods of time here. I think she would be bored.* His strange eyes moved to Tia for an instant and Phoebe's heart sank. She was going to have to do this solo.

He gave her that unnatural smile of his. *I promise it will be pleasurable for you and you will return unscathed.*

What was meant to put her mind at rest only sent her alarm bells clanging all over the place. She looked at Tia for a little help.

Tia just shrugged and pulled a "nothing she could do" face. *Don't keep her long, Vionne. It's been a tiring day,* was the best she could do. She finished on a wry smile aimed just at her.

Of course, Vionne said, inclining his head, but his lips curled at the corners strangely and he looked amused.

It was a side to him that surprised her. She wasn't sure why. She guessed because of the whole language barrier thing she'd labeled these Murrs as having no game or sense of humor. It made her warm to him slightly.

I assure you I am not that bad company.

It made her blush being caught out with the whole mind-reading thing yet again. *Suppose not,* and she allowed him to take her elbow and lead her to the waterfall doorway. *I'll get you back!* she threw over her shoulder as she stepped through.

Tia gave her a grin and a childlike wave.

· · ·

WHAT IS there to do in an underwater town then? Phoebe projected, as she walked next to Vionne into the vestibule at the front of the palace. The door closed behind them, closing them in. Nothing apart from swimming came to mind. *Not that I care particularly. I just want to go home,* she added quietly.

I can still hear your personal thoughts, you know, Vionne said, sounding a little wounded.

She put her hands on her hips. *You shouldn't listen.*

You have no filter!

This drove Phoebe into immediate rage. *Sorry I have no brain training for weirdo mind readers! What do you expect me to say when I am kept here against my will?*

We rescued you.

It was kidnap!

It is not kidnap if you are my Siren.

For once she was absolutely stumped for words. Tia was right and it made everything fall into place. *I still get a choice... and, anyway, I'm not. I have someone.* Her eyes tracked down to his ring. She didn't know a lot but she knew which color it was meant to be. *What does that even mean?* she said, pointing at the large red ring.

Vionne sighed and shook his head absently. *Honestly, I don't know.* Then he stood up straighter, resolved again. *Look, let's just spend a couple of hours. We will meet with Dante, and you will be returned if you still want to go.*

I'll want to.

His eyes took on a calculated look. The process that changed the water atmosphere worked at the wave of his hand. The water became heavy and took her feet softly off the ground. He bowed his head and held open the door for her to swim outside.

They swam side-by-side out of the palace gates. Three little kids zoomed past on what looked like transparent space hoppers with fairy lights inside. They looked adorable, like little pixies in their little shimmering body-hugging costumes.

Phoebe smiled in spite of herself: *What are they? They look like fun.* She realized that he was watching her closely with that intense gaze. He made her feel like he was studying her all the time.

Would you like to try one?

Really, I can? Yes, I would, she said, delighted.

Follow me. And he began to swim off in the direction of a gazebo-like dome.

When she arrived a few seconds behind him she saw rows and rows of hovering hoppers of varying sizes. *What are they?*

There is no human word for them only an approximation.

Phoebe frowned, not understanding at all. An image of her zipping across the ocean floor hit the front of her mind and took her breath away. It was quickly followed with a surge of excitement.

Vionne cocked his head to the side.

For a moment she was in shock. *What just happened?*

The same thing happened again. *You did that?*

After watching her mouth closely, he smiled a very human-looking smile. He was copying her and getting better at it. *Our language.*

She looked down in amazement when she finally under-stood. *No words, only pictures.*

And feelings of the spirit – perhaps the strongest language of all.

The look he gave her then made her swallow hard. If this was an example of Murr moves, then he was very good at it.

He grinned again. *Thank you, I'm a fast learner.*

That actually made her laugh, which she really didn't want to do. She didn't want to like him as much as she was. Scratching her head, she quickly changed the subject and began swimming up and down the lines of machines. *So, who do they belong to? Shouldn't we ask someone?* Her hand ran over the handles that had a squidgy jellylike feel.

They don't belong to anyone.

Phoebe stopped and looked at him. *Like a council scheme or something?*

Vionne shook his head. *No they belong to no one and everyone. They are the best way to get around. They're fast and as long as you leave them in a gathering point for the next person you will always have transportation.*

For a moment she was stunned. A lump came up in her throat and she didn't know why. *That is the loveliest thing I've ever heard.*

The children whizzed past again and she heard their tinkling laughter. *Is it safe?* she said doubtfully.

Vionne pulled one out with delicate, pulsing, pale green lights. *You are in the softness of the water and all the working parts are in the bubble. I would say so.*

The deep, intense gaze held hers for a moment too long until she dragged her eyes away. *Bubble Bikes...I shall call them Bubble Bikes.*

Vionne laughed and pulled out another, larger one for himself. *I will have it declared that they be known forever as Bubble Bikes in honor of the Princess Phoebe Bonaci.* Then he straddled his bike and whooshed out of the dome.

Still dazed after the unbelievably sweet compliment, she called after him, *How do I do it?*

Get on, squeeze and think go! he called back.

The little bike bobbed up and down in front of her. *Get on, squeeze and think go,* she repeated. She slid her leg over and nearly fell forward except she gripped with her knees and yelped as it juddered forward. Then she closed one eye and thought, *go!*

Her mouth opened to scream in reflex, but no noise came out. In her head she sounded like a banshee. The bike felt super fast until she got used to it. The main bubble was so soft her knees burrowed into it and her feet found some-where to rest. It was really very comfortable. By leaning forward she speeded up and sitting up straighter slowed her down.

Vionne was zooming off ahead of her. *Right, man-fish, here I come.*

She heard his laughter and he went even faster and the race was on. It got a little hairy when they got to a busier part of town and people on similar bubbles were coming towards them. However they seemed to have driving etiquette and either stayed left or those even faster went upwards. They hurtled through the narrow streets, hunched low, urging their bikes faster. There were other bikes and larger craft everywhere.

Phoebe felt alive and had the most fun she'd had in ages.

Up ahead, Vionne pointed his finger up and began to go higher. *How?* she squealed.

Lean back slightly.

She did and she began to climb. Soaring above all the green and blue domes and traffic congestion. Her heart slowed and she felt she could relax. Below them looked like a toy town.

Vionne must have slowed a little too as she caught up with him. *We'll go down there,* he said, pointing. *Put your weight on the handles.*

She did and it worked. They glided down to a clearing with gold-colored rocks that glittered with crystals. As the rocks came nearer, it suddenly occurred to her that she didn't know how to stop. *Vionne!* The ground rushed to her, she closed her eyes and gripped with all her might.

Then nothing.

When she cracked open one eye to see, the sandy bed was about eight inches from her nose. The bike had just stopped dead before impact and she was left there, hovering almost up side down.

Vionne was holding his stomach with laughter. *You could have just let go.*

Phoebe let go of the handles and scrambled forward softly but very unladylike. *You could have warned me.*

Vionne was gathering himself together. *Just think 'slow, stop', or tilt your weight back with your legs forward.*

She was now just treading water, scowling at him. *You did that deliberately.*

He got off his bike and put them together near a rock where they obediently bobbed together. Then he put two fingers together to indicate a little.

Phoebe couldn't keep a straight face and begrudgingly thought he really was an okay guy. His sense of humor and mannerisms were so human in so many ways.

Vionne took her hand and led her between tall seaweeds that grew straight up from the floor and looked like curtains. The other side of it made her hold back and pause. It was so beautiful. Her eyes roamed the glittering crystals in the rocks, the little shoals of brightly colored fish dotting around beds of pink and yellow anemones and archways of weeds. She tried to take it all in.

Vionne swam ahead and sat on a carefully placed piece of driftwood.

It was then she realized that everything around them was cultivated.

Vionne's smile was becoming more human every time. *I'm glad you like my garden.*

Phoebe's eyes were still roaming over everything. *It's beautiful.* She swam over and sat next to him.

As are you.

Phoebe turned to face him and looked into his speculative

coal-black eyes. *I'm not going to get with you, Vionne, so you can stop with the charm now.*

He grinned again and looked down at his ring. *I think you speak the truth. Out of all the Sirens, you are the most unusual.* He sounded so sad that Phoebe put a hand over his.

Honestly, V, you lucked out. I am a weirdo.

His eyes darted to hers while he gauged what she'd said, then he threw his head back and laughed. *Most unusual,* he said, and continued to laugh. *Out of all the things I have learned from the humans, laughter is by far is the most joyous.*

She couldn't help but laugh along with him. Despite an air of sadness, he was so upbeat and great company. *Maybe in another lifetime.*

As usual, he'd heard every word and smiled appreciatively. *You have chosen; that is rare for our kind.*

Phoebe didn't really understand but he seemed so regretful. *Don't you get to do what you want?* She was thinking of him going to Seattle with the sole purpose of kidnapping her.

His shy grin made her warm to him a little more. *A little, maybe. But royals of our race have destinies.* He fidgeted with the ring on his finger.

What does it mean – that colour. I've never seen it?

He shrugged a little. *Honestly, I'm not sure. I've never seen it either. It changes so it proves who you are, but red normally means something bad. Like foul play, or something like that.*

Yeah, probably my fault. I'm used to being the black sheep.

He frowned as if he'd felt her sadness and moved a piece of hair from her face. It gave her the chance to really study him. The strong jawline and high cheekbones slashed with the dark Murr stripes that looked completely hot and tribal. This close he really was fabulous looking –model-beautiful but bad boy dangerous.

Thank you!

She scowled and hit him in the shoulder. *Stop that! It's so infuriating when you do that.*

He laughed again as if it was completely natural to him. *Well, as you are going back to the man of your heart shortly, would you like to go out somewhere lively tonight?*

What, here in Murrtaine? She thought skeptically. It was hard to imagine anything as cool as that here. *What, dancing and everything?*

You've never partied until you've tried it Murr-style. He rose from the bench, taking her with him.

Intrigued, she was really starting to enjoy her little stay in Murrtaine.

PHOEBE AND TIA wore the slinkiest, sheerest, mesh outfits they could find in their new wardrobe, and none of them left much to the imagination. It seemed that Murr women didn't suffer the same insecurities as their human counterparts. Probably because Macci-D's hadn't got a franchise down there yet.

Beautiful, Vionne said, when he came to pick them up with his brothers, Dax and Caan.

The three brothers didn't look half bad either; bare-chested and emblazoned in stripes. They wore loose dark gauze trousers each in varying shades of grey. The way the material moved in the water was completely flattering to their powerful legs and cute butts.

Once they cleared the vestibule, Phoebe was in a constant state of wonderment at nighttime Murrtaine. The place was simply magical. They took a leisurely swim through the narrow toy-town streets, with Vionne explaining things along the way. Tia, of course, had seen it all but followed along amiably.

The streets bustled with the fascinating residents. Whole

families went in and out of shops with delightful names like Apothecary and Soothing Parlor, indicated by symbols that flashed into your mind as you walked by. Colored lights twinkled in long reed beds like fireflies. The larger lights in the eaves of the buildings cast a friendly blue-green luminosity in the streets. Everywhere glowed right up to the membrane of the huge dome. She couldn't even feel surges in the water because of its protection. It was a wonder it couldn't be seen from above. The lack of noise reminded her of topside after a fresh layer of snow. Everything felt safe and secure like a warm blanket.

'*She's getting smitten.*' Tia sang from next to her.

Phoebe was about to answer back with something not entirely flattering when the welcome sound of music filtered through the water. Instead she looked at Tia in excitement. *Where are we going?*

The nearest thing in your language, I guess, is The Nave, Vionne said.

Tia shrugged, meaning it was new to her too.

Phoebe hadn't been this excited about anything since she'd got to Seattle and that felt like a lifetime ago.

The music was coming from a tunnel that disappeared underground. *Ready?* Vionne said.

Phoebe nodded. He was building it up so she was reaching fever-pitch with excitement.

Stay close, it will be crowded.

Phoebe grabbed Tia's hand. Her eyes glittered too. The other two brothers stayed close behind them as they swam the roughly hewn tunnel. Youths hung around the entrance, seemingly in conversation in front of the huge, circular door reminding her of a bank vault.

You could still feel the vibrations around it.

We have to wait a moment, Vionne said.

Phoebe wondered why. The whole idea of the thickness

of that door was disconcerting and, for a moment, she thought of making an excuse and going the other way. Then it hissed and the door opened and two of the biggest-looking Murrs stepped out. Her eyes went from what only could be described as a loincloth to their faces, so far up it gave her neck ache. They both bowed reverently, immediately recognizing Vionne as the prince. She'd be lying if she said it didn't give her a buzz to be treated like a VIP.

Vionne picked up her hand and the huge bouncers' eyes followed her all the way in.

Let no one else in while we are here, Vionne said as he passed them.

One inclined his head but didn't take his eyes off her. Phoebe felt like dinner and shuddered.

CHAPTER 47

$\mathcal{I}$nside, The Nave felt like a dream. It began with the loud clank of the thick door closing behind them then, a moment later, the water seemed to dissolve around them. Gravity took over and their feet landed softly onto the sandy floor.

Phoebe looked anxiously to Vionne. *It's called a Water Quantifier – technology enabling many things. For this evening's purposes, more freedom of movement and greater conduction of sound. You'll see.*

She smiled, still a little unsure. At least the bank vault door made perfect sense now. It was creating some kind of non-air lock in the lobby to allow this to happen. They continued to walk further into the club.

It was obviously the 'in' place for all the beautiful Murrs. They were dressed in the customary next-to-nothing costumes, but they'd enhanced their markings with vivid colors that they carried on into their hair, making a stunning contrast to the black or white. They only seemed to do two colors of hair; pure white or jet black. There were no shades in between. The stripe under each cheekbone looked particularly cool. The placement of stripes on all Murrs was very similar. When she looked down at her own they were different, but similar to Tia's.

You and your sister have inherited your father's Bonaci markings, Vionne said. *They are very beautiful, much more delicate than ours.*

Phoebe found herself blushing under his stare for the hundredth time that day. *Thank you,* she said, looking down.

The music was still a dull throb of bass – anything else was probably severely hampered because, despite appearances, they were under water. It was a bit of a let down and she felt a little disappointed.

Vionne tilted his head at a curious angle.

What? she thought, guessing he'd read her mind yet again.

You Sirens ... always such a love for music. He smiled that increasingly natural smile of his. *Give it chance. We have a few surprises up our sleeves.* Then he looked at his bare arm and frowned.

It made Phoebe burst out laughing.

Vionne grinned. *Now everyone is in, it will begin.*

Blimey. That really got her interest going and scared her a little too. She looked over at Tia to see if she knew what was going on but she just shrugged.

They picked their way between the many clubgoers further into the club. The main room was a vast cavern that went upwards as far as the eye could see. It reminded her of a huge church spire. *The Nave.* The connection made sense now.

The colored lighting that gave everywhere its distinctive glow continued up the walls and were interspaced with crystals or cut glass that bounced the light beautifully. *How far does it go up?* she asked.

Wait and see. It's part of the surprise. Vionne's eyes appeared to glitter under the lights. He was enjoying her excitement as much as she was and she warmed to him a little more. She found herself saying 'if things were different' more and more as the day wore on.

Come, we have time for refreshment before it begins.

Phoebe exchanged a look with Tia. *It was getting built up so much, it had better be good.* Then it occurred to her, how did you go out drinking when you were already underwater? She was under the impression that they extracted the necessary fluids for survival through their gills and so they didn't actually need to drink.

There are no optics or pumps, Phoebe said, trying to work out how they did it.

Don't look at me. I'm normally pregnant when I'm here. I didn't think Murrs actually drank alcohol, Tia said. *How does a girl get drunk around here?* she said to anyone who would listen.

Dax and Caan laughed strangely. *Its not called that here.* Dax said.

Vionne called them over. *It's called taking the breath. Here, I'll show you.* He touched her gently on the arm and pulled her closer to the bar. *Five pieces please,* he said, to the barkeeper.

The ripped barman, who looked more like a striped Chippendale, put five glass tubes in front of them. They tapered at one end like the mouthpiece of a whistle. No kind of money passed hands.

Phoebe was about to ask about the financial system when five tubes miraculously rose out of the bar about eighteen inches apart. Then Vionne gave them each a mouthpiece.

Phoebe hung back a little waiting for someone else to do it first.

It's a mouthpiece, look, Caan said, slotting his over the tube sprouting from the bar. *Just put it in and breathe.* He put his mouth to the tapered end and inhaled – making a trail of bubbles go upwards around him. It was all the more weird as it was the only giveaway that they were under water.

Phoebe watched him closely. He released his lips from the tube and stood back with low eyelids. Bubbles streamed out from behind his ears. *Hits the spot,* he said, nodding.

It made her giggle. She had them pegged as being so straight.

Come on Phoebes, lets get breathed! Tia said, and lowered her head to a pipe.

Phoebe laughed. The others joined her. People were coming over, having a couple of tokes with their own mouthpieces and moving away. This was how they did it. This was their social wind down poison. You just purchased the mouthpiece which you kept as your own and partook of the pipes as and when you felt like it. There were even tubes rising out of the small circular pods where people were sitting.

She moved a little closer, still unsure. *What exactly is it?*

Mainly Oxygen, Vionne said, now looking really relaxed. *Mixed with a few other gases like nitrous oxide.*

Laughing gas! Dax butted in.

Completely harmless to humans and Murrs, Caan added.

Phoebe looked at Tia, who was already holding her mouth trying not to giggle. Then she looked around the table pods at everyone else looking relaxed and breathing every now and again.

It's like alcohol without the hangover, I believe, Vionne said. *Try it a little. It will begin in a minute and will heighten your experience.*

There were a thousand questions to that, but she could tell Vionne was holding back for the surprise. *Okay, here goes then.*

Phoebe slotted her mouthpiece over the pipe and put her lips to it.

You will feel an immediate, gentle flow but if you want a hard shot just press the button here on the bar. I suggest you get the feel of it first, Vionne said.

Phoebe concentrated on what she was doing and opened her mouth. The air in the pipe was surprisingly cold and filled her mouth quickly. Her eyes darted to Vionne's.

His hand gently rubbed her back. *Don't be alarmed, just imagine you are on the surface and breathe.*

Her heart was pounding. She counted to three and took in a little, then a little more. Bubbles began to tickle around her neck. Nothing untoward seemed to be happening so she became a bit braver and breathed normally through the pipe. Vionne's smile was widening as he watched her closely.

Then she realized why. Two seconds later, it hit the front of her head.

She must have slid down the bar as Vionne was right there, steadying her by the arm. She'd let go of the pipe that was just hanging there with a small stream of bubbles coming from it. Her heart was hammering and then a warm feeling washed over her so strongly she had to close her eyes for a second.

When she tried to open them she found that she couldn't – well, barely.

Vionne was openly grinning at her with the others at his shoulders.

Her lips were tingling, *Wow! I can't ...* and she put out her hand to steady herself on the bar. The only way to describe it was that she'd gone from zero to majorly tipsy in about one minute. It really was good stuff. Shame she hadn't used it in the clubs above ground, she would've saved a fortune on drinks.

Her heart jumped when a claxon sounded, filling the whole place. Before she knew it she'd grabbed onto Vionne's arm, and looked around for the beginnings of panic. No one seemed bothered by it. *What's wrong?* she said a little frantically.

Here we go, Dax said.

It's starting. Are you ready? Vionne said, taking her by the arm and leading her away from the bar to the huge spire area.

Hey, what's happening? Tia was saying, hanging onto Dax and Caan on either side of her for support.

Then the sound that had been muffled beats before became clear and amplified – like rock concert loud. The other clubbers were leaving their seats too to cram into the same central area. The Smiths, "How soon is now" began to play. *I love this song.* Even so, she did feel it was a little slow for a nightclub.

Vionne was smiling as if he was enjoying just watching her response.

Looking around at all the faces they all appeared to be looking upward, just swaying and waiting. *But waiting for what?*

Phoebe looked up to see if there was anything to see. Then the song reached its chorus and the whole place erupted into song and they all joined in.

Then the gravity switched off. In fact, it went 'moon landing' weird and everyone started to rise up.

Ready? Vionne said, sliding his hand around her back as if he was about to serenade her.

She was just too amazed and excited to resist as they became weightless. It was as if every sense in their bodies was catered for and enhanced.

The room filled with everyone singing collectively, and they began to slowly swirl around the walls of the room getting higher and higher.

Phoebe's heart soared with the music.

Vionne pulled her more tightly into his side as they

spiraled upwards around the walls. She could hear Tia's squeals and whoops of glee behind her. *Whoo, best club ever!*

Vionne took her hands. *Lean back,* he said, linking his lower legs around her calves. She did it without question and opened her eyes. The lights in the walls appeared to be bouncing and moving like shooting stars. Everywhere, different colors like a swirling milky way. People were rolling, tumbling and twisting as if they were bathing in pleasure. Some were in tight embraces and kissing their partners. Others were simply enjoying the experience alone. The water was becoming a whirlpool of decadent enjoyment spurred on by song after song, not too fast and not too slow. It was the pinnacle of communal experiences – the utmost pleasure. *Mind-blowing!* Phoebe projected to no one in particular.

With Vionne's legs still holding hers, she let her arms float above her head until she felt his strong hands hold her gently at her hips and pull her back in. Her body came flush against his and, for a moment, she got lost in his eyes. He ran a thumb across her lips and then brushed them with his. He almost kissed her, but stopped himself just in time.

With the sound of the claxon the moment had gone. The music returned to its muffled background beats and the partygoers slowly swirled down until their feet gently landed on the sandy floor.

Phoebe continued to stare into Vionne's eyes as if mesmerized.

That was bloody brilliant. Will it do it again? Where's the DJ? I'd love to see how they do it down here, Tia was going on in the background. But Phoebe was only half listening. She had seen Vionne for the first time – really seen him and now she just felt desperately sad.

It will repeat a few times, he projected absently. What he was really saying was evident on his face. Would she stay here with him to enjoy it?

The sadness came because they both knew the answer was no. The strange dance they'd just shared had been so intimate. It was so close, in all honesty, she couldn't do it again without feeling like she was cheating on Drew.

Drew! It was the bucket of cold water she needed. *I need to go.* She broke his stare and ducked under his arm to make her way to the entrance and the steel door.

Vionne quickly caught up with her. *Wait. We will all go.*

Phoebe stood in front of the huge door in the lobby, tapping her foot in impatience. *Make them open it. Now!*

The others all caught up and Tia was looking at her as if she'd lost her mind. *Get me out!* she shouted.

A door closed behind them and the steel door hissed and opened in front of them. She swam out through the tunnel as soon as she was able, but somehow, she just couldn't swim fast enough.

She could hear them asking each other if she was okay. Thankfully, Vionne remained quiet, but she knew he was there. He swam a little apart from her, not crowding her but everything about him was overwhelming. Every part of her was aware he was there.

Phoebe closed her eyes and imagined Drew there in front of her but every time her heart skipped, she would be transported to the feel of Vionne's arms in the huge whirlpool; spinning, twirling, with his strong legs propelling them faster and higher. The brushes of his hand, of his lips, tempting and tasting. She simply couldn't get the whole evening out of her head.

· · ·

WHEN THEY ARRIVED BACK at the palace, his brothers went on with Tia and Vionne caught her arm before she went into their room. *Phoebe please.*

Phoebe swung around on him sharply. *You! You drugged me. It's all your fault!* That was it. It was some weird compulsion Murr crap he'd played on her.

He stared down at her with a look of puzzlement. She wanted him to get angry and defend himself so she could stomp off and take the high ground. Instead he was processing what she said – no, not what she said, what she felt. And that was a whole lot more reliable than what she was shouting at him.

She sagged in defeat. *Please, Vionne.* He inclined his head and walked away.

Tia, who she only just noticed, was leaning against a wall a little way off. *Great night,* she said with a giggle. Then she hiccupped, slid down and landed on her backside.

VIONNE DIDN'T GET VERY FAR before he was intercepted by his brothers. He didn't want to stop. The evening hadn't ended as he expected and he didn't feel much like explaining.

Brother, stop, Dax said, quickly catching up with him.

He continued to walk with long, angry strides. *If you have something to say, say it as a Murr and be done with it. I'm in no mood for humanisms,* he projected so both brothers could hear.

The picture that hit his mind brought him abruptly to a standstill. *Father!* The image was of his father ashen, painfully thin and laying on his bed. Stricken, he hurried with Dax and Caan to his father's chambers. *How long has he been like this?*

His soother said he has hidden it from view for some weeks.

CHAPTER 48

Drew had an unbearable wait. He knew where Phoebe was, but there was no way of getting to her. It called for drastic measures.

He knocked and waited at Dante's study door. The king rarely came out these days.

"Come in."

It was one of the rare occasions when Dante was alone. He was surrounded by huge volumes of old books and seemed to be studying when he approached the desk. "Is there any news?"

Dante sighed and put down his pen. "Not yet. Darl is ill."

That wasn't what he'd hoped to hear. "How does that affect things?"

"Not sure yet. I'm checking the source is accurate. If it's true and Darl dies, that makes Vionne lord advocate. Where at one time I thought I could count on him, now … I'm not so sure." He looked him dead in the eye. "His people will look on him as a king – a king who happens to have two Sirens."

"You think it was intentional?"

Dante shrugged. "Honestly, I don't know. The only thing I

can say is that Vionne loves his father and would not harm him. But, he is also a shrewd leader and will know when he has an advantage."

A wave of desperation washed over him. The idea that had taken seed a few hours ago seemed all the more urgent to try now.

"What's on your mind?" Dante asked.

Drew shifted uncomfortably, not sure how to say it exactly. Whatever way he looked at it, it seemed like madness. But his whole life was like that lately. "I wanna see if my body can go under water."

Dante just continued to stare at him as if he had something else to say. Then he eventually said, "Are you mad?"

"Yes, no, probably. Look … my body has changed. It is possible, isn't it? That I'm changing into one of you?"

Dante let out a mirthless blast of laughter, sat back in his chair and considered what he'd said. "I suppose it is possible, I hate to break it to you, buddy, but body shifts aren't exactly standard kit for an Atlantean – for anyone, come to that. It could be suicide. There's the water pressure, for one."

"I have to know … I need to do something."

Dante lounged back and shook his head. "To compete for Phoebe, I suppose," he said on a deep sigh.

There was a knock at the door.

"Come in."

Alfonzo entered and Drew took that as his cue to leave.

He held up his hand to halt him. "What I have to say affects you." His eyes quickly flickered from Drew to Dante. "The conclusive results on your blood tests are back from the lab."

Drew's heart hammered.

"And?"

"They have never seen anything like it, and whilst he has definite human markers—"

"Spit it out, man!" Dante said.

"There is another DNA marker multiplying fast and it is Atlantean."

Drew thought his heart would literally beat right out of his chest.

Dante's eyes narrowed. "Are you saying he is changing?"

"Yes, he's changing and at an alarming rate. So fast that they were able to watch it under a microscope."

He wasn't sure where it came from, why it mattered, or how he was so calm, but he had to know. "If it's Atlantean, then what family?"

Both the other men openly stared at him as if they were seeing him for the first time. Then Dante looked at Alfonzo. "You heard him."

"Bonaci!" When no one else uttered a word he continued, "If the more powerful Bonaci DNA continues to multiply at its current rate, he will be pure-blooded within twenty-four hours. There hasn't been the like since the destruction of Atlantis."

Drew was dumbstruck and looked at Dante for some kind of response. He wasn't sure if he'd be angry, upset or what.

He just slumped back in his chair with the air knocked out of him. Then he frowned. "Are you thinking what I'm thinking?" He said to Alfonzo.

He was nodding. "A Bonaci prince."

Dante half laughed when he looked back at Drew. "Looks like you will get your water test."

DREW WANTED the test as soon as possible. Enough time had passed already and no one was going to get Phoebe.

Despite the mounting evidence, Dante refused to test him in the sea outside the castle. "It's too deep," Dante said. "Even if by some miracle you do manage to breathe the water the pressure could kill you."

Instead he had one of the holding tanks filled in the dungeons under the castle. It was just like a glass box for a Houdini escape at just six by eight feet in size. "At least this way if you drown we can get you out quickly," he said. "This isn't a test to see if a Siren accepts you. It's just to see if you can survive under water, so we don't need any theatrics."

Drew didn't want any fuss anyway. He just wanted to know once and for all if the changes he'd undergone meant something so he could go and rescue Phoebe.

Dante came up in his face. There wasn't much difference in height. "You think you know what it's like but you don't. You will drown, okay?"

"I know what I'm doing."

"Do you though?" Dante half laughed. Then he shook his head as if he wasn't sure if he was brave or mad.

There were a few chuckles around the room. Cesaré and Keenan were there. Both knew what to expect. They were joined by two dark men introduced as Phoebe's half brothers, Luca and Dino. That meant they were relatives of his now, like cousins or something. Lacy, Isla and Lily were there too, stripped down to their swimsuits.

"You can't do this on your own, none of us can. You need a Siren to initiate you – to open your gills."

Drew's hand went up to his ear and he felt behind it. There was nothing there. It was the first time it hit home what he was actually trying to do.

"It should be your mate that does this. Do you understand what I'm saying? Are you sure you still want to go through with it?"

Drew took a deep breath. He kind of got it, the marriage thing. He didn't have time for petty jealousy now. "It's not why I'm here." He turned to the girls. "No offence."

Dante motioned for Dino to undo the hatch at the top of the tank. A harness was put on him and attached to a pulley, which would haul him up and lower him into the tank. He put an arm on his shoulder. "Listen to me carefully, we'll go with Isla as she has already gotten quite acquainted with you with the mind walk – and her man ain't here," he said with a smile. Then he got serious again. "When you're in the water you'll let the water into your lungs and Isla will attempt to breathe for you. If it's gonna work it will happen at that point." Then he narrowed his eyes. "And if it doesn't or you attempt to harm her in any way … well, we'll get you out as soon as we can, but it will be Isla who has priority."

Drew nodded. He knew he was expendable. It appeared to be the story of his life.

Dante signaled with his hand and Keenan began to wind the hoist. There was no time to respond before his feet left the ground. Suddenly the amount of strong men in the room made sense. It was to hold him in there or get him out, one of the two.

His feet touched the tepid water. They'd warmed it up a bit. Then he was slowly lowered in. Before he completely disappeared into the green water Drew held Dante's eyes. "If I don't make it out, promise me you'll go get her from the Murr bastard and take care of her as your own?"

Dante nodded. "She's already pledged to me. Don't worry, I will take care of her."

Drew couldn't say any more as his mouth, nose and eyes went beneath the water.

The harness was unclipped and hauled out so he couldn't harm himself or the glass when he was panicking. Then Dino shut the hatch with a loud clank. Isla climbed up ready to join Drew but Dante held up his arm for her to wait. "Wait for him to lose consciousness. I don't want to risk you getting hurt in there." Even a panicking human can cause damage when their life depended on it. It wasn't strictly clear what he was at that moment.

They all waited the longest five minutes.

BEING CLOSED in the glass box was terrifying. The few inches of air remaining were soon topped up with water so there were no air pockets. Dante had warned him they would do it. Something to do with what a man would do when he was desperate. It would just prolong what must happen, he'd said.

Drew could just make out shapes through the thick glass, and some gurgling voices with indiscernible words.

He ran his hand behind one of his ears. There was nothing there. Panic took hold for a few moments. *What was he doing? Was he on some level trying to kill himself? No, he wouldn't accept that.*

If he didn't do something, no one else would. Despite what Dante said, he would have diplomatic talks with Vionne and Phoebe would be given to him in some kind of treaty.

His chest was beginning to burn and his head felt like it was going to explode. He shook it wildly. He looked up at nothing but iron and glass. In his desperation he pushed off the floor to put his mouth to the glass and cursed Dante. There wasn't so much as an inch worth of air.

He bashed the glass hatch with the heel of his hand. Then he went to the front of the box and kicked out with his foot. His pulse was so fast he was sure it would burst out of his ears. It was at this point he knew for sure he was going to drown.

No one was coming and he lost all reason.

· · ·

IT WAS NEVER PRETTY WATCHING a man drown. Dante had seen it several times, but this was one of the worst. He had no way of knowing whether he would come out the other side.

Lacy and Lily covered their eyes and looked away. Only Isla continued to watch with her icy detachment. She was definitely the right choice for this. Instead of turning away from the grizzly scene she walked up to the box and put her hand on the glass.

Drew was thrashing and kicking out like a mad thing. Isla looked over at Dante. "There is no restriction as to what I can do?"

Dante shook his head. "This isn't a marriage test. Just get him breathing and fast."

She nodded once and turned back to the glass.

After a moment, Drew's thrashing lessened. His arms and legs slowed and he hung, knees bent, in the water. His hair splayed out all around him and his eyes remained eerily wide open.

He had been in there well over five minutes and should have drowned by human standards, but he still wasn't breathing the water. However, holding his breath longer was still a good sign. Whatever she was saying to him was getting through.

His face now looked pained, then resigned, and his eyes slowly closed.

"It's time!" Isla said. Luca rushed up the ladder and pulled open the heavy hatch.

Dante helped Isla up the steps. "Be careful, okay, Darres is gonna be pissed off at me as it is.

Isla grinned. "You're shark bait!"

She reached the top and slipped into the water through the hatch.

Drew's head was hanging forward and his long hair was

everywhere. Trying to not get tangled in it, she found his chin, pushed his head back and moved the hair away from his face. Then she put her mouth to his and did what came naturally. She blew. Little puffs at first. Then long bouts of a few seconds then a break. A little like CPR.

Anything, Dante projected, thankful for the bond he had with her.

Nothing, she projected back.

Dante shook his head in disappointment.

"He's already been in there too long for a human," Alfonzo said at his shoulder.

"Get him out!" Dante ordered.

Dino and Luca rushed up the iron steps followed by Keenan and Cesaré, who waited for him to be passed out to them.

No, wait! Isla said, stopping them all in their tracks. *He twitched, I'm sure of it.*

His whole body was now glowing as if someone had plugged him into the mains.

"There, his arm moved," Keenan said, from right next to the tank.

Dante came closer. There it was again. Then his eyes flashed open, his head flew back and a noise nothing short of a roar echoed through the water and around the stone walls. They watched helplessly as he grabbed hold of Isla by the hair and the waist and bit her neck hard.

One minute it was the end, then every nerve receptor ignited. His heart rushed, his head span and he slaked his unbelievable thirst with the warmest spiced nectar he had ever tasted. Need seared through him – to drink hard, and to fuck. His hips squashed the lithe body next to him and he dug his fingers into soft flesh.

Stop! Stop, Drew, please, or I will have to hurt you.

It took a few repeats for it to sink in. Gradually it occurred to him that it was a voice he wasn't that familiar with. *It wasn't Phoebe.* He could feel the prickle of adrenalin and it was someone else's.

Drew's vision homed in on cream skin and blond hair.

Please let go slowly, Drew. You're tearing my skin. The spike of fear subsided and was replaced by pain. *Hers.*

His mind was slowly coming back online and the overwhelming primal instinct began to recede. *Isla?* It all came crashing back to him now. It was the voice of the mind walker. She was the one chosen to initiate him in the water too. *Fuck! What had he done?*

With the realization of where he was, his teeth retracted slowly and his erection died. He looked around, he was still in the tank. Isla was close as there wasn't much room. Before he could apologize there was a loud clunk above his head, arms came into the water and she was hauled out double-time. He felt oddly bereft.

It was then it hit him. He was still alive and he was breathing. His hand went to his ear and it was there. Somehow during the whole process the ridge of skin had appeared and opened like a small mouth.

He paused with his arm as it passed his face. *Stripes.* Exactly like the ones he'd seen on Phoebe.

His thoughts were interrupted by Dante. *Drew, can you hear me?*

His head came up sharply as he tried to see through the glass.

I'll take that as a yes ... You have your answer. How do you feel?

Now he actually thought about it, he felt great. He moved all his fingers and toes. All seemed in working order. *Isla.* He'd hurt her.

We're gonna get you out slowly. Don't make any sudden move-ments because we will put you down, Drew. We clear?

He just nodded, not sure what anyone could hear any more. They were acting like he was dangerous or something. He guessed he did just bite the throat of the woman who'd helped him.

A strong arm reached down, which he took and used to pull himself up. He felt stronger somehow. Other hands grabbed to pull him over the side and he was bundled down the steps. He was met by a wall of protective testosterone.

"Cough!" a voice said, and he felt a heavy slap on his back. The momentum knocked him forward and he doubled over, heaving and spluttering as the water left his lungs. A sports bottle was shoved in his face. He took it gratefully and glugged. He straightened up and his vision cleared.

Dante, Alfonzo and Cesaré stood watching him. Keenan and the Bonaci brothers were either side of him. They looked cautious, like they didn't know what he'd do.

"Amazing," Cesaré said.

"I think he's okay. His eyes are changing back to normal," Dante said and the other two nodded.

Drew brought an arm up and studied it. It was still stripy. He went to speak but it hurt like hell and only came out a croak. He held his throat.

"It'll pass," Dante said. *You can speak in your mind. I am strong enough to hear you.*

Where is Isla? I wanted to tell her I'm sorry. None of the girls were left in the room.

"She's gone to get medical attention."

I'm sorry; I had no idea what I was doing.

Dante nodded as if he was calculating whether he was sincere. "It is a very intense experience meant for mates. Your problems are yet to come." He smiled ruefully.

"Darres will kill him," Keenan said, as if he was loving every minute of it.

Drew cast him a dark look.

"It will be our job to keep him alive. The test proves we have our Bonaci prince."

Keenan huffed and walked towards the door. "You can't be serious. He was a human enemy five fuckin' minutes ago."

Although he was essentially right, Drew's vision narrowed and his teeth shot down into his mouth.

Keenan just pointed. "You see. Can you trust him around the women and children?"

Dante pushed his hand through his hair and walked up to

Keenan to speak quietly. Now with new super senses, Drew heard every word. "No one touches this man unless I say so, we clear?"

Keenan swore under his breath and walked out. The others started to leave behind him.

Dante returned to Drew who was standing there, still dripping onto the floor. *Thank you.*

"Don't thank me yet. You have to survive Darres. He'll be pissed at me then he'll come at you."

Drew nodded, understanding perfectly. Still it gave him a little confidence knowing the king was backing him. It would also give him more standing when it came to being a Siren's mate.

Dante seemed to read his mind because he smiled. "There could be your real problem."

Drew frowned.

"In Atlantean law, when a Siren chooses a mate, she brings him to the point of drowning then breathes her life's spirit into him to open his lungs. It's that point – the being first that's important. You just did it with another Siren. I'd be proper shitting myself if I was in your shoes." He was still shaking his head and laughing as he left the room.

Drew stood alone in the room, thinking on what he said. He had so much to learn if he was going to be of any use to Phoebe. He was still some ticking time bomb sent by the Scythians. *Whatever.* When the time came for a diplomatic party to go to Murrtaine, he'd just proved he could go with them.

Darl lay cocooned in sea moss in his sunken bed in the floor of his chambers. He was pale and gaunt when Vionne knelt next to him. *Is he awake? I came as soon as I heard.*

His father's eyelids flickered and he turned his head

slightly. Vionne reached out and took his hand. It was so light and thin; the skin was like tissue paper. *My son...I'm so glad you are here with me for my last moments.*

No... we will get you well. You have had these episodes before. Terror was already slicing through Vionne's heart. His father had always been the strength of his family – the rock they all leant on. At almost six hundred and fifty years old, he was believed to be the oldest person alive, Murr or Atlantean. Because of his great age he was often considered the wisest. For Vionne, he was the hero he'd always looked up to.

Darl shifted to look at Vionne more directly. The soothers rushed to help prop him up. Then he took Vionne's hand in both of his. *Listen to me, Son, my time has come. The Ether is calling me. I can feel it. I am not afraid and nor should you be. I have lived a very long and full life. I have been blessed with many sons and daughters. My only regret is that I couldn't see you married to your Siren before I go.*

Father, Vionne interrupted, not able to stand to hear him giving up on life.

Please, Son, I don't have much longer. I must impart what I have to say.

His voice got so weak Vionne had to lean right over the bed. Dax and Caan knelt next to him and Darres hovered just behind. Several of his sisters were around the bed, now openly weeping by swaying their bodies to and fro.

Darl gripped his hand to get his attention on him. *I too was fortunate, Vionne, to marry a Siren ... many years ago...*

His father was becoming delirious. He looked at Caan, who shrugged his shoulders.

I have lived a long time, my son, and was around your age the last time the daughters' spirits were sent to the earth.

Is he saying he married one of the Sirens five hundred years ago? Dax asked.

It sounded ridiculous, but he didn't want to upset his father and so he returned his attention to him. *Go on, Father.*

Ashaya was her name. She was so beautiful. I rescued her from the rocks near Dante's castle. The privateers of the day were using her to lure ships onto the rocks to steal gold returning from the new world.

Her beautiful song could be heard even beneath the waves and I was pulled to it just as the sailors were. The moment I saw her I knew she was mine. My ring confirmed it. She was terrified when I came out of the water but, in time, she came to trust me and came back with me to Murrtaine. Never were two beings so in love.

And her sisters? he asked.

It was never known for sure. The families warred over two who were kidnapped several times. One was believed to be held to ransom by a secret society some called The Illuminated. I was to be king as I was first pledged but the last was never found. Then rumors abounded that she had been ducked and burnt as a witch.

But surely you still had yours, Vionne said. It may not have been enough to fulfill prophecy but surely enough to make a king.

Darl patted his hand. *I railed against it too, but you see a king's strength only comes through his Siren and when one of them goes something is missing in each of them. It was as though a light had gone out in her eyes. Something was taken from her when her sister died.*

What happened to her, Father? She wasn't my mother.

Darl took a deep, fortifying sigh. *No, she was not. She died shortly after – just faded away with a broken heart. Your mother, Orb rest her soul, was Murr and I loved her dearly.*

What if she wasn't burnt? What if it was a ruse to take your power?

No one ever came forward as a reliable witness, so it is possible, but it was hard not to believe it when I saw my young, vital Siren shrivel before my eyes. Darl was staring into the middle distance, lost in memories. *The light is so close I can touch it.* His hand rose weakly to point.

Quickly, bring him something to help him rest. He is overwrought.

It is too late, one of the medics said.

Plenty of time for sleep, my son. Marry...promise me you will marry your Siren.

There was no time to explain what a lost cause that was. All he could do was pat his father's hand and say, *Rest assured, father, that I will do all in my power to secure the government.*

His father's focus returned and he looked at him again. *Do not allow another generation to be disbanded. Time has run out... time is now...they are coming, my son. They are on their way.*

Caan put his arm around his shoulders. *He rambles now, Brother. You have said all you can.*

The five families can come together if you take the lead, Vionne. You are the unfulfilled branch. Your oath, Son...give me your oath.

Vionne wasn't even entirely sure what he was swearing to but he gave it. *I swear, Father.*

Darl relaxed back into his soft bed, at last satisfied. *That is well. A prince's oath is solemn and binding before the Orb.*

Any guilt quickly evaporated as his father's body went taut and then relaxed slowly as the life left him. Vionne watched helplessly as the last bubbles trickled out to nothing from behind his ear.

Vionne sat with his three brothers, stunned. His sisters started to wail opposite them. Somewhere, a great bell sounded for the whole of Murrtaine to hear the sad news. The great Darl, Lord Advocate of Murrtaine, had at last passed into the Ether.

Vionne bent his head and prayed to the Orb for his father

to find peace. He also prayed for strength, all the more needed, when his brother said, *You have to do it now, Vionne. You cannot break a vow.*

Lastly, he prayed for the strength needed to break Phoebe's heart.

CHAPTER 50

The whole court at Ballygowan castle was stunned to hear the news of Darl's death. The man was legendary and believed immortal. Those who'd dealt with Murrtaine had never known anyone else and trusted him implicitly. Now power was about to shift to his son and no one knew where that left them, particularly Dante. Of all the trials in his turbulent reign, this felt the most dangerous. Vionne not only had Phoebe but Tia too, and that terrified him. He prayed he had read the man well and that, deep down, he was an honorable male.

Dante was dying of frustration. The respectable mourning period was two weeks, so apart from sending his deepest condolences there could be no other communication. Darl's many sons were being called from the furthest Murr outposts and it was left to him to announce the news to the Atlantean world.

Drew was champing at the bit for action. Dante promised him a summit would be arranged as soon as the mourning period was over to discuss the return of the princesses. At the very least, their bonds needed to be renewed. Both he and Drew were bound to them and could become gravely ill if they weren't replenished. Even so, he kept to himself that the chances of both princesses returning were slim. Medications, such as the one Jay was on, were available. The only hope was that Vionne chose to recognize that Dante was the rightful king and representative of Atlas here on earth and that both Sirens were already his.

DREW WAS in his below ground chamber pacing like a caged animal. He had fully recovered from his ordeal in the tank and longed to get Phoebe back to safety. Isla was inside him now too. She was like a quiet strength in the shadows urging him on. He'd forever be grateful to her, but she had her great love and he had his.

Vultures were circling. He could feel it.

The castle was filling up with so-called mourners, but the vibe felt more like excitement than sadness. Like no one really knew what was going to happen next. There was a lot of talk of the Americans being close to knowing the whereabouts of Murrtaine. Whispers that Dante couldn't hold his kingdom against the pure-bred Murrs. That scared him the most of all. Phoebe needed to get out of there before everyone went in all guns blazing.

Then there were the Scythians. He had his own score to settle with them. His vision went, his teeth descended and he clenched his fists at the mere thought of getting his hands on one of them. Those bastards had taken everything. He was nothing; with no future and no past. The person he was now was all down to Phoebe. He wasn't sure how he knew exactly but she had made him and it was that that drove him on. He may be nothing, but he was perfect for her. With all the weirdness that surrounded him here there was no one else like him; apart from her. They were complete. And no one, especially not some alien overgrown fish, was going to take her away from him.

Fuck this! He threw open the door and strode along the rock corridor to the great hall which had become a waiting room for the dignitaries of the Atlantean world.

The hall was packed. Perhaps it was the way he marched through the crowds, but the chatter died down and everyone started to turn to look at him. He walked right over to Dante, in conversation with Cesaré and Jay. Lance was there too, standing a little way off with Lily. Everyone was there; lounging, drinking and chatting like nothing was going on. Even Connor, her so-called Protector was there. Drew turned slowly, taking them all in, disgusted.

"Is there something I can do for you, Drew?" Dante asked.

Drew nodded. "Yeah, you can. You can all get off your lazy butts and do something about Phoebe's kidnapping."

It felt like there was a collective intake of breath.

Drew's vision narrowed and people started to move back. He was getting used to the changes in him and he was starting to like it. Cesaré took a step in front of the king and Lance walked towards him. He admired him for that; he was the only one with the guts. "It's not that simple, man. He won't see it as kidnap, just keeping what's his."

His teeth punched out of his gums and he almost combusted in rage. Except for Jay, he said the first sensible thing all day. "He overstepped the mark taking Tia, whatever he thought."

There were other murmurs of agreement.

"How can you all live like this?" Drew shouted, turning around to glare at everyone.

Lance came right over and touched his arm. "Calm down, we'll think of something."

Drew pulled apart. "How do you know who she's meant to be with, Dante? She chose me!"

"It's the price you pay for loving one of them," Dante said, quietly. He sounded like he was genuinely sorry. "They don't get to have their own life ... none of us do."

"Well it's fucked up!"

Dante just nodded. "I don't make the rules, much as I'd like to."

The thought of what could be happening to her and by who made him want to kill something. Several of the guards began to close in. Dante put up his hand to stop them coming any closer. "I have sent word to Vionne that I request a summit to discuss his accession and the safe return of the queen and her sister."

Drew blinked. At least something was happening.

"We will leave for Murrtaine as soon as he sends word."

"With me."

Everyone seemed to talk at once. Someone said, "He wouldn't survive the trip." Another said, "None of them had spent any real time under water."

"I will insist the meeting is over quickly."

"I don't like it," Keenan said. "You're the king, make him come here."

Dante smiled ruefully. "I'd like nothing more, but what's to stop him turning up without the girls. We will go to him and make sure we bring the girls back with us."

His words gave Drew hope. His eyes returned to normal and he felt human again. The look he gave him was full of purpose and strangely comforting. As if he knew exactly what he was feeling and was with him. "I thought no human had seen Murrtaine?"

"No Atlantean has either," Dante said. A smile began to creep across his face. "And we have a new prince to introduce to the Murrs. The newest member of the Bonaci family."

.   .   .

PHOEBE HADN'T WOKEN until way past lunchtime the next day. Who knew that just laughing gas and air could give you a hangover, but that was how she felt. Maybe it was the late night, but more likely it was the guilt and confusion she felt about recent events and how she had reacted to Vionne. There was no flowering it up. The minute she was on the swirly dance floor they hadn't kept their hands off each other, and the killing blow was she'd liked it and wanted more.

A young maid had been assigned to them and brought breakfast. She and Tia sat at the opaque oval table nibbling bits of things (she didn't even know what they were) in silence.

The queen mother, Naomi, would like to enter, the speaker voice said.

She looked at Tia with a face that said, "What now?" who gave her a similar look back. They could both do without this visit – and Tia knew her. Apart from a brief introduction, she didn't know her at all. She would have liked to have been on top form for something as heavy. *Enter,* she thought in a tone that really meant, *If you must.*

Her mother glided in and the maid quickly set another place at the table. Naomi bowed her head gracefully and sat. *We're not very talkative today, Mom,* Tia said, flashing Phoebe a look.

Naomi smiled enigmatically. *I understand, Darl will be a great loss.*

Phoebe and Tia both looked at each other with a frown. *What?* they both projected.

Naomi quickly realized they had no clue and explained: *Did you not hear the great bell?*

Yes, it woke me up. Phoebe said. Tia nodded. *And me.*

Phoebe couldn't help thinking of Vionne and his brothers. They must be devastated. And she thought she couldn't feel any worse today.

I came straight here now things have changed. Naomi was stirring something in a bowl that looked like cereal.

The girls looked at each other uneasily. *What's changed?* Tia said.

Dante was to have met with Vionne but now there will have to be a funeral and offerings to the Orb for two weeks of mourning. Vionne will have a state ceremony to become lord advocate in his father's place.

Is he okay? Phoebe asked.

Naomi looked at Phoebe a moment too long before she answered, *He feels the loss of such a great man. We all do, but he will be fine in time. His father was very old so it wasn't a great surprise. It will be a great comfort that you are here.*

She was looking straight at Phoebe with a meaning she didn't want to acknowledge, making her feel a hundred times worse.

What happens now? Will he still meet with Dante? He's not gonna be happy, Tia said.

Phoebe thought of Drew alone somewhere. She wasn't sure if she preferred the idea of him going back to his old life in Seattle or being all alone at the castle. He hated it there. She hoped Lance was there for him and maybe Connor. What she wouldn't do for one of his strong talking-tos. At least when they left for the meeting she'd know for sure.

Dante has sent word that he will accompany a delegation here to Murrtaine.

Tia's eyes went wide. *What? That's never happened. Outsiders have never come here before. Well, apart from us.*

It is true, no Atlantean or Human has ever stepped foot beneath the canopy. I can't make my mind up if he pays Vionne a great compliment or is very foolish indeed.

Phoebe was confused. *What do you mean?*

Well. Naomi appeared to be choosing her words carefully. *Dante is king. Some would say after Vionne brought both of you here, he should have returned you both to the castle to show his fealty.*

Phoebe racked her brains to work out what that actually meant.

Tia looked worried. *Vionne has total advantage if he comes here, the idiot. None of them at the castle has spent any real time under water. Can they last down here?*

Naomi bobbed her head as if she wasn't sure at all. It made her grateful that Drew was probably thousands of miles away.

Don't you get it? Tia said, loudly snapping her out of her thoughts.

She shrugged and shook her head.

We were brought here because of you. To see if you were his. And now ... Tia and her mother exchanged a look that was definitely a private conversation.

What? Phoebe asked uneasily.

Now his dad's gone and he has two Sirens.

The penny finally dropped. *What, he's going to try to take Dante's crown?*

Why not? It's what all the stupid princes want. Personally, I don't give a shit who's king as long as me and mine are okay, what's bothering me is that we'll be lucky if just one of us gets out of here.

Sheer horror crept over her when she grasped what she meant. Tia might escape as she was Dante's true wife, but everyone assumed she had not met her destined mate. *It's not Vionne though,* she said desperately. *It's Drew. His ring was purple. You saw it. Everyone saw it.*

Tia batted that away with her hand. *That was bollocks and you know it. Something must have been wrong there. He's human, Phoebe.*

Naomi stood and held up her hands to stop the heated conversation before it went too far. *Come, come, let us wait and see. It may not be as bad as you think.* Although the look in her eyes said she wasn't so sure.

Tia got up and flounced off, throwing her hands up in the air.

Phoebe was left playing with food she hadn't touched. Naomi sat slowly back into her chair. *I know we don't know each other very well, my dear, but I would like to get to know you.*

If she had air in her lungs she'd let out a blast of laughter. Instead she had to just roll her eyes. *You don't understand. How could you?* She went back to playing with her food.

Weirdly, she wondered if it was possible to cry underwater with the Water Quantifier thingy. Would anyone see her tears?

Naomi's face softened as if she understood. *We come from a world made up of strange laws and traditions. It is full of rules for mates and often keeps mothers away from children even if they don't want to be.*

Phoebe studied the strange woman's face. She was trying to explain in a roundabout way why she hadn't been with her. It wasn't important. Not when she was about to be bargained like some pawn in a silly game between princes. *Strikes me, in this world we don't get anything we want,* she said spitefully.

Ah, you are referring to your Human, Naomi said, nodding her head slowly. Every time she tried to act human, she just came off looking weird and awkward. She did everything too slowly; as if it was taking great effort.

Phoebe just shrugged. *Well, for your information he's not human, not any more.*

Naomi was nodding again. *A transformation.*

She was still nodding. Phoebe wanted to scream at her to

stop. Instead she changed tack. *Thankfully, he's well out of all this.*

Naomi stopped nodding at last. In fact, she was eerily still.

What? You know something?

Naomi seemed to snap herself out of her daze. *There have been rumors from the castle.*

What rumors?

Naomi paused again. *Some are saying ... that a human has dragon eyes and has been breathing the water.*

She didn't need to explain further. It had to be Drew. *Recently? But how? Doesn't he need* me *for that?*

Naomi rose from her chair and took too long to answer. Phoebe's heart thumped in sudden fear. Her cheeks burnt and she was shaking all over. *Well, doesn't he?*

Not necessarily, Naomi said at last. *An Atlantean needs a Siren. But he is not Atlantean,* she tacked on as if it made some sort of difference.

Phoebe's blood was now on a steady boil. *Who?* she said through gritted teeth, made all the more difficult as her canines threatened to tear her own lip.

Dante was there with three of your sisters.

Who did it! she shouted, but it came out like a snarl and her vision completely tunneled.

Naomi looked alarmed for the first time. *I believe they nearly lost him ... but it's okay, he was saved.*

Phoebe took a menacing step towards her mother. *Get out ... Get out!* she shrieked.

Naomi almost ran to the door and called "open" as she ran. The waterfall appeared immediately. Just before she stepped through, she said, *I didn't mean to upset you.*

Leave!

Naomi nodded and stepped through, leaving Phoebe

numb with shock. Her brain was racing. *How could he do this to her now when she needed him the most?*

Tia walked back in carrying two scraps of material in her hand. *Which one ... Where's Mom?*

Phoebe flopped down into a chair and put her head in her hands. Tia flung down the clothes and dropped down to her knees in front of her. She let her hand fall away so she could see her transformed eyes, but instead of scaring her off she just looked more concerned. *What's the matter, Phoebes?*

The tears came then and Tia pulled her into her shoulder. Her body shook with huge, racking sobs as her heart broke. She rocked her, shushed her and let her cry herself out, rubbing her back gently. *Hey, you gonna tell me what's wrong now?*

It's Drew; he's breathing the water.

Tia pushed her hair back from her face. *Well that's great, isn't it? Proves he's not human after all.*

Phoebe pulled away from Tia and got up. *No it's not fucking great. Who did it, Tia?* she said, glaring at her.

Tia sagged with understanding. *Oh god, yes, of course.* She stood up and hugged her, which started the tears off again. At least Tia had been Dante's first, the one that actually meant something.

She went back to bed and cried till she had nothing left in her. She was numb – not sure whether she would ever be able to feel anything ever again.

CHAPTER 51

The next two weeks passed slowly. Phoebe heard no
more about Drew. She didn't ask. Naomi made
herself scarce and Vionne was now much too busy and
important for guided tours. Tia seemed to have stepped into
that role – dragging her around, showing her any places of
interest she'd seen on her previous visits.

The funeral was later that day, followed by the meeting
with Dante tomorrow. Phoebe was dreading it but at the
same time wanted it over with. Anything was better than all
this blasted waiting.

That morning she wondered how Vionne was getting on.
He was probably closeted with his brothers. Apparently, he
had hundreds of siblings, but Darl had named him as his
successor. She guessed that spoke reams about how close
they were.

So much for being wooed. She guessed she hadn't exactly
encouraged him.

The maid delivered a message. The princes Dax and Caan
would be escorting them to the funeral at 11.30 a.m. Then

she placed new outfits on both of their beds and left them to it.

Phoebe picked up the shimmering material and held it to her body. It was beautiful; deepest indigo. Tia's was a similar design but in darkest green. Both were made of the material that never looked wet and hugged their figures perfectly.

They dressed and stood opposite each other. *Book ends,* Tia said with a grin.

Phoebe managed a smile. They did match perfectly, and yet they managed to reveal their personalities subtly. Almost as if the utmost care had gone into choosing them.

Princes Dax and Caan would like to enter, the tinny voice they referred to as the door lady said.

Come in, they both projected.

The young men came in and bowed low. Guess they were in serious mode. There was none of their teasing banter this morning. They did look very cool in loose trousers of dark grey, bare feet and chests. Somehow it made them look buff but elegant at the same time, like male ballet dancers. Phoebe totally approved of the look.

Dax offered his arm to Tia, and Caan offered her his. She imagined Vionne would escort her, which was silly, but asking after him came out before she thought about it. The men exchanged a look and she could have kicked herself.

Caan smiled politely and said, *You will see him soon.*

Phoebe blasted red. Also noticed by the brothers.

We're hoping you can cheer him up.

He was a bore before, now he's an automatron.

Both brothers laughed at the joke. Phoebe smiled weakly. She hadn't thought Vionne boring and looked at Tia, who was watching her, puzzled too.

They exited using the waterfall and followed the walk-ways for what felt like ages, to the furthest point of the palace. The last glass vestibule meant they left the artificial gravity behind and stepped out to a huge circular pavilion. Beautiful gardens surrounded it with colored sea plants and tall reeds. It all looked Japanese to Phoebe.

To prove her point they swam over a tiny hump-backed bridge to the open door and entered the pavilion. There were hundreds of people, but the thing that hit her was the silence. With no verbal chatter it was eerie. Everyone there was Murr.

No outsiders are permitted, Caan projected next to her.

It should have felt like an honor, but it just made her feel uneasy. Thankfully, Naomi spotted them and hovered near her seat in the front row, indicating where they should go. Dax and Caan maneuvered them smoothly through the many guests treading water. There were three rows of seats that went almost all the way round, leaving a long gap for an aisle, rather like the shape of a keyhole. A white casket was positioned in the center of it.

Soon the doors closed and the gravity was switched on. Phoebe and Tia floated down and took their seats next to their mother. Everything became clearer again. Tia was right; the feeling never got old. Dax and Caan suddenly became serious again, bowed and left to find their seats nearer the end of the row.

There was Vionne. He was sitting quietly, staring ahead of him, when his brothers joined him. He nodded his head to acknowledge them but looked a shadow of the man she'd met a couple of weeks ago.

He was still handsome and muscular in similar trousers to his brothers and very little else. For a moment his eyes met hers. They were there and they were gone. No words, just a feeling of devastation. Somehow she knew it was a feeling he'd deliberately transferred to her. He was letting her know in his own language how he felt and why he wasn't over there with her.

It reignited her feelings of utter confusion, and she was glad when a white-haired Murr stood looking official, signifying the funeral was beginning. He was the only male in the room without dark grey or black trousers on. His were white with a silver shimmer to them. He also had on a skintight top in the same material, reminding her of a 1960s TV spaceman.

He held his hands aloft, as if summoning something. Then he projected. *Please open your minds to the life of Darl, son of Kevian-the-great, pure descendant of Atlas Terranova. He leaves behind one hundred and fifty-three sons and one hundred and twenty daughters.*

Then every mind in the room projected the same thing: *We welcome the life of Darl.*

Phoebe and Tia looked at each other, then around at everyone else; they'd all shut their eyes. Phoebe reached for Tia's hand, sat back into her chair and did the same.

A moment of absolutely nothing passed. It went on for so long Phoebe thought they were meant to be praying or giving a two-minute silence out of respect or something.

Then the pictures came. They blasted through and bombarded their minds one after another. It happened so fast it was hard to make sense of them at first. A baby in his mother's arms, a toddler, a little boy swimming with his friends with dolphins. By the time he was a teenager, Phoebe felt that they were literally seeing Darl's life.

It astounded her. Over six hundred years flashed before their eyes – weddings, laughter, children being born and growing up, happiness and love and, finally, peace. She'd been witness to a family album of pictures that spanned many human lifetimes, all with the emotions that went with it.

A whole life that had ended in peace, with a picture of Vionne's beautifully sad face. The vision panned out and rose upwards, until she could see an elderly man viewed from above. He was cocooned in a soft bed with Vionne, his brothers and many other siblings, surrounding him and comforting each other. Then the scene evaporated like mist on the wind.

Phoebe sat dazed for a good minute. She'd seen the last moments of a man's life as his spirit left his earthly body and disappeared heavenward.

She found she was crying. Naomi's arm came around her shoulders. *So beautiful. So amazing.*

Wow, what a send-off, Tia said from the other side of her.

The show was over. Everyone in the room appeared to be as subdued as they were and remained perfectly still.

She looked across at Vionne. His eyes were cast down into his lap. He looked so alone.

The master of proceedings stood and held his arms up again. *We convey Darl to the Ether with our esteem and love. Let him be at one with our mother universe and our forefathers.*

As it has always been, the minds in the room chorused after him.

A loud hum sounded as a trapdoor beneath the casket opened and it began to sink down slowly. With all that looking up at the Ether, she was a little surprised to see the coffin going down. That was soon forgotten as it was engulfed in an impossibly bright light and then it was gone. It just disappeared and the door in the floor closed again with a hum.

Both Phoebe and Tia were left staring at where the body of Darl had once been. Everyone else seemed to relax, get up and mill around.

Phoebe and Tia looked at each other. *Guess that's it,* she said.

Tia shrugged. *Just like that,* she replied, raising her eyebrows.

When Phoebe thought about it, the whole thing had been

kind of perfect. Everyone joined in by seeing and celebrating a long and happy life and then waved him off as he went God knows where – some high-tech incinerator, probably.

Her eyes strayed to Vionne. He was touching people on the shoulder and they were touching foreheads with his. He was obviously thanking them and they were showing affection in that Murr way he'd used with her. It was so loving and tactile, much better than the standoffish way of humans.

Then he looked over. It was unnerving how he always seemed to know when her attention was on him.

Tia was already talking to someone with her mother so she walked over to him. He said something to an older man and he left them alone. *Hello, stranger,* she said, not able to think of a single thing to say.

He gave her the most brilliant face-lightning smile she'd seen on anyone – let alone a Murr. *You've been practicing,* she said, not helping breaking into a grin herself, then immediately feeling terrible in the circumstances.

He didn't seem to notice. *I'm getting good, aren't I?*

She laughed and nodded, relieved. He really was. *Do you wanna get out of here?* she said on impulse.

For a moment he looked a little surprised, like he would turn her down.

Of course you're a busy guy now, and she went to turn around.

He touched her on the arm. *No it's okay. I just need to tell my brother Axyl where I've gone.*

That was one she hadn't heard of. She watched him go over to a guy standing next to the brother she knew was Darres. They looked identical except Axyl's hair was shoulder-length and Darres had long black hair to his waist. *Twins.*

The doors opened and the gravity machine got switched off. Vionne swam back over. *Come on.* And he took her hand

and led her out through the gardens and away from the palace.

When they slowed their swimming through the cute windy streets to a more leisurely pace, she asked. *How come I don't know that brother – like I know you've got loads, but he looks like a twin of Darres?*

Vionne turned his head and smiled at her. *You are right, he is a twin. He is already a ruler of our outpost in Antarctica. I can learn much from him. My life is no longer my own and I cannot easily take time off. He is a good second-in-command.*

They swam a little further in silence. She was learning so much about this strange race of which she was now a part. She didn't realize there were other underwater cities.

There are many, Vionne said, grinning. *Murrla is Axyl's. It is smaller than Murrtaine. This is more like the capital city.*

You shouldn't keep reading my mind. It's rude, you know. But she wasn't angry and bumped shoulders with him. It was dawning on her just how important he was now. *I don't want to get you into any trouble.*

He smiled. *I am a ruler, Phoebe. I can do anything and yet go nowhere. I can talk to anyone as long as I say nothing. I think I can take a last afternoon with you.*

It was so sad; it brought a lump to her throat. She saw what a great gift he was giving her. It was the last of his freedom.

He tugged her along faster. *Shall we get right out of Murrtaine?*

Fear shot through her for a moment. She was God knows how far below the surface, but she kind of felt a level of protection from the dome. At least she couldn't get eaten by anything.

Vionne's laughter had become a wonderful sound in her mind. *Come, I'll protect you. This is my back yard.*

She laughed along with him and they swam over to one of

the little depots that held the Bubble Bikes. *Ooh, yes! I love these.*

The water outside is going to feel a lot colder than in Murrtaine. Would you like a suit?

She shrugged. Honestly, she had no idea.

They swam over to a rack where there hung rows of shimmering body suits in varying sizes and shades of blue. *Do you wear them?*

No, Vionne said. *Very few do. Maybe the very young or the elderly. It is very cold waters here and you do have some human blood,* he said, raising a brow.

Hey, only a little. If you're not, I'm not.

He laughed. *I'll take one just in case.* He took the scrap of material off the hanger and tied it around his neck like a scarf. *What is it the humans say? Lightweight?* Then he hopped on his Bubble Bike and sped off.

She swore she'd get him, jumped on another and followed him.

It didn't take them long to get to the perimeter. The membrane itself was invisible, but small red lights placed at three-meter intervals on the seabed and an AI voice alerted them it was there.

Slow down, Vionne said, as he crossed the line.

Phoebe squinted her eyes and did the same. Cold water hit her immediately and she almost fell off her Bubble Bike in shock. Vionne spun around, jumped off and swam over, pulling her into his arms. She was fine in a few minutes, but she let him hold her just the same. When she couldn't let it last any longer without it being obvious she was enjoying it she looked up into his eyes. *I'm okay.*

His expression didn't change. He let her go, pulled off the suit wrapped around his neck and held it out to her. *Here, put this on.*

Grateful for the distraction, she took it and wriggled into

it like a wet suit. Except this one was extra stretchy like a second skin, and thin as gossamer. She straightened up and tried to look at herself from all angles. It felt great. *Does it look okay?*

Vionne was watching her with heavy-lidded eyes that made her take a swallow. *For a lightweight!*

Her eyes went wide and she lunged forward to give him a dead arm but he was too quick. He was back on his Bubble Bike and speeding off in a flash. She laughed and followed.

The suit was amazing. The cold water simply disappeared. They continued at top speed for another five minutes, until Vionne eventually began to slow down. *Where are we going?* She called.

I'm taking you to meet some friends. He was grinning, making it all the more intriguing.

She was scanning the seabed to see if she could see any other Murr activity or architecture.

Vionne dismounted his bike. *We'll leave these here.* He nestled it between two rocks, then bent down and picked up a stone about the size of a brick. He started banging it against a large rock but, after a few, Phoebe could tell they weren't random. He was banging in fast little stanzas, leaving spaces.

Phoebe got off her bike, fascinated.

We need to go up, he said, pointing a finger.

It was so exciting. He took her hand and they started their assent. She wondered how on earth he would find anyone in all this expanse of water.

I know them, they generally pass through here every few days or so.

Even though he'd just read her mind again, she was too intrigued to pull him up on it.

They were nearing the surface. The sun was glittering and rippling a few feet above their heads. *I'm going to send out a blast. Don't be alarmed.*

Before she could respond a light blinded her, but it was ridiculous because it came from inside. Then an amazing feeling of warmth came. It was essence of Vionne – like a signature of who he was. It happened again. He was sending out a signal that he was here.

For a moment she watched him in awe, until he pointed. She followed the line of his arm. Three dark shapes were coming in fast.

CHAPTER 52

At first Phoebe was scared as they became distinguishable and fish-shaped; she thought they were sharks. Then, as they approached, she realized with joy that they were dolphins. They went up to the surface then they dove down to where they were waiting.

She gripped Vionne's arm.

Don't be frightened. Like dogs to humans, dolphins are a Murr's best friend – except we don't try to own them.

The dolphins circled and one swam right next to Vionne's arm and made several clicks and whistles. Vionne responded and let his hand run across the creature's back in a long stroke. It was magnificent seeing Vionne swimming, twisting and diving with the creature in what could only be described as a water dance. She'd never seen anything so beautiful. It knocked anything at a theme park into a cocked hat. This wasn't choreographed; it was two mammals interacting with joy at seeing each other. It moved her deeply.

Vionne swam in a large backwards arc and came up in front of her. *Come and meet them,* he said, taking her hand.

However, when they approached, the dolphins swam up to the surface.

Her heart sank. She must have scared them off.

Vionne squeezed her hand. *Give them time.*

He was right. After they surfaced for air they dove back down, cavorted and twisted all around them.

One came particularly close and clicked.

Put out your hand, Vionne said.

She almost squealed in delight as it pushed its bottle nose under her hand. *What's his name?*

It's a she. The others are her sons.

Phoebe looked at the other two. One was a lot smaller than the other. *Cute baby.*

The other is a cheeky teenager. Their pod is a mile or so away in that direction. He pointed to their left.

She answered my call, he said, tickling the mother under the chin.

Do they have names?

Not that you would understand in human terms. I have a picture for her that means something along the lines of ocean friend.

Phoebe was enjoying running her hand all over the silky skin. *I shall call her Boo then. That's Junior and little Boo.*

Vionne grinned. *As you wish. I don't think I will ever get to grips with human vernacular.*

Junior was nudging at her side. She laughed and gave him the same attention.

They want to take us with them.

She wanted to ask where, but Vionne was already swimming off as fast as their Bubble Bikes, holding onto Boo's fin with little one darting off behind.

Junior nudged her and spun like an impatient dog. *Be gentle then.* A little fearfully, she took hold of his fin as he whooshed by to catch up with his mother.

It was the most exciting, exhilarating experience of her life. They breached the water so they could breathe and dove down. Most of it, she was sure, was just for the hell of it – until she caught a glimpse of activity up ahead.

Fins were breaking the water and birds were circling ahead. This time, when they dove down, they had company. Tens and tens of dolphins joined them.

First of all her heart thumped in fear. Maybe she would be treated as an intruder.

Meet the family, Vionne blasted.

Junior spiraled down beneath the pod and shot back up with her through its center. When they came to the surface, he took off with her at least fifteen feet out of the water in a graceful arc.

The other dolphins were swimming with them, getting swept up in the joy of meeting new faces and mimicking their actions.

It was so wonderful and so deeply moving it made her cry.

Eventually, after the last dip and soar, Boo turned and Junior followed, back in the direction they came.

When they returned to the crop of rocks they'd left, Vionne let go of Boo and Phoebe let go of Junior. *They're tired,* he said.

She wasn't surprised. They had been balls of energy.

The dolphins were clicking and she wondered what they were saying.

A noise that started of as a soft rumble was getting louder. Fear shot through her as she looked at Vionne.

Go, little friends, Vionne said, reaching for Phoebe's hand as the noise got louder and nearer. It was beginning to sound like rhythmical banging on an oil drum.

Vionne pulled her over to a crop of rocks and they waited, looking upwards.

The wonderful meeting was over with Vionne's order for them to go back to their pod.

They understand by your emotions, Vionne said. *Animals are far more advanced than humans give them credit for.*

Phoebe felt a lump in her throat as, with a final phrase of clicks, the three swam off. She watched them all the way until their grey dots disappeared completely.

The noise was really loud now and a huge, dark shadow passed overhead. Then it made sense.

A ship.

Stay perfectly still, Vionne said. *It will pass.*

He was right. The loud thumping was a long way up at the surface. It went over and passed into the distance. Vionne was watching it closely though and she sensed he was troubled but didn't want to rattle her.

When at last he turned his attention back to her, she said, *Thank you, Vionne, so much.*

There was a moment where he just studied her eyes. *It was my pleasure to share it with you.*

Puzzled, she wondered if he meant he'd never shared that with anyone.

Never, he said, simply. *Well, we snuck out as children. Does that count?*

She smiled. He really was a charming man. Then she frowned. He really wasn't a man at all. However, he *was* male. That was for sure. Then her eyes drifted to the direction the ship had gone and she thought of Murrtaine and what they had to go back to. Trouble seemed to be in all directions. *Are you okay?* she asked.

He leaned back against the rock and nodded.

He was toying with the ring on his finger that was still red. It was an odd color and she knew it couldn't be good. *Dante comes tomorrow.*

Yes.

Honestly, she didn't know what that would bring. Some pretty heavy politics, for sure. She was more worried about the shit storm that would follow with Drew. Then she slammed that thought down, not willing to go into that tailspin of emotions.

He will use this as evidence that you should go back with him. He looked at his ring and then where the ship had gone too. Like the ring wasn't the only thing on his mind.

The ring she kind of understood. Drew's ring had turned purple. That meant she was his. A red ring, well, she had no more of an idea what that meant than he did.

I would have legal grounds ...

She nodded. He didn't need to finish. *Who else will come with him?* She tried not to look him in the eye, but in the end she couldn't help it.

You think your Protector will come? I heard he breathes the water now.

He's my mate. Not my Protector. Her hackles were beginning to rise. *His ring is purple,* she finished spitefully.

Vionne's head tilted to the side as if there was something he didn't understand. *And yet you never breathed for him in the water, he chose someone else.*

The truth hit her like a slap around the face.

I won't ask you how a human purported to be of pure blood manages to breathe the water. He pulled her to stand in front of him so she couldn't avert her eyes.

It was way too close for comfort and she tried to push away, but he held her fast. She was between his legs with his huge body surrounding her completely. She glared into his heavily striped face and, for a moment, she was disarmed by the look in his deep, pool-like eyes. The anger just ebbed out of her. Until she said eventually, *You would be easy to love, Vionne.*

He pulled her in closer so their skin touched. *Let me give you what you have been cruelly denied. Let me breathe for you.*

She stared into the savage, masculine face, millimeters from her own and she could literally feel his need to do this for her.

There is no drowning, no violence in the act for us, Phoebe. Just a sharing of self. A gift. It has only become debauched by the Atlanteans. We are pure. Everything here, and he held out his hand indicating the ocean, *is as it has always been for thousands of years.*

She knew he included their home planet in what he was saying and it did make perfect sense. And, if she was honest, he did fire up something inside her that she did find harder and harder to ignore. Flames that needed dousing. *I am in love with him, Vionne.*

Whatever spell he was holding her with never wavered for a moment. He either didn't believe her, didn't understand or didn't care. Otherwise he wouldn't have said what he said next.

Let me show you who I am from the depth of me. You will know me and know for sure I would never hurt you.

His lips were getting closer and closer and she knew she should push him away. They brushed hers and then did the same with his tongue. Luxuriating warmth enveloped her tempting like an invitation. His smell seemed to overrun her senses and his taste was just so intriguing she found she wanted more. On some level she knew he was pulling her in with some kind of thrall-inducing pheromones. He was from a whole other species, her species, but it was just a kiss. He was so insanely hot that it couldn't hurt to find out – *could it? Just the once?*

Just the once ... he repeated.

Drew had done it, after all.

Her arms moved up his arms to his corded muscled

shoulders.

I can't live here, she said as a last-ditch, lame attempt to get a hold on the situation. It was pathetic really as she told herself again he was only asking for a kiss.

I would never make you stay.

That was enough and she parted her lips. It was like dropping the drawbridge to an invading army. In less than a moment he was inside, plundering and owning her with his tongue. Pulling her into his body with his strong arms, her legs were off the seabed as he held them with his and spun and twisted with her in the water.

The kiss wasn't gentle and loving, but demanding and hot and, after the initial shock, she matched it. It went on fiercely for several minutes until he eventually slowed.

Phoebe knew the moment he would do it when she opened her eyes to find his open and soulful. There was something so strong in the depths of them that held her in his power. Yet so calming and infinitely attractive too, that he didn't invoke any of her physical changes. Her vision stayed riveted on him and her canines remained hidden.

When the first of the breath came, it was like a seeking mist across her tongue. It meandered slowly down her neck, warming; like a good brandy. It crept through her veins and neural pathways. The feeling was pleasurable but so acute it was overwhelming. Her heart began to hammer so hard she thought it would explode. In fact, if he hadn't gradually tapered off the stream she was sure she would have passed out. He literally left her seeing stars.

It was in that moment that everything made sense. It wasn't just pleasure, it was imparting aspects of him. It was thoughts, feelings and impulses, all the more overpowering because he was such a strong male. He was passionate and open and he had given all of himself to her in a single breath. It was awe-inspiring and humbling at the same time.

Even the time she'd experienced the breath with Dante, it was a mechanical act for the state. He probably saved the real thing for Tia. This was something different. Vionne had meant every molecule of himself to find a home in her. Maybe it was because he was a pure-bred Murr, she wasn't sure, but he was there inside her now, untainted, honorable and kind. It brought a lump to her throat.

Vionne was watching her cautiously. He was worried how she would react; she could feel it.

The afterglow of him still surrounded her like a nest. *You feel wonderful,* she said, sounding sleepy or a little drunk.

My pleasure, he said, still gauging her reaction to him.

Her mind was gradually clearing and becoming a little more alert. He was waiting. He expected her to return the gift. She wouldn't give him false hope and she shook her head.

As angry as she was with Drew, she was a one-man girl. If there was ever a chance with her and Vionne, she would find out what had gone on with Drew first and whether he still wanted her. It cleared her mind instantly. It was like a knife to her heart to think one of her sisters had taken her place with him.

He's a lucky man. The smile he gave her then was regretful. *Unfortunately, I love you all the more for it.*

She shivered. Either his breath was wearing off, or the cold of the seawater was seeping in. Another thunderous rumble was coming closer. It seemed to wake them both up. *Let me get you back to the warm waters of Murrtaine.*

He tied her Bubble Bike to his and motioned for her to straddle his behind him. After what they'd just shared, it seemed silly to say no. Besides, when she put her arms around his huge chest, he was warm. With her cheek to his back she found herself wishing the journey would last forever.

CHAPTER 53

*D*ante knew it was useless saying no to Drew. He was exhibiting all the behaviors of a mated Atlantean male. He'd have been the same in his shoes. He did send ahead and warn Vionne though – particularly because of the security risk Drew posed knowing the whereabouts of Murrtaine.

Vionne didn't seem too perturbed as long as Drew was blindfolded. His confidence was unsettling.

Two marine bugs were sent to carry them. Dante, two water breathing princes, Cesaré and Keenan, and Sirens, Lacy and Lily rode in one, and Drew, Isla and eight of the honorable guard he'd insisted he bring in the other.

The guards wore Murr technology breathing apparatus to make the journey. It just looked like a thin bubble on their faces with a gill-like valve at the bottom. The soldiers were brave because he sure as hell wouldn't fancy wearing them. But he couldn't go unprotected. It was a strong show of vampire protection, although down there in Vionne's domain he wasn't sure what use they'd be.

He'd been through some hairy moments in his reign, but

this one made him the most nervous. He would be at a dangerous disadvantage to a male who had been groomed for leadership his whole life, hundreds of meters below crushing ocean. There was no access to oxygen should any of them need it without Vionne's say-so, but he was left with little choice. Tia's life and the future of his kingdom rested on this.

Dante hung back until they all disappeared, one by one, into the tunnel from the fountain in the great hall. Isla went with Drew to get him started breathing again. There was a whole lot of difference breathing salt water under pressure. The tank had been a piece of cake in comparison.

Vionne had sent them all special pills for them to take for the water pressure, which he'd distributed to everyone except the Sirens. Being almost pure-bred, they wouldn't need them.

Dante was the last to go. Jay and Lance approached him. They had to be content with staying and being the center of operations. Even with the Murr breathing apparatus they couldn't last long enough to make the journey.

Jay came up first and Dante hugged him. Despite all their differences, he was like a brother. He would be as worried about Tia as he was. "Don't trust the fucker," Jay said, quietly, in his ear.

Dante nodded and looked over at Alfonzo, Sebastian and Max hovering a little way off. "Stay in touch." For once, Dante was grateful for the recently made bond that Jay had made with Tia. It was another link to land in case all else failed.

He touched Lance on the shoulder and he gave him a single nod back. He understood. Reincarnated from an ancient race of humans bound to the Atlantean crown, he'd fight along side them if need be to save his Siren.

It was time to go.

After taking a last look at each of their faces, Dante disappeared down into the depths of the tunnel.

THE MARINE BUG slowed and they were sucked through the membrane dome protecting Murrtaine. None could fail to be in awe of the technology of such an undertaking. The city was magnificent. Drew gawped along with everyone else at the domes and spiral buildings that looked like they were made of blue smoked glass, all visible through the jelly walls of the craft they were carried in.

The two marine bugs came to a halt not far from the palace at a raised docking area. Crowds of the strange-looking local people were gathering. They'd had more visitors in the last month than they'd had in a lifetime. He didn't blame them. Guess they looked weird to them too.

They alighted through the hatch in the floor and huge Murr guards swam with them to the large palace doors. Down here they looked even bigger. On land they were almost seven feet tall. In water their lower legs grew and added at least another six inches.

They entered the glass vestibule and the door hissed shut behind them. One of the guards pressed a button in the wall and their feet slowly came down to the ground.

They all looked at each other in wonder. The water seemed to have disappeared.

A guard went to take off his mask but Dante stopped him by grabbing his wrist. He shook his head. Then he looked around catching everyone's eye. *Those of you who can hear me, don't be fooled. We're still under water. They're using something to make it feel like we're not.*

Drew frowned. It can't just be for their benefit. They must live like this all the time when they come inside.

The two guards who were leading the way hadn't

explained anything. All they said was to follow and that Vionne was waiting for them.

It refocused them on the purpose of the visit and they fell into strong marching strides along the strange oval corridors. All the way, Drew looked left and right to see if he could see Phoebe. He'd hoped she would have been there to meet him. It made his blood boil again to think that she was a prisoner here.

They came to a standstill at a blank, glistening wall. A woman's voice said, "His majesty the king would like to enter." They all looked at each other uneasily, not sure what would happen next.

'Lord advocate will see you now,' the voice said.

They all took a sharp step back as the wall shimmered and moved until it looked like a curtain of falling water.

They hesitated until their escorting guard stepped through, showing the way. Dante, Cesaré and the girls went through, Drew next, then everyone else after.

They stepped into a huge chamber that looked like everything in it was made up of smooth opaque white material like glass or some kind of plastic.

Vionne rose from behind a desk where he was working at a monitor that floated in the air. With a wave of his hand it dissolved like a hologram. *Not plastic. Everything is an organic substance we grow and polish into the things you see.*

Drew looked around at the other faces. Either they had all thought the same thing or the guy had singled him out and read his mind.

Vionne came forward. Clasped Dante's arm at the wrist and pulled him close to touch his forehead with his. He towered over Dante. It reminded him of a large dog dominating a smaller one.

No one else reacted, as if it were a normal greeting. Drew found himself hoping he didn't do it to him. It was the first time he'd seen him properly and the guy was huge. All the Murrs were scary-looking with their permanent war paint, but were all built as well without an ounce of fat. Down here it was easy to make the comparison to the Atlanteans – a very similar, slightly watered down version. He couldn't help but look down at himself.

Vionne greeted the other princes similarly, but much more quickly as if it was a formality that needed to be followed. Eventually he came to Drew and he put out his hand for a simple human handshake.

The big Murr paused and the corners of his mouth curled into the beginnings of a smile. The guy was assessing him and finding him amusing. It made his blood begin to rise.

The large black pools he had for eyes narrowed horizontally as Drew's vision clouded orange and did the same vertically.

Vionne's grin widened. *Dante, please warn your hybrid human pit-bull that we read all thoughts and emotions, not just projected speech.* His eyes never wavered from his as he spoke.

Drew realized that the rumbling growl he could hear was coming from his own throat.

Dante was soon at his elbow and Keenan the other. *Tone it down, or you'll have to wait outside,* Dante projected.

Drew still had what little vision he had locked onto Vionne. *Read this, asshole. I'm not leavin' without Phoebe.*

Keenan was right there, ready to jump in between them. Vionne hadn't moved a muscle. Drew was just waiting for it; he didn't give a fuck about the size difference.

Come, Cousin. Let us concentrate on the matters at hand so we can get back to managing our kingdoms, Dante said.

The words seemed to strike a chord with Vionne as he averted his eyes and nodded. *Come,* he said, and they all followed him through another wall into a room with a huge oval table occupied by several other Murrs.

The Murrs at the table were introduced by name while they all took their seats. Drew mentally noted that the two called Dax and Caan were his brothers. *I apologize for any anxiety caused, but after watching that area of the USA for many years, we received certain intelligence that my Siren would be there. We were not expecting to find the queen. I made a calculated decision to bring her to safety,* Vionne said.

Drew was seething. His mind stopped moving after *my Siren.* He tracked what little vision he had to Dante, hoping he wasn't buying this bullshit either. Dante inclined his head, giving nothing away.

Please fetch the queen, Vionne said to one of the palace guards standing at the door. He immediately bowed and went. *We will have a moment of private discussion. I do not want to keep you all any longer than necessary out of your environment. It is not safe.*

Those final three words were said directly with his soulless eyes resting on Drew. *What about Phoebe?* he thought, having no idea whether the big bastard could hear him.

Drew felt a pressure on his neck that felt like fingers pushing down on his currently unused airway. No one else saw, but Drew knew it was a warning. He could crush his windpipe here and no one would know until he expelled his lungs topside. He had no projected speech and so he couldn't tell a soul – no one who'd listen anyway.

The rest of you will be given apartments to rest and refresh before the journey back.

Everyone except Dante began to rise from their chairs. Vionne hadn't yet released his grip. The blood surging around Drew's veins in anger was now being restricted and giving way to dizziness and nausea. *You have wasted your time in coming here, human. You are merely a Protector with no loyalty, of which she is fully aware.* He shot a look to one of his guards. *Remove him.*

Drew was pulled to his feet and Dante frowned, but Vionne got his attention on him again. *Your man pup will be shown to apartments with the others. I'm sensing a little animosity.*

Dante glanced at him one last time and projected quickly. *I won't be long,* and Drew was ushered out.

THE MOMENT they were alone Vionne said, *What the hell is he, Dante?*

Dante guessed correctly that they'd been having a whole other conversation before his guards had removed Drew from the room. *By the last blood test – Bonaci. Whatever you think, Vionne, he's a good man.*

Vionne did momentarily pause at that. With that name, he would have just joined the dots and worked out that Drew could very well be Phoebe's most compatible.

Are you aware that he was responsible for bringing both her and the queen to that clinic?

It was clear what was going to happen here. Vionne would bargain Tia for Phoebe and he held all the cards. It was time to be frank with him.

He started with a summary of what he knew of Drew so far. How he'd been inducted and brainwashed by the Scythians. How he could very possibly still be working for them even if he didn't know about it. How the vampiric trend was spreading through the court and he was at its center. Then he concluded that, despite all that, his bloods had been checked and re-checked and they all came back saying the same thing; that since knowing Phoebe his blood was changing until he was almost pure Bonaci – the only House not yet accounted for at the council by bond to a Siren.

That appeared to stun Vionne to silence. No doubt he thought he could brush Drew aside with a greater claim. *What do you understand of a blood-red ring?* He held up his left hand, showing his divining ring, now at its resting white. Dante's was identical as no Sirens were present. *When I near Phoebe it is as red as blood.*

Dante considered what he said carefully. The only other instance he'd heard of was unsubstantiated. It was rumored that Malleven – the prince who'd abducted Lacy, disgraced his cousin, Cesaré, and married Lily – never wore his ring because of the same reason. Most believed the color meant disqualification because of foul play. It could very well mean the same thing here. Perhaps it wasn't even Vionne's fault. *My scholar, Max, believes it's a reaction of the Orb in some way.* He didn't want Vionne to think he was accusing him of trying to tamper with the fates. *You should know that Drew's is purple around her.*

For a Murr who normally showed no facial expression, Vionne's went through a whole range, ending on a scowl. *A human – and a second one at that. I believe your man is correct. The Orb is angry. It is an omen. Bloodshed will come.*

Dante put up his hands to slow down Vionne's thinking. *Let's not get hasty here. Phoebe is ...let's just say she's different.*

Vionne didn't look nearly as surprised or curious as he should have been. He hadn't been playing all his cards up front. Tutelage by a father who was arguably one of the most wily and shrewd rulers to have ever lived wouldn't have been wasted.

Let's cut the bullshit now, Vionne. I felt movement in the bond with Phoebe yesterday. What is it you know?

I wasn't idle during the mourning period of my father either. I conducted my own study. Murrtaine has the most extensive Atlasian library in the world. I have also seen Phoebe's transformation. Then he lowered his eyes. *I know what she is.*

CHAPTER 54

For a moment Dante didn't say a word. Vionne could of course be bluffing. Both men were strong and wanted to know what the other was thinking. The push of Vionne's mind at the edge of his consciousness meant he was attempting to scan him for anything he could find out. He was soon blocked.

Strong mental barriers were something he'd worked on ever since he'd become king. It was a necessity. His mind had to be like a fortress as he was linked to most of the Sirens. He hoped he wasn't too late. Something had already happened between Phoebe and Vionne. A lone new signature was attached to the bond. Thankfully, Phoebe hadn't done anything stupid – yet.

Dante smiled then. It hadn't been reciprocated. Not in the way Vionne wanted. Everything had been engineered to get Phoebe here. There was no point in saying that she was one of his wives and that Vionne was breaking Atlantean law by holding her. He was going for the trump card of compatible mate. That was the reason Vionne had seized his opportunity and grabbed her in the first place. Pledged she may be, but married to a mate, whom the Murrs held dear, she was not, and that made her the most valuable woman alive.

Vionne understood all this more than anyone. Murrs lived by all the old ways.

To attempt to bluff would only lose his respect and any chance of negotiation. *Are you going to share what you know?*

Vionne tipped his head ignoring Dante's avoidance of the real issue. *She is a Nyx.*

A Nyx, Dante repeated. He racked his brains for all that he'd learned from the history books, but all he could come up with were mere myths or legends. *A Night Goddess, a shifter?* Dante shook his head. It was ridiculous. She was Phoebe Ray – Ray for sun, brightness and light. As he recounted the significance of her surname compared to the other Sirens, he knew it sounded wrong. She did more resemble darkness and night. He finished by grasping at straws. *She only transforms her face. No, you are wrong, Vionne. And, besides, there is no doubt she is a Siren.*

Vionne tipped his head again. *Yes, she is, but in previous generations there were rumors of Sirens having the ability to change. Blood is the catalyst. I believe she has used that ability to change the human into what she wants.*

It was astounding, but it so fit what was going on. Vionne had definitely hit on something.

You see a Nyx not only has the ability to change herself but things in her immediate vicinity. I believe it is governed by extreme emotion.

The Scythians couldn't have known that. We didn't even know it. Dante shook his head, dismissing it. They are a small organization. What could they hope to achieve, honestly?

You're probably right, but they are an age-old enemy sworn to obliterate us. They see us as the demons cast out of heaven. It would be better to concentrate on who they could be in league with to bring about their aims?

Dante thought about what Vionne was saying. It was sound reasoning. To really be in with a shot they would need to be in league with someone else – something big. Their hatred of anything Atlantean ruled out helping another family, as a Siren would only strengthen them. *The Human governments* came to him like a bolt of lightning. It all fit with the secret correspondence he'd been receiving from his father, the Duke Ormond Delissi. It had been the reason he'd moved his court away from Ireland and had been having secret talks with other friendly governments. He didn't mention it yet. He wanted to find out whether Vionne had any new intelligence.

The UK and US, to be exact. My sources tell me there has been a lot of activity in Washington, D.C. and Whitehall.

I have heard they have renewed their search for Murrtaine and are close.

Vionne nodded slowly as if it was what he feared. *There has been increased shipping and air activity in this part of the Atlantic.*

They both sat quietly for a few moments, until Dante had to say the reason for his visit: *It is no longer safe for the girls to be here.*

I am in no doubt Phoebe should be mine, Dante.

Dante frowned. He could very well be right. *If what you say is true, and she is a Nyx, I think she chose her own mate and voided you,* he said, pointing at Vionne's ring.

The question we should be asking ourselves given who owns the boy is, is it legal?

Dante's heart sank. Vionne was right.

The tinny voice saying, *Prince Caan wishes to enter,* at least gave him some breathing space.

Caan entered through the bubbling wall and bowed in front of them.

We're in the middle of important negotiations, Caan, Vionne said.

Forgive me, but in light of recent events, I cannot keep silent any longer. It is something I should have told you long ago.

Dante shifted uneasily in his chair, not knowing if this was a clever ruse to derail discussions. Vionne's face gave nothing away when he said, *Go on, Brother.*

It was reported to me about a year ago that supplies of blood had gone missing from the infirmary stores. I carried out a full investigation and the culprit was found. Not much was taken so I didn't see any point in burdening you or Father with it.

Dante looked at Vionne, enquiringly. *You knew nothing of this?* He could already guess why. Murr blood had always been revered as a wonder medicine by humans and Atlanteans alike for centuries. No one had any proof it was the real thing. Most wasn't. *Who did he sell it to?*

Caan was standing eerily still. *He assured me it was humans and that he would never have tipped the balance for an Atlantean family.*

Dante turned angrily on Vionne. *What stunt are you trying to pull here, Vionne? What if this is what they were giving Drew over the months at the health center? If any part of that supply was your own, then it would have driven them together like a magnet.*

For the first time Vionne looked visibly shaken. *That alone should not have transformed him and doesn't explain Phoebe's physical changes. Could any of the supply have been my own?* he said directly to Caan.

There was a long pause until Caan finally said, *It was the royal supply that was plundered.*

Dante closed his eyes. This was a theft to order for someone on land who knew precisely what they needed. They must have known a lot about their culture, where they were in point of time, about destined mates, everything. The Murr who stole it was probably oblivious of the motive.

He shook his head. Everything started to fall into place. It was genius. They took a human –Drew, with no allegiance to anyone, and made him like a pheromone beacon to attract the only Siren left. He opened his eyes again. *Could they have known she was a Nyx?*

By the look on Caan's face, Vionne hadn't shared knowledge of what she was.

Vionne shook his head. *I believe they had no idea. None of us did until recently.* Then he looked heavenward in misery. He'd just made the same connection as Dante. *Drew's ring thought it was me.*

Dante had to agree, however fantastic it seemed. Whoever had ordered the theft knew the chances of the last Siren's mate being a Borge were high. They could even have tried several donors over time. They'd infused it into Drew until they hit on the right one – effectively making him seem like a destined mate, masking or cloaking his own genetic make-up. It was enough to snare the Siren destined to be with the original blood donor.

The blood could have belonged to any one of the Borge princes if it weren't for Vionne's blood-red ring. It told them who it was as surely as if it had been purple. The infused blood had to affect the detection powers of a divining ring as it embeds itself with its wearer. The Scythians may not have even thought that Drew would wear one. It was probably just some lucky coincidence

His mind raced. Whether they knew or not, these people had hit on a way to tamper with a ring's outcome. The only other time he'd known that to happen had been engineered by Malleven Mancini, but he didn't think he was behind this. *I don't think it was their intention. They hate us and seek to rob us of power.*

If they don't want a Siren for themselves and they could have killed her at any time in Seattle before we knew of her, then why let her and Drew continue on?

The realization hit them both at the same time.

To find Murrtaine!

And he is here, Dante thought and closed his eyes at his stupidity. They now had the final coordinates.

TIA HUGGED the three sisters when they arrived at the apartment. Phoebe hung back. Until she knew which one of them it was, they were all the enemy.

When they were all brought up sharp by her open hostility, they stood in a line opposite her, puzzled. Except one of them, her face showed nothing at all. Tia stood off to the side looking decidedly nervous from one side to the other.

You! Phoebe said simply. Her eyes zeroed in on Isla and her teeth tingled.

Play nice, Tia was saying. Lacy and Lily looked at each other anxiously and Isla was readying her stance.

Phoebe was no longer interested in the other two. Isla was too still, too relaxed, too damn ready for trouble.

Drew would like to enter, the AI voice said.

Saved by the bell-end, Phoebe said, still glaring.

Tia giggled nervously.

Drew would like to enter, it said again.

Go away, Drew, she shouted as hard as she could think. *Just fuck off!*

I do not understand the response, the AI voice said.

You can fuck off an' all, Phoebe shouted back.

Tia was beginning to enjoy herself and pulled up a chair.

The girls all turned to look at the wall where they came in which was making a thudding noise and beginning to bow.

Warning ... Forced entry. Permission has not yet been granted.

The sisters were watching, wide-eyed, and Tia was now laughing hysterically. Even Phoebe's anger was slowly subsiding into shock.

The noise was a boing like a huge ball hitting the ground and a large bulge kept appearing in the opaque wall.

Come on, Phoebes, be nice, the guards will come, Tia pleaded, holding her stomach.

Phoebe rolled her eyes, *Oh for fuck's sake, let him in!*

As soon as she said the words, the waterfall appeared and Drew came tumbling into the room.

He scrambled to his feet and ran a hand through his long hair, putting the long mess back in shape. *Phoebe,* he said. His eyes were shockingly feral, he was heavily striped and his teeth were visible.

Meow! Tia sung, appreciatively from the sidelines.

Phoebe scowled at her and, for a moment, was unsure where to go or what to do.

One of the others said, *Should we go and give them some space?*

Not yet, in case it gets ugly, Tia said, clearly enjoying herself. *Pull up a chair.* The others followed her lead, relieved to be off the hook for the time being.

Phoebe! Drew called loudly. He had no idea what he was doing. She was sure she was just picking up stray thoughts.

He took a step forward, but she held up a hand. For a moment she took him in. He looked wild and desperate to get to her – super hot, in fact. A photographer would have had a field day for an album cover.

Then she remembered he'd locked lips and breathed with one of her own sisters, *Why are you here, Drew?*

He straightened as if he was surprised by the question. His thoughts were a jumble but eventually he managed to put a couple of readable sentences together. *I'm here for you. I've been going out of my mind.*

It was unbelievably cute, but her anger snapped back into place. *No you misunderstand me. You're 10,000 leagues under the sea breathing fucking water!* she ended up shouting.

His whole body sagged and his head fell forward while he gathered together what he needed to say. It must have been incredibly difficult for someone unused to telepathic speech.

Realizing the risk of violence had passed, Tia signaled silently and the others slipped out leaving them alone. However, when Drew looked up, his eyes had gone feral again. *What was I supposed to do, Phoebe? Stay back there at the castle like a dumb fuck, while some fish-guy takes what's mine?*

Phoebe could feel her hackles rising too. How dare he think he owned her? Although it did satisfy something deep inside to think he'd been beside himself with worry. He'd been willing to make the dangerous journey to stop Vionne having his wicked way. She kind of liked the whole damsel in distress image. But that thought soon evaporated into the image of him getting close to one of her sisters. The act was so incredibly intimate that she had to look away.

Drew took a tentative step closer. *You okay? Nobody hurt you, did they?*

She shook her head and turned her back on him, struggling not to cry.

Did he touch you? he said from right behind her.

She swung around and glared up into his eyes. *I haven't been unfaithful to you if that's what you're asking?*

His whole demeanor relaxed. Her eyes narrowed. *I've done nothing worse than you.*

As she watched the confusion cross his face into realization, she wished she could have taken it back.

Breathing? he said simply. Although he looked like she'd kicked him in the stomach.

Yes breathing, nothing much, eh? She could no longer look at him.

Drew grabbed her to him roughly by her shoulder and the back of her hair. They glared at each other, barely noticing the change in their eyes. *He breathed for you?* he said, like he was trying to get his facts straight.

Yes, she thought quietly. She knew exactly how gutted he felt because she felt it too. Except hers had been an impulse and he had risked death to come and get her. Suddenly she was ashamed and she felt tears despite being under water.

He was calm now, searching her face as if he'd find the answers there. *Did you do it for him?*

No.

He took another moment, as if he was gathering his strength. *What stopped you?*

Because even though you hurt me, Drew, I love you.

He closed his eyes momentarily, as if relieved. Then he cupped the side of her face with his hand and ran a thumb through the tears on her cheek. *I love you, Phoebe. From the moment you came to the club. I've never felt like this about anyone.*

Phoebe stared up into his eyes as they returned to normal, wanting to hear him say things like that over and over. He bent his head and put his lips gently over hers. They were warm and gentle, and for a few moments they reveled in the closeness. She was almost lost in a kiss that was gathering momentum when she came to her senses. She pushed him away hard in the chest. *Did you give me up to those people?*

For a split second he looked completely confused.

At the clinic! It was your idea. You took me there. If Vionne hadn't saved us ... She shuddered at the thought of what could have happened.

Yes, but...

The contents of her stomach rose up into her mouth and she covered it with her hand. Then she pushed past him in the direction of the door.

Phoebe! he called. *It wasn't like that. There's so much you don't know ... I didn't even know.*

The waterfall door opened and she jumped through.

CHAPTER 55

*V*ionne had always liked Dante. Despite what people said about him being crazy and impulsive, he was a good king and had defeated the odds to remain on the throne as long as he had. In light of the new information about the immediate threat to Murrtaine, it was no time for petty squabbles between princes. The safety of thousands of Murrs was at stake. The humans knew that if Murrtaine and its power fell into their hands, the Atlantean race would fall into obscurity. They would merely marry and mate into the human population and disappear for ever. Until eventually no one would be any the wiser.

As much as it pained him, he would let Phoebe go – for now.

He regarded Dante shrewdly. He had taken a big risk coming to Murrtaine. A less scrupulous prince could have had him killed and taken the Sirens for himself and Dante was fully aware of that. And yet still he came. It showed he was either a good judge of character or a madman. He chuckled as he suspected the latter, if all accounts were true. *I will make terms with you, cousin. Then you can be on your way.*

Dante waited apprehensively and shifted in his chair.

I will give you safe passage back to the castle with both sisters.

Dante's relief was palpable, but his eyes narrowed, waiting for the catch.

Nor will I lay claim to your crown all the while the fates charm your rule.

And your price? Dante asked.

Vionne looked Dante dead in the eye and smiled humorlessly. *Together we mount the largest evacuation of Murrs ever undertaken. You will help me make the necessary arrangements to move Murrtaine back to its original site.*

IT WOULD BE a mammoth undertaking on an epic scale with very little time. However, Dante could do nothing else. Vionne had negotiated wisely. Not putting his own ambition before the good of his people. He was indeed his father's son.

Yet, as he was about to rise, he sensed that Vionne was not done. He relaxed back into his chair. *There is something else.* Now would come the demand for Phoebe at some future date. He was sure of it.

The human must be left here.

For a moment Dante was speechless. Then he got it. The boy was nothing but a homing beacon that they were zoning in on as they spoke. He had to be here when they found the remains of the old city if they ever had a chance to relocate. It would be impossible for him to go with them.

A chuff of mirthless laughter left him. It was genius really. Vionne had single-handedly taken care of everything in one fell swoop: his people relocated, the trail cold. Drew would undoubtedly be killed, leaving the fates to then work uncorrupted. He had to hand it to him; the plan was faultless.

Except for Phoebe, Dante reminded him. *She will be heart-*

broken. You think she will thank you for having the man she loves killed?

Vionne dipped his head. *You are absolutely correct, but it will not be my idea.*

MESSAGES WERE RELAYED throughout Murrtaine that they were in a state of emergency and must pack everything that they could carry and be ready to leave at a moment's notice.

The castle was forewarned of the impending danger, and that the king would be returning with the Sirens as soon as possible. His men had already been submerged for more than two hours and were showing signs of fatigue.

It was decided that Dante would deliver the blow to Drew with Vionne as a united front. It was something he hated doing. Despite Drew being the biggest pain in the arse for as long as he'd known him, he did actually like the guy and he knew he would do anything for Phoebe. That's what made this all the more harder. His great love would be used to get him to do what needed to be done and there was absolutely no way around it.

PHOEBE AND TIA had been given about five minutes' notice and now waited on the small platform a few feet away from the Marine Bug. Cesaré and a few of the guards were to travel in the one in front of them, followed by the other three sisters and more guards in the next one ready to dock.

Phoebe was still furious with Drew, but it had subsided into anxiousness. She was disappointed that he seemed to have given up trying to say he was sorry so quickly; she was hoping to hold it over him a bit longer yet.

She craned her neck to see if he was in the party with her

other sisters. Her blood boiled at the thought. But a quick scan revealed he wasn't there either.

What's the matter? Tia said.

I can't see Drew, Phoebe said, looking around her. *I don't like it.* Something felt very off. They'd been welcomed by crowds of Murrs when they arrived. It was the height of the day and literally no one was around.

Tia shrugged, seeing it too. *Don't worry, Dante isn't here either. He probably wants him to travel with him.*

Phoebe nodded doubtfully and hoped that was the reason. There was something that didn't feel right about the whole thing.

Vionne's brother, Dax, appeared and her heart lifted a little. *Is everything OK?* she said anxiously.

Dax nodded. *It is time for you to leave. Much is happening here in Murrtaine. It is no longer safe for you here.*

What about Dante and Drew? The lieutenants of the little craft were now urging them to board. *They are just concluding some business with Vionne and will be following shortly. Now you must go.*

Phoebe hugged him and, with a last look at the palace, went up through the hatch into the bug. Tia followed a moment later and they moved off with a soft purr. The second bug followed along behind them with still no sign of Drew or the king.

DREW HAD TRIED to see Phoebe again after their bust-up but she refused to see him. Then he heard the news that they would all be going home and he figured he'd work it out with her later. She just needed time to cool down. It made him feel slightly better when he was summoned back to the council room. The looks he was getting from the locals were making him nervous. He hoped it was the call to congregate to leave.

When he was shown into the room there was just Keenan, three other guards, Dante and the big Murr.

Take a seat, Drew, Dante said, indicating one directly opposite the two of them. It felt like he was being hauled up in court in front of two judges.

He sat uneasily and glanced at the door where Keennan and his men waited. *Aren't we going?* he said.

Another tall, spindly Murr entered dressed completely in white carrying something resembling a hairdryer in his hands. His eyes darted to Dante nervously.

Soon. We just need to check something and have a talk with you before we leave.

Drew moved back into his chair as the Murr approached. The big Murr's face remained unreadable.

The one with the hairdryer held it out ahead of him and, starting with Drew's head, moved it slowly down his body. Straight away a blue, grainy hologram appeared in front of the Murr's face, like a floating screen.

It continued down his body and travelled the length of his leg – his bad leg – until it stopped at the knee.

The Murr looked at Dante and Vionne, who immediately rose from their chairs. They came closer to examine what the Murr was showing them.

What? What is it? Drew said.

Dante's face looked as though he'd received some news he was dreading.

Someone mind telling me what's going on?

Can you play it back so he can see? Dante said to the Murr holding the machine.

In a moment the screen of blue lines appeared in front of Drew's face. *What am I looking at?* he said to Dante, frowning.

Look at the red thing, Dante said.

He could see it there, nestled among the blue lines. It was

the size and shape of a bullet, but it appeared to have moving parts. He looked at Dante again. *Yeah, I see it. What is it?*

Vionne spoke for the first time. *It is a scan of your left knee. It holds a device the size of the end of a pencil.*

Drew looked from him, to the image and back again, not getting it at all.

This is why you were taken to the medical center, Drew, Dante said, sounding gutted. *It's how they probably got you to come in when it hurt; they could monitor you, and...*

Know your whereabouts at all times, Vionne finished for him.

Drew sat looking at the image, speechless for quite a few moments. Until the enormity of what it meant hit him. *A tracking device?* His eyes moved to Dante's in despair. *They've been tracking me the whole time.*

Dante smiled weakly and nodded. *Probably since you left them as a boy.*

Phoebe? he said, suddenly panic stricken.

Dante put his hands up to calm him. *It's okay, she has just left with her sisters. She is safe for the time being.*

Drew put his head in his hands. *I could have led them straight to her.*

You could and you did. You're a time bomb waiting to go off, Vionne said.

Drew looked up at him through his hands. There was no compassion on his face, just hard implacable lines, and efficiency in what he must do. No wonder Phoebe liked him; he was a born leader. It was written all over him; in the way he spoke and carried himself.

Drew nodded in understanding. He'd known for a while he wasn't worthy of her. She was a princess and he was a nobody from questionable beginnings, who didn't really know who he was anymore. *You want me to leave her.*

Yes. Vionne said, flatly, devoid of any emotion or sympathy.

Dante flashed him a look of annoyance.

It's OK, I get it. I'll get away and I won't go near her. He was rambling as his mind raced. He didn't know where the hell he'd go or what he'd do. All he felt was the misery of knowing that he could have got the one thing he loved most in the world killed.

It's not as easy as that, Dante continued cautiously. *It isn't just Phoebe.*

Drew stopped his emotional nosedive and looked up at Dante in surprise. He couldn't understand what else there could possibly be. He just wasn't that important.

Were you given transfusions at the clinic, Drew?

Drew touched his forehead, struggling to think straight. *Probably,* he said looking up hopelessly. *I had a serious illness as a kid. I think I had them regularly.* He frowned. It was all so grainy now. *I think I did. The memories are patchy. But the knee thing ... that was definitely much later. I fell off stage.* Then he shook his head when he remembered the alien thing in his knee. He wasn't sure what was real any more.

Dante turned to Vionne. *The tracking device could have come later.* He shrugged, *or the stage injury could have just been an implanted memory to cover the fact they needed to bring you in a lot more often when you got to the right age. We're pretty confident that you weren't being given human blood, Drew.*

You were given Murr blood to attract a Siren, and, from that Siren, you led them here. Vionne said bluntly, still without a trace of movement in his expression.

Drew just looked between them while he tried to catch up with what they were saying.

For centuries the humans have looked for Murrtaine for the power that lies beneath it. Dante explained.

The Orb. Vionne added. *The source of our power and wealth.*

It's what gives the earth its seasons and affects the weather. It would be catastrophic for it to get into the wrong hands.

We believe the Scythians, who inducted, trained and hid you as a boy, have made a deal with the human governments. Our destruction in return for our hidden power source Dante said.

It was all too much for Drew to take in. He'd barely got past the idea; he could have got Phoebe killed.

The US and UK Navy are almost here, Drew. We are evacuating Murrtaine as we speak.

The realization hit Drew like a lead weight in the stomach. *Go, get out. Don't worry about me.* He would take his own chances. He knew they were telling him the truth. Dreams and nightmares that had plagued his sleep for years were really memories. He swore if he got the chance to kill the bastards who'd brought him up he would.

You can't leave, Vionne said.

Drew frowned.

We need to relocate a whole city, Drew ... They must find this one, Dante said.

What's left ... and you, Vionne added.

There is no time to remove the device and we're not sure if it would disable and kill you anyway.

Drew listened and stared at Vionne for a long time. It wasn't just some characteristic lack of emotion. The guy hated him. For some reason only known to him, he was enjoying this.

The corners of Vionne's mouth curled into a humanlike smile proving he was right. Then it all fell into place. The Murr blood given to him must have been his, meaning the Siren must have been his. He was looking at Phoebe's most compatible mate and he'd stolen her.

At that point he felt drunk on recklessness and grinned

back, knowing he could read his mind. It made him feel strangely powerful that he would get the chance to face his enemies here when everyone had left. And, despite their obvious rivalry, he was able to do this last thing for Phoebe. *Just tell me what you need me to do.*

CHAPTER 56

The castle was already in a state of high alert. The heads of all the families had congregated for fear that Dante would not return and the Murrs seized control. As soon as Dante surfaced from the fountain, he began issuing orders telepathically.

Jay was the first one to help and, for a moment, they locked eyes. In that minute, without any comment, Dante knew he was there for him, and no matter what had passed he could be relied upon. It moved him deeply. *Get my father on the phone, Jay. Tell him to sort this fucking mess out. They are about to find Murrtaine and he needs to delay it. He must set up a meeting, a conference call, anything to stall them.*

"Got it," Jay said.

Alfonzo and Sebastian were next and he quickly brought them up to speed. He explained who Drew was and why they'd left him behind.

"The people are leaving Murrtaine already in a steady stream," Alfonzo said.

Where are they heading?

"They are heading in this direction."

Good. Have the catacombs below made ready. The castle will shelter them until their new home is ready. Call the Maltese prime minister. Tell him to speed up operations.

The two men bowed and left immediately.

Phoebe caught his eye as she came into the hall. She'd been one of the first back and was darting in and out of the pockets of people searching until she stopped, agitated, in front of him. "Where is he?"

Dante scratched his head. He had a life and death situation here growing more serious by the minute, but the girl wasn't going to be brushed off. So instead of flowering it up, he just came out with it. *He volunteered to stay behind.*

He watched her quickly survey the room and knew she could tell everyone else of the party was back. "Why would he do that?"

Because there is nothing else that could be done. He has some sort of tracking device imbedded in him. Phoebe. The humans have found Murrtaine. He has to stay long enough for all Vionne's people to escape.

Phoebe was watching him carefully for any lies, but there was no point in misleading her. "Okay, what then? Is someone going to get him?"

Dante didn't answer straight away. Connor, who'd silently approached at his nod, put a comforting arm around her shoulder to lead her away, but she pulled out of his grip without even noticing who it was. "No! I want to know what's happening."

When the human forces go in, nothing of value must be left. Those in command must think that everyone and everything perished without a trace.

He paused to let his meaning sink in.

Confusion quickly changed to horror, but there was no softening the blow. There could be no false hope. *They will attempt to go in and be destroyed along with Murrtaine. The Orb itself will see to it.* As her face began to crumple, he delivered the killer blow. *Murrtaine and several thousand years' worth of history will be gone.*

"And Drew," she whispered. Then she pulled out of Connor's grip and ran for the fountain.

With a deep sadness, Dante quickly alerted Keenan who looped his arm around her waist as she went to shoot past and caught her. She screamed, scratched, kicked and sunk her teeth into his forearm. He ended up having to pinch the back of her neck and shake her to get her to let go. Then he held her at arm's length like a pup so she couldn't reach him and struggled in midair. It didn't last long as the strength in Keenan's blood began to hit her. She dissolved into spasms then sobs.

Dante felt bad when Keenan held her out to his eye line. *I am really sorry, Phoebe, I genuinely am. There was nothing else that could be done.*

"You killed him," she kept saying over and over again.

In the end, Dante just nodded to Keenan. *Take her to her room. Leave someone to watch her outside and I'll get a nurse along in a minute to give her something.*

"Vionne is on the line," Alfonzo said, dragging him back to the present crisis.

He nodded wearily. *I'll come now.*

IT WAS spooky being the only one left in a city. Especially when it was one you didn't know and looked so strange. Drew was sure he'd seen nothing like it, not even in the movies. After swimming the tiny streets for a while making sure everyone really had gone, he headed back to the palace figuring that would be where any invader would head to first.

He entered the vestibule that hissed behind him creating

the lock that enabled the strange gravity system to work. He guessed all these systems would still work until someone switched them off or the power source ran out.

His feet gently touched the ground and he walked into the corridor that led to the grand glass hallway. It really was magnificent. A huge aquamarine vaulted atrium as far up as the eye could see. If ever there was proof of aliens then this was it. No human could possibly be its architect.

Drew turned a slow circle. *Where to now?* He couldn't simply sit; the silence would drive him mad. Maybe they had some sort of TV or alien type entertainment somewhere. Four oval corridors went off in different directions. He closed his eyes and spun and pointed, then opened his eyes. *There!* That would be the direction he would take.

The palace was huge, like White House size big, except inside it felt more like a rabbit warren of tunnels. He let his hand drag along the wall as he walked and was surprised at its texture. It felt soft and spongy, almost alive.

Every now and then little colored lights would light up beneath the surface, and after a little play, he discovered they all did something, like make the lights brighter, the temperature cooler or open one of the weird waterfall doors.

Most of the rooms looked like strange reception rooms, but one he came upon was completely circular with a spiral shelf like a shell going around its walls and a single cylinder island in its middle. Drew stood in the middle and spun around. What possible use could a space like this be for? It did occur to him that maybe it was a kid's playroom but dismissed it as he hadn't seen any evidence of kids in the palace at all.

He turned to face the pedestal in the middle. It turned white under his gaze and raised a few inches higher, making him jump back in shock. When it returned to the previous height and blue-green color, he took a step towards it again, and it changed as it had done before. He relaxed a little, amazed that it appeared to be eye-activated.

After a long moment he ventured a hand out to gently touch its surface and was made to jump again as a hologram of a woman appeared about a foot tall.

Immediately, Drew grabbed his head as a white-hot pain started at the top and moved down and felt like it sliced through to the base of his neck. Then it stopped abruptly.

Drew stood up straight again, swallowing hard as the pain subsided. His eyes fixed on the hologram, except now it was changing and images were flashing lightning fast like a fast-forwarding film. It took a full minute for Drew to realize they were his own memories. The thing, whatever it was, had taken them from his head and was logging them away in front of his eyes. For a moment it filled him with horror until he thought, *Stop!*

The pictures froze in front of him at a particular point in time. It was his old bleak school. The bare wooden rooms with bunks, a thin mattress, a single blanket that brought back a familiar sinking feeling. It was how he felt all the time back then. He'd just forgotten; hollow and empty.

Forward...stop! he commanded again. There, the endless drills, the hardened monks in the robes that hid their endless tattoos. He remembered that. He'd seen them when they'd been forced to fight to toughen or speed them up or else be severely punished. The place was no more than a death camp for children – hopeless, homeless, aimless children. Trained and driven to be mindless vessels controlled by these hate-filled men. *Who am I?* he whispered.

The hologram came back, *Drew Stone. Male, Bonaci. Mate to Parthenope Riadne Teles Bonaci. Known as Phoebe Ray. Bonded to Airla Leukosia Artemisia Bonaci.*

Stop! It was going too fast for him to process. It had classed him as Bonaci, but it also thought he was bonded to

Isla. He closed his eyes. No wonder Phoebe had been so pissed at him. It was devastating to think he wouldn't get the chance to explain.

Maybe it was for the best in the end. He'd heard somewhere bonds were severed by death, and yet there was also talk of partners going into the Ether together. He liked the idea of that. If it were true, he'd wait for Phoebe and hope she didn't think too harshly of him. His blood boiled at the big Murr waiting in the wings. However, he was a strong prince completely secure in who he was, which was more than he could say for himself.

Drew sighed inwardly. Well, if this thing was truly some kind of oracle, then it should be able to answer anything it was asked. It still hadn't really answered his question. It was the fundamental thing all orphans wanted to know. *Who am I,* he repeated. *From my blood – my heritage,* he added.

The thing was silent for a long moment. It appeared to be thinking or drawing information from its memory banks. It was then he noticed the pastel-colored lights flickering all around the spiral going up and around the strange conical room. He looked in wonder at what appeared to be some kind of super computer. Then he faced it, resigned that it was probably a question that couldn't be answered.

The image changed to what looked like red blood cells. He hadn't been that great at science but even he could see there were weird purple-thistle-looking things attached to each one.

The hologram came back. *Results inconclusive.* Then silence, as it appeared to be thinking again and the blood cells reappeared, rotating so they could be viewed from all angles.

DNA ... Human ... Northern European origin. Then it went on to say something about mitochondrial genomes and a load of shit he didn't understand, but he did get the bit that said, *Bonaci blood markers,* It was what he knew already. However, the last bit made his heart sink. A *small percentage of Borge.*

Explain Borge? He shot back, already feeling the fear of an answer he wouldn't like.

Family line of Murrtaine. Pure blood of Atlas decent.

It continued in the background while his brain whirred. The big Murr had been right. Up to then he'd always believed it was to do with Phoebe that his body was changing. That it was somehow due to what they did together that made him less than human; now he knew that the catalyst was very probably the blood of the guy that hated him. Or maybe it was the mixture of the two.

At least he had his answer now. He'd been born human, recruited into the weirdo Scythian cult and had his blood fucked with. No wonder by the time he met Phoebe he welcomed her alienisms with open arms. It made him feel sick that the Murrs' blood was in him in the mix though.

No point wasting energy on anger now.

His memories came up again, grainy like an old black and white film. They were fairly recent, the last four or five years. Seattle. The medical center.

The image slowed and his heart thumped. He remembered the procedure and had taken little notice of the drip stand with blood at the time. The hologram answered. *Indeterminate.*

The oracle here might not know for sure how his metamorphosis happened, but he sure did. Those bastards had injected him with something that had started all this off. And Phoebe? Well, she had changed everything, and for that he was grateful.

There was a deep clang above him and the lights flickered. His heart banged in his chest. *Guess it's show time,* he said, looking at the pointy ceiling above him.

The hologram flickered in front of him. *Prepare, earth son of Borge. The end has come and the sky chariot is almost here.*

She wasn't making much sense, but she sounded so human – almost caring. There was no point in running or taking cover. This was as good a place as any to die. The invaders were already there. *I'm ready, lady. Do you have a name?*

The face looked beautiful in the hologram right then – almost angelic. She smiled. The ground started to shake beneath their feet and cracks began to appear in the ceiling above their heads. Debris and large chunks of the walls began to fall. Drew's eyes darted around him. *Good bye angel,* he said. He liked the idea of his last conversation being with an angel.

The hologram grew. She went higher and wider until she was life size and looked down on him like a Madonna. *My name is, Orb.* Then she disappeared leaving Drew in the silence that followed.

Then nothing happened. There was total silence for what appeared to go on for minutes.

A white light blinded him. The flash was so hot and flashed out sideways, flattening everything as far as the eye could see. The last thing he was aware of was a feeling of security. It was as if he was encased in a bubble – a soft cocoon that rose up slowly. Until a shaft of light shot out from deep within the earth like a meteor and launched up past him in an arc towards the sky.

The light gradually dimmed, and he was aware of nothing else.

CHAPTER 57

*E*veryone had seen the light at the castle. It shook the great window so badly people cowered and actually thought the two-feet-thick glass would crack.

Dante sat with Vionne in front of a bank of monitors. Many had TV news channels on from around the world reporting on the deep-sea explosion and strange comet that appeared to come from the midst of it and go down somewhere in the middle of the Mediterranean. However, some were CCTV of the catacombs filling up with Murr refugees and others the eyes of the tiny drone subs that scoured the waters between the castle and Murrtaine checking for stragglers or, by some miracle, Drew.

It is done, Vionne said, simply.

Dante nodded, still looking at the screen showing nothing but the seabed covered in a crystalline white dust. It was all that was left of the great city that had stood for several thousand years. "Everyone is safely in the catacombs," he said. It was small consolation but to their knowledge there had been no casualties – well except one. "Brave guy," he whispered to himself.

Vionne heard and nodded sagely. *Indeed.* Then, after a respectful moment, he said, *What now?*

"Now we build. The Maltese prime minister is a cousin – Dubonnetti bloodline. The Island of Filfla has long been used as a secret bunker and he has gifted it to the royal family in the hope of a strong relationship between us."

Vionne's eyes went wide with surprise. It was surprising how human-like his expressions were getting. *What is this place?*

"It's a small, mostly barren, uninhabited islet five kilometers south of Malta… Close to the site the comet went into the sea," he said, allowing him to join the dots.

Vionne nodded and slowly smiled, understanding perfectly.

"We will wait, of course, until the seabed is scoured by the world's operatives for any remains, and when they find nothing, we will start the building of New Murrtaine. I will move my court to Filfla, with Murrtaine for ever nearby. What say you, Cousin?"

VIONNE LOOKED at the world's cameras on the tiny island surrounded by crystal waters and was very pleased. He was sure his father would be proud of the outcome under the circumstances. Miraculously, the Orb had chosen the site close to Dante's, the weather was calm and the sea a millpond, indicating all was well and as it should be. The human had given him much.

And now for Phoebe, arguably his most difficult task of all.

He sensed her the moment she came into the great hall, now his breath was inside her. All that was needed was for her to complete the bond and he had his Siren wife as he'd promised his father.

As he turned to face the gaunt, pale, bedraggled girl, he realized it wasn't just any Siren he needed, but this one. The girl he was already falling deeply in love with.

His ring thrummed on his finger and his eyes strayed down to his hand.

After saying hello to the girl, Dante saw the same thing. "You have your wish," he said, with a small rueful smile.

He was right, of course. It was a hollow victory to win by default, and to see the girl standing with tears streaming down her cheeks in front of him.

Phoebe had seen the purple ring too and the implications of what it meant made her collapse like a deck of cards. Dante jumped to his feet to catch her and she sobbed into his chest moaning, "Drew … Drew," over and over again.

All Vionne could do was look on and wonder how on earth he could ever fix this.

"You! … You did this!" she screamed, pointing her finger at Vionne from Dante's encasing arms. He shushed her gently and tried to lead her away but she struggled. Refusing to let him off, she pulled out of Dante's grip. "And you, you're no better." Then she turned back to Vionne, channeling all the venom she could muster. "I will never, ever, ever, speak to you again. Do you hear me? You killed him. You did it!"

"Listen, Phoebe," Dante tried to reason.

She snapped her head around to Dante. He'd helped him in all this and was almost as much to blame.

"There's more than you know. Vionne was always your true mate. Let us explain to you," Dante said.

But she put up a hand and turned with a "Don't waste your breath." Her heart shifted and almost stopped when she saw the group of strangely familiar men descend the marble staircase with an older man following Alfonzo and Sebastian.

She looked back at Dante and saw him and Vionne slowly stand. He signaled to several of the guards who rushed forward between them. "Delissi?" Dante said, eyes fixed on the older gentleman.

Phoebe remained glued to one man amongst all the others dressed completely in black. His gaze was confidently on her until he neared and smiled.

"Malleven," escaped her on a whisper. Then everything swamped her like a tsunami. Every memory, every breathless feeling washed over her. She knew this man and she knew him well.

"What is this?" Dante demanded.

Malleven came forward to stand next to Delissi. "Malleven has to come to claim his mate and council seat."

Others were rushing to Dante's side. Minor scuffles were breaking out between them and Malleven's men, until Delissi raised his arms and shouted, "Silence!"

When everyone eventually stood still and became quiet, Delissi spoke to the whole assembly. "A prior claim has been made between the prince Malleven Mancini and the Siren, Parthenope Riadne Teles Bonaci, also known as Phoebe Ray. I repeat, mate by full bond. As he is also married to Lilian Gale he therefore demands to be heard by ancient right of challenge to the crown."

"You yourself know I am married and bonded to this Siren," Dante said, nonplussed.

"We all witnessed it," someone else shouted.

"I claim my right by First Breath," Malleven said, emphasizing his words slowly in his strong Italian accent.

The room erupted into shouts and arguments. In all the pandemonium Dante looked at her, horrorstruck. "You know this man?"

Phoebe, whose crying had stopped abruptly, looked aghast at Malleven and then back to Dante, unable to speak.

She did know him. She knew every inch of the strong, dark body. The moment her eyes had locked with his when he'd entered the room a shroud had fallen away from her mind, and she knew. Every day from the moment she'd bumped into the brown man as a little girl. Then again when she'd stumbled upon him in the warehouse. How he'd taken her and introduced her to Malleven and how he made her never want to leave.

Even now, everything about him beckoned her to him. She took a small step forward and a guard appeared next to her. She turned and hissed at him, eyes zeroing to orange and canines punching into her mouth. She snarled at everyone around her to leave her alone and especially to Dante and Vionne, whose faces betrayed how deeply shocked and broadsided they were. "Yes ... I know him. Drew's gone, I choose him. Do you hear me?" she screamed. Her voice was hoarse, but everyone heard her. "I choose him!"

Despite feeling like her insides had been carved out with a serrated edge, she went and stood next to Malleven in defiance and no one made any attempt to stop her.

"Call the other sisters," Delissi shouted. "We will conclude this now."

DANTE LOOKED on in a state of utter bewilderment. He had ignored his intuition that no power had passed to him from Phoebe in his haste to proclaim to the world that he had all five Sirens. He'd been rash and felt secure. Now he lived to regret it. The mystery of her lost month was solved; Malleven had outplayed him and covered his tracks well.

All the sisters except Phoebe assembled in a row in front of everyone. It looked as though they were being sold at market. He hadn't seen anything as abhorrent since he'd first seen Tia tested in the tank all that time ago.

His heart stalled as Tia was the last to join them and their eyes met. He hadn't managed to mend their rift since the day he'd spent with Ruby. *I love you,* he projected while he still had the chance.

He allowed his mind to quickly scan the room and knew that Jay wasn't there. It seemed even his oldest friend had abandoned him now he needed him the most. The extent of his predicament was slowly sinking in. The Santalinis stood guard between them, but allegiances could change in a moment.

Then his eyes rested on his so-called biological father. Guess he finally knew if he was with him or not, despite the kindly gaze resting on him now.

"What of the charter? Each family signed in this very place recognizing Dante as king," Cesaré shouted angrily.

Dante touched him on the arm. He already knew the answer to that. With Malleven legally married to a Siren, Lily and Phoebe apparently bonded to him, the charter could be broken if they all no longer backed him. Phoebe had just made her allegiance clear.

Delissi didn't dignify the outburst with an answer. He merely resumed his quiet, authoritative tone, "You may now take a moment to speak to your wives each in turn. The king by right of station will go first."

After a moment of gathering his thoughts, he projected to all the sisters together. *Listen to me, everyone. I know you can hear me – even you, Lily. I am strong enough to reach you all because I am king. I am rightful king, first pledged to a Siren before most of you were found.*

"Let him speak aloud before the whole assembly," Malleven was saying, "So all may judge the truth of it."

Delissi turned on Malleven. "It is not words that are judged, but who can be heard and who would listen. It is the five Sirens that stand judge and jury today. Bonds are made, but wisdom, love and respect maketh a true king."

Malleven's eyelids lowered and he remained silent, but a muscle ticked in his jaw.

The room hushed.

I've followed the ancient laws, but wherever I could I bent them to accommodate you, knowing how restrictive they were. He paused, knowing his time would be up shortly. Whatever he said had to be short and sweet and very definitely hit home. *Know this, I love and respect you for the individuals you are and, if you choose me, I promise to do all in my power to accommodate your wishes so that you can all be happy.*

Dante noticed the big Murr, Darres, had returned from checking his people in the catacombs. In fact, all of the mates were there. He decided to make sure they could hear his address too. *I appeal to all those bonded males to communicate with your wives and argue my case, because you will have no such luxury under him. I doubt he will even let you live. You all remain married and in government because of me and my reign. I impose nothing except allegiance. The Orb has already blessed us with children. If you think he will allow that then you're sorely mistaken.*

His eyes went from Darres, to Keenan, Cesaré, Lance and finally Vionne. Each of them moved closer and stood with Dante. It was the proudest he'd ever felt and he confidently returned his gaze to the girls. *If you want to continue with your current freedoms, then I beseech you to stand with me.*

"Time is up," Delissi said, quietly.

Then he slowly turned to Malleven, whose men were still alert and ready for any threats to the safety of their fellow Magi brother.

"I have nothing to hide here. I will speak aloud so all may hear there are no spells, bribery, collusion or trickery."

The crowd muttered and the Magi brothers held their fists up and readied themselves for attack.

"Tia Storm, we have barely met, but it is no secret the trials you have endured in your intolerable situation. And yet you are meant to be the wife of his heart."

Dante felt his blood begin to boil but Cesaré rested a hand on his arm. *Stay calm. He goads you.* He nodded slightly with clenched teeth.

Then what happened next left them speechless. Without a word, Lacy broke ranks and walked towards Malleven. Keenan leapt forward so his guard mates and brothers had to jump on him and literally haul him back. "He's using magic. He's doing what he did before!" He was shouting and struggling but nothing could be allowed to interfere. It took at least six big men to hold him down.

Malleven smiled benignly as Lacy came and stood next to him with her eyes fixed ahead of her. Keenan was right, he was definitely using some kind of weird hypnotism.

"This is unfair!" Cesaré shouted to Delissi. "Stop this farce, immediately."

Delissi held open his arms. "Malleven has spent no time with the girls to prep them. The test stands."

Cesaré threw up his arms in frustration. It was Dante's turn to calm him down. *We can do nothing, Ches.* The two of them continued to watch the scene unfold like some horrific car crash.

Malleven grinned wickedly at Isla. She was his true mate who'd left him to die in the water and chosen Darres. She closed the gap and moved closer to Tia and held her hand. Malleven's grin widened and he moved on to Lily.

"My flower. How honest and true you are." The comment was clearly sent as a dig to Isla, who looked visibly shaken. No one had ever seen her so rattled. "Your time here is over, come back to me." He held his arms wide for her to go to him.

Dante watched as she frantically looked for Lance. Then some kind of exchange happened between them as the guy went to move towards her. Malleven saw it too. "Of course, all allowances will be made for your happiness. That goes for you all."

Don't believe him, Lance. You're as good as dead if you go with him, Dante projected.

The guy turned his head toward him and, in that moment, his eyes shimmered over gold and he understood. Malleven had already got to him. He didn't stand a chance.

"I can't let her go alone." It made Dante a little relieved that he appeared still to have his own mind. Then he was gone, taking Lily's hand and moving to the growing group on Malleven's side of the room.

He now had Phoebe, Lacy and Lily. Three out of the five and you could say the controlling share, but everyone in the room knew, without the five, any king would be ineffectual.

Delissi stepped forward and put what they were all thinking into words. "Search your hearts and put petty squabbling aside. We are deeply into the final days. If Atlas were to return today what would they find? I will tell you; nothing but a pitiful excuse for a nation. Now I ask you one last time, search your hearts and do what is best for the nation."

Dante's heart thumped. Everything was on Tia and Isla. Tia was his. Despite all their recent differences, he knew she loved him. Isla, on the other hand, hated Malleven, but he was her true mate. He clung on to the fact that out of all the Sirens she had been the only one to reject her most compatible. That, he believed, was a true testament to the nature of the man and the strength of the woman.

"It is time to choose," Delissi said.

· · ·

TIA HELD both of Isla's hands and looked deeply into her frightened eyes. It felt like the whole world was watching them. The pressure was immense. If it were just for herself it would have been a no-brainer. She would always be Dante's. But when she looked at her three sisters, already standing with Malleven, it wasn't so easy. *Isla, I know you hate him, but look at them.*

They both turned their heads and saw Phoebe, an empty shell, no longer crying. An unscrupulous prince could do anything with her now. She had lost her great love and didn't care what happened to her.

Then there was Lily, standing with Malleven to her left, seemingly oblivious as to what he was truly capable of. She was holding onto Lance's hand tightly on her right as if holding onto him meant she would never have to let him go. Except a man like Malleven would never share. Tia didn't know what he'd done to make her trust him so much, but she knew they were three lambs to the slaughter.

Lastly, her eyes rested on Lacy, the most beloved of all her sisters, probably because they'd known each other for the longest. There was no way that girl would have left Keenan of her own free will. It must be the same hold he'd had over her when he'd abducted her before.

"I must hurry you," Delissi said.

Listen, Isla, we can't just leave them to him.

Isla's hands were shaking in hers. *But you don't understand what he is like. He's the Devil and I ...*

Tia looked deeply into her eyes. The girl was terrified.

... I'll be useless. I can't resist him. My life will be torture and he will kill Darres for sure.

Tia couldn't begin to imagine what it must be like to have a mate's pull with someone you hated with every fiber of your being. And she was right about Darres. Her mate would undoubtedly follow her to certain death.

She shook her head in frustration as nothing else could be done. She turned to find Dante's eyes and said, *Forgive me*, pushed away from Isla's hands and walked towards Malleven.

There was a collective intake of breath. No one could believe what they'd just witnessed.

Malleven visibly swelled with pride and he looked at the last of the sisters.

Come, Isla, Tia projected urgently. *We need your strength and knowledge of him.*

Isla frantically called to Darres, who moved from Dante to her side. Then, after closing her eyes for a long moment, the pair of them walked towards Malleven.

Tia's heart broke.

The guards surrounding Dante all began to look at each other, not knowing what to do. Keenan was still struggling and had to be led from the room. Dante looked so alone.

Delissi moved to the center of the room and shouted, "I proclaim a new era with a king who has all Sirens." Then he turned to Dante, his son, who hadn't yet moved a muscle in obvious shock. "All royal children must remain with their mothers."

Dante's eyes shot to hers. *Protect them."*

She nodded as her eyes misted over with tears.

"You may keep the fortune you came with and take with you anyone who would stand with you and leave this place."

Tia had never felt so helpless and wretched in her whole life. Jay was nowhere to be seen and Dante was so alone.

THE ONLY PEOPLE surrounding him in his last moments at Ballgowan castle were Alfonzo, Sebastian, the Sirens' brothers, Dino and Luca, Cesaré and Vionne. They spoke in urgent whispers.

"We stand with you."

"He will destroy the nation."

Dante came to a decision quickly. "Cesaré, you come with me, as to stay would be certain death for you. The rest of you must go with him."

They all protested angrily, but Dante held up his hand and spoke telepathically to Vionne. *I will go to the place we spoke of prepared by our cousin. You stay and see to it that the inhabitants of Murrtaine are taken care of. That is imperative.*

Vionne bowed his head. *I will.*

The rest of you, please stay and protect the sisters and the children. You will work for me in secret. The Sirens' Protectors will try to go with them but I doubt he will keep them.

After looking at each other, they reluctantly nodded.

"What will you do?" Alfonzo said, grabbing his arm as he went to walk away.

"I will be okay. Don't worry." He felt remarkably calm despite his state of shock. He was grateful for his newfound faith in the Five Moons. "The Orb is with me, I know it. I will return."

After a long moment of searching his eyes, Alfonzo said, "Come," and the group of men left him to walk towards the Malleven camp.

"You must leave now," Delissi said.

Dante sought Tia's eyes one last time and with a parting *Stay safe,* he left with Cesaré.

The room remained quiet, in complete shock.

CHAPTER 58

*J*ay followed Ruby into the large sitting room at the Dubonnetti estate, west coast of Ireland. It felt like a very long time ago since he was last there. It held so many memories, some bad but an awful lot that were good. It had been where he'd spent most of his childhood as a friend of the family and where he'd formed the strongest relationship of his life with Dante.

It was with a deep sadness that he entered the room that didn't look like it had changed at all in all that time.

"Ah, my boy. Drink?" Christian said, decanter in hand at the large sideboard.

While he poured, Jay looked around, acknowledging each of the brothers in turn. It was hard to imagine being brought up with these men now. "Paulo." He nodded back. He was basically a nice guy underneath, just easily mislead. "Stephan." He hated Dante with a vengeance for sending the great love of his life blind and had attempted to kill him at least once. Antonio was missing. No great surprise there. He was now openly in a relationship with Malleven. Then, lastly, there was Marco. He sat moodily apart. Jay just cast him a look with no greeting. There was too much bad blood between them to ever get over. Amongst a list of things, he was solely responsible for condemning him, Tia and Dante to a life of misery these last few years; all being bound together.

Christian handed him a drink. Ruby sat down, making herself at home far too easily. It made him pause. "Why am I here?" he said, turning back to Christian.

Christian's expression became serious. "I wanted you out of harm's way today. I won't beat around the bush, Jay. I have some sad news to impart."

Jay took a sip of his drink and looked around at the brothers, none of which were meeting his gaze. "What's going on?"

"Take a seat, Jay."

"Just get on with it," he said, losing patience with the theatrics.

Christian nodded as if he expected nothing less. "Today, Malleven Mancini will be turning up. And he looked at his watch. "Around about now to challenge Dante for the crown."

Jay was so taken aback he almost laughed. "You're serious? He could never win. The sisters have to choose him, don't they?" He shook his head, dismissing it as ridiculous.

Christian looked as if the whole thing was very regretful. "It would seem that way, but we have learned through a reliable source," and his eyes flashed to Paulo, "that he expects to tempt them all onto his side by any means possible."

Jay understood then that Paulo must still be in contact with his estranged brother, Antonio.

His immediate thought was for Tia and the children. He turned to walk out of the room but Ruby jumped up and caught him by the arm. "Don't, it's no good, Jay. He'll kill you." For a moment he hated her: the black hair, the ebony eyes, the soft, luscious curves of her body that just trapped him and were everything opposite to Tia, the love of his life.

"She is right," Christian said, coming closer. "I have a plan, that if it works, can maybe keep Dante alive." It was enough to stop him in his tracks. However, Marco was watching him closely and he'd never forgotten how he had betrayed them all – not forgetting selling Tia to the humans. "Do you hate your brother that much?" he said, not helping himself.

Marco shrugged. "Whatever. Looks like I just swapped one druggy waste of space brother for another."

If they'd been anywhere else he would have cuffed him across the face. He was, of course, referring to his blood addiction. "I'm no brother of yours." And he went to continue out of the room, except for Christian's parting comment of, "Actually, you are," bringing him up short.

He turned on his heel to face Christian, his patience now gone. "We've been through all this," he said, wearily.

"We have, but I haven't told you everything."

Jay remembered the conversation they'd had all that time ago in his office where Christian had first told him about the Darkly Begotten prophecy. He held his arms out at a loss. "What's happening now is none of my doing."

Christian tipped his head in agreement. "Not directly, no. It's time to fulfill your own destiny, Jay. When the dust settles, you will make your own claim."

Ruby shook him gently to look at her. "You can be king, Jay."

Jay looked down at her but he wasn't seeing. He still couldn't believe what they were saying.

"I'm not even really Atlantean. Don't be ridiculous."

"Am I Jay?" Christian said, tilting his head to the side at his question. "You are the dark progeny foretold many years ago. You are bonded to a Siren. The others will follow, given the chance to leave Malleven once he has shown his true colors. He won't see you coming. It is so simple, it's brilliant," Christian said, not holding in his delighted laughter.

Jay scratched his head, shook it and put his hands on his hips. "I am not a true brother though. The claim would be instantly rejected."

Christian was already shaking his head. "It won't though, you are indeed my son."

Jay couldn't keep the horror from his face as he searched Christian's for any kind of joke or lie. "Dante and I had our DNA tested years ago. You saw the results."

Christian conceded with a nod. "Indeed I did."

Then Jay started to see where he was going with it and realization crept over him. The results *would* come back negative. Dante's mother was already pregnant with him by Delissi when she married Christian. Christian had had an affair with Jay's mother who'd acted as his oracle. So he and Dante shared different mothers and different fathers, but that didn't have to be the case of the other Dubonnetti brothers that they never thought to test. Christian could very easily be his biological father. "Except, no stripes," he said, holding out his arms wide. Even the weakest bloodlines often had them.

"Recessive genes," Christian said, with a nonchalant shrug.

Just as the thought occurred to retest, Christian preempted him and produced a paper from his pocket. "Done, several years ago."

Jay took the piece of paper from his hands that explained everything. He and Dante had always thought there was a reason for his father taking him in the way he did. He just wasn't that charitable.

His mind raced. He needed to process what he'd learned. If Dante had been deposed then. whether he believed this or not, maybe he could be in a position to help him.

"Malleven will soon become a despot that no one can deal with, and when he does, we will swoop in and take everything from him. The crown will then sit on the rightful Dubonnetti head.

Jay looked down into Ruby's moist eyes glittering with excitement and was left with no other choice. "Okay."

EPILOGUE

$\mathcal{D}$rew opened his eyes and the light and the sting of salt blinded him. A wave washed over him and moved him over what felt like gravel. He scrambled onto his knees, coughed up his lungs and was cold right through to the bone. For a moment his eyes streamed with pain of razor blades hacking down the back of his throat. He sat back on his lower legs, held his neck in his hands and looked around him.

His vision slowly cleared. He was on a rugged beach.

There was literally no one around and he needed a drink urgently. As he scrambled to his feet he noticed what he was wearing. The shimmering material of the Murrs barely covered his lower half to his knees. He needed a change of clothes badly.

Hungry, thirsty and with a banging dehydration headache, he scrambled over the craggy rocks of the shoreline until it gave way to a crescent of sand. Wooden bungalows followed it a little way back.

Drew had absolutely no idea of the time, just that it was probably early as there didn't seem to be that many people around. Just a couple of dog walkers and a man with a fishing line on a stone wall jutting out into the sea.

He jogged past the first building. Washing was pegged out on a line behind it. With a quick look around him, he jogged through, pulling a pair of black track pants and a navy blue t-shirt with him. At the next group of shrubs, he slowed to a stop and pulled the t-shirt over his head and stepped into the pants.

He was now behind a row of small wooden buildings. Keeping in the shadows he jogged silently looking for an outside tap – anywhere where he could take a quick drink and not disturb anyone.

There. It was next to a coiled hosepipe. Drew turned on the tap and put his mouth straight under the stream. It was instant balm to his raw sore throat. When he straightened up and looked at the building, he noticed that it wasn't as cared for as the others. He peered in through the window. It was furnished but didn't appear to be lived in. He circled the house, keeping an eye out for any signs of life until he found a small window at the side to what must be a pantry. He scanned around and saw a wooden box. Grabbing it and checking around again for onlookers, he put it next to the wall. Then he stepped up and went in head first through the window. His landing wasn't pretty. A broom fell and crashed into a metal mop bucket. With a lot of cursing, he scrambled up from his crash landing, froze and listened in case anyone was in the house.

There was no sound. He clicked open the pantry door and opened it slowly and silently. When he thought the coast was clear he padded out in his bare feet and checked out all the rooms. There were two sparsely furnished bedrooms, a small lounge and a kitchen. He'd guessed right. It must be someone's vacation home or something.

In no time at all, he found a can of beans and had a coffee

pot on. There was a small radio on the windowsill, so he switched it on. A jingle played, then a US male with an exaggerated happy voice announced, "it's going to be a great day in Kennebunkport with wall to wall sunshine."

He stopped pouring the beans into a saucepan to think. *Where the fuck was he?* It didn't sound like Ireland.

He began rummaging through the kitchen drawers looking for anything that might give him a clue where he was. Halfway down, he found a bunch of opened letters stuffed back in their envelopes. He went straight to the last couple of lines of the address: Kennebunkport, Maine. *Fuck! He was in the United States.*

Somehow, in the explosion, or whatever it was, he must have been thrown clear, or drifted and ended up on the east coast of the US. The distance he'd covered was astounding.

Then everything became startlingly clear. The woman in the hologram was no super computer. She'd revealed his life to him. The former brainwashing had disappeared and he remembered everything – the constant training, drills and, above all, the channeling of brutality into cold, hard determination by the bastard who'd tutored him.

She'd said her name was Orb. Everyone he'd ever met in the Atlantean world had spoken of the Orb in hushed, revered terms, like it was a mystical power source or something. For some reason she'd valued him enough to protect him from the blast that had destroyed Murrtaine and spat him out here.

His eyes narrowed. This was no accident, he was sure. She was helping him find his destiny. Phoebe was safely at Dante's castle. He was no longer human – the Orb herself had confirmed it. By now his blood would be pure Bonaci. No other Atlantean had that. Only the Murrs had untainted blood. He'd been trained in a war camp and he remembered all they'd taught him.

He was a survivor. He'd always been that, but for the first time in his life he knew who he truly was and what he was meant to do. He would find and destroy the Scythians so they could never inflict their beliefs on any other young boys. Or hurt his new race that he undoubtedly now belonged.

Then he would come at the big Murr. He stabbed his kitchen knife into the wood of the counter. *As an equal!*

* * *

Can't wait to find out what happened in Phoebe's lost month? Then read **Lost Moon** straight away. Available absolutely free only from T's website: https://mailchi.mp/d18c89c14f50/tstedmannovellas

CONTACT T

To receive your two, 21st Century Sirens Novellas, and be the
first to know anything relating to T's books, leave your
details here: https://mailchi.mp/d18c89c14f50/
tstedmannovellas
And please don't forget to leave a review wherever you
bought your book, I really appreciate the feedback.
Much love
T
www.tstedman.com
Facebook
Twitter

GLOSSARY

Characters in family groups

Bonaci

Alfonzo Bonaci – Head of the Bonaci royal family and uncle to the Sirens

Sebastian Bonaci – Brother to Alfonzo and father to the Sirens

Luca Bonaci – half brother to the Sirens

Dino Bonaci – Full brother to Luca and half brother to the Sirens

Tia Storm – Siren – First wife and most compatible to Dante – queen – bonded to Jay

Lacy Rain – Siren –Mated and most compatible with Keenan Santalini and second wife to Dante

Isla Snow – Siren – Mated to Darres Borge, third wife to Dante (Most compatible to Malleven)

Lilian Gale – Siren – Mated and most compatible to Lance McCabe – bonded to Cesaré Florianna by First Breath and therefore the only Siren not married to Dante

Phoebe Ray – Siren – Mated to Drew Stone, fourth wife to Dante – bonded to Malleven by First Breath – Most compatible eventually to Vionne Borge

Royal Children

Xavier – Son of Dante and Tia
Alexia – Daughter of Dante and Tia
Roman – Son of Dante and Tia
Zander – Son of Dante and Tia
JJ – Son of Jay and Tia

Borge

Darl – Lord Advocate of Murrtaine and father to Vionne, Dax, Caan, Axyl and Darres
Vionne Borge – Murr and eldest son and successor to Darl
Dax Borge – Son of Darl, brother to Vionne
Caan Borge – Son of Darl, brother to Vionne
Axyl Borge – Son of Darl, brother to Vionne, Dax, Caan, twin of Darres and ruler of Murrla
Darres Borge – Son of Darl, twin of Axyl, brother to Vionne, Dax and Caan – Mate to Isla Snow
Naomi – Wife to Sabastian Bonaci – Mother to Sirens

Royal children

Keefa – Son of Darres and Isla Snow
Dannon – Son of Darres and Isla Snow

Dubonnetti

Dante Dubonnetti – King and most compatible mate and married to Tia Storm (and all other Sirens except Lily)

Duke Ormond Deliss – Biological father to Dante and Ambassador for the Atlanteans in Washington DC
Christian Dubonnetti – Stepfather to Dante and head of the Dubonnetti royal family
Marco Dubonnetti – Half Brother to Dante and Jay Gardiner
Paulo Dubonnetti – Half Brother to Dante and Jay Gardiner
Antonio Dubonnetti – Half Brother to Dante and Jay Gardiner – Lover to Malleven Mancini
Stephan Dubonnetti – Youngest – Half Brother to Dante and Jay Gardiner

Florianna

Cesaré Florianna – Head of the Florianna – Bonded to Lilian Gale by First Breath – king's right hand on his council
Sandro Florianna – Eldest brother to Cesaré
David, Roberto and Mario – Brothers to Cesaré
Malleven Mancini – Cousin to Cesaré – most compatible with Isla Snow, married to Lilian Gale, bonded to Phoebe Ray – Challenger for the Kingdom

Santalini

Andreas – Elder of the Florianna royal family and uncle to Keenan Santalini
Keenan Santalini – Most compatible and mated to Lacy Rain
Ruby Santalini – Sister to Keenan and married to Jay Gardiner
Marius Santalini – Eldest brother to Keenan
Adriano, Drago and Louis – Brothers to Keenan
Reeve Santalini – Fellow guard and cousin to the brothers

The Humans

Jay Gardiner – Protector/Lover bonded to Tia Storm –
Married to Ruby Santalini
Lance McCabe – Most compatible mate to Lilian Gale –
Reincarnated from the male heir of the sect of the Five
Moons (Incarnates)
Max Brunswick – Advisor to Dante for Atlantean history
and language.
Glen – Bass player in Drew's band Blunderbuss
Drew Stone – Mate to Phoebe Ray

The Scythians

Lord Croll – High Priest and commander
Seville – Mentor/Trainer and handler to Drew Stone

Those filling council seats and whom they represent

Dante Dubonnetti – King and head of council representing
the Dubonnetti
Cesaré Florianna – King's right hand and representing the
Florianna
Keenan Santalini – Representing the Santalini
Darres Borge – Representing the Borge/Murrs
Lance McCabe – Representing the Human population
Sebastian and Alfonzo Bonaci – Representing the Bonaci in
the absence of a Bonaci mate.

Protectors (Appearing in this book)

Sean McPhearson – Protector to Tia Storm
Cash Reynolds – Protector to Tia Storm
Connor – Protector to Phoebe Ray
River – Lily's Protector and Lance's band mate

Nathan – Lily's Protector, Lance's brother by adoption and fellow band mate

Terms particular to the Atlanteans

Divining ring – worn by all princes and forged particularly for them. Can only have one wearer. Forged from the Orb itself. Determines whether a Siren is nearby and the wearer's status to her by its color
Opaque white – default resting color
Turquoise/green – a Siren is nearby
Purple – the Siren nearby is the wearer's most compatible mate
Red – the wearer is excluded or disqualified from bonding with the Siren nearby. They should not marry or mate a Siren for fear of displeasing the Orb

Elixir – Potion taken by princes and those humans in contact with a Siren to prevent an extreme reaction or even death in the event of breathing her essence.

First Breath – The breath passed from a Siren for the very first time. Her power passes to the recipient only on the very first exchange. Usually reserved for the king.

Murrla – satellite Murr city situated near Antarctica

Scythians – Ancient warlike religious order of fighter monks rumored to kidnap small boys to indoctrinate and train them. Human supremacists, their sole aim is to destroy the Atlantean nation

The Arawans – the sect or The Way of the Five Moons – is the ancient religion of Atlanteans. Came with them from Atlas.

The Magi – ancient order of magicians and alchemists of which Malleven belongs. Mainly Human in origin but have worked alongside the Atlantean nation since the beginning of their colonization.

The Orb – the ancient power source of Atlanteans. Believed to rest beneath Murrtaine and came with their ancestors from Atlas.

ALSO BY T STEDMAN

21st Century Sirens Series

Soul Breather

Blood Sister

Protector (Novella)

Shield Maiden

Tiger Lily

The Dark Valentines Collection

Diablo

The Watchers

* * *

Non-Fiction

My Migraine Story